A Splendid Defiance

Stella Riley is a young, talented British author. Born in 1950 in Staffordshire, she was educated at Cannock Grammar School. After taking her Certificate of Education, she taught full-time for the next nine years, working as a music specialist in various junior schools. In 1978 she and her accountant husband moved to the Oxfordshire/Northamptonshire borders, where she now divides her time between teaching at a nearby village school and her writing. *A Splendid Defiance* is her second novel. Her first novel, *The Marigold Chain*, was published in Fontana in 1983.

STELLA RILEY

A Splendid Defiance

FONTANA PAPERBACKS

First published in 1985 by Fontana Paperbacks

Copyright © Stella Riley 1985

Made and printed in Great Britain by
William Collins Sons & Co Ltd, Glasgow

Historical/Author's Note

Although Justin Ambrose, the Radford family, Ned, Lucy and Thankful Barnes are my invention, their world and its events are not. Life in and around Banbury Castle was pretty much as I have described it and Will Compton, Anthony Greene, Hugh Vaughan, Will Tirwhitt, John Fiennes and John Lilburne all existed – as did the spy, Hannah Rhodes.

Chapter One

Sharply silhouetted against a sky of dazzling blue, two ancient stone giants brooded over a forest of pointed gables. One was the cruciform elegance of St Mary's church, its square Norman tower settling gracefully over delicate traceried parapets and stone-tipped lancets; the other was the uncompromising bulk of the Castle, a crenellated mass of grey-brown austerity, its only ornament the fluttering Royal Standard that gleamed gold on a ground of cobalt and scarlet.

Beneath the bright banner, Justin Ambrose leaned against the sun-warmed stone of the ramparts and stared moodily out across the town. Only fifteen weeks in the place and already he felt caged – and who knew how much longer it would be? Back in the summer of 1642, everyone had said it would all be over with the first big battle. That had been almost two years ago. Now people had given up saying that it would be over by Christmas, by the spring, before the harvest; they had even, with the pendulum of success swinging first one way and then the other, given up predicting who would win. Meanwhile, Englishmen devastated English fields and towns, neighbour against neighbour and sometimes father against son, as they fought and killed and died.

And for what? It was a question that Justin was beginning to ask himself more and more often in the daily tedium of his present backwater. It had been easy in the first headlong enthusiasm to know why you were fighting. But time dulled it; that and seeing your country torn apart by civil strife and your career blighted by a spiteful word. The issues merged and became blurred. That was when you wondered if it was worth it.

Justin's thoughts slid effortlessly into a well-worn groove. A misplaced word about Lord Digby, that beautiful, smooth-tongued Royal favourite, and here he was in the comparative exile of Banbury. Nearly four months of collecting supplies for Oxford by ambushing the occasional Parliamentary convoy and provoking or being provoked by the Roundhead garrison at Newport Pagnell – neither of which could be described as a fitting occupation for one of Prince Rupert's cavalry captains; and neither of which was likely to produce the promotion he both hoped for and needed.

The truth, of course, was that he was bored. Despite being a largely hostile, Puritan town, life in Banbury went on in a rarely-ruffled rhythm. One day, on the whole, was much like another and there seemed little chance of anything happening to change it. The war was being won or lost elsewhere while Justin dealt in bread and coin and barrels of powder; a merchant, a carrier and sometimes a thief – but only infrequently a soldier.

A solitary horseman reined in and was challenged by the guards below. He was smothered in dust and his horse looked winded. Justin's gaze sharpened. A messenger, perhaps? More specifically, a messenger from the North where the Scots and Parliamentarian allies were besieging York and might even have taken it unless Rupert had arrived in time. The guards stepped aside and the rider was admitted. Justin left the walls and ran smartly down to catch the new arrival just as he was dismounting in front of the stables.

'Have you news?'

'Yes.' The battered, broad-brimmed hat with its draggled, once-white feather was pulled off to reveal a face that, beneath the dirt and exhaustion, was very young. 'I've despatches for Oxford but I need a new nag. This one's done.'

'And so are you, by the looks of it,' observed Justin. 'Have you come from York?'

The boy nodded and his expression altered subtly, as if he had suddenly aged. 'It . . . the news isn't good.'

There was a brief silence.

'Good or bad, it will wait till you sit down and take a drink,' said Justin. 'Come on.'

He led the way through to the inner bailey and the room that he and the other officers of the garrison used for practically everything except sleeping. Walrond and Tirwhitt were poring over duty lists, Vaughan and Frost were playing dice and Tom Mayhew was servicing his pistol. All looked up as the door opened and then stared at Justin's companion. No one moved.

Justin ushered the boy in and nudged the door shut with his foot before crossing to the barrel of ale in the corner.

'Sit down,' he said, coming back with a pewter tankard. A sweep of his hand indicated the other men. 'Captains Charles Walrond, Will Tirwhitt and Hugh Vaughan. Lieutenant Edward Frost and Ensign Tom Mayhew. I'm Justin Ambrose.'

The boy managed a ragged bow. 'Gentlemen. My name is John Anderson — cornet to my Lord Goring's regiment of horse.'

Hugh Vaughan's dark eyes met Justin's light ones.

'York?' he asked.

'Yes.'

'Ah. Then perhaps we'd best send for the Colonel and Sir William. Tom, will you . . . ?'

'Yes.' Ensign Mayhew was already half-way to the door.

Lieutenant Frost slapped a hand on the heap of papers that the youthful gentleman's wake threatened to send whirling to the floor and grinned.

'Keen, isn't he? Makes you dizzy just watching him.' He paused, his gaze travelling from Justin to Cornet Anderson and back again. 'Something tells me that all is not well.'

'Does it?' Justin hooked a stool forward and sat down. A faint smile dispelled a little of the grimness about his mouth and he cocked an eyebrow at Captain Vaughan. 'Quick, isn't he?'

'Very.' Hugh's attention remained fixed on their guest. 'Bearing sad tidings is no pleasant duty, I know, but perhaps it will help you to hear that things in this area have gone none too badly in his Highness' absence.'

'No,' said Justin with sudden savagery. 'The King merely allowed himself to be talked into ignoring Rupert's advice with the result that we've given away Reading and Abingdon in exchange for a useless, tactical victory over Waller at

Cropredy. Not too bad at all, really.'

'Justin.' Captain Vaughan drew a long breath and loosed it. 'It doesn't do any good, you know.'

'No. I can think of only one thing that might – and that's to cut out Digby's meddling tongue before its inept whisperings lose us the war.'

'You don't know it was Digby,' offered Ned Frost, judicially.

'Who else would it be?' retorted Justin. 'But you're right, Hugh. It's no use talking and I'm losing my sense of humour. Tell the lad about Cropredy Bridge – and make it sound encouraging. That way he may stay awake till the others get here. I'm going to see about some food for him.'

When he returned bearing bread and cold meat, he found that his arrival had been preceded by that of Major Sir William Compton and Lieutenant-Colonel Anthony Greene. Like Captain Vaughan, these two had both been at the Castle since 1642 when, four days after Edgehill, they had helped remove it from the hands of Parliamentary Colonel John Fiennes. Younger brother of James, Earl of Northampton, Will Compton had held the place ever since – with the help and experience of Anthony Greene. For while the Lieutenant-Colonel had turned forty and had seen action in foreign service, Sir William was still, in July of 1644, only nineteen.

He was casually waving Cornet Anderson back into his seat and telling him to finish his ale. 'For I don't doubt that you've earned it and we'll be in your debt for whatever news you can give us. You've been at York with Prince Rupert?'

'Yes, sir.' The boy put down his tankard and squared his shoulders. 'He'll be marching south again soon. There – there's nothing else to do. York is lost.'

Shock, incredulity and incomprehension registered in varying degrees on the faces before him. Then Lieutenant-Colonel Greene said, 'Lost? Irretrievably?'

'Yes, sir.'

'How? Didn't Prince Rupert get there in time?'

'Oh yes, sir. He did – and he relieved the city,' said Cornet Anderson quickly. 'He made one of his fast marches round to the north and we got to York while the enemy must have thought us still at Knaresborough. Only . . .

'Yes?' prompted Sir William.

The boy's eyes dropped to his hands.

'Well, the rebels had us heavily outnumbered but everyone was saying that they wouldn't attack us because of the York garrison.'

It was Will Tirwhitt, disabled at Brentford by the loss of an arm, who said helpfully, 'And did they? Were you taken by surprise?'

'No – at least, not then. But the Prince said that we must engage them early next day and my Lord Goring went into York to tell Lord Newcastle to bring his men out to rendezvous with us. Only they were late and the whole morning went by and the Prince was fretting at the delay.'

'I'll wager he was,' said Justin grimly. 'Cursing all creation, was he?'

'I don't know, sir. He marched us out to Long Marston and deployed us for battle before the York men came up. But by that time the light wasn't good because there was a storm brewing so the Prince said we could stand down and get something to eat. It must have been nearly seven o'clock and, after all the delay and everything, it seemed he'd decided not to attack – and it didn't look as if the enemy would because they'd been manoeuvring all day as if they expected us to strike south again.' He paused and his hands suddenly tightened on each other. 'And then all hell broke loose. They attacked and the storm came all at once. The Prince was riding up and down the lines through the rain like a man possessed. It wasn't even his own horse.' He stopped again and then said wearily, 'It was horrible. Our wing didn't do too badly but the Prince's cavalry just broke and scattered. And Lord Newcastle's men kept refusing quarter until – until they were all lying there in the mud.'

This time the silence seemed to close around each one of them like a fist.

'So York could not be held and the North is lost,' said Lieutenant-Colonel Greene at last, voicing all their thoughts. 'What is Prince Rupert doing?'

'Rallying the men, sir. Lord Newcastle,' added the boy on

11

a perceptible note of contempt, 'is taking ship for France.'

'And what of Rupert himself?' asked Justin. 'It's his first real defeat. How has he taken it?'

'It's hard to say,' came the slow reply. 'But they killed his dog, you know . . . and I expect he was upset about that.'

There was more, quite a lot more, but Sir William insisted that Cornet Anderson eat before telling them. An hour or so later, it was decided that Lieutenant Frost would accompany him the rest of the way to Oxford, an arrangement that, as they were all well aware, suited Ned very well since it gave him the chance to see his Lucy.

Justin saw them off and then, because nothing required his attention and because he felt a need to escape for a while, he strolled out of the south gate and into the Market Place.

It was fairly quiet, as it usually was in the late afternoon, except on Thursdays, when the colourful bustle of the market brought it to life. The whole town was quiet, wrapped in Puritanical disapproval of the inmates of the Castle. It was not unpleasing to the eye, with its irregular hotch-potch of timber and plaster houses, some of which were pargeted with floral or geometric designs. Even the gaol which faced the Castle from the south side of the square was an attractive building with three gables and the new Town Hall was a masterpiece of decoration. The whole place, sleepy beneath the July sun, presented a picture of charming tranquillity which accorded well with its reputation for cakes and ale. But the other side to the town was visible too; an iconoclastic fervour typified in the stump of broken stone in Cornhill that had once been the market cross and the remains of the barbican, demolished two years earlier because its proximity to the Castle gates provided cover for a besieging enemy. Not, of course, that there had been a besieging enemy and there was no reason now to suppose that there ever would be.

Justin walked westwards up Parson's Lane, trying to decide between a solitary mug of ale at the Reindeer and an hour with Nancy Lucas. Anything to stop his mind from revolving fruitlessly around the circumstances that could have made his former chief seek battle in needless haste and then break his own rule by failing to take the initiative. The Reindeer would not do. It would have to be Nancy. Cheerful, vulgar Nancy, who had moved herself and her three girls into Banbury along with the garrison and whom the townsfolk loathed to the point of obsession. It was a foolish attitude, reflected Justin idly, for Nancy and her girls fulfilled a useful dual function. They kept the garrison happy and saved all those respectable daughters, wives and sisters from annoyance.

He passed the gateway to the Reindeer, stepped over the gurgling trickle of the Cuttle Brook and swung into the narrow, cobbled depths of Pebble Lane. It was hot and airless and it stank of rotting vegetation thrown from the jumble of cottages that flanked it. Justin quickened his pace. Cleansing once a year was not enough and it was a long time until Easter. No wonder all towns suffered from the plague during the summer months.

From up ahead came the sound of scuffling feet and loud, inebriated laughter punctuated by snatches of inane persuasion.

'Little dove . . . pretty dove . . . give Jackie a kiss. Oh come on! No need to be scared . . . we'll not hurt you.'

'No – *hic!* We like little doves . . . we like to hear 'em coo.'

Justin recognized the voices all too easily and, though irritation was uppermost in his mind, reluctant amusement tugged at the corners of his mouth. He banished it and strode on.

'Potts! Danvers! What the devil do you think you're doing?'

Two dishevelled and far from sober troopers sprang to unsteady attention while their quarry tried to efface herself in a corner. With a single, cursory glance, Justin observed the white cap and wide, plain linen collar that told him all he needed to know and his gaze returned coldly to Messrs Potts and Danvers.

'Well?'

Trooper Potts licked his lips uneasily and wished that, if he and Rob had to be caught, it could have been by one of the other officers.

'We didn't mean no harm, Captain.'

'No. You never do, but you do it, nonetheless,' came the stinging reply. 'I take it that you are off-duty?'

Trooper Danvers was hurt. 'Aye. Course we are.'

'I beg your pardon?'

The trooper flushed. 'Yes, Captain Ambrose.'

'Thank you. And you've been in the Reindeer. Is that your only excuse?'

They agreed that it was. Then, with more valour than wisdom, Potts added, 'But she were on her own, Captain – and she smiled at us.'

'I don't care if she were naked as Eve and enticing as the bloody serpent,' retorted Justin. 'You have strict orders to leave the townswomen alone and, since you seem to have such difficulty remembering it, we will have to find some way of improving your memories. Now get back to the Castle and I'll see you in my quarters at eight o'clock. And if you present yourselves looking as slovenly as you do now, you'll regret it.'

'Yes, sir.' They spoke in gloomy unison.

'Be off with you!' Justin suppressed his grin until they had set off back down the alley. And only then, with renewed irritation, did he remember the girl.

She was still huddled against the wall and scarlet with an embarrassment that owed itself more to her rescuer's words than her attackers' importunities. A bulbous stone bit into her back but she did not notice it. Indeed, if the ground had opened to receive her, she would have been glad. She wished it would; she wished he would go away without speaking to her; she wished she did not know him, and that was as pointless as the rest.

She had never spoken to him, of course, for her brother, Jonas, would not have his womenfolk contaminated that way, but she had seen him. He had been into the shop twice about cloth for the garrison and thereby caused Jonas long hours of heart-searching on the matter of principle versus profit. She had expected principle to win for, with Jonas, it usually did. But looking now at Captain Ambrose, she was not so sure. He looked as though he could overcome anything and his air of collected assurance was frightening.

He was a tall man, perhaps a little under six feet and built with the lean compactness of a hunting cat. Thick, dark-brown hair fell in waves about his shoulders and framed a severely-sculpted face that was too forbidding to be considered handsome. His cheekbones were high, his jaw determined and his mouth hard but it was his eyes, now resting on her with polite indifference, that produced an involuntary shiver and made her wonder why she had expected them to be dark. For they were not dark at all. Fringed with heavy, sepia lashes, they were a remarkable, light grey, as clear as spring water and as cold.

His clothes she remembered rather better but that was only natural for cloth was her family's business. In fact, though far removed from the sombre garb she was accustomed to, the Captain dressed with an elegance more restrained than flamboyant. His broad-brimmed hat of black felt supported only one plume which, though curling and very white, did not trail to his shoulder. His coat was of well-worn, buff leather, its only adornments being an exquisite lace collar and a fringed sash of gleaming blue silk and his boots and baldrick had clearly been chosen for their practicality. He was as neat as wax and did not look as though he were ever anything else.

'Well, Mistress? Are you hurt?'

The crisp voice, edged with impatience, made her jump. She tried to speak, found her throat too dry and swallowed.

'No.'

He nodded. 'Good. Then I hope you will accept my apologies on behalf of the garrison. Such incidents are as distasteful to us as they must be to you and we do our best to prevent them. Unfortunately it isn't always possible.'

'N-no, I can see that.' She realized that she ought, in common courtesy, to thank him but his manner made it hard. She drew a deep breath, stepped away from the wall and recoiled nervously as her foot encountered something unexpected.

'The contents of your basket,' offered the remote voice, helpfully. 'I hope nothing is damaged. Allow me to assist.' This as she stooped hurriedly to pick up the small, carefully-wrapped packages that littered the ground at her feet.

'Oh no – please – there's no need. I can manage,' she said disjointedly. 'They are only samples of damask for Mistress Welchman at the cake shop.'

Justin retrieved a parcel that had fallen at some distance from the rest and dropped it into the basket. Then he picked it up and held it out whilst waiting for her to rise.

She did so a little unsteadily and took it gingerly from him.

'Thank you. And thank you also for arriving when you did. I am very grateful.'

'I'm glad to have been of service,' came the cool reply. 'But, if you'll take my advice, you won't use this particular short-cut when you are alone. And a wise maiden does not smile at soldiers even when they are sober. It leaves you open to misinterpretation.'

'I only meant to be friendly,' she murmured defensively.

'Yes. That is what they thought,' agreed Justin drily. 'You will do better, therefore, to remain unfriendly. That way, you will be saved from annoyance and I from the trouble of administering a reprimand. Do I make myself quite clear?'

She nodded, overcome with a sense of guilt that was all too familiar and a feeling of mild resentment that was not familiar at all.

'Good. Now, you said you were going to the cake shop, I think. Where is it?'

'Just around the corner, in Parson's Lane,' she replied, her voice very low. 'At the sign of the Unicorn.'

A swift smile suddenly transformed the shuttered face.

'Yes? Well, that sounds appropriate. And, to keep it that way and absolve the honour of His Majesty's army, I'll see you to the door. Come.'

'It's all right,' she said, alarmed. 'It's only a step. And you were going the other way. Please don't trouble yourself.'

The smile disappeared and was replaced by exasperation.

'It's no trouble, I assure you. Come.'

So she fell reluctantly into step with him and walked along in silence at his side, praying that no one she knew was watching. It was only as they emerged into Parson's Lane that she summoned enough courage to ask hesitantly, 'Those men, what will you do to them?'

16

'In the end very little,' he replied, with a hint of grim humour. 'But I doubt you'll find them making the same mistake again.'

It was not until later, when she was half-way home, that the girl remembered how unicorns are supposed to meet their doom and thus understood the previously obscure implications of the Captain's remark. Shuddering, she wondered if all the King's men were equally shameless.

Home suddenly took on an entirely new complexion and became a refuge. She sped towards it on quickened feet.

Chapter Two

'Abigail!' Rachel Radford's voice held its usual note of complaint. 'Where on earth have you been till now? You should have been back an hour ago.'

'I'm sorry.' The girl closed the door and advanced slowly into the stuffy gloom of the shop. 'I tried to be quick but Mistress Welchman . . .'

'You let her keep you gossiping, I suppose,' said Rachel, incisively. 'Then ran through the town like a hoyden, if the state of your hair is any indication. Really, I don't think you have the remotest idea of properly modest behaviour or industry – or even what is due to your brother's position. This is an honest, God-fearing household and it's time you stopped acting like a child before you shame us all.'

'I'm sorry,' said Abigail again. She put her basket down on the edge of a polished trestle and added placatingly, 'She chose the most expensive one.'

'Not there!' Rachel snatched up the basket and put it on the floor. 'It will scratch the surface. How many times must I tell you?'

Abigail repressed a sigh and looked silently down at her hands.

'Well? What are you waiting for? There's the table to be set for supper and Betty to be watched if she is not to burn the meat. Do I have to tell you everything?'

'No, Rachel. Of course not.' Abigail turned dutifully towards the door which led to the rest of the house.

'And make sure you tidy your hair before Jonas sees you. I don't know how you managed to get so untidy. Have you ever seen me with my hair falling all about my face?'

Her hand on the latch, Abigail turned slowly back.

'No,' she said. It was true.

Tall and elegant, her fair hair drawn back with an immaculate smoothness that Abigail could never achieve for

18

herself, Rachel was an object-lesson in neatness. She was also deft, efficient, well-versed in all the domestic skills and – were it not for the severity of her expression – beautiful. A person, in fact, to whom it was impossible not to feel inferior and hard not to envy.

'No,' sighed Abigail again, escaping unobtrusively through the door.

She looked in on her mother before going upstairs and felt guilty all over again for what Rachel would call time-wasting but the feeling fled at the smile that greeted her and she responded ruefully, 'Am I really very late?'

'A little, perhaps. Did Rachel scold you?'

'Yes. It was my own fault. I should have come in the back way.'

Alice Radford sighed. She tried very hard not to dislike her daughter-in-law but it was not easy and she frequently wished that Jonas had chosen a less formidable girl, one whose warmth might have softened his own unyielding disposition instead of echoing and strengthening it as Rachel did. The house had been cheerless enough when her husband had been alive but now it was a tomb. It was not for herself that she minded. Rachel was always civil to her and it was only proper that she should assume the running of the house but it did not seem fair that Abby should be constantly criticized and harangued for faults that were not really faults at all, until she spoke of coming in through the back door like a servant. It had begun to seem, thought Alice sadly, that Abby's life was going to follow the same, joyless pattern as her own and that was a pity.

Abigail watched the once comely face settle into lines of familiar anxiety and came quickly across the room to kiss her mother's cheek.

'It's all right,' she said. 'Don't worry. I'm becoming quite brave you know and I daresay Rachel doesn't mean half of what she says. Where's Sam?'

'Upstairs checking the stock. Jonas thinks there was a mistake in the last delivery and he's probably right. This war upsets everything. I don't know how we are to avoid ruin.'

'By selling cloth to the garrison?'

'Abby!'

'I know. But everyone else sells them things so I don't see why we shouldn't. They just double their prices.'

'And wait months for payment, no doubt,' said Alice. 'No. Jonas will never do it.'

Abigail's eyes grew thoughtful.

'Oh, I don't know. He might.' And then, quickly, 'But I must fly. He'll be in soon and I haven't even combed my hair – let alone laid the table.'

Alice smiled. 'I'll do the table. Rachel needn't know – and it will be interesting to see what she finds wrong with it. You just go and tell Sam to put away the book he's doubtless spent all afternoon reading.'

A few minutes later, Abigail entered the attic store-room to discover, without surprise, how wise Alice was in the ways of children. Samuel showed no sign of mercantile activity. Instead, he was seated, chin in hand, on a box by the window, his head bent over the open pages of a slim, leather-bound volume that was almost certainly nothing that Jonas would have approved of. Abigail smiled and flicked the door-latch with her finger.

The dark head jerked up and round as he stumbled to his feet. Then defensiveness gave way to relief and he grinned sheepishly.

'I wish you didn't move so quietly. You scared me half to death,' he complained. 'I thought it was Her Maleficent Frigidity.'

'Shh!' Abigail glanced over her shoulder. 'One day you'll call her that and she'll hear you.'

'So? I don't much care if she does.'

'You will when she tells Jonas – and, talking of Jonas, do you realize what the time is? I hope you've counted those wretched rolls.'

Samuel shrugged. 'Of course. It didn't take five minutes. And you'd better be ready for ructions at supper because we're twenty ells of worsted short.'

'Oh no. Are you sure?'

'Yes. What's the matter? It's not your fault.'

'I know.' She managed a wry smile. 'But it will put Jonas in a bad mood and Rachel is bound to tell him how long I was going to Mistress Welchman's and . . . .'

'And he'll be unpleasant,' finished her brother simply. 'Yes. I know. But it's only words, after all. You shouldn't let them upset you.'

'I know. And I try not to, I really do. But it isn't just Jonas, is it? It's loud voices and angry scenes and never knowing what to say to people. I feel such a terrible coward. Are you ashamed of me?'

Samuel came carefully through the racks of merchandise, his twisted foot dragging lightly along the floor.

'Don't be silly. How could I be? Being scared of Jonas doesn't make you a coward – he's enough to give anyone the shudders. And we're a pair, aren't we?'

They were and in many ways for, with only a year between them, they had always been each other's closest companion. Samuel's lameness was not a barrier to physical activity for he had made sure, with sheer hard work, that it should not be but it was a barrier between him and other boys of his age and this he had never had the inclination to overcome, preferring the company of his sister or of books. In quiet defiance of Jonas (who considered the ability to do more than read, write and count superfluous and thought most books the devil's own invitation to idleness) Samuel read anything he could lay his hands on and, at seventeen, had managed to beg and borrow a surprisingly broad education.

It was a shame, thought Abigail, as she hurriedly tidied herself to go downstairs, that the war had made it virtually impossible for him to attend a university but if the war had not stopped him, then Jonas would have so perhaps the idea had never been more than a dream.

She peered at herself in the tiny mirror above her washstand and sighed. Jonas said that a larger glass was unnecessary for the purposes of neatness and would only lure one into the sin of vanity. And that, she reflected wryly, might well be true if one was fortunate enough to have anything to be vain about. Sadly, that did not apply to her for, though there was nothing actually wrong with her face, it did seem to be easily forgettable. Captain Ambrose, for example, would probably have the greatest difficulty in

21

recognizing her again for she did not think he had really looked at her even once . . . but that ought definitely to count as a blessing.

The little, wayward curls that Rachel had so objected to were now strained tightly back under her cap in the forlorn hope that they would stay there but the effect, though properly neat, was not a significant improvement. It was tempting to wonder if the fault lay in her colouring but that was mere folly. Everyone could not be fair and Sam, whose eyes and hair were as night-black as her own, made nonsense of the theory by being as vivid as she was pale.

She stepped sharply back from the glass, suddenly aware of the trend her thoughts were taking. Truly, it seemed that God was wise. It was just a pity that the undeniable absence of one sin was but the gateway to another and was vanity really any worse than envy?

She arrived at table just in time to take her place with the rest of the family and, though her narrow escape from lateness drew a reproving frown from Rachel, nothing was said of it because Jonas was speaking.

Of moderate height and spare, angular frame, Jonas Radford looked exactly what he was: a well-to-do merchant whose deep religious fervour bordered on fanaticism. His black hair was cropped short, his clothes were of the best quality but sombre and his face, though ascetic and proud, was dominated by a pair of burning dark eyes. He was, in fact, an extreme copy of everything his late father had been. Abigail had never been other than afraid of him.

Tonight, however, something had clearly occurred to please him for he accorded Abigail a nod that was less taciturn than usual and forbore to catechize Samuel on the state of the stock-room. With an aspect that was almost smug, he waved them all to their places and folded his hands to recite the Lord's blessing.

'You said you had news, husband,' prompted Rachel, as she served him liberally with roast meat. 'Will you not share it with us?'

A tight, unaccustomed smile touched Jonas' mouth.

'Indeed, indeed. And it is news worthy of great rejoicing.

On the second day of this month, the Lord God saw fit to smite the Popish, Malignant enemies of His Kingdom in such force that it is doubtful if they will ever recover.'

'There was a battle?' asked Samuel.

'Not just a battle,' corrected Jonas. 'A glorious victory over evil, a triumph of righteous, Godly men over wantonness and vice. "So the Lord awaked as one out of sleep and, like a giant refreshed with wine, He smote his enemies in the hinder parts and put them to a perpetual shame."'

'And where,' asked Samuel, prosaically, 'did all this happen?'

'At a place called Marston Moor, just outside the city of York, which has now been saved from its own iniquity.'

'God be praised,' murmured Rachel. 'Do you think that this will shorten the war?'

Jonas' fingers curled around his tankard and the satisfaction deepened in his eyes.

'I do, for there is more. Our stout fellows in the North have done greater work than to inflict a territorial defeat. They have vanquished, once and for all, the mainspring of our enemies' hopes. The Wizard Prince – that hell-spawned foreigner whom the devil protects and no bullet can kill; that devourer of children, ravisher of women, destroyer of towns and soul of unnatural vices – is now disgraced and finished. His cavalry were smashed and he preserved his own worthless life by taking shelter in a beanfield. And as for his familiar the beast that has struck terror into grown men and been the subject of sermons in church – it is now no more than a dead dog. It was found on the field . . . a true token of the Lord's favour.'

Unpleasant sensations were taking place behind Abigail's serviceable dark blue bodice and she quietly laid down her knife. She caught Samuel's eye, saw her own distaste mirrored there and then sat staring down at her hands, hoping to escape notice.

She had, as always, reckoned without Rachel.

'Is there something amiss with the food, Abigail?'

'No.' Abigail looked up quickly and her fingers moved unconsciously towards her discarded knife. 'There is nothing wrong. It's just that I'm not very hungry.'

'If you dawdled less, perhaps you would be,' came the sharp response. 'Or perhaps it was Mistress Welchman's cakes that delayed you this afternoon and are now spoiling both your appetite and your ability to be pleased by your brother's tidings.'

'No.' Growing rapidly whiter, Abigail withdrew her hand again to the safety of her lap where its trembling could not be seen. 'No.'

'No?' frowned Jonas. 'Is that all you can find to say? What is the matter with you? I think we are entitled to an explanation.'

Abigail's mind was already gripped by the paralysis that always took possession of it at moments like this. She could neither tell the truth nor frame a convincing lie and a blank refusal was unthinkable.

'I expect,' remarked Samuel, calmly, 'that, like me, Abby finds it difficult to celebrate over the remains of a dumb animal.'

Jonas' gaze swung round to encompass him.

'That dumb animal had the powers of Satan behind it.'

'Rubbish,' said Samuel, provocatively cheerful. 'The only powers it had were the ones that our armies endowed it with to explain their own failures.'

'Sam!' whispered Alice, her anxious glance flicking from Rachel's set face to Jonas' angry one. 'Apologize to Jonas at once.'

'Was I rude? I'm sorry. I didn't mean to be.'

'No,' cut in Rachel, acidly. 'You meant to do just what you did – divert our attention from your sister's shortcomings.'

Samuel smiled innocently into the eyes of his foe.

'I don't know what you mean, Rachel. Are we talking of Abby or of Ruth? If it's Abby, I don't think she has any shortcomings and if you mean Ruth, I wouldn't waste the effort. As far as I'm concerned, her husband is welcome to her. I just hope he's Perseverance by nature as well as by name.'

Alice gave a small, inarticulate moan and abandoned all attempt to finish her food.

'That's enough!' snapped Jonas, flushing with indignation. 'I will not have such unseemly talk at my board – nor such flippant insolence to my wife. Since you can say nothing that is fit to be heard, you will withdraw to your room and study the Twenty-Fifth Psalm. You may return at evening prayers and recite it for us.'

'Jonas, please!' said Alice. 'I'm sure he meant no harm.'

'I beg your pardon, mother, but you really must allow me to deal with these matters as I see fit. Samuel lacks humility and his heart is clouded with false values which he must learn to root out and destroy lest they lead him to eternal damnation.'

Samuel slid off the bench and came to his feet.

'Don't worry, mother. It's all in a good cause and, as Jonas will no doubt agree, nothing is ever achieved without suffering.' He limped out of the room.

Abigail swallowed and continued, steadfastly, to regard her trencher. Sam was good and kind but he had sacrificed himself to no avail for Rachel was not one to accept failure meekly. She would return again and again to the attack until she found her mark.

As it turned out, she was not granted the opportunity for Jonas again took up the theme of God's grace and favour to the just cause of the Parliament and His obvious displeasure in that of the King. Abigail did not know if Jonas was right or merely optimistic but, for the first time that she could remember, she was grateful both for his eloquence and for the wifely submissiveness that prevented Rachel from interrupting it.

At nine o'clock precisely the maidservant Betty came in from the kitchen and Sam from upstairs to join in the customary evening prayers. These were longer than usual for Jonas indulged his talent for lay-preaching and began with a fiery sermon on the omnipotent justice of the Lord.

'For on those who turn not from the crooked path and compound their sins daily without repentance,' he enthused, 'the wrath of the Almighty shall fall without mercy. To Him are the secrets of all hearts made open and happy are they that deserve His charity. But the unworthy, the wanton and the deceitful shall surely perish in their woe.'

Uncomfortably conscious both of her secretive deceit and her unshakable determination to compound it, Abigail flushed uneasily. The wrath of God would be as nothing compared to the wrath of Jonas if he found out that she had been consorting, however unwillingly, with members of the Royalist garrison. Even her mother would probably be shocked and Rachel . . . Rachel would make her life unbearable for weeks. The only person she might possibly tell was Samuel and there seemed little point in that. The best course was surely to forget it had ever happened and pray earnestly that nothing of the kind occurred again.

Head bent, she listened to Samuel repeating his psalm. And when it ended and Jonas finally dismissed them, she went thankfully upstairs to the safe fastness of her bedchamber.

Five days later, Captain Ambrose walked into the shop.

It was early and, under Rachel's critical eye, Abigail was still engaged in polishing the wide trestle that Jonas used for cutting the cloth. Neither of them expected custom at such an hour and so, when the door opened, both turned in quick surprise. Rachel's habitually chilly expression hardened and Abigail took three steps backwards into the nearest dark corner.

'Good morning,' said the Captain.

His tone was bland but the sardonic lift of his brows did not live up to it and neither, observed Abigail, did the exaggerated courtesy of his bow. She watched the beautiful, white plume of his hat brush the floor and decided that it was just as well that she had given the shop a thorough sweeping.

The grey eyes continued to regard Rachel.

'It's a fine morning, isn't it?'

'Very,' agreed Rachel, according him a curt nod of acknowledgement. 'Is there something I may do for you, Captain?'

'Why yes, Mistress Radford,' came the gentle reply. 'You may summon your husband.'

Rachel's mouth tightened. 'I don't know that he can see you now.'

'Then perhaps you had best find out.'

'You don't seem to understand, Captain Ambrose. My husband —'

'Is a very busy man. Yes. I know. That is why I took the precaution of calling so early, before he is forced to go out. I hope, however, that I am not too early?' The brisk voice became tinged with delicate malice. 'Never say he is still abed!'

'Certainly not,' snapped Rachel. 'But he has a good deal of urgent paperwork to do and then a meeting of the Common Council to attend and . . . '

'Then I'll wait,' announced the Captain, cheerfully. He sat down on a stool. 'I'm sure your lady clients will find me invaluable when they come to choose their lace.'

It was a subtle threat and Rachel knew it. Her colour rose and she hesitated before finally accepting defeat.

'Abigail, go and tell Jonas that Captain Ambrose is here.'

Abigail started violently and saw the strange, light eyes turn to gaze across at her. She froze and then recognized, with a completely illogical lack of pleasure, that they were utterly indifferent. As she had suspected, Captain Ambrose had no recollection of ever having seen her before and was almost certainly not seeing her now.

'Abigail! Are you going to stand there all day?' Rachel's voice could have cut bread.

'No. I'm sorry.' Abigail turned quickly and therefore missed the sudden flicker of alertness in the Captain's face. 'I'll go now.'

'That,' said Rachel, sarcastically, 'would be a great help. You did say now?'

Abigail blushed and fled.

Jonas did not know if he was irritated or relieved to hear that Captain Ambrose awaited him in the shop. He hated the garrison and everything it represented but a review of the last month's figures had revealed a far from satisfactory state of affairs and he was regrettably aware of needing the Captain's business. This, however, did not cause him to greet that gentleman with any degree of cordiality and, as soon as Rachel vanished into the house, he said frigidly, 'I begin to find your persistence annoying, sir.'

'Yes, I'm sure you do,' agreed Justin. 'But the remedy is in your own hands, you know. And you won't be the first to sacrifice your principles in exchange for hard cash.'

Jonas' gaze sharpened. 'Is that how you would pay? No promissory notes?'

'No. We have the money. What we don't have is endless time to discuss the matter. If the men are to have decent coats this winter, we need the cloth now so it can be made up. And if you won't supply it, I must apply to Oxford.' Justin came to his feet and smiled coolly. 'Well? What is it to be?'

Jonas stared at the worldly elegance before him and longed for the personal and political satisfaction of refusing but with the townsfolk spending as cautiously as they had been since the war began, he needed the extra trade and needed it badly. Bitter rage burned in his breast and his frustration channelled itself into hatred of the man in front of him.

'Very well. Broadcloth or worsted?'

The Captain expressed a preference for broadcloth. Jonas named his price and the Captain laughed.

'Oh no, Mr Radford. I realize that the damage done to your finer feelings will require compensation but I am not willing to be robbed. Try again.'

'Robbed?' echoed Jonas, incensed. 'Why, you Godless son of Apollyon, do you think I cannot guess where you get the "hard cash" you boast of?'

'On the contrary, I'm very sure that you can. But I am equally sure that you will find our transaction less painful if you avoid thinking of it.'

Jonas' answer was a diatribe against Cavalier lawlessness and vice. Captain Ambrose listened unmoved until he paused for breath and then said, 'This is war, Mr Radford. The rebels, I beg your pardon, the Parliament attacks our convoys and we theirs. It is unfortunate but necessary. I doubt any of us takes pleasure in it.'

'Pleasure is all you and your kind think of!' spat Jonas. 'Is nothing safe from your accursed levity? You profane our town with your very presence, corrupt our young people with your vile example and slander our honesty whilst shamelessly admitting your own villainy but God, who sees all, is not deceived. And you might remember that, if war makes thieves —'

'Peace hangs them. Quite.' Bored grey eyes met smouldering black ones. 'But I'm not here to justify either myself or my cause and I don't have all day to waste while you preach. Eighteen shillings the yard and not a farthing more.'

On the other side of the door, Abigail drew a long, appreciative breath and turned an awed gaze on Samuel.

'Aren't you glad I brought you down?'

'Yes.' Samuel paused and a grin began to grow on his face. 'Where did you meet him?'

She gasped. 'What do you mean?'

'Oh come on. I know you and you're a terrible liar. Where did you meet him?'

Abigail sighed. 'In Pebble Lane.' She favoured him with a brief, whispered résumé.

When she had finished, Samuel gave a low whistle.

'I'll bet you were scared when he walked into the shop! Did he say anything?'

'No. He didn't even recognize me.'

Samuel fixed her with a long, shrewd stare.

'Did you want him to?'

'Of course not.' Abigail fidgeted with her cuffs. 'I was extremely relieved that he didn't.'

'Yes. You sound it.'

A faint, reluctant smile dawned and she said, 'All right. It's silly, I know, but I've suddenly realized that I'm eighteen years old and as memorable as a glass of water. I don't much like it.'

'No. Who would?' Samuel folded his arms and appraised her thoughtfully. 'You're exaggerating, of course. But if you really want to make your Captain notice you —'

'Don't be ridiculous!'

'— or anyone else for that matter,' he continued placidly, 'there's a perfectly simple way to do it. If, of course, you're interested.'

Abigail hesitated and then jettisoned her pride.

'I'm interested. What is it?'

'Smile. You'd be surprised how much it improves you. And so, I daresay, would Captain Ambrose.'

Chapter Three

It was one of those typically English days of mingled sunshine and showers and everyone was damply irritable. Captain Ambrose sent out his third scouting party of the morning and prowled restlessly along the hedgerows where the foot lay in sulky concealment, checking that none of them had seen fit to alter their dispositions. They hadn't, of course. They knew better. The Captain nodded curtly, reminded them to keep their powder dry and stalked back to where Lieutenant Frost had managed to find shelter half-way up a tree.

Fair-haired, blue-eyed and invariably light-hearted, the Lieutenant was the younger son of a respected Warwickshire family of genuine but largely cautious loyalty. Ned, however, was too young and much too insouciant for caution. Just now, he looked down with tolerant amusement on Captain Ambrose and said, 'Sit down, you impatient devil! You're wearing yourself out and making the men jumpy – and they'll not come any the quicker for it.'

'I know.' Justin's grey eyes dwelt thoughtfully on his friend's sprawling figure. 'But one of us has to set an example.'

Ned grinned. 'You're just jealous of my new sash – made, I'll have you know, by my Lucy's own fair hand and the exact colour of her bright eyes.'

'And given,' mocked Justin, 'to a hero who lurks up trees.'

'So? I'm dry and moderately comfortable, though a cushion wouldn't go amiss. And, since you only get to be a hero when you're dead, it's not a distinction I've any ambition for.'

'Rupert isn't dead.'

'The exception that proves the rule. We can't all be disinherited young princes with romantic pasts, and if someone pointed a loaded pistol in my face or yours, you can

31

be certain that the damned thing would go off perfectly. They only misfire when it's a Wizard Prince with the luck of the devil.'

'He wasn't very lucky at Marston Moor.'

'He was outnumbered two to one. What do you expect? No one can win all the time and he'll soon get his reputation back.'

Justin's eyes grew hard. 'If that bastard Digby lets him.'

'Oh, a pox on Digby! I'll tell you what, you're becoming obsessed by him and he's not worth the trouble. All right, he got you sent here and you don't like it much but there are worse places to be, you know, and for all it's damned dull, it still has to be done. You're not the only trained field officer to be tied to a garrison and, if you really want to get back into the war, why don't you write to Rupert? He's still recruiting up North and no doubt he'd be delighted to have you with him.'

'No.'

'But —'

'No!' A sudden spurt of temper flared in Justin's face. Not even to Ned would he explain that pride kept him from asking, that and the fact that he knew only too well the plague of letters that tormented the Prince at every turn. 'I take your point. I'm here to do a job and I'll do it and, for the time being, Digby can go hang but one day, I swear I'll . . .'

'Captain Ambrose! They're coming, sir.'

Justin swung round to face his returned scout.

'How far?'

'About a mile, sir. Six heavy carts, about fifty horse and a handful of dragoons.'

'Good.' His mood lightening at the prospect of action, Justin smiled suddenly. 'Get yourself up to my troop in the wood over there and tell Lieutenant Chamberlain to have the men mounted and ready. I'll be along in a minute. And now,' he added, turning back to Lieutenant Frost, 'perhaps Zacchaeus will come down and see to the foot?'

'Who the devil's Zacchaeus?' Ned was already half-way to the ground. 'Sounds like some canting Puritan.'

'Quite – and an indication of the company I've been

keeping lately. You know what to do?'

'Yes,' said Ned, laconically. 'Stock Plan A. My villains could do it in their sleep.'

'So could mine.' Justin untethered his horse and came lightly to the saddle. 'Worrying, isn't it? By the time this war is over, the country will be awash with professional foot-pads.'

With the wait almost over, the men forgot their cramped wetness and began to regain their normal ebullience. It was a Parliamentary convoy of powder and ammunition, passing from Brackley to Gloucester, and who better to intercept it than the stout lads of the Banbury garrison. They had a reputation as far afield as Westminster for supplying the Royalist capital with anything and everything that came their way. And they were proud of it.

The routine ambush was a simple affair that made use of the ample, natural cover between Banbury and the village of Middleton Cheney and relied largely on shock tactics. The only vital ingredient was a sense of timing and Justin knew that Ned's was as good as his own. Lieutenant Frost might be essentially frivolous and talk for the sake of talking but he was also a first-class infantry officer who could be relied on to do a good job.

From the edge of the copse, where his troop waited motionless and silent behind him, Justin watched the convoy weave into sight and progress slowly into the net. The sun was out again, glancing fitfully off helmets and breast-plates. Only fifty horse, but well-armed and well-mounted. The train was squeezed out by the narrowness of the road into a long ribbon of colour and jingling harness but they had anticipated that and Ned's men were spread well back. Justin watched the column advance between the innocent-looking green hedges and felt the stirrings of familiar, tense excitement. Only a few more yards and Ned could close in behind them. He unsheathed his sword and raised it in signal to his own troop . . . almost there . . . now! And, delaying only for the fraction of a second it took to see the foot swarm noisily out of their ditches, he brought down his hand and with a cry of 'For the King!' led his men out into the open.

Blades flashing in the light, they formed a close-packed charge to thunder down across the open country and smash into the startled mêlée of rebel horse on the road. It broke before them but that was not enough. Away to his right, Justin saw that Ned had accounted for the rear-guard of dragoons and was re-forming his division, musketeers behind pikemen, at either end of the cart-train. Meanwhile, the Parliamentary Captain was struggling to re-group his force and it was no part of Justin's plan to let him. Summoning his own men to follow, Justin set his horse at the hedge and over they all went, dividing neatly on his shouted command into twin wings that wheeled and converged on the enemy.

A bullet tore its way through Justin's sleeve, scorching his arm and then the time for firearms was past and the smoke-filled air rang with the clamour of hand-to-hand combat. For ten brief minutes, he was restored to his natural element and then it was over. The rebels fled in disorder, leaving some twenty of their number dead or wounded on the field and after speeding them on their way with a little desultory pursuit Justin returned to find Ned in secure possession of the carts. The whole operation had taken less than half an hour and they had lost only three men.

Ned grinned up at Justin, noting the carefree expression that was only ever present at moments like this and which rendered the usually shuttered face younger and less formidable.

'Enjoy it?' he asked, passing one powder-blackened hand over his brow and leaving a generous smear behind.

Justin smiled. 'Yes.'

'So did I.' Ned pulled the helmet off his fair, damply-curling hair. 'And the best is yet to come.'

'Oxford and Lucy!'

'Yes. Tomorrow, I hope. Coming? I'd have thought there must be at least one amongst the reputed realms of your former mistresses that you'd like to see again. God knows there's little in Banbury to tempt you to use these fabled talents of yours.'

Justin refused to be drawn but could not resist a single

mischievous thrust. 'Very true, but if you really want to see me in action, you could always introduce me to your Lucy.'

As it turned out, neither of them went to Oxford – Justin because he declined to go and Ned because large-scale enemy activity between Broughton and King's Sutton forced him to turn back. After a frustrating day playing grandmother's footsteps with two Parliamentary scouting parties and a narrow escape from a hair-raisingly large cavalry force, Ned brought his gunpowder back to the Castle and saw it safely bestowed. Then, in a mood of rare aggravation, he went in to make his report.

He found Sir William and the other senior officers gathered about the dinner table. The food had gone but the wine was still out and the room was hazy with smoke from Hugh Vaughan's pipe. It was Justin who noticed him first and, with a suggestion of tension in his face that was absent in his words, said, 'That was quick. Did Lucy throw you out?'

'No.' Ned walked across to look down at Will Compton. 'I couldn't get through. The country's crawling with rebel troops and I was damned lucky to get back here without a fight.'

'Where?' asked Will. 'And how many?'

'Just south of Bodicote. They've cordoned off all the lanes and stationed about a hundred horse and foot on the Oxford road. Without the advance scouts we'd have been right into them. As it was, we doubled back to try other routes only to find enough men posted at each to delay us until their main body could come up and finish us off.'

Sir William looked at Colonel Greene.

'What do you think?'

'I think we'd better send out some reconnaissance parties,' came the grim reply. 'And not just to the south, either. If they're closing in, and with the King's army away at Evesham, it looks as though they could be, it would be nice to know it. I'm only surprised they didn't do it sooner. What's today – the nineteenth?'

'The twentieth,' said Justin. 'It's probably taken till now for their wonderful Committee of Both Kingdoms to make a

35

decision. I doubt if its right hand knows what the left is doing half of the time.' He got up. 'Shall I send my fellows out now or at first light?'

'Now,' said Sir William. 'But tell them to be careful – no silly heroics.'

Knowing that Justin would not go to bed until his scouts came back, Hugh Vaughan elected to sit up with him but neither of them felt much desire to talk. Once, the Welshman said, 'Have you had any experience of sieges?'

'Only from the outside. Have you?'

'The same. I was at Breda.'

The grey eyes widened a little.

'Were you? Well, I doubt any little affair we have here will rival that, even supposing we have one at all.'

Captain Vaughan surveyed him enigmatically.

'You're ambitious, aren't you?'

'Yes. Is that wrong?'

'No. Not at all,' replied Hugh, tapping out his pipe. 'Just don't go ill-wishing the rest of us for the sake of it, there's a good fellow.'

The first reconnaissance party returned at about four in the morning and by six the others had all followed suit. An hour later Justin had collated the information into a concise list of figures and Hugh had drawn up a rough map marked with a number of small crosses. They did not discuss their findings. There was no need. Rebel troops were quartered in force at Broughton and Warkworth and, in lesser numbers, to the east and west. The investment of Banbury, it appeared, was not just a possibility. It had already begun.

It was the opinion of all that every effort should be made to bring in stocks of food before their situation became common knowledge in the town.

'That gives us just under three hours,' announced Sir William grimly. 'There's a meeting of the Common Council at eleven and I wouldn't wager a groat on the chances of the secret lasting through that. There's hardly a burgess or alderman that isn't hand-in-glove with Old Subtlety.'

'Who?' asked Justin.

'Viscount Saye and Sele,' supplied Will Tirwhitt, his thin, clever face creasing with sudden, wicked amusement. 'Lord of Broughton Castle and Keeper – in name only, just at present – of Banbury. Our host.'

The next two hours passed in a whirlwind of organization and activity. Justin began by listing the slowly incoming stores but, at a quarter before eleven, he handed this task over to Ensign Mayhew and departed on what he had come, with irony, to regard as his personal crusade. He collected the small, purposely-hoarded store of gold from Sir William, took two troopers and a hand-cart and set off for the sign of the Ragged Staff on Shop Row, for when the Council meeting ended and the merchants returned hot-foot to cancel supplies to the garrison, Justin had a presentiment that Jonas Radford would be one of the first.

He had timed his visit better than he knew for, not only was Jonas absent but Rachel had just set forth to call on a friend recently brought to bed of her first child. Consequently, he entered the shop to find it staffed by what must surely be two junior members of the Radford family, the shy, diminutive girl he dimly recalled seeing before and a dark-haired youth whose fine-boned face was vivid with intelligence.

When the door opened, Abigail looked automatically up from the array of ribbons she had spread out for the perusal of Mistress Atkins and felt her breath leak slowly away. Samuel, perched on a stool with a copy of Godwin's *The Man in the Moon* lying open on top of the sales ledger, shot her a briefly quizzical glance and then calmly took control.

'Good morning, Captain. What may I do for you?'

'Good morning.' Justin removed his hat and bowed courteously towards the two girls. 'I have come to collect the broadcloth that I ordered a few days ago. Is it ready?'

Samuel blinked, looked enquiringly across at his sister and, as he had expected, got no help whatsoever.

'I'm sorry, sir. I'm afraid I don't know. Abby?' He spoke her name with an intonation designed to wake her up. 'Has Jonas said anything to you of the Captain's order?'

Abigail shook her head and then managed to produce the

37

information that there were a number of packages awaiting collection in the hall.

As once before, her soft voice struck a chord of vague familiarity in Justin's memory but he was too intent on the business in hand to pursue it. Beyond wondering why the girl looked habitually scared, he paid her no further attention and said pleasantly, 'Ah, then we must hope that mine is amongst them. But I interrupt this lady's business. My apologies, ma'am.'

Barbara Atkins dimpled at him.

'Oh, no need, sir. I'll be gone in a trice if I can only decide between these two shades of blue.'

Captain Ambrose crossed to her side and, picking up the brighter sample, deliberately produced his most devastating smile. 'Why, which but this one, Mistress? It is the only one not made utterly drab by the brilliance of your eyes.'

'Oh!' Bab blushed and peeped at him through her lashes. 'You shouldn't say such things, sir!'

'Perhaps not. But how may I help myself when confronted with such inspiration?' teased Justin. 'And should I apologize for speaking no more than the truth or blame you for making my day immeasurably brighter?'

Torn between utter shock and a sort of grotesque fascination, Abigail watched the Captain unleash the full battery of his charm on the goldsmith's golden daughter and have it returned in full measure. Five minutes later Mistress Bab was out in the street, clutching five yards of gaudy ribbon that her father would almost undoubtedly forbid her to use and Captain Ambrose turned back to business without batting an eyelid. Samuel examined him with respect.

'Quite remarkable,' he said. 'I thought she was here for the day. Is it military training or can anybody do it?'

Justin's brows rose in mild amusement.

'Anyone with a modicum of natural cunning. Since you can recognize it when you see it, you shouldn't have any trouble. Now, about my cloth?'

'Ah yes, of course.' Samuel met his sister's astounded

gaze with a grin. 'I'll go and check.'

Abigail pulled herself together and directed a darkling glance across the room.

'I'll go,' she said quickly and went.

Samuel gave way to a helpless splutter of laughter.

'I'm sorry! It was the look on her face when she realized that you weren't just – just —'

'Exercising my wanton wiles?' supplied Justin helpfully. 'Yes. I hope she didn't find it embarrassing?'

'I should think she found it highly informative,' came the frank reply.

Justin picked up *The Man in the Moon* and directed a thoughtful gaze at its reader. 'You're not very like your brother, are you?'

'No.' Samuel looked him in the eye. 'But that doesn't mean I've any Royalist sympathies. I haven't. Quite the reverse. It's just that we're not all narrow-minded fanatics.'

There was a pause. 'That was straight from the shoulder, wasn't it? Have you ever thought of joining the army?'

Samuel's gaze grew bleakly withering.

'And what would be the good of that? I'm —'

'It's there,' said Abigail, emerging from the house. 'It's been cut and priced and everything. Only, well, there's rather a lot of it.' She looked dubiously at her brother.

Justin allowed satisfaction to inform every muscle.

'That is no problem. I have two troopers and a cart outside. If you will permit me to call them?'

'By all means,' said Samuel, bitingly. He rose from his stool and leaned his hands on the trestle. 'What a good thing you brought them.'

Abigail's startled eyes flew to his face but he did not meet them. Instead, as the Captain turned to leave the shop, he limped quickly towards the door to the house, muttering, 'You deal with it from here. I'm going upstairs since I'm obviously not needed.'

Under the Captain's eagle eye it was the business of only a few minutes to move the cloth out and on to the cart.

39

Then, despatching his men back to the Castle, Justin pulled a purse from the pocket of his buff-coat and set about paying his account.

It was a simple transaction and Abigail dealt with it efficiently enough until, as he handed her the money, he said abruptly, 'Perhaps I'm mistaken, but I seem to know you from somewhere.'

The purse slid through her fingers, struck the edge of the table and fell, scattering guineas all over the floor.

'Oh!' gasped Abigail, diving after them under the trestle and coming face to face with Captain Ambrose, whose reflex had been the same. 'Oh no!'

The clear grey eyes were bright with amusement.

'Pebble Lane,' he said simply. 'What a good job you don't deal in glassware. Do you always drop things?'

This seemed unfair and for one, exhilarating second, Abigail actually found herself framing a retort. Then her nerve failed and she said weakly, 'No. I – you took me by surprise.'

'Yes. I gathered that. I only wish I knew why. I don't bite, you know.'

She flushed and bent her head over the guineas.

'There's one by your knee,' she said.

'So there is.' He retrieved it and then reached out to pluck another from the folds of her skirt. 'And one by your – oh God – not again! What the devil's the matter now?' This as Abigail shot back a foot and dropped the coins for a second time.

Justin stared into wide, dark eyes filled with apprehension and his momentary exasperation melted. Dropping his brow on the arm that rested against his upraised knee, he gave way to unexpected hilarity. Abigail eyed him with dawning resentment. Then, snatching up all the coins she could see, she clutched them protectively to her chest and stood up.

'I don't,' she said finally, 'see what's so funny.'

Captain Ambrose drew a steadying breath and arose from beneath the table only to dissolve afresh when he looked at her. 'No. You wouldn't. But I daren't explain in case you hurl the money across the floor again and we have to spend another half-hour on our knees together.' He picked up his hat and bowed mockingly before setting it on his head. 'Goodbye, and give my love to Jonas. I think – indeed, I'm sure – that you'll find him sorry to have missed me.'

Chapter Four

It took Jonas Radford a full ten days to get over the fact that Captain Ambrose had outflanked him. Indeed, it might have taken longer had not the last day of July brought a small and rather ludicrous skirmish to divert his attention. The change came as a welcome relief to Samuel and Abigail, on whom the bulk of his displeasure had fallen. But though Samuel was disposed to laugh at the tale of enemy captains at Nethercote attempting to duel with faulty pistols, Abigail was not. The episode brought the war close again and she began to realize how much she hated it.

Rachel hated it too, though not for the same reasons, and as soon as she realized that Banbury might soon become a battleground, she began urging Jonas to leave it. She met, surprisingly, with a stone wall of resistance. The Lord, said Jonas, would protect the righteous and he was not leaving town just when the lions and lilies of the Royal Standard might at any time be struck from the Castle flag-pole. Rachel deferred silently to his wishes, relieved her frustration by carping at Abigail and, two weeks later, played her trump card by demurely announcing that she was pregnant.

After his initial burst of typically circumspect joy was over, Jonas discovered that the news had produced a chink in his armour. He began, reprehensibly, to consider the summer plague figures and the possible danger if the Castle should be besieged in earnest. Of course, there was plague every year but he had not previously had an unborn child for it to threaten and, though there was no question of the Cavaliers holding hostile, unwalled Banbury, there would be noise and fighting, overcrowded billets and difficulty over food. He found the prospect worrying and it disturbed his rest.

It was perhaps unfortunate that, while Jonas was torturing his already tortured conscience with thoughts of Aaron and Isaac, Nancy Lucas walked into the shop. Endowed with ample curves of which she liked to show as much as possible, thick unruly curls and bold, brown eyes, Nancy ran a modest but cheerful brothel near Sugarford Bar and was Royalist to the core. Her appearance in the Radfords' genteel establishment sent two respectable matrons scurrying into the street and produced a climacteric of shock that temporarily succeeded in depriving Jonas of breath.

Then he choked, bringing Abigail's head sharply up from a tray of muddled embroidery silks, 'Whore of Babylon! How dare you cross my threshold?'

Nancy eyed him calmly.

'Why shouldn't I? I'm only a customer – same as anyone else.' She grinned. 'I wouldn't stop you crossing mine if you wanted to.'

Jonas' colour rose and he spluttered incoherently. Nancy laughed and turned easily to Abigail. 'Now, my duck, I want some cambric and I want the best. What's that on the second shelf?'

'It's a little stiff,' offered Abigail nervously. 'The one above it is softer.'

'Abigail!' roared Jonas, furiously. 'Have you lost your mind? Contaminating yourself with the filth of the gutter by addressing this – this painted harlot!'

'Now hold on!' snapped Nancy. 'She ain't done nothing but show herself better mannered than you. And I didn't come here to listen to hard names. I came to buy some cloth.'

'Then you wasted your time. Do you think that I would touch your tainted money?'

'Why not? It's no worse than yours,' she retorted. 'After all, we both supply the needs of the garrison, don't we? The only difference is that you sell 'em cloth on the sly and I sell 'em —'

'Get out!' Jonas' voice shook with rage. 'Get out before you tempt me to violence.'

'What, would you soil your hands?' mocked Nancy. And then, 'Lay a finger on me, Master Long-nose, and I'll blacken both your eyes for you. But you needn't have a fit. I'm going.' She gathered up her brilliant, emerald skirts and smiled at Abigail. 'Keep your chin up, love. I know he's a miserable old sod – but he ain't no more than a puffed-up pig's bladder underneath. You remember that.' And she strolled unhurriedly from the shop.

It was a full minute before Jonas was capable of speech but then he rounded on his errant sister and made up for lost time by reducing her to emotional pulp.

On the following afternoon when Abigail was returning from Mistress Carter's, hard by the derelict Bear Garden, she met the redoubtable Nancy again. Her arm was seized, she was pulled into the shadows and a broad voice said, 'There – I thought it was you! I saw you go by an hour ago, so I kept an eye open for you coming back.'

Swallowing hard, Abigail digested the fact that she was standing in the doorway of Banbury's only house of ill-repute. She said weakly, 'I've been fitting a dress on Lizzie Carter. I'm sorry, I can't stay. If someone were to see me and tell Jonas —'

'Come in, then,' said Nancy. Then, as Abigail shook her head and tried to escape, 'Oh come on! It won't take a minute and I'll see you get away all right. I want to ask a favour.'

'Of me?' Abigail gazed timidly around Nancy's front parlour and was surprised to find it much like any other. 'I don't understand.'

'Well, you help in the shop, don't you? And there must be times when old long-nose ain't there? So I wondered if you couldn't buy twenty yards of cambric for me and drop it in here when next you're passing.' Nancy paused. 'I know I've got a cheek to ask but me and the girls need new shifts and shifts is important in our line of work, see?'

Abigail coloured a little. 'Oh yes.'

'I don't want you to get into trouble, though. That wouldn't be right.' She smiled wryly. 'Like I said, I got no business asking and it ain't as though I know you or anything. But I had a feeling you wouldn't mind talking to a whore and you can always say no. I reckon I'll understand. Old long-nose your brother, is he?'

'Yes.' Completely out of her depth, something prompted Abigail to add, 'I'm sorry for the way he spoke to you.'

Nancy grinned. 'Don't worry about that. I'm used to it but

44

I appreciate your saying it. There's not many who'd bother and I shan't forget. Now: I mustn't keep you so just say whether you think you can help me or not.'

Abigail smiled shyly into the warm, brown eyes and drew a long breath. 'Yes. I think I can. I'll try.'

A few days later, on August 22nd, violence erupted in the town when the Parliamentary forces tried to establish outposts in the suburbs. They were beaten back by troops from the Castle but for several hours the streets rang with booted feet, shouted commands and the rattle of musket-fire. Like everyone else, Jonas barred his family in behind shutters and locked doors and by midday he had decided to send his wife and mother to the comparative peace of his sister Ruth's house at Grimsbury.

'And what about Abby?' asked Samuel, indignantly. 'Isn't she to go as well?'

'How can she?' replied Jonas coldly. 'Someone has to run the house and I imagine that you will expect to be fed?'

'There is no need for Abigail to leave,' added Rachel. 'She will be perfectly safe with the two of you. Indeed, I am only going myself because of my condition.'

Samuel eyed her sarcastically, opened his mouth to argue and then closed it again as Abigail kicked him beneath the table.

'I'm glad I'm not going,' she told him later. 'Just the thought of living with Rachel and Ruth for goodness knows how many weeks is enough to give me an ague, but I'm sorry for mother. She won't enjoy it either.'

Rachel and Alice left for Grimsbury the next day, escorted by Jonas, and Abigail seized the opportunity to run up to Sugarford Bar with Nancy Lucas' cambric. She found the neat parlour full of baggage and Nancy up to her ears in packing.

'I'm taking the girls up to the Castle,' was the brisk explanation. 'Once the Roundheads get into the town, our lives won't be worth a docken. Your brother and his Praise-God friends will see to that. So I asked Justin Ambrose to get permission for the four of us to move in with the garrison and I don't reckon we've got long.'

'Do you know Captain Ambrose well?' asked Abigail.

'As well as he lets anybody know him. But he's got a good heart, that one.' Nancy paused in her labours and said warmly, 'Thanks for helping out with the stuff, love. If there's ever anything I can do for you just ask. Right?'

Just before dawn on the morning of Sunday August 25th, Nancy's suspicions were made reality when two companies of Parliamentary foot entered the town and quietly took possession of St Mary's church. The first the Radford household knew of it was when it was awoken by a party of troopers wishing to search for billeted Cavaliers. Majestically robed in his nightshirt, Jonas threw his doors joyfully open and made his guests welcome with cherry cordial.

It was the house-to-house search rather than the seizure of the church which resulted in a belated alarm being raised in the Castle and by that time the Parliamentary cavalry had come up to join the advance infantry. Then Thursday's events were repeated in greater magnitude as the garrison sallied forth in force and took up positions in gardens and outhouses all about the town.

Abigail attended to breakfast with shaking fingers and smashed three eggs on the kitchen floor when a stray shot tore through one of the upstairs windows. She helped Betty prepare the vegetables for dinner and cut her hand along with the turnips when the small pieces of Parliamentary artillery in the church tower opened fire on the Castle. And by mid-afternoon when Samuel came in, full of eager excitement, her nerves were vibrating like lute-strings.

'The garrison cavalry drove ours to the edge of the town,' he told her, cheerfully. 'But it won't do them any good because they can't hold a position without infantry and that's been pushed back inside the Castle. Twice.'

'Oh?' Abigail sank wearily on to the settle. 'Then why is there still fighting in the streets?'

'Well, naturally the Cavaliers are trying to regain their hold on the town. They have to. It's only common-sense. But they'll never do it. There aren't enough of them. Colonel Whetham has just arrived from Warwick.'

'Good,' said Abigail. 'Who's he?'

'Commander-in-Chief of the Parliament's artillery-train,' replied Samuel, grinning. 'He's brought three companies of foot, a cannon royal and a murdering piece.'

His sister stared at him for a moment without speaking. Then, with irony, she said, 'Wonderful. That's all we need, isn't it?'

First light on Monday morning found the Royalist garrison tired, irritable and securely besieged from without. Sir William Compton and Colonel Greene waxed contrapuntally articulate on the subject of unobservant sentries before placing four troopers under arrest and then gave orders for continuous cannon- and musket-fire to prevent the enemy digging breastworks and siting their guns. It was uphill work but the afternoon brought a diversion in the form of an impromptu cattle drive after two beasts in the Castle pasture were shot. It increased the population of the outer ward by seven cows, five sheep and a goat and it raised a cheer from each of Will Compton's three hundred and twenty men.

Tuesday the twenty-seventh dawned hazy with the promise of heat. Busy with a stream of tasks, Justin found himself appraising their defences in a way he had never troubled to do before.

The Castle was some three hundred years old and concentric in design. It occupied a large area. Its outer defences consisted of a moat fed by the Cuttle Brook and an earth mound lying parallel to it, inside which ran the seven-foot-thick curtain wall. This, unfortunately, did not follow the line of the moat but it was studded with interval towers and was equipped to the north and south with twin, square-fronted gatehouses. Against the inside of the wall the garrison had banked up earth, thus enlarging the wet ditch that surrounded the quadrangular, four-storey building of the inner court.

All in all, it looked as good as any other English fortress of its age and type, until, that was, one noticed the places where the stone had crumbled and never been repaired. Then it suddenly became what it was: a dubious, even flimsy defence against the engines of modern warfare, containing stocks of food that, even with rationing, would last little more than a month.

Justin was assisting Hugh Vaughan with the recalcitrant firing mechanism of a saker when he heard the unmistakable sounds of arrival in the rebel camp and, stopping work, looked down on a well-drilled troop of horse. At the head of the column, an unmarked rectangle of silk proclaimed the presence of a full Colonel; and, echoing its azure brilliance, a great silver-fringed banner bearing the legend EXURGAT – ET DISSIPA BUNTUR.

'Hugh, whose colours are those?'

Captain Vaughan peered abstractedly between the machicolations and then straightened quickly.

'The honourable member for Oxfordshire. Well, well, he's taken his time, hasn't he?' And then, in response to Justin's patient stare, 'It's Lord Saye and Sele's son, John Fiennes.'

'Ah.' A faint smile touched Justin's mouth. 'I met his brother Nathaniel once. When he surrendered Bristol to Rupert.'

Hugh grinned. 'Yes? Well, this one's better. And what he lacks in flair, he makes good with haste and sheer, bloody persistence. If he's got command, we're in for an interesting time and sooner than we expected, too.'

This prophecy was fulfilled within two hours when the rebel drums beat out the chamade and a blue-sleeved trumpet rode slowly up to the south gate, accompanied by a cornet bearing a white flag. The Castle, bristling with a discreet show of force, was ready for him. In rigid silence and with the utmost formality, the trumpet was conducted to the Governor's quarters where Sir William sat in state, flanked by Colonel Greene and Captains Ambrose, Vaughan and Walrond. All four had removed every trace of the morning's toil from their appearance and were garbed with temporary splendour.

The envoy, a pink-faced young gentleman in his early twenties, cleared his throat and began.

'Colonel Fiennes presents his compliments to Sir William and suggests that, before hostilities are commenced in earnest, it may be possible to reach an accommodation for the preservation of life. He therefore seeks that you will look upon the forces ranged against you and determine the wisdom of ceding the Castle for the use of the Parliament. In return for this, Colonel Fiennes will issue passes and permit you to march out with all the honours of war.'

'Now that is generous of him,' murmured Will. 'The full honours of war, no less. Very generous, indeed, especially as we won't have earned them.'

A glint of appreciation warmed Captain Ambrose's eyes but he remained ramrod-stiff and even resisted the temptation to glance at Hugh. The envoy, meanwhile, was attempting to continue.

'The Colonel further empowers me to —'

'I think,' said Sir William, coming abruptly to his feet, 'that we have heard enough. You may thank Colonel Fiennes for his courtesy but tell him that we hold this place in trust for His Majesty and, while there is one man left alive within it, he need not expect to have it delivered to him. And, in case you find trouble in remembering that, you may give him this letter. Captain Ambrose. Escort this officer from the Castle. Captain Vaughan, I believe you have your orders?'

Walking beside Justin to the gate, the trumpet said good-humouredly, 'Ah well. So much for the preliminaries. Now we can get on with the action. I don't suppose you could recommend a decent billet, could you?'

Laughter stirred in the grey eyes. 'No. I couldn't. And we've got all the whores.'

'Well, of course,' grinned the envoy. 'But we have all the daughters of Banbury.'

'You're welcome to them,' said Justin, his hand on the gate. 'Goodbye.'

The trumpet was half-way back to his own ranks when Hugh applied a match to his favourite culverin. Then the air was rent by a single, throaty roar as Singing Jenny bellowed out the Castle's defiance to the enemy at her gates.

Colonel Fiennes heard it and, wasting no more time, opened a heavy cannonade which continued till dusk and began again at dawn the next day. The garrison answered in kind but, before night brought temporary respite, a hole

49

some four yards square was already apparent in the west wall.

Few in the Castle slept that night, the men because repair work had to be done hastily under cover of darkness and the officers because they were in council. It had taken Captain Ambrose's field experience to identify the latest Parliamentary reinforcements as Colonel Boswell's regiment of foot and Colonel Purefoy's horse, but three of the six pieces of ordnance that accompanied them needed introduction to no one. Capable of firing a hundred-pound stone, fireball or the explosive device known as a grenado, mortars could batter walls, blow up buildings or fire towns. One would have been a problem; three could spell catastrophe.

However, due to skilful garrison marksmanship, the rebels were still trying to plant their new pieces on Friday and, by then, their determination was so great that Captain Ambrose had scant difficulty in slipping out with twenty men to fire the houses on the north side of the market-place.

It was an order that Will Compton had been reluctant to give but the houses stood too close for comfort and it was only prudent to remove them. They were already deserted for even the most obstinate citizen had seen the folly of inhabiting no man's land once the siege became active. Although he knew this, Justin conducted a swift, thorough search before fulfilling his mission.

He found the spaniel pup, a shivering bundle of liver and white fur, in a corner of the corn chandler's scullery and scooped it up with scarcely a glance or second thought. When the floors were lightly dusted with gunpowder and the torches laid, he led his men smartly back to the Castle with the dog tucked snugly into the breast of his coat.

Ned Frost eyed the bulge speculatively and expressed the hope that it was salt to replenish their dwindling stock. Justin grinned and, with the air of a travelling conjurer, produced his trophy.

'I think I'll call him "Hallelujah-that-Perdition-hast-not-taken-thee", ' he shouted over the din of reciprocal cannon-fire. 'What do you think?'

'That I'm damned if we want any Roundhead curs in this

castle,' retorted Ned. 'And the name's bigger than the animal.'

'True.' Justin examined the pup with absent interest. 'Very well, then. We'll rear him to know his duty and call him Rex. Better?'

'Much. Where are you going now?'

'To charm Nancy into milking the goat. Even a mascot has to be fed, you know.'

At a little after midday, the first of Colonel Fiennes' mortars came into play and its chosen missile was the most destructive it had to offer, the grenado. The first great powder-packed shell whizzed harmlessly over the Castle to explode in an eruption of earth on the near bank of the Cherwell. After ten, breathlessly active minutes on the ramparts, Hugh Vaughan bethought himself of other measures and flew down the steps, to collide violently with Justin at the base of the west turret.

'Fire-hooks and buckets!' he shouted. 'If the next one hits, it could —'

'I know.' Justin gestured curtly to where his troopers were already drenching the thatch of the outbuildings. 'But I'll wager a bottle of claret that the next one is —' His words were drowned by a whining crescendo that culminated in a deafening, earth-shaking blast. '— short,' finished Justin, imperturbably. 'The bastards are quick, aren't they?'

Hugh swore and dashed back the way he had come.

Fired less precipitately, the next grenado dropped neatly into the outer ward, ploughing up the ground, setting light to the stables and injuring three of Justin's men. Watching the surgeon shake his head over a lad of no more than nineteen, Justin felt the clawing of familiar nausea. To lead was to kill: a simple fact that one expected to get used to – only to find that, at best, all one learned was control.

The mortar spoke twice more before dark. One shot fell wide, the other deprived the castle of its master-gunner, who was painfully killed by flying splinters of shattered stone. Captain Vaughan, grazed, scratched and bloodied by the same explosion but otherwise miraculously whole, knelt unmoving beside his sergeant until the man died and then returned to his duty with white-faced savagery.

Night fell but not peace for the rebels continued to site their artillery by torchlight. Inside the Castle, fatigue was beginning to take its toll for many of the men had scarcely seen their beds in a week. Most of the officers had not seen them at all, but snatched a few minutes' rest when and where they could. That night, they were again called to a council of war.

After reports on damage, casualties and provisions had been dealt with, Colonel Greene said, 'You know the situation. The west wall is already damaged and the enemy have a large artillery-train and something in excess of fifteen hundred men. We might hold out a day or a month but, since this is one fortress His Majesty can't afford to lose, Will and I would prefer to minimize the risk by summoning help.'

'From where?' asked Justin. 'With the King's army in the West, Oxford won't have any troops to spare.'

'No.' Anthony Greene turned a quill thoughtfully between his fingers. 'So we must gamble on the fact that Rupert is still at Shrewsbury. Gentlemen, I'd like your recommendations of who to send. Two men with courage, discretion and a knowledge of the country in question.'

At an hour before dawn, two shadowy figures stripped of their hose and shoes and each bearing one half of a letter to Prince Rupert, slipped quietly over the curtain wall and disappeared into the gloom. A little later, the rosy glow of daybreak revealed two more Parliamentary cannon firmly planted and in working order. Then the morning's brief tranquillity was over and the air became heavy with smoke, dust and a cacophony of sound.

Shortly after noon, a grenado blasted its way into the Castle precincts, firing the old mansion house and killing one of the few women. The others set up an immediate clamour to be let out.

'Let out? Let out?' screeched Nancy Lucas, over the din of booming cannon and wailing females. 'Why, you lily-livered puddings, I'll give you let out! You ought to be ashamed of yourselves!'

'For what?' yelled back one common-law wife hysterically.

'For not wanting to end up fried like poor Sal?'

'If the silly bitch had stayed put like she was told to, she'd be as safe as you or me,' snapped Nancy. Arms akimbo, she raked them with a contemptuous stare. 'And what do you think's going to happen to you if you do get out? Smiles of welcome and a nice, cosy billet with some miserable poke-nose? Don't think your wedding ring'll save you, Madge Burke, because it won't. Far as they're concerned, you're all as big a whore as I am. And you, Katy Muldoon, hasn't no one ever told you what they do to Irishers?'

'Nancy, what the devil's going on here?'

Nancy swung round to meet Captain Ambrose's bright gaze.

'Well, thank God for that! Perhaps you can persuade these daft little flowers they're better off where they are.'

With the blaze in the outer ward still uncontrolled, Justin had better things to do with his time but he checked his temper and produced a delicate blend of reassurance and charming appeal. It worked on all but five and these remained stubbornly unconvinced, leaving him with the unenviable task of laying the matter before the Governor. Twenty minutes later a message was on its way to the rebel lines, politely requesting a brief cessation and safe-conduct for those women wishing to leave.

Having sent it, Justin looked round to find Nancy at his elbow, her full mouth set tight and her brown gaze savagely acrimonious. He smiled and said, 'Quite sure you don't want to go too? It may be your last chance.'

'A pox on that!' came the forthright reply. 'Me and my girls'd as soon set fire to ourselves.'

Colonel Fiennes' reply, when it came, was an elegantly-phrased refusal.

'Snuffling, misbegotten pigs!' spat Nancy. And then, looking shrewdly at Justin, 'No more than you expected?'

'No.' He turned to get back to work and then paused, looking back at her. 'Pity there aren't a few more like you, Nan. The war would have been over months ago.'

Her colour rose a little but she laughed and cast him a

glance of roguish invitation. 'Going to see something of you then, am I?'

'With regret, no.' The grey eyes met hers with understanding. 'There's no time even for sleep, you know, and I'd hate to prove a disappointment. But thank you, anyway.'

Smiling wryly, she watched him go. It was not the first time he had refused her, indeed, he had yet to accept but, though she was sorry, it was not a matter for offence. She liked him too well for that.

A cannon-ball crashed against the curtain wall and sent a shower of earth spattering over her.

'Sod it,' said Nancy, to no one in particular, then strolled inside without even bothering to brush the dust from her skirts.

Chapter Five

Not far away, at the sign of the Ragged Staff in Shop Row, another lady thought occasionally of Captain Ambrose and wondered how he did. She would have been startled and perhaps a little reassured had she been able to see him, for imagination showed him conducting his work in a state of flawless elegance. Other officers might end their day streaked with dirt and sweat but not Captain Ambrose. Like Rachel and Colonel Fiennes, he was enshrined in Abigail's mind as a paragon of perpetual neatness.

She herself was rarely neat these days but, with other things on his mind, Jonas carped less than usual and Rachel, of course, was no longer there to see. Left to hold the fort, Abigail had found it a relatively simple matter while there was only Samuel and Jonas to care for. But on August 27th, Colonel Fiennes had arrived in Banbury and Jonas, in his capacity as the town's most senior remaining official, had volunteered his home as the Colonel's billet. It was perfectly logical for the house was large and conveniently situated; but for Abigail, who never knew how many to expect for dinner or when she would be free of visitors long enough to clean the floors, it was a source of constant domestic crisis.

Bred only four miles away at Broughton Castle and son of the district's traditional overlord, John Fiennes was already distantly acquainted with Jonas. Dark as a gypsy, he was just thirty, of medium height and possessed of a quiet forcefulness that crushed opposition like a well-oiled millstone. Abigail went in awe and trepidation for three days before his unfailing courtesy disarmed her and she learned to appreciate the many small aggravations his presence spared her. Colonel Fiennes might be the cause of endless muddy feet and hasty culinary improvisations but he kept Jonas in check and the common soldiery at bay and that was a lot to be grateful for.

With him came efficient, serious-minded Major Lytcot

and insouciant Robert Woodley, whose duties as a trumpet meant that he had always to be within call. Of the Major Abigail saw very little; of Rob Woodley, she saw more than enough for he seemed to have a marked predilection for the kitchen and was constantly underfoot.

On the morning of Thursday September 5th, deafened by the roar of cannon and unnerved by spasmodic explosions which set every dish rattling on its shelf, Abigail was wrestling with her preserves when an arm slid familiarly around her waist. A jar of apricots shattered on the red-brick floor and she wheeled round, flushed and furious, to meet Mr Woodley's unabashed smile.

'Sorry,' he said. 'I didn't mean to startle you.'

'Then keep your hands to yourself,' she snapped, too irritable to be shy. 'And stop creeping up on me if you don't want to starve.'

'I didn't creep. I've been calling out to you ever since I came in. I'm surprised you didn't hear me.'

Abigail stared at him, speechless. An explosion tore at the air and a plate toppled off the dresser.

'Hear you?' she shouted. 'Of course I didn't hear you! I'm amazed I can still hear anything. What's going on out there? It sounds as if the entire town is being demolished.'

'No, no,' said Mr Woodley, soothingly. 'Just a few cannon and mortars over at North Bar. Nothing you haven't heard before.'

'But those explosions?'

'Grenadoes. We've fired over thirty this morning, big ones, too. Hundred and twelve pounders.'

'Then I'm surprised the Castle is still standing,' said Abigail acidly. 'It ought to be no more than a heap of rubble if the noise is any guide. Or do your gunners miss a lot?'

Mr Woodley folded his blue, trailing-sleeved arms and grinned at her. 'You are in a bad mood, aren't you? But it suits you. You ought to try it more often.'

'That,' said Abigail, 'is not at all unlikely. I suppose you came for the Colonel's meal?'

He nodded, saying with winsome boyishness, 'Are you really angry with me? I'm truly sorry about the apricots.

56

May I help you clear them up?'

'No you may not,' said Abigail, her mouth trembling on the brink of laughter. 'You may pick up your basket and go – before Jonas comes in and finds you here.'

'At once, Madam!' He saluted smartly and seized the basket from the dresser. 'But I wish you'd smile. I shall worry all afternoon if you don't.'

'Oh, go away!' Betrayed into an involuntary gurgle, she grabbed a stray apricot from the table and threw it. 'Now!'

He laughed, ducked, blew her a kiss and went. Abigail was left with a sticky floor and a sense of wonderment mingled with regret.

By the time Samuel drifted into the kitchen half-way through the afternoon, the noise had abated not at all and her head was throbbing.

'Those guns!' she wailed. 'Don't they ever stop?'

'Not today, apparently,' said Samuel, reaching for an apple and retiring with it to the settle. 'But think of mother at Grimsbury and count your blessings.'

'Yes.' Abigail sighed and collapsed beside him. 'Is Jonas in the shop?'

'Mm. He's brooding over the empty pages of his sales ledger.'

'We've had no custom again, then?'

'Well, of course not. Who's going to buy cloth while the town's being blown to bits? And who is there left who can afford it anyway? Virtually all the families of any substance have decamped – except for old Atkins, that is. And he's having a wonderful time buying up bits of plundered jewellery and pretending he's never seen it before.' He stopped suddenly. 'Listen – do you hear it?'

'What? All I can hear is gunfire.'

'Yes, but it's changed. And the mortars have stopped.' He paused, head tilted to one side. Over the roar of the cannon came a sharp rattling sound, like stones flung hard against a wall.

'There! That's musket-fire. The garrison must be making a sally.' He got up and limped quickly to the door.

'Where are you going?' Abigail arose, full of suspicion.

'You can't go out there. Jonas will have a fit.'

'Let him,' said Samuel and was gone.

The evening meal of mutton pie, roasted vegetables and stewed apricots was less well cooked than usual but Samuel returned for it safe and sound and without Jonas being any the wiser. He took his seat just as Abigail placed the last dish on the table and, after giving her a conspiratorial wink, assumed an expression of unnatural and provoking gravity.

Abigail, who had formed the habit of seeing to the gentlemen's needs and then retiring to eat in the kitchen with Betty, took a last look at the table and was about to withdraw when the Colonel stopped her.

'Mistress Abigail?' He rose from his seat and regarded her with his usual unsmiling courtesy. 'It is churlish of us to banish you from your own board. Won't you join us?'

She coloured a little and glanced nervously at Jonas. 'It – I – you are very kind —'

'My sister is honoured, sir,' cut in Jonas smoothly. 'But she has no wish to intrude and will do very well in the kitchen.'

John Fiennes surveyed him steadily for a moment. Then he said, 'Possibly. When we have added company, such discretion is admirable but when we do not, there is no question of intrusion and it would please me to have her join us. Major Lytcot, a stool, if you would be so good.'

Flatteringly placed between the Major and the Colonel, unable for different reasons to look at either of her brothers and uneasily aware of approaching indigestion, Abigail struggled mechanically through her dinner and thought nostalgically of the kitchen. Then, thankfully, the talk turned to things military and she was able to relax and listen.

'They lifted seventeen of our men on that last sortie,' Major Lytcot was saying bitterly. 'One has to admit that they are very well led.'

'Quite.' The Colonel gazed thoughtfully at his stewed apricots. 'Anthony Greene, of course. We know all about him, sacrilegious, stubborn and wily. Take him, gentlemen, and we have taken Banbury.'

'I wondered if they might not be running short of

powder,' mused the Major. 'The two messengers we caught slipping out last Saturday said nothing of it and nor did the letter they were carrying, but it might bear further investigation.'

John Fiennes' expression darkened.

'We'll be short of it ourselves if we have to repeat today's performance too often. Eighty grenadoes and twice that in cannon-shot and we're still not inside. I do not find it satisfactory.'

'We might try an assault,' suggested Rob Woodley diffidently.

'We might try flying over the wall, Mr Woodley,' came the blighting reply. 'But at the present time I do not think it likely that we will.'

'No, sir.' Rob buried his round face in his ale mug and managed to send Abigail a glance of comic gloom.

'The Lord will provide a way,' stated Jonas. 'He will not suffer us to come so far only to be defeated. The Castle must fall and when it does —'

'When it does,' interposed Colonel Fiennes, rising from his seat, 'we shall all give thanks. In the meantime the Committee of Both Kingdoms grows impatient and looks, not to the Lord, but to me. Mistress Abigail – the dinner, as always, was excellent and I thank you for doing us the honour of sharing it with us. Major, a word with you in my room, if you please.'

'And me, sir?' Rob rose and fixed his superior with a wide, blue stare. 'Will you be requiring me at all?'

'I think not.' A hint of humour showed for the first time in John Fiennes' eyes. 'You may therefore devote your surplus energy to helping Mistress Abigail, if, that is, she can find a use for you. Goodnight.'

'Well, if you won't go for me, won't you at least go with me?' asked Abigail pleadingly. It was Saturday morning and there was not a vegetable in the house. 'You know how I hate going there. Mr Barnes looks at me in such a strange way.'

'He looks at everyone in a strange way,' retorted Samuel. 'You make too much of it. And, since you know I can't leave the shop while Jonas is at Grimsbury, you might as well make up your mind to collecting the vegetables yourself. Goodness knows why you should be scared, anyway. His mother's always there, isn't she?'

This was true but Abigail found it no comfort as she drove the small cart slowly to nearby Bodicote where Thankful Barnes ran his forge and small-holding. It was a poor place, scrupulously clean but cheerless and bare of all save the most basic essentials, a reflection, Abigail knew, not of financial straits but Puritan fervour. Even in religiously independent Banbury, the Barnes family was known for the radical nature of its views. But it was not this that caused Abigail's reluctance nor even her dislike of the smith's sour-faced mother, though that was great enough, having often witnessed the old lady's treatment of her grandchildren. It was something that came from Barnes himself, a creeping, insidious fear that made no sense at all but made her wonder, shuddering, what kind of life his late wife must have led.

He was standing outside the forge when she arrived, a big, ox-like man in his middle thirties but looking older, with whitish hair and narrow pale eyes that settled on her and lingered.

'Good morning,' said Abigail. 'I've come for our order. Is it ready?'

The smith crossed slowly to stand beside the cart.

'The boy's doing it now. Won't take no more than a minute. Meantime, perhaps you'll come in and pass the time of day with my old mother?' He held out his hand to help her down.

Intent on avoiding his oddly mesmeric gaze, Abigail fidgeted with the reins and made a stammering excuse of having little time.

'But you have to wait for the vegetables, don't you? And my old mother'd be that pleased to see you, Mistress.'

The words were innocuous but something in the broad, country voice was not. Before she could answer, the reins were taken from her grasp and twisted about the bar.

'Come, Mistress. Let me help you down.' His hands were on her waist, lifting her like a wisp of straw, burning through

60

gown, corset and shift to her skin and then hesitating before finally releasing her.

The kitchen was dark and smelled of the onions that hung on strings from the oaken beams. Mistress Barnes was scouring her oven and, in a corner, eight-year-old Charity was silently cutting rags for a rug. She looked up as Abigail entered and smiled faintly before turning back to her task.

'See who's here, mother? It's Mistress Abigail, come for the vegetables.'

'I see her.' Zelah Barnes offered no greeting but stared at her visitor rather as though she were a dirty cooking-pot.

Something stirred in Abigail and, lifting her chin, she said, 'I am so sorry, Mistress Barnes. You are busy and I have come at a bad time. Please don't let me disturb you. I can easily wait in the —' She was half-way to the door when the smith stopped her.

'Now where's the hurry, Mistress? Endurance is only just starting to load the cart. And mother's never too busy for you. It's just her way. Isn't it, mother?'

'If you say so.' The voice remained harsh with disapproval. 'Ye'd best sit down, Mistress, and take some ale.'

'Oh no, no, thank you.' Barnes' hand was still on her arm and Abigail subsided hurriedly on to a stool. 'It's very kind of you but really I must not stay. I am expected back and . . .' Her words trailed off helplessly as mother and son seemed to close in on her.

'I hear you've got his Lordship's son in the house,' said Zelah.

'Colonel Fiennes? Yes.'

'And two other young officers. And your mother and sister away at Grimsbury?'

'Yes.' Unable to comprehend Zelah's interrogation, Abigail looked from mother to son and then wished she had not. The pale eyes were fixed on her as if they would break into her mind and crack it open, as if – and she recognized the fact with a sense of paralysing shock – they could see through her clothes to her body. New fear rippled cold down her spine and she stood up, shaking. 'I have to go.'

'Of course.' Thankful Barnes towered over her, huge,

muscular, apparently respectful. 'You have heavy responsibilities. We understand, don't we, mother?'

'I understand,' came the cryptic reply. '"The serpent was more subtle than any beast of the field which the Lord God hath made." Do you pray, Mistress?'

The question made Abigail jump. 'Yes. Yes, of course.'

'With a clean heart, made pure and open to the Lord?'

'I think so.'

'Temptation is in your path, Mistress. You should make sure of it.'

The oppressive gloom of the kitchen enclosed Abigail like a fist. Her palms grew damp with sweat and the smith's face wavered before her eyes. 'He knows I am afraid,' she thought, hazily, 'and he is glad.'

'Smith! Ho there! Smith, I say!'

The call checked Abigail's wandering senses and she blinked.

'Mr Woodley?'

A dark figure appeared in the sunlight of the doorway.

'Smith? What on earth do you think you're playing at, man? I've been calling myself hoarse out here!' And then, differently, 'Why Mistress Abigail. I'm sorry. I didn't realize you were here.'

'It's all right.' Somehow Abigail reached the door and clutched Rob Woodley's arm. 'I was just leaving.'

He drew her outside, his plain countenance marked by a frown. 'What's the matter? You're as white as a sheet. Are you ill?' And then, moving as though to take her back in, 'I think you ought to sit down for a moment.'

'No!' She shouted the word, careless of what anyone thought. 'I want to go home.'

Rob stared at her. 'All right. Is this your cart?'

She nodded.

'Good. Come on, then.' He crossed the yard with her and helped her up on to the seat. 'Now wait there. I'll just have a word with the smith about these firing pins and then I'll take you back.'

'Yes.' She fumbled with her purse. 'Give him that. The money for the vegetables.'

Five minutes later, with his horse tied to the back of the cart, Rob was driving them both back to town.

'Now,' he said calmly. 'What was all that about? You looked frightened to death.'

'Did I?' Beginning to recover herself, Abigail managed a tiny shrug. 'How silly. I merely felt a little faint. The kitchen was so stuffy, you see and —'

'Liar,' he said placidly. 'You've never been so glad to see anyone as you were to see me just then, and I'm not vain enough to suppose it was personal. But if you don't want to explain, that's your business.'

'Yes,' agreed Abigail. 'It is. And I don't.'

By the following Wednesday it was clear that the Cavaliers were indeed running short of gunpowder and rumour also held them cowed by sheer force of numbers and dogged by the virulent new fever. Morale in the besieging forces therefore ran correspondingly high only to be dashed when, after investing the Castle on three sides, they were beaten back by a garrison sally. By then Colonel Fiennes was also low on gunpowder and, despite being now in command of some three and a half thousand men, he considered his infantry inadequate for the task in hand. He sent requesting Lord Manchester to repair these deficiencies but was not even remotely surprised when all that arrived were five hundred dragoons and those from Lieutenant-General Cromwell.

Colonel Fiennes was not entirely disappointed. Dragoons were accustomed to serving as infantry and would probably do well enough, but the identity of the Lieutenant-Colonel commanding them produced a number of mixed emotions for his name was one known the length and breadth of England. The man ought to be an asset, mused John Fiennes dubiously. He had been a popular Puritan hero ever since he had been pilloried for distributing anti-episcopal pamphlets. Yet, a niggling worry gnawed at the Colonel's mind and suggested the wisdom of keeping this new officer under his eye.

When approached to extend his hospitality, Jonas' reply

was immediate and affirmative, but his response to the suggestion that his sister should also be consulted was one of blank surprise.

'There is no need for that, Colonel. Abigail knows her duty and will be happy to assist in any way she can.'

'Even so,' said the Colonel, quietly, 'I think we will do her the courtesy to ask. Will you be so good as to call her?'

Abigail entered the room reluctantly for, though Jonas had said nothing save that her presence was required, his expression boded no good. The simply-phrased request, therefore, took her completely unawares.

'Well, Abigail?' prompted Jonas sharply. 'The Colonel is waiting.'

'Yes, I'm sorry. Of course we have room, sir. And naturally the gentleman is welcome to lodge here.'

'Thank you.' John Fiennes inclined his head gravely. 'When the Lieutenant-Colonel sees how well you look after us, I am sure he will be as grateful to you as I am but I feel I must point out to you both that this is no ordinary officer you will be taking in for he is possessed of a certain notoriety. In short, he is John Lilburne.'

'Lilburne?' echoed Jonas. 'Free-born John?'

'The same.'

Jonas' eyes glowed. 'My house will be honoured. The victory now is surely ours for God has sent us a sign.'

'God has sent us a firebrand,' corrected the Colonel drily. And then, half to himself, 'I only hope he will also help me to control it.'

Abigail met their new guest for the first time at dinner that evening and was quick to notice that Samuel was already enslaved. They had both expected the fanatical Mr Lilburne to resemble Jonas but they had been wrong. Free-born John was no cold, gloomy pontificator. He was elegantly clad, bursting with animated, joy-filled humanity and less than thirty years old. Abigail met a wide, intelligent gaze, was greeted warmly and without reserve and found herself smiling.

It seemed to her that the war-talk took on a different flavour that night. They discussed the news from outside:

Lord Essex's defeat at the hands of the King at Lostwithiel and the victory of a renegade Scottish Earl and his tiny band of Irish cut-throats over the Scots allies north of the border. But there was no anti-Royalist ranting of the kind so often indulged in by Jonas and, indeed, more than a hint of criticism of the Parliament until, that was, Colonel Fiennes quietly put an end to it.

John Lilburne accepted the check with a faint smile and shifted his ground. 'Have you heard of our difficulties with my Lord Manchester? Fearing an absolute victory over the King, his Lordship declined to march on Newark and told me to my face that he'd like to see me hanged for taking Tickhill.'

'Oh?' Colonel Fiennes toyed idly with his ale. 'And is that why Lieutenant-General Cromwell sent you to me?'

The clever gaze widened.

'Not at all, sir. You requested reinforcements and, since Lord Manchester will not have his troops used, Lieutenant-General Cromwell supplied you from his own.' A sudden gleam of amusement dawned. 'Though it was perhaps politic to remove me for a time. If I am not mistaken, there is a quarrel brewing.'

'And no need to ask whose side you are on, I suppose?' It was Major Lytcot who spoke.

'None. Oliver Cromwell is a great man and if he were allowed to control the war without interference from ham-fisted Moderates such as Manchester and Essex, it would be over by Easter.'

'I see,' said the Colonel. 'And then?'

'And then the Lord's work can begin,' said Lilburne simply. 'The instatement of civil liberty and freedom of conscience that are the right of every true-born Englishman.'

Throughout the meal, Samuel had remained almost totally silent. Even afterwards, when Lieutenant-Colonel Lilburne expounded his views on free elections and universal franchise, he still said nothing. It was only as Lilburne made to retire that Abigail saw her brother move to detain him. 'I would like to know more – if it is no trouble.'

Free-born John looked searchingly back at him and then

smiled. He said, 'It's no trouble. Come.'

After Lieutenant-Colonel Lilburne's revelations about Lord Manchester, it not unnaturally came as a surprise when part of his Lordship's regiment arrived in Banbury on the following Sunday, along with some fifty miners from Bedworth. Colonel Fiennes, however, wasted no time in idle speculation. He had longed to try a new approach and now had the means to do it. The colliers were immediately set to work undermining the curtain wall of the Castle.

As soon as he knew what was afoot, Samuel vanished from the house and took himself off to watch. He returned in the late afternoon to find Abigail smothered in flour and rolling out pastry.

Without even glancing up, she said despondently, 'It's cracking. I knew it would. Patchwork pie again.'

Samuel grinned, draped his cloak over the back of the settle and sat down. 'It's disaster all round then. Colonel Fiennes has had a bad day, too.'

'Oh?' Abigail lifted the pastry with stealth and cunning. A good third of it fell back on the board.

'Yes. His miners swear a lot.'

'I know how they feel.' The pastry was kneaded savagely back into a submissive lump. 'Have they dug a tunnel yet?'

'They've dug half a dozen,' said Samuel, his voice warm with amusement. 'Unfortunately, the ground they've chosen is like a bog so all they've achieved is to locate two underground springs and drain part of the moat. They are wet, dirty and tired. And the garrison, needless to say, have been laughing themselves silly. One of their officers is something of a comedian and, after he tired of offering advice, he got his men to rig up a couple of catapults. That was when the language deteriorated. In fact, the whole situation grew rather ripe because, having little gunpowder, our enterprising Cavalier decided to make do with dung.'

'What?' Abigail stopped work and stared at him. 'They used what?'

'Dung,' repeated Samuel, unsteadily. 'Cow dung, horse dung – I don't know. They catapulted it down on those poor, wet miners. Colonel Fiennes wasn't amused.'

'I'm not surprised,' said Abigail, striving to retain her composure. 'Would you have been?'

'Yes,' choked Samuel. 'And guess who organized it?'

'How should I know?' she began, and then stopped, her awed dark eyes meeting Samuel's hilarious ones. 'You're joking!'

'Not me. Your Captain Ambrose is the one with an over-developed sense of humour but he'd better watch his step on the next sortie because there isn't one of our officers who wouldn't like to see his head on a pike.'

Chapter Six

The night was cloudless, the moon just entering its dark quarter and all lay calm and still in the rebel encampment.

'It seems a pity to wake them,' said Ned Frost, regretfully. 'This is the first bit of peace we've had in a week.'

'Quite.' Justin finished buckling the straps of the back-and-breast which covered his buff-coat. 'They're tired and know that we are too, so they won't be expecting us. Perfect.'

They had had it planned for three days, waiting only for the right moment. Other sorties had combined success with a certain degree of reckless spontaneity but now every musket-shot and ounce of energy had to be made to count and every potential advantage made into a reality. Tonight, Friday September 20th, was important for the enemy was making extensive preparations for an assault.

The episode with the miners, whispered the garrison, grinning, was to blame. On the very next day, Colonel Fiennes had attempted to salvage his dignity by sending another formal summons to surrender but it had not helped him. His trumpet passed from the collective snigger of the outer ward to the lofty tones of Sir William Compton who, having wondered that Colonel Fiennes should require a second telling, had bidden Trumpet Woodley be gone before he received another manner of answer.

That had been that. Outside the Castle, moves towards the first assault had begun forthwith while, inside it, Colonel Greene began planning his counter-measures.

In the courtyard, a hundred hand-picked men awaited their final instructions from their Colonel.

'The word for tonight is to be "King and Castle" and our sign, the white band on each man's right arm. Your aim, as you know, is the destruction of guns and scaling ladders and anything else that comes within your reach. We will, of course, be taking no prisoners and there is to be absolute silence before the attack. That is all, gentlemen, except to wish you good luck and good hunting.'

From the entrance of the tent, which for the last three nights had replaced his comfortable room at the Ragged Staff, John Fiennes brooded on the dark bulk of the Castle. His gun crews were sprawled, dozing, about their batteries and his pioneers had been given leave to withdraw from their earthworks. There could be no sortie tonight. If his men were exhausted, then the Cavaliers were doubly so and his own pervading sense of unease, mere folly. He would not listen to it. There could be no sortie tonight.

Suddenly, the tranquil darkness was shattered. From the crenellated battlements, a shower of whizzing, flaming arrows rained down on to the gun-emplacements. Beneath them, illuminated by the glare, bodies of well-drilled infantry came hacking through the outposts. A Puritan to the core, Colonel Fiennes rarely forgot himself but he was soldier enough to do so now. He bellowed three regrettably curse-stricken orders at his lieutenant and dived inside the tent to arm himself.

The alarm was already being given as Justin led his troop through the vedettes and men were emerging from all directions startled, unarmed and in varying states of undress. All was confusion and tumult but the small band of Cavaliers had their work cut out to gain the batteries and Justin, helping to block the path to a cannon royal while his men spiked it, suddenly found himself confronted with a furious officer in black.

'You!' snapped John Fiennes, staring over crossed blades into Justin's face. 'This is a pleasure I'd scarcely dared hope for.'

Grinning, Justin disengaged and replied with a *botta lunga*. 'I'm flattered.'

'Don't be. I intend to see you hanged.'

'The road to hell,' observed Justin, sidestepping to avoid a thrust to the shoulder, 'is paved with good intentions. What you need is opportunity. I, too. What a shame your miners wouldn't stay.'

Colonel Fiennes attempted a feint and then whipped up his guard before Justin could follow parry with attack.

'Do you have a name,' he asked, between set teeth, 'or are you merely the bastard you've shown yourself to be?'

The grey eyes narrowed and grew hard as granite. Then, with a swift, invisible twist, Justin sent the other man's sword spinning from his hand and pushed him back against the banked-up earth of the ditch. Not far away, the Royalist drummers were beating the Retreat.

'Ambrose,' he said with freezing clarity, the tip of his blade hovering motionless some two inches from the Colonel's throat. 'Justin Ambrose. And you, I suppose, are John Fiennes?'

'I am.'

'Good. I want your word, Colonel. Safe-conduct for fifty yards with no bullet in the back. Otherwise I'll have to kill you.'

'Very well. You have it.' There was no hesitation. Colonel Fiennes disapproved of pointless heroics, and only a fool would argue with thirty-five inches of steel at his throat. 'Fifty yards.'

'Thank you.' With a curt nod, Justin withdrew his sword and turned to go. 'And give my love to Nathaniel.'

Through a fog of sleep, Justin became slowly conscious of two things: one was a persistent voice and fist on the far side of the door and the other was of something wet and warm against his face. The first, he was tired enough to want to ignore; the second caused him to force his eyelids apart.

Velvety brown eyes regarded him with pleased approval and a soft, pink tongue gave his chin a congratulatory lick. Then the paws on his chest altered their position and Rex sat down, plainly satisfied with both their achievements.

'I suppose,' remarked Justin bitterly, 'that you think you're clever?'

A feathery tail stirred and two long ears brushed his ribs. In the last three weeks, the little spaniel had improved tremendously both in size and confidence. He had also become a general favourite, which basically meant that, no matter who else went hungry, Rex was always assured of more titbits than he could manage. Though he was willing to associate with everyone from Sir William down to the humblest soldier, his chosen home was the rag rug on Justin's hearth and there was no one who did not know it.

'Captain Ambrose!' The fist hammered again on the door. 'Captain Ambrose, sir!'

Justin drew a long breath, put the dog to one side and sat up, rubbing his eyes. 'Yes? Come in.'

The door opened and a young trooper poked his head round it. 'It's a quarter before six, sir, and you're wanted below. Sir William says —'

'Yes, yes. I can guess.' As yet, the effect of Justin's three-hour sleep was to make him feel a good deal worse than if he had done without it. 'Tell him I'll be there in ten minutes.'

The head vanished. Justin heaved the leaden objects which he knew to be his legs down to the floor and surveyed the trail of coat, shirt, breeches and boots that marked his last progress from door to bed. He dimly recalled a determination to shed his clothes which he now rather regretted since it meant that he had to summon the energy to put them back on. Rex jumped down, sat on his master's best silk sash and barked encouragingly.

'All right,' groaned Justin. He rose, mother-naked, and fixed the spaniel with a gimlet stare.

'You win. Just don't overplay your hand, that's all.'

The council of war, held in the Governor's quarters to the accompanying roar of the usual cannonade from outside, was brief and to the point. The losses of the sortie were set against the degree of havoc it had wrought amidst the rebel emplacements and the venture pronounced relatively successful. A list of provisions showed an absence of salt, flour, vegetables and preserved meat. Supplies of ale, biscuit and cheese, even with more stringent rationing, would scarcely last the month. Stocks of great and small shot far outstripped the amount of powder available to fire them and two of the drakes had been damaged beyond repair.

The simple truth was that if help did not come the Castle

must fall; not today nor even, perhaps, next week, but eventually. Yet a subtle sense of pride invested the council table. They had been cut off from the outside world for nine long weeks and they had been under constant attack for the last four, but the will to resist was still strong. They were not finished yet.

The meeting had ended and some of the officers had already returned to duty when Sir William tossed two news-sheets down on the table and invited those who remained to read them.

'A couple of our fellows brought them back from the sortie. Mayhem in Aberdeen, the Great Cuckold pushed into the sea at Lostwithiel and the continuing saga of a certain Oxfordshire siege. Yes, gentlemen, England thrills to our tribulations and Anthony here has become a Great Man.'

Lieutenant-Colonel Greene smiled. 'I could do without it.'

'Nonsense, man! This could earn you a knighthood. Have you found it, Justin?'

'Yes.' Justin looked up from the latest issue of the Parliament's weekly news-sheet, *Mercurius Britannicus*, and raised one ironic brow. 'According to this, we should have surrendered a week ago but you're undoubtedly right about the knighthood. They've given so much space to – what was it? Ah yes, "that Rabid, Arch-cur Greene" that they've had to give Rupert a rest this week.'

He dropped the paper back on the table with a gesture of distaste. 'I wonder what nasty little mind concocts this stuff?'

'Don't be superior. We do it too, you know, in fact, we did it first.' Hugh Vaughan waved the Royalist *Mercurius Aulicus* at Justin. 'The only difference is that Birkenhead's stuff is better written.'

Ned peered over Captain Vaughan's shoulder.

'What does *Aulicus* say about us?'

'That we're all heroes. We've wiped out half the rebel army and are causing Master Fiennes to shed tears of blood because he can't get back in as easily as he came out. Here, read it for yourself. I'm off.'

Hugh was half-way down the stairs when he realized that

72

Justin had followed him and, turning, he said, 'You're very disapproving today. Why?'

Justin shrugged. 'A man's private life should be his own. Ridicule his military errors, by all means – if he's made them, then he deserves it. But it seems unnecessary to brand Essex a fumbling eunuch because both of his wives turned out to be whores, and being six feet four with an appetite to match, doesn't make Rupert a modern-day Gilles de Rais. I object to men like John Birkenhead making a fortune out of such lurid rubbish.'

Hugh stared at him. 'I'm sorry I asked.'

Justin's face relaxed. 'Take your revenge then. Tell me about John Fiennes' defence of the Castle back in '42.'

'What defence? We took the place inside two hours.'

'So I've heard. But how? The little I've seen of him suggests neither a fool nor a coward and yet he surrendered immediately to a straight assault. Why?'

There was a pause and then Hugh sighed.

'You might remember a fellow at Edgehill who brought his men over from their side to ours right at the last minute. He had a rather inappropriate name – Sir Faithful somebody-or-other.'

'Sir Faithful Fortescue,' supplied Justin. 'Yes. It was the Earl of Peterborough's regiment.'

'It was part of it,' corrected Hugh with dry humour. 'The rest, to Master Fiennes, eternal misfortune, was garrisoning Banbury Castle.'

The great Parliamentary assault began on the morning of September 23rd and followed a forty-eight-hour bombardment in which thirty yards of the west wall were reduced to rubble. Only the thick lining of earth within the breach lay between Colonel Fiennes and his goal. But, with his plans for the assault well-advanced, he was content to wait a little longer and he watched with satisfaction as his stores of scaling ladders and furze grew steadily larger. Through the permanent screen of smoke, the garrison watched it too and made what repairs it could in anticipation. No one inside had any illusions about what their fate would be if the Castle was

73

taken. Quarter and the right to march away belonged only to those who surrendered.

By an hour after dawn on Monday morning it was clear to the garrison that this was the day appointed. The cannonade had slackened off a great deal and there was much activity in the rebel camp, with men massed beneath fluttering blue or orange colours, the discharging of muskets and the glinting of pikeheads. Captain Ambrose watched it all from a variety of vantage points and then turned to find Nancy Lucas at his elbow.

'What are you doing up here?' he demanded. 'This is no place for women.'

'Maybe not. But I reckon you'll be glad of us before the day's out.'

'Possibly. But not on the battlements.'

'Give me a musket and we'll see about that,' laughed Nancy. 'Oh – don't worry. I shan't stay once it looks like the fun's about to start.'

'Fun, Nan?'

'Yes. I enjoy it. And don't try telling me that you don't, too.'

The ghost of a smile touched the hard mouth. 'No. Everyone enjoys the things they are good at.'

'Oho! So you're good, are you?' she teased. 'Whatever are you going to do when it's all over?'

'Look for another war, I expect. It's what soldiers do, you know.'

A thoughtful gleam entered the lively brown eyes.

'But you aren't just a soldier, are you? You are gentry.'

'Thank you.' Justin inclined his head politely. The smile had gone. 'I do my best.'

'No, you don't. You're as rude as be-damned if it suits you. But you're a gentleman for all that.' She tilted her head consideringly. 'Because of it, probably.'

'That is a fascinatingly shrewd observation. But being what you term "gentry" doesn't preclude my also being a soldier.'

Any of his men would have recognized that tone. It was bland as milk and it spelled danger.

'No, it don't,' agreed Nancy. 'But it does mean that you ought to have a home worth going back to. Have you?'

There was a sudden, cold silence which seemed to stretch out on an invisible thread before it was broken by the distant tuck of drums. Justin glanced swiftly over the wall and then turned back to Nancy. 'They're moving. Get below.'

'I will, when you've answered my question.'

Temper flared unexpectedly in the light eyes. 'Don't bargain with me, madam. I gave you an order. Now go!'

By nine o'clock the rebel forces had completed their dispositions and were drawn up in bodies roughly two hundred strong, ready for a five-pronged attack. Sir William and Colonel Greene surveyed the situation with grim calm and then ordered the cream of the garrison's marksmen to the breach in the west wall. The rest, armed with muskets, pistols and even baskets of stones, lined the battlements and turrets. Drakes, sakers and culverins lay primed and ready and, on every side, spirals of smoke rose from lengths of slow match, already lit and swinging gently in expert fingers. With the last possible precaution taken and prayers for their safe delivery already said, the time of waiting became, as always, one of silence and strained, watchful eyes.

The rebel drums proclaimed the march. Stentorian voices from five points around the Castle bawled their commands and, slowly, the Parliamentarian host began its advance. Tension on the battlements reached its peak. The divisions of Colonel Fiennes' own troop broke into a psalm.

'*Let God arise, let his enemies be scattered . . . as wax melteth before the fire, so let the wicked perish at the Presence of God.*'

It was too much for their natural rivals to bear. A growl rumbled through the ranks of Lord Northampton's green-jackets and one burly trooper shouted, 'Damn me, boys – we can do better than that!' And tensions dissolved into a rollicking, local parody.

'*On the seventh day of the seventh month, most lamentably*
The men of Babylon did spoil the Tribe of Banbury.
We called up all our men of war – young Vivers, Cook and Denys

Whom our Lord Saye had placed under his son,
Master Fiennes.'

Lieutenant Frost grinned companionably at Justin.

'And if that pronunciation of his name don't make the Colonel fighting mad, nothing will!'

'I doubt it's new to him,' said Justin absently. And then, turning to his men, 'This is it, boys – but no one fires till I give the word. Understand?'

Having halted briefly well out of range, the rebels came on at the run, encumbered just a little by the bundles of furze and scaling ladders they brought with them. For those moving in from the north and east, there was little useful cover and this made the work of Captains Vaughan and Ambrose relatively straightforward. But to the south and west, Sir William and Colonel Greene faced approaches sheltered to within twenty yards of the moat by low stone walls and the blackened ruins of houses. The parlous west wall could naturally expect to bear the brunt of the attack.

The Royalist artillery fired their opening volley, bringing forth screams and confused shouting, and veiling the enemy advance in a swirling, acrid haze.

'Steady, my lads,' yelled Justin, peering keenly through the smoke. 'Steady . . . give them time . . . now!'

The harsh crackle of musket-fire ripped the air; more screams, blue scarves crumpling earthwards; others taking their place and running on.

'At will!' Justin levelled his own flintlock cavalry pistol and picked off a tall, helmeted officer. 'What are you waiting for – a chance to count their bloody buttons?'

All around the walls, hands moved rhythmically through their familiar ritual. Charge of powder, bullet, wad . . . all down the barrel and rammed home; prime the flash-pan, close and blow; match to cock, adjust, take aim; open the flash-pan . . . fire! Round and round; an automatic repetition. Spare bullet between your teeth . . . keep the match clear of your bandolier; that man is – was – a neighbour . . . but that's pointless. Don't think . . . steady your aim and fire.

Answering volleys of cannon-shot and grenadoes were now

coming at the upper part of the Castle from the Parliamentarian artillery in the church tower. An unlucky shot took Hugh Vaughan in the shoulder and he was carried inside unconscious. Meanwhile, on the north side, the first men had gained the moat and were throwing their bundles of furze into the mud to form a crossing. Behind them, rows of musketeers formed up to give them covering fire.

They needed it for they had no other protection and the garrison's shot fell about them like hail, taking a heavy toll.

'Justin?' Dirty and already hoarse from the smoke and shouting, Ned Frost paused briefly in his labours. 'What's that their file-leaders are shouting?'

'Encouragement,' replied Captain Ambrose, swiftly reloading his pistol, 'in the form of prize money.'

Ned stared at him. Then, 'Hell. Fiennes is a bastard.'

'A very astute bastard.' Justin glanced down at the breach, frowning a little. 'And it's the ones down there who stand most chance of winning it. I think you'd better go and give Captain Tirwhitt a hand. He looks hard-pressed.'

Ned groaned at the unintentional pun. 'All right – if you're sure you can manage?'

'It will doubtless be marginal,' said Justin, suddenly smiling, 'but we'll do our best.'

The day wore on in fits and starts. Attacks were fierce when they came but the murderous fire of the garrison prevented them being pressed home and, by late afternoon, the pace began to abate as fatigue and hopelessness grew like weeds in the Parliamentarian ranks. The ground edging the moat was strewn with some three hundred forlornly twisted corpses and littered with unused scaling ladders, numerous firearms and even a couple of muddy, tattered colours.

At around seven in the evening, a heavy silence settled over town and Castle and, through it, Trumpet Robert Woodley rode slowly forth in pursuit of his duty and tried not to see what lay around him on the ground. Then he put the trumpet to his lips and sent the notes of the summons spinning clear and true through the air. Faces appeared above him on the battlements of the south wall; Sir William, Lieutenant-Colonel Greene and a selection of captains – including the one responsible for the incident with the miners.

Justin looked back at the young envoy with remote pity. The lad looked positively green and small wonder, but he had himself well in hand and he made his request for the Parliamentary dead without a single tremor or mistake.

When he finished speaking, there was silence. Then, with crisp and utterly dispassionate clarity, Will Compton said, 'Sir, you may present my compliments to Colonel Fiennes on the gallant showing of his men and inform him that the fallen may be reclaimed, upon terms, under my personally guaranteed amnesty.'

'Here it comes,' thought Rob, savagely. 'He was bound to say it, of course, but I hope the words choke him.' Aloud, he said, 'And the terms, sir?'

'That everything lying within pistol-shot of the Castle walls be ceded to us. All arms, colours and ladders. And the bodies of your dead will be stripped and delivered to the Market Place. It is, as I am sure Colonel Fiennes is well aware, in perfect accordance with the rules of war.'

Rob knew it but he could not help wondering how receptive they might be to bargaining. As if reading his thought, Sir William ended his hesitation by saying coldly, 'We are not open to negotiation of any kind. Perhaps you wish to consult your superiors?'

'No,' snapped Rob. And then, striving for the correct tone, 'That will not be necessary. Colonel Fiennes anticipated your terms and is prepared to meet them. We will expect the bodies of our dead to be in the Market Place by eight tomorrow morning, if this can be done?'

Will inclined his head.

'It will be done. As to a temporary cessation for the burials, would until midnight tomorrow suit you?'

'Admirably.'

'Very well, then. Until midnight tomorrow. Ah . . . and Trumpet?'

'Sir?'

A hard smile touched the Governor's mouth.

'Tell the Colonel to send me no more summonses.'

Chapter Seven

On the day after Colonel Fiennes watched three hundred of his men laid in the earth to the slow beat of drums and the chanting of psalms, the garrison sallied forth and slew thirty more in a sudden, fierce sortie on the east side.

By the end of September, the Committee of Both Kingdoms was showing its impatience not only in the usual batches of advice but also by sending the means to implement it. The engineer Jacob Keilenbury arrived to give Colonel Fiennes the benefit of his expertise and, to ensure that his time was not wasted by lack of labour, he came equipped with an order which authorized the conscription of local workmen to act as pioneers. The Colonel, who had watched the Bedworth miners try and fail, was not impressed. He bequeathed his tent to the engineer and moved, moodily, back into the Radford household.

He did not, however, lose his temper until the following morning brought the last straw in the form of the Royalist penny-news-sheet. He crushed *Mercurius Aulicus* in his fist, hurled it furiously at the wall and slammed out of the house.

Faintly stunned by the suddenness of it, Abigail watched Major Lytcot depart hurriedly in the Colonel's wake and then stooped to pick up the offending paper.

'Open it up,' said Rob Woodley, hovering hat in hand between duty and curiosity. 'If we're in for a bad day, it would be nice to know why.'

'Can't you guess?' asked Samuel. 'John Birkenhead strikes again. Lay it on the table, Abby, and then we can all see it.'

The relevant article was long and combined enthusiasm for the courage and audacity of the Royalist garrison with extravagant sympathy for its Parliamentary besiegers. The sting lay, as always, in the tail. '*All this while, we see nobody takes any care of Master Fiennes who – if they beat him again – is resolved to tell his father of it.*'

79

'Oh dear,' grinned Samuel. 'Do your fellows read this?'

'Well, of course they do. Thousands of copies are smuggled out of Oxford every week and our supposedly loyal supporters in London pay anything up to three shillings for 'em. The Lord,' concluded Rob, gloomily, 'works in mysterious ways.'

When he had gone, Abigail looked blankly at Samuel and said, 'I can understand that this kind of thing must be irritating but I don't see what there is in it to make the Colonel quite so upset. They write worse things about Lord Essex all the time.'

'Oh, Essex!' Samuel shrugged dismissively. 'He hardly matters any more. He's too old and too cautious and he ought to retire from the field, or be made to.'

Abigail's eyes grew faintly troubled.

'I suppose Colonel Lilburne told you that?'

'Yes. And he's right.'

'But it sounds so hard. Lord Essex has been Commander-in-Chief ever since the war began and —'

'And look what he's achieved,' interrupted Samuel, sardonically. 'He's a dyed-in-the-wool Presbyterian and more Moderate than any of them.'

'He's done his best,' said Abigail defensively. She felt as sorry for the unknown old Lord Essex as she would have done for any perpetual scape-goat. 'And what's so wrong with being a Moderate? They only want peace, after all.'

'We all want peace,' he replied impatiently, 'but not at any price. The King is stubborn and if we lose or make peace on his terms, we'll be back with a Church that's Catholic in all but name and a Parliament that's only allowed to sit while it's doing the King's will. We have to win and we won't do it with men like Essex and Manchester whose loyalty is clouded with sentiment.'

There was a pause and then Abigail said slowly, 'I've never heard you speak like this before. John Lilburne has changed you.'

'No. All he's done is to show me that this war has a point. I always used to think that things would go back to being much as they were, but John has opened my eyes to the fact that, if we are prepared to work at it, we can have real freedom of conscience and the right to help direct our civil government. But first we need a strong Parliament and, for that, we have to win the war.'

'It all sounds too easy,' said Abigail, broodingly. 'It will mean enormous changes, even I know that. Think how much time Colonel Lilburne has already spent in prison because of his views. It could . . . if you were to help him, it could be the same for you.'

'I don't care if it is,' said Samuel firmly. 'This is what I want to do and, for once, it's something I can do without Jonas or my foot getting in the way.'

'Does that mean that Jonas knows?'

'Don't be silly. He may be all admiration for John's religious views but can you honestly see him supporting any move towards an extended franchise? He's too fond of his own importance.'

Worry began to gnaw at Abigail and she said, 'What are you going to do?'

'Not much, at present. Distribute a few illicit pamphlets – that sort of thing.' He smiled at her. 'Don't worry. In a few months, I'll be able to do it all openly.'

'Will you? Supposing we win the war and so on, where does the King fit in to all John Lilburne's plans?'

The smile faded. 'Where he's always fitted in but with less actual power. Win or lose, he'll still be the King, won't he?' demanded Samuel in exasperation. 'Since you're obviously set on being difficult, I'm going out.'

'I'm not being difficult. I'm trying to understand,' snapped Abigail. 'Where are you going?'

'Down to the lines. I think I feel like doing some digging.'

The first week of October struggled by, then the second and the siege moved sullenly into its thirteenth week. Colonel Fiennes' engineer dug long, long tunnels from North Bar to the Castle; the garrison kept its ear to the ground and counter-mined. The engineer maintained a patient façade and changed location only to meet with the same reception. Colonel Fiennes permitted himself a little subtle sympathy and the engineer lost his temper. The days fell into an uneasy rhythm. In the town, men whispered of the devil's magic and said Will Compton never slept. John Fiennes scorned the first and began to believe the second.

'It's only a matter of time,' he told Major Lytcot. 'They're tired, virtually out of powder and probably starving. We can take the place in two weeks simply by waiting, instead of which we're decimating our troops just to satisfy the notions of our civilian masters at Derby House.'

The Major nodded gloomily. The times were uncertain and careers had foundered on smaller ventures than this. Success yesterday meant nothing and failure today could ruin you. Look at Waller. Look, as the Colonel must be doing, at Nat Fiennes – court-martialled for surrendering Bristol. It was a grim warning.

Untouched by these worries, Rob Woodley was endeavouring to brighten the monotony of his days by luring his hostess into mild flirtation. This was not easy because Abigail rarely recognized what was required of her but he persevered and was occasionally rewarded by a glimpse of something very appealing. Abby might not be pretty in the usual sense but she had the most remarkable smile he had ever seen and might, were she not so steeped in her brother's Puritanism, have developed other qualities. For, although he supported the Parliament heart and soul, Rob saw no sin in laughter and no virtue in sartorial austerity. Jonas Radford curdled his blood.

He realized this on a day when, having nothing better to do, he passed an idle hour teaching Abigail a song. It was an innocent pastime for she was busy making a custard and the door stood open to the scullery where Betty was preparing vegetables. But to Jonas, who entered the parlour in time to hear his sister timidly repeating Suckling's words, it was as shocking as if he had found her naked in the street.

Why so pale and wan, fond Lover?
Prithee, why so pale?
Will, when looking well can't move her,
Looking ill prevail?
Prithee, why so . . .

He erupted violently into the kitchen and the comfortable tableau dissolved. Abigail froze, clutching a basin, and Rob rose abruptly from the settle.

'How dare you?' breathed Jonas. 'How dare you sully my house with immoral rubbish! Are you both lost to all sense of decency or shame?'

'Oh come now!' Rob expostulated. 'There was no harm in it. It was only —'

'I know what it was and it has no place under my roof,' replied Jonas harshly. 'Neither have you any business here alone with my sister and I shall speak to Colonel Fiennes of your behaviour this evening. In the meantime, you may return to your duties.'

Rob hesitated. It seemed unfair to leave Abigail to bear the brunt but the fellow had told him to go and it was difficult to know how best to refuse. He compromised by making a magnificently untruthful apology. Then he left.

Abigail's eyes rose slowly to meet those of her brother. She said, 'I'm sorry, Jonas. I didn't think.'

'Think? You never think! You encourage familiarity like any common trollop. Do you know who wrote the words you were singing? A Royalist lecher who gambled himself into so much debt that he committed suicide. And you see no harm in it!'

'I'm sorry,' said Abigail again. Her hands were beginning to shake and she set the basin carefully on the table. 'I didn't know.'

'Is that supposed to be an excuse?' snapped Jonas, lashing himself into greater rage. It was not difficult for, at times like these, he dimly recognized that he did not like Abigail, that there was something alien about her which must be crushed.

'Look at yourself! With your hair falling out of your cap as usual, is it any wonder you are taken for a loose woman? "Wide is the gate and broad the way that leadeth to destruction." No sister of mine shall take that road while I have breath in my body.' He reached out and his fingers closed hard on her arm. 'Aside from that which I heard, what other liberties have you permitted that impious young fool?'

'None.' White-faced and breathless, Abigail struggled to

at least appear calm. 'None at all. I swear it.'

'He has not touched you?'

'No. Never.'

There was a pause while Jonas fought to control his temper and then the bruising grip relaxed as he forced her to her knees on the brick floor.

'I shall try to believe you. But we will pray together that God will deliver you from the sins of the flesh and teach your heart the purity that it should have. For I fear, Abigail, I greatly fear that you have the seeds of wantonness in you.'

On the following morning, while Jonas was out visiting his wife at Grimsbury, Abigail entered the shop to find Samuel huddled over the sales ledger, his eyes heavy and his face flushed.

'Sam, what's wrong? You look awful.'

'I feel awful. I can't get warm and my chest hurts and the rest of me aches as if I'd been beaten with a cudgel,' he said fretfully. 'I suppose it's just a touch of ague but I feel like death.'

'Bed,' said his sister, decisively. She crossed to the shop door and locked it. 'Go on. I'll send Betty for the apothecary.'

The apothecary came, shook his head and spoke of the baleful influence of Mars before recommending a purge. Abigail's stare told him that he had made a mistake. He progressed to Saturn, produced a vial of Peruvian bark and left. Abigail persuaded Samuel to swallow the potion and when, four hours later, he showed every sign of growing rapidly worse, tried a cordial of her mother's. It was as useless as the other. By the time Jonas returned, Samuel was burning with fever and restless with delirium.

For the first time in her life, Abigail was immune to her elder brother's disapproval. Ignoring his remarks about the closure of the shop and the fact that the evening meal was far from ready, she said, 'Sam needs a doctor.'

Jonas scoffed, blustered and eventually produced the information that the town's physician was no longer in residence.

'Then ask Colonel Fiennes. The army must have one.'

'One what?' asked the Colonel, entering unnoticed behind them. 'Is there some way in which I can help?' It was Abigail to whom he spoke and Abigail who explained what she wanted. Thirty minutes later the army surgeon was at Samuel's bedside.

'It's the new fever,' he announced, regarding Abigail from under bushy red brows. 'We've had it in the ranks but there's nae reason tae fear. The laddie's young and strong and wi' proper care he'll do weel enough. Keep him warm and quiet and dose him wi' the poppy if ye have tae – but carefully, mind.' He picked up his hat. 'The King's man, Harvey, has put a fancy name tae it – something tae do wi' its influence, I believe – but I canna recall just what. Good day tae ye, Mistress. Ye can call me again if there's need.'

While Samuel lay in the town and battled with Dr Harvey's 'influenza', Captain Hugh Vaughan lay in the Castle and began to recover from the shot wound that he had received during the assault. It was the one bright spot in an otherwise cheerless world for by the middle of October the Castle's powder was almost gone and the entire garrison had been existing solely on horse-meat for a week. Every face was fine-drawn, its pallor printed with the flat marks of exhaustion. Every day reactions grew that little bit slower and less reliable. The end was very close and inescapable.

'They don't seem to be trying very hard these days,' remarked Ned to Justin as they crossed the outer ward to check the guard one night.

'They don't have to try at all,' came the dry response. 'They only have to wait. Now what do you suppose he's doing?'

'Who?'

'Potts. There, look, creeping down into the cellar. The bastard's supposed to be on duty, isn't he?'

'Yes.' Ned peered through the gloom. 'Shall I go?'

'No, I will. You see if any of the others have decided to take the night off.'

Silent as a shadow, Justin crossed the courtyard and vanished inside the remains of the west turret. At the foot of the steps, light flickered and steadied into a gentle glow. Justin started carefully down and then stopped abruptly as a soft vibration of sound reached his ears.

'Potts, what the hell do you think you're doing?'

Trooper Potts jumped, swore and nearly upset the lantern. The light eddied and swayed, settling first on the Captain and then on the row of rough boxes along the opposite wall.

'Well?' snapped Justin.

Trooper Potts' face crumpled into lines of acute depression. 'It's the pigeons, sir.'

'I can see that, damn it. What I'd like to know is what both they and you are doing here? You're supposed to be on watch.'

'I came down to let 'em go,' came the morose reply. 'I ain't got nothing to feed 'em on and they'm good birds, even if they ain't my own.'

He stroked the one he held and Justin stared, his breath catching raw in his throat. Then, with careful restraint, he said, 'They wouldn't, by any chance, be carrier pigeons?'

''Course they are. I told you, they'm good birds.'

'And not your own?'

'No.'

Captain Ambrose sat abruptly on the steps and dropped his head into his hands. 'Oh God,' he said unsteadily. 'I don't believe it.'

'Justin?' Ned Frost came hurtling down the steps and narrowly missed falling over his friend. 'What's the matter? Are you all right?'

'Yes.' The Captain sat up, still gripped by ironic laughter. 'Did you know that, during all the weeks we've spent desperately trying to get a messenger out of here, our friend Mr Potts has been keeping carrier pigeons?'

Ned's eyes widened. 'Christ! You haven't?'

Potts sniffed. 'Well I have. Got a friend in Oxford, see.'

'Oxford,' repeated Justin gently. 'Really? Ned, go and get some paper, will you? We're going to send a few messages.' Ned vanished and Justin continued to regard the trooper with fragile tranquillity. 'I'm not going to ask how you've done it or for how long,' he went on mildly. 'But just tell me

86

one thing. Why, in the name of heaven, didn't you have the sense to confide your little secret to one of us?'

Mr Potts looked back at him with a mixture of surprise and impatience. 'Well, it's obvious, ain't it, sir? I thought the poor little sods would end up being eaten.'

Another week dragged by. Seven long days and nights in which the rebels tunnelled like moles to the Castle walls and the garrison counter-mined to catch them in their works.

'Hell,' said Ned Frost wearily. 'Did I say they'd stopped trying? Why do you let me open my mouth?'

'Can we stop you?' Justin finished tying a scarf round a gash in his left arm and leaned back, closing his eyes. 'How many times is it now? I've lost count.'

'Eleven,' supplied Hugh Vaughan, weak and paper-white but idiotically determined to resume his duties. 'It makes you wonder what's holding the walls up. God but I'm tired!'

Silence fell. Fresh from their last muddy fight in the dark confines of the earth, filthy, tattered and light-headed with exhaustion, they snatched a brief respite before returning to duty.

'What day is it?' asked Justin, less out of interest than an effort to stay awake.

'Thursday,' said Hugh. 'The twenty-fourth, I think. Fourteen weeks.'

There was a pause. And then, in a tone of detached surprise, Justin said, 'It's my birthday.'

Two gaunt and dirty faces turned slowly in his direction.

'Congratulations,' offered Ned. 'I'd wish you many happy returns only it don't seem exactly appropriate.'

'And we can't even drink his health.' Hugh became mournfully Welsh. 'There's a pity. What is it you are, Justin *bach*, thirty?'

Distant amusement touched Justin's mouth.

'Twenty-six.' Sleep was informing every muscle and he added dreamily, 'A glass of canary, a loaf of fresh bread, and a piece of cheese from anywhere except Banbury. That's what I'd like.'

Ned groaned. 'Don't. Talk about something else.'

'Yes.' Hugh settled his head on his hand. 'Tell us your life story.'

The light grey eyes flew suddenly wide.

'Another time, perhaps. It's remarkably dull and just now we have to stay awake. In fact,' said Justin, rising from his chair, 'we ought to be getting back to work. There's a lot to be done before dark.' And, picking up his coat, he left the room.

Ned gazed owlishly at Hugh.

'Now look what you've done. You know how shy he is.'

'Mm.' Hugh heaved himself to his feet. 'Odd, isn't it? He's been here six months and we know nothing about him.'

'We know he's fought abroad, served here under Rupert and has the devil's own reputation with women,' replied Ned, yawning again. 'Isn't that enough for you?'

'No. I can't say it is. But then, I'm the inquisitive type.'

A couple of hours later, Ned climbed the ramparts to find his mysterious friend scrutinizing the rebel camp through a perspective-glass.

'What is it?', he asked. 'Any sign of activity?'

'Yes, rather a lot, in fact. Here, see for yourself.' Justin passed him the glass. 'A body of Purefoy's horse came in about an hour since looking as though they'd had a busy day and now there are men out working at all the batteries.'

Lieutenant Frost focused on a mortar emplacement and then slowly lowered the glass to gaze blankly at Justin. 'I must be dreaming. They can't really be doing what I think they're doing. Can they?'

Justin stared enigmatically back.

'Well, if they're not, you and I are sharing an illusion. I think . . . I think it might be as well if we asked Will to come and take a look.'

Sir William looked for a long time before saying weakly, 'They're preparing to move the artillery. All of it.'

'That,' agreed Justin, 'is what we thought. The only question now is where they are moving it to. Ned, don't say anything. We know about your predictions.'

'Let's wait and see,' said Will. 'It could be a ruse or a new plan of campaign – anything. They'd be mad to give up now.'

'Unless they know something we don't,' amended Justin. No one replied and he did not elaborate. There was no need. If John Fiennes was raising the siege, it was either because he had been ordered to meet an emergency elsewhere or because he knew a sizeable Royalist relief force to be on its way. And either one would represent a miracle.

Gradually, word of what was happening spread through the Castle and men began to appear, silently, on the ramparts until the walls were lined with strained, watchful faces. Below them, in the slowly deepening dusk, the black muzzles of cannon trundled one by one from the emplacements while, here and there, tents sagged like pricked bladders before disappearing from view.

It grew dark but no one in the Castle slept. Unaware of time, they continued their vigil and stored up a memory that would last forever: a pattern of moving, torchlight flares, vivid against the black night, that marked the progress of their enemy's withdrawal to the north.

The dawn arrived with grey reluctance over gaping trenches, empty works and the last, unburied litter of the deserted camp.

Sir William turned at last to Justin and spoke. 'Scouts,' he said simply. 'I want to know if the town is clear.'

An hour later, with the tension around the walls dissolving into cheerful, speculative chatter, Justin delivered his report.

'There's no sign of the horse or the artillery but the western end of the town is still alive with infantry. Five hundred or so, maybe more. Their officers are still trying to collect them before moving out. What now? A sortie?'

'With the only two horses we haven't eaten and no gunpowder? Hardly.'

Justin sighed faintly. 'No. I suppose not. But I'd give a lot to know if there's something approaching on the Oxford road that's sent their main force scurrying for Warwick.'

'So would I,' grinned Will. 'So send out your scouts again and then get some breakfast. It could be a long day.'

It wasn't. Shortly before eight o'clock, sounds of firing were heard from no more than half a mile away and, soon after that, Justin's men brought word that a body of eight hundred Parliamentarian horse was retreating in disorder towards the village of Hanwell, that the remaining infantry from the town was following them and that all were being hotly pursued by four regiments of Royalist cavalry.

'Whose?' demanded Will. 'The Oxford horse?'

'Yes. Also Lord Wilmot's and the Earl of Brainford's.'

The dark eyes widened. 'But they were with the King. My God! His Majesty has sent his own troops to relieve us.' And then, 'You said four regiments?'

Justin smiled wryly. 'Yes. The other belongs to my Lord Northampton. Big brother to the rescue.'

'James?' A faint flush touched Will's hollowed and unshaven cheeks. 'And about bloody time too. I just hope he's brought some beer.'

The last scene in the drama was played out shortly before noon when Colonel Gage led the Queen's Own regiment of foot through the streets of Banbury to the south gate of the Castle where Sir William and his officers waited on the drawbridge. Although they had all washed, shaved and changed into the least shabby of their attire, they presented an undoubtedly scarecrow appearance, but Colonel Gage affected not to notice it and his salute was expressive only of profound respect.

'Gentlemen,' he said clearly, 'I have the honour to report that the siege is raised and the enemy in full retreat. God preserve His Majesty!'

Chapter Eight

'Missus, oh, Missus! Whatever are we going to do?' With her cap sadly awry and a smear of mud on one cheek, Betty confronted the Radford ladies. 'It were an accident for sure but I don't know how to tell you!'

'The cat's been at the meat safe,' thought Alice, rising resignedly from her chair. It was a little over a week since the Royalist relief force had withdrawn and she and Rachel had been home for three days. Three days of scrubbing and polishing in an attempt to set the house to rights again; three days of bearing with Jonas' profound ill-humour and a period of almost continuous anti-Royalist disturbance in the town. Now, to cap it all, hysterics in the kitchen. 'Calm down, child, and tell us properly. What is it?'

'It's Master Sam, Missus. He's been took! There was trouble in the Market Place and I got knocked down so Master Sam, he goes to pick me up afore I gets trampled on. Then somebody hit him, so he hit 'em back and then there was soldiers arresting everybody and they took Master Sam!'

The blood drained from Alice's skin and she sank back into her chair. Equally pale, Abigail threw her sewing aside to kneel beside her, saying rapidly, 'It's all right, mother. It's a mistake. They'll have thought he was part of the apprentice demonstration but they'll soon release him.'

'But they'll put him in a dungeon!' wailed Betty.

'Then perhaps the experience will teach him a lesson,' said Rachel, whom pregnancy had softened not at all. 'If he had kept away as he was told, he would be safe at home now.'

Abigail stared at her. 'How can you be so callous! You know he's done nothing wrong and, with the fever barely off him, he can't last a night in a damp cell without being ill again.'

'He should have thought of that before,' replied Rachel coldly. 'I can't see the Malignants bothering to make

91

enquiries before morning or believing him innocent when they do. Not if he was actually caught participating in a vulgar brawl.'

'What was that?' Jonas had entered in time to hear the latter part of this speech. 'Samuel has been fighting?'

'Yes,' said his wife composedly. 'In the Market Place, amongst those stupid apprentices and farm-boys. He was arrested, of course, and Abigail appears to feel that he should be got out. No doubt she would like you to go down to the Castle and beg for his release.'

Abigail met her brother's smouldering stare stoically.

'Please, Jonas? Sam's still far from well. He has such a cough.'

'Are you out of your mind?' he thundered. 'I go and plead with recusant scum? I'd sooner see him dead at my feet.'

'If you don't go, you probably will,' retorted Abigail, for whom three months of responsibility and having to deal with strangers had done more than she yet realized. Bemused by her own recklessness, she continued. 'But you needn't plead. Just explain.'

'Explain what? That my brother is an idle young fool who spends his time where he has no business to be? That he was not creating a political disturbance – merely a private one? Perhaps you would like me to perjure my immortal soul by congratulating those sons of Satan on their continued presence in this town?'

'No. Of course not. I only —'

'She only wants to see Sam brought out of that place as quickly as possible,' finished Alice. 'And so do I. He has been so ill, Jonas. Surely it wasn't much to ask?'

Jonas put a visible curb on his temper.

'It is a great deal to ask. If Samuel has been imprisoned, it is because it is God's will and I cannot interfere with that. To do so would be a double offence both in doubting His purpose and in abandoning my conscience to ask favours of His enemies.'

'But —'

'No. I have heard enough,' he snapped. His glance fell on Betty. 'And you, girl, go about your duties. It is past five o'clock and I would like my dinner.'

A strange and alarming sensation crept over Abigail and she clenched one hand over the other as it rose like a steadily expanding bubble in her chest. As the door closed behind Betty, she heard herself saying, 'How can you be so selfish? Sam is in prison and all you care about is food. It's disgusting!'

Three voices spoke her name, in fury, shock and fear, but Abigail heeded none of them. 'It isn't principle, Jonas, or even respect for God's will. You're just sulking because the Castle didn't fall and you're too proud and stubborn to humiliate yourself.'

She snatched her cloak from behind the door. 'Well, I'm not. I'm used to being sneered at.'

'Go to your room!' ordered Jonas, dangerously flushed. 'I will not tolerate such insolence and will deal with you when you have recovered your senses. Go to your room, I say. Abigail! Where do you think you are going?'

She finished tying the strings of her cloak with fingers that shook only a little. 'I'm going to get Sam and I shan't come back till I have. Enjoy your dinner.' She was gone before he could stop her.

Outside, the freezing November wind took her breath away and she held her cloak tightly against it. It was dark but lamps hung outside most of the houses and she darted along, unafraid, borne up by a dimly recognized wave of pure temper. It was her first sight of the devastation in the Market Place that brought her to a halt. Almost every house seemed to have suffered some kind of damage, windows shattered, chimneys blown off, walls pitted by musket fire or demolished by cannon. On the north side of the square, the entire row of buildings nearest to the Castle wall had been reduced to no more than a heap of charred and blackened timbers. She had been told, of course, but nothing had prepared her for the eerie menace of the deserted ruins and she picked her way through them with a fast-beating heart then ran for the Castle.

'Halt! Who goes there?'

The sentries' challenge startled her and administered the

final prick to that comforting bubble of anger. Abigail opened her mouth and found that her teeth were chattering.

'I want to see C-Captain Ambrose.'

The guards examined her wonderingly.

'Now then, Mistress,' said one of them, kindly. 'A respectable lass like you has got no business wandering about on her own in the dark. You go on home and come back tomorrow morning.'

'No,' said Abigail stoutly. 'I want to see him now.'

'What is it, Corporal?' The voice of the duty officer came, disembodied, through the gloom and the guards stepped back, saluting.

'It's a young woman to see Captain Ambrose, sir.'

Abigail looked up into a pleasant, mobile face framed with curling, fair hair. 'Please! I don't mind waiting but I must see him tonight.'

'Then you shall, my dear, and without any delay at all.' Ned grinned at her, taking in the pale, pointed face and wide, dark eyes. Not Justin's usual type, he decided, but a taking little thing for all that. 'Croft?'

The trooper stepped forward. 'Sir?'

'Take this lady to the officers' room and if Captain Ambrose isn't there, find him for her.'

The outer ward was a shambles but Abigail was too preoccupied to spare it more than a passing glance. Treading carefully between lumps of fallen masonry, broken timbers and other assorted debris, she reached the safer ground of planking laid across the ditch of the inner bailey and followed her escort inside.

Trooper Croft rapped smartly on the nail-studded door and, on a command from within, opened it. Then, not without a certain discreet relish, he announced that there was a lady to see Captain Ambrose. There was silence. Then a lilting voice said, 'A lady, is it? Well, well, I fear she's come a mite late. The Captain's been in his bed this hour past.'

A burst of laughter followed this remark. Abigail felt her cheeks grow hot but she pushed back her hood and stepped into the light of the doorway. 'Then he'll have to get up again. And the officer at the gate told this man to find him for me.'

This time the silence assumed epic proportions as six pairs of eyes riveted themselves on her small, soberly-clad person and six brains reluctantly reshuffled their ideas. Then Hugh Vaughan rose and said winningly, 'I beg your pardon, Mistress. If Lieutenant Frost has given his word, then the Captain must, of course, be woken. Croft, see to it.'

An expression of horror informed the trooper's face.

'Me, sir? Now?'

'Of course.' Hugh's smile was maliciously understanding. 'And, if you'll take my advice, you won't neglect to mention Lieutenant Frost. Now, Mistress, will you come to the fire while you wait? Tom, shift your idle carcass and give this lady your seat. As usual it's the best in the room.'

Ensign Mayhew grinned and removed himself to the other side of the hearth with Cornet Bentley and Lieutenant Poultenay. Captains Walrond and Tirwhitt continued abstractedly with their game of cribbage and Abigail found herself handed to a chair while the dark-haired Welshman pressed her to accept a cup of wine.

'Oh, n-no, thank you.' Jonas considered wine to be an invention of the devil. 'I'm sorry. I didn't mean to disturb you.'

'But you haven't,' responded Hugh gallantly. 'Now do take a little wine. There's a chilly wind tonight and you must be frozen.'

This was undeniably true. Jonas' sister banished him from her mind, accepted the cup and took a tiny cautious sip. It proved rich, soothing and pleasant so she smiled shyly at her host and politely finished it off.

Hugh's eyes widened but he said nothing, merely refilling the cup whilst shooting a quelling glance at his junior officers. Then he returned it to her, saying, 'Perhaps you are wondering why Captain Ambrose has taken to his bed at such an unseemly hour?'

'Oh no,' protested Abigail weakly. 'Well, not very much.'

'He's been rather busy, you see,' smiled Hugh. 'I doubt he's had more than five hours' sleep in the last forty-eight hours.'

'Oh.' Guilt temporarily overcame her concern for Samuel.

'I didn't know. Perhaps I shouldn't have —'

'Not at all,' he assured her. 'It's just that he may be a little . . . a little less than his usual, sparkling self, that's all.' He heard Tom Mayhew choke at the understatement, and then the door opened.

Heavy-eyed, coatless and far from immaculate, Justin leaned against the door-jamb and directed an irritable grey stare at Captain Vaughan. 'Well? If this is Ned's idea of a joke, I'll break his damned neck.'

Hugh tutted approvingly and stepped aside to reveal Abigail. 'This lady wishes to talk to you,' he said.

She had time to notice that, like the others, he looked shockingly fine-drawn and then her breath leaked away beneath his frown. She came to her feet, spilling a little of the wine. 'Oh God,' said Justin, unpleasantly. 'It's Mistress Butter-fingers. Take that cup, Hugh, before she throws it at you.'

A flicker of resentment stirred in Abigail's breast but she handed the cup dutifully back. Captain Ambrose, meanwhile, detached himself from the door-jamb and demanded, with neither courtesy nor grace, to be told what was so cursed urgent that it necessitated dragging him out of bed.

Abigail's heart sank and she cast a glance of agonized appeal at Captain Vaughan. 'Well, I . . . it's a little difficult . . . I'd rather not . . .'

Hugh responded promptly but with total misunderstanding. 'I think that the lady would prefer to talk in private. But since Will is coming down to talk over the reconnaissance reports with me, it's a little awkward for us to give over this room to you.'

Justin regarded him out of eyes that could have quarried stone. Then, on a brief explosion of breath, he said, 'Oh very well. It's all one to me, so long as it doesn't take all night. Well, Mistress Radford, are you coming?'

'Coming where?' asked Abigail, startled.

'To my quarters. If it's privacy you want, there's nowhere else in this hen-coop that you're likely to find it.'

Considering that he had left his bed to dress hurriedly and come straight downstairs, the Captain's room was remarkably tidy. A lot tidier, thought Abigail, with a faintly shocked, sideways glance, than he was himself. It was also larger than she had expected, being situated at the top of the south-west turret and reached by means of a narrow spiral stair. Despite the cold stone walls, it had a comfortable, lived-in look and its cosiness was epitomized by the spaniel which stirred sleepily on the bright, rag rug before the fire. A row of books sat atop a large, carved chest and a pair of inlaid pistols hung on either side of the splayed window; there was a blue sash looped over the washstand mirror, a buff leather coat on the back of a second door and the Captain's sword reposed on the room's only stool.

'I shouldn't be here,' thought Abigail, in sudden panic. 'Jonas will kill me if he finds out.'

Justin removed his sword and deposited it in a corner. Then, turning to pull the bedclothes into some semblance of order, he told her to sit down and demanded again to be informed what she wanted of him.

Abigail hovered and hesitated.

'For God's sake!' exclaimed Justin, dropping irritably upon the bed and regarding her with acute disfavour. 'Sit down and stop being coy. I'm not in the mood for it.'

She obeyed him rather quickly. 'I'm sorry.'

'Don't be sorry. Just come to the point.'

His tone made this difficult but Abigail did her best.

'It's my brother. He was arrested in the Market Place this afternoon but he didn't do anything and I came to ask you to let him out.'

Comprehension dawned slowly and the blurred gaze registered astonishment. 'You mean he was taken for rioting? No, no. It's too good to be true.'

Abigail stiffened. 'I'm afraid I don't find it funny.'

The dark brows soared and his reply was deliberately blighting. 'My dear child, I'd be amazed if the members of your household found anything funny. Quite apart from your religious persuasion, your dismal brother and his appallingly sour-faced wife are enough to kill anyone's sense of humour. However. If you've hauled me out of bed just to ask a favour for Jonas, I can only say that your nerve outstrips your intelligence. To put it bluntly, I don't care if he rots.'

Abigail dissected this remarkable speech before brushing it aside. 'What has Jonas to do with it? It isn't him you've got.' And then, staring at him, 'Is that what you thought?'

'Not being on intimate terms with your family, what else was I to think?' he said acidly. He leaned back, brooding on her over folded arms. 'Mistress Radford, my patience is limited and diminishing by the second. Will you please tell me, in plain language, just who the hell it is you came to rescue?'

The quiet savagery of his tone shook her and she hung her head, a lump forming in her throat. 'My younger brother, Samuel. You met him when you came for the cloth.'

'Did I? I don't recall . . . or no. Perhaps I do.' He paused and sat up again, his mood shifting a little. 'The lad who reads Godwin?' She nodded mutely and he eyed her with distrust. 'If you're going to cry, I'd advise you to go and do it over the gentleman you met downstairs. It works on him.'

'I'm not doing it on purpose!' Abigail raised a mistily indignant gaze. 'I don't know why I came!'

'Neither do I,' he agreed. 'It should have been Jonas. Where is Jonas?'

She sniffed. 'At home. He wouldn't come.'

'Really? You do surprise me.' For the first time, a hint of interest, albeit mocking, replaced the harsh boredom in Justin's face. 'Does he know you are here?'

'Yes. But he didn't send me.'

'I never imagined that he did. He wouldn't take his own life as a favour from me, let alone Samuel's. In fact, I can't understand why he allowed you to leave the house.' She flushed and began to toy with the folds of her cloak. Justin's mouth relaxed a little more. 'Don't tell me you defied him?'

She nodded, suddenly dispirited and rather tired. 'Please, none of this matters. I know you don't like Jonas but —'

'No, I don't. Do you?'

Abigail blinked. 'He's my brother.'

'That's no answer. It could probably have been said of Nero or Attila the Hun.'

The white-capped head drooped again and the slender fingers were visibly unsteady. 'I should love him, but I can't. To my shame, I don't even try. I'm afraid of him.'

There was a long silence. Then Justin said crisply, 'I think you had better explain exactly why I should order Samuel's release. You said he wasn't part of the riot?'

'No. He only went to watch and then he saw our maidservant being trampled and tried to help her. He has no patience with senseless violence.'

'Hasn't he, indeed?'

'No. And he's been very ill these last weeks so he really shouldn't stay all night in your dungeons.'

'My what?' In spite of himself, Justin was betrayed into a choke of laughter and immediately felt the better for it. 'You've been listening to nasty stories. We don't keep our prisoners chained to the walls any more and the dungeons here are knee-deep in water and have been quite unusable these twenty years. Your brother is probably snug in the gatehouse.'

'Oh,' said Abigail, deflated.

'Oh,' agreed Justin, hauling himself to his feet. 'You'd better wait here. I won't be long.'

The great dark eyes flew to meet his.

'What are you going to do?'

'What do you think? The only thing that promises me any sleep tonight. No. You can't come.' This to the spaniel which had leapt up at his first move and was waving its tail like washing in the wind. 'You can stay and entertain Mistress Radford.' He directed a swift, unexpected smile at Abigail. 'Make yourself at home.'

He left the room and she sat listening to the receding ring of his boots on the stone steps, her eyes stinging with the relief of it. Outside, a distant challenge and the tramp of feet announced that the guard was being changed; inside, the fire crackled merrily and the little dog put his paws on her knee. Abigail slid from the stool to the rug and put her arms around him.

She was still there when the Captain returned. There was no sign of Samuel and for a moment she stayed where she was, staring at him. Then he said, 'It's all right,' and the fear drained out of her.

Justin leaned against the door, thinking how very young she looked sitting there on the floor with the dog. Young, fragile and vulnerable, her one potential beauty tortured and hidden beneath that unflattering white cap. Her clothes were ugly too, despite being of the best quality cloth. The broad, linen collar encircling the slim throat was too starkly white for her pale skin and the dark blue damask gown was cut to conceal rather than reveal. He thought, 'She ought to wear apricot or jade.'

Then, dismissing the notion, he said, 'There seemed no point in dragging your brother all the way up here so he's waiting for you below with my friend Mr Frost. Why didn't you tell me he was a cripple?'

She came quickly to her feet, her eyes opening very wide. 'I didn't think of it. He isn't a cripple to me. Is he all right?'

'Perfectly. He's been educating both his fellows and my guards with the teachings of Free-born John.' He lifted one brow in gentle enquiry. 'He appears, so I am told, to have been speaking as if from first-hand knowledge.'

'Ah,' said Abigail, torn with guilt. 'Yes. It seems only fair to tell you that Colonel Lilburne was our guest while he was here last month. And Colonel Fiennes lodged with us all the time.'

Something flickered in the grey eyes. 'Did he indeed? Well, well.'

'Do you want to change your mind about Sam?'

'If I did, could I be blamed?'

'No.' She gazed down at her hands. 'I never realized before how bad things must have been for you here. Everyone looks as though they have been ill, especially you.'

'My finicky appetite. I find it hard to stomach horse-meat when I'm acquainted with its source. But there's no need to look so stricken. I don't hold you personally responsible.'

'I hate this war,' said Abigail abruptly. 'I wish it had never begun. Don't you?'

'Yes, but that's futile,' he shrugged. 'And I don't hate what I do, I merely regret doing it in England. Also, although

I can't say I enjoyed being sealed up for fourteen weeks under siege, I can scarcely blame you for it, even if you did feed John Fiennes while we were starving.' His face held a gleam of humour. 'You may have your brother.'

She examined him wonderingly with eyes that gathered sudden, unsuspected brilliance. Then the pale mouth widened into a disconcertingly sweet smile and she said, 'Why, you're kind!'

Faintly stunned by the metamorphosis, Justin said carelessly, 'No. Merely malicious. I want to see Jonas cringing under the knowledge that he owes me a favour.'

She did not believe him. Because she did not, she gave him the only thing she thought might please.

'Colonel Fiennes did not like Jonas either.'

Her reward was a choke of laughter.

'Then that must have made his stay enjoyable for both of them. What a happy household you must be when you're all together. I gather that Samuel isn't enormously in tune with Jonas either? And that reminds me, I think you said that Samuel dislikes what you called "senseless violence"?'

'Yes. What of it?'

'Only that he has badly skinned knuckles and a rather spectacular black eye,' replied the Captain blandly. 'Anyone who didn't know better would undoubtedly be convinced that he'd been in a fight.'

Chapter Nine

'It's looking good, isn't it?' asked Ned of Justin as the latter paused beside him on his way across the outer ward. 'Or, at least, better than it did.'

Justin's gaze travelled round the restored neatness of the courtyard and came to rest on the nearly-completed stable block. 'Yes. The men have done well, a fact we may all live to be grateful for.'

'Mm. Pity about the weather, though. I reckon there's snow on the way and if I'm right it's going to put a stop to all our fine plans.'

'For the moment, perhaps. But it will also deter Colonel Fiennes and his friends from returning to sit at our gates so we shouldn't lose anything by it.'

'You might not,' grinned Ned, 'but spare a thought for others, will you? After fourteen weeks of incarceration and six spent shifting rubble and plugging up holes, I can do without being cut off from Oxford by heavy snow.'

'Oh, I see,' said Justin acidly. 'For a moment there you actually had me believing that you were eager to implement our designs for the outer defences.'

Ned cast him a shrewd glance. 'What's the matter?'

'Nothing that can possibly compete with the loss of your love life. Simply that the Lieutenant-Colonel is going to Oxford, presumably to be rewarded with a promotion.'

'So? He deserves it, doesn't he?'

'Of course he does,' snapped Justin. 'But would you necessarily say that Charles Walrond deserves to go with him?'

'Ah.' Ned's eyes grew thoughtful. 'Well, no. It ought to be Hugh. Naturally.'

Five minutes later he found himself regretting this piece of tactlessness but by then it was too late for Justin had stalked off without a word the instant it was said. Ned sighed and decided that the poor devils who had the misfortune to be working with the Captain that morning were deserving of sympathy.

In this he was mistaken for it was not Justin's practice to vent his moods on the men and he took particular care to be no more exacting than usual. It did not occur to him that, after one look into his face, the troopers were also employing their own brand of caution. He merely noted their reserved formality and put it down to a dislike of digging.

Once the charred remains of the burnt-out houses had been cleared away from the south wall, it had seemed only sensible to use the space to the Castle's advantage and the excavation of a second moat was clearly the best means of doing so. It was a large undertaking and, despite having a hundred men working on it for the last month, Justin saw no possibility of its being more than half finished before the winter set in. As for Sir William's plans to modernize the outer defences by building two new bastions that would bring the curtain wall forward to run parallel with the original moat, these could not effectively begin until the spring came.

However, with the general pattern of the war looking brighter than it had since before Marston Moor, the work seemed justified. The Parliament might have won an inconclusive victory at Newbury but they had failed to take Banbury and the warp and weft of their high command was currently being torn apart by the extremely public quarrel between Oliver Cromwell and my Lord Manchester. They had been defeated in the South-West and, best of all, their Scots allies were being lured homewards by the Marquis of Montrose and his band of mad Irish who had recently defeated the Covenanters at Fyvie Castle with bullets made of melted-down chamber-pots. All in all, it was small wonder that the Committee of Both Kingdoms had decided to send commissioners to treat with the King at Oxford. But then, thought Justin with cynical realism, they probably don't realize that we're fighting on credit.

His own pay was two months in arrears and some of the men were owed even more. The only way many of them kept body and soul together was by using legitimate tax-collecting missions as an excuse for wholesale plundering. It was a situation that bred brutality and indiscipline but which could not be helped for the alternative was a high rate of desertion.

A cloaked and hooded figure on horseback came slowly across the Market Place from the bridge and made its way to the south gate. Justin surveyed it with absent interest and then restored his attention to the duty rosters and requisition lists that had just been handed to him. The rider was no messenger but a woman; someone's sister or mother or wife, no doubt. He scrawled his name at the foot of each page and handed the papers back to Sergeant Cole.

'We don't seem to be getting very far very fast, Sergeant.'

'No, sir.' Ramrod stiff, the sergeant kept face and voice strictly expressionless. 'Shall I speak to the men, sir?'

'About what?'

'Digging faster, sir.'

A disquieting gleam informed the grey eyes.

'Can they? After five days' frost and with the ground hard enough to break three spades this morning? You must make a few allowances, Sergeant.'

Sergeant Cole's chest heaved but he repressed his natural indignation and responded with only a wooden, 'Yes, sir.'

Justin grinned. 'Oh come off it, Archie! What have I done to make you sulk? Think pioneer work beneath your dignity, do you?'

'No, Captain Ambrose, I do not!' snapped the sergeant, goaded beyond endurance. 'But I do think you've got no right coming out to my boys looking ripe for murder. It makes 'em edgy.'

There was a pause and then Justin's mouth twisted wryly. 'Was I? I wasn't aware of it. But I know I haven't said anything to reinforce the impression.'

'No, sir. That's just the trouble,' offered Archie Cole with a hint of grim humour. 'You didn't say anything at all.'

Justin did not see Lieutenant Frost until the pair of them met in the officers' room a few minutes before the dinner hour. A wary look entered Ned's eyes but it was Justin who spoke first.

'Ned, I beg your pardon. I was bloody rude, I know, but I hope I don't have to tell you that I didn't mean it.'

'Oh,' said Ned faintly. 'No. Neither did I.' And then, pulling himself together, 'Let's forget it and have a drink. How's your ditch?'

'My moat,' corrected Justin, 'is going to be a masterpiece and the pride of my existence. What of your stables?'

'Finished. When the war is over, I think I'll apply for Inigo Jones' job and offer them as a testimonial.'

'To what?' asked Hugh Vaughan, newly come in. 'You do realize that your beautiful new roof is leaking?'

'What?' howled Ned, hurling himself across to the window. Then, with good-humoured relief, 'You lying devil! It isn't even raining.'

'No.' Captain Vaughan sat down, crossing one elegant leg over the other and looking critically at his colleagues. 'I do think you might have dressed for dinner.'

Justin gazed mockingly back at his lace-edged burgundy satin. 'Do you? But what price then your moment of glory?'

'Speaking for myself,' said Ned, passing Justin a cup of wine, 'I'm saving what little decent clothing I have left for an occasion worthy of it.'

'Ah.' Hugh smiled. 'You'll be sorry.'

Intrigued, Ned was still pressing for an explanation when the door opened and it walked into the room on Will Compton's silk-clad arm.

'Gentlemen,' said Will, demurely, 'allow me to present Mistress Anne Rhodes.'

Smiling like a cat with the cream, Hugh rose and bowed. Ned simply stared and Captain Ambrose drew a long breath of pure appreciation.

She would have been beautiful in any circumstances but in the mundane clutter of the room she was sensational. A magnificent, queenly creature in her mid-twenties, she had skin like magnolia and hair the colour of burnished chestnuts and she was exquisitely and provocatively gowned in pearl-trimmed, delphinium taffeta. Dense, slate-blue eyes set under heavy, long-lashed lids rested first on Lieutenant Frost and then, with interest, on Justin.

The air was charged and fragrant with musk, and dinner, usually a light-hearted and rather haphazard affair, was suddenly transformed.

'So you have come from Warwickshire,' said Hugh a little later as he refilled her glass. 'A perilous journey, surely?'

'I had no choice.' Huskiness touched the low contralto. 'My late husband's family have been very good but with the house seized by the enemy, how could I stay?'

Ned gazed at her with dazzled sympathy. 'And where will you go?'

'I don't know. I thought perhaps Oxford but I have heard that it is desperately overcrowded.'

'Oh it is,' Ned assured her. 'It's impossible to find a lodging these days, even if one is willing to share.'

Will Compton hid a smile. 'I'm sure Mistress Rhodes is immensely comforted by that information.'

Ned flushed. 'Actually, I was about to —'

'So it's just as well she already knows that she may count on our hospitality for as long as she needs it.'

There was a startled pause and then Anne Rhodes smiled, her gaze resting for one seemingly intimate second on each face in turn. 'You are all so kind. I cannot believe my good fortune, but please don't let me intrude upon your work. I know – all England knows – what loyal and courageous service you give His Majesty and I would hate to feel myself in the way of it. Indeed, if there is anything that I can do to help, I hope you will not hesitate to ask.'

There was a threefold murmur of graceful acknowledgement into which Justin said pleasantly, 'A generous offer and one worth remembering, but you must not encourage us to take advantage of you, Mistress.'

Considering slate-blue eyes met gleaming grey ones.

'Are you likely to, Captain?'

'Given the right circumstances, all things are possible,' came the deceptively innocent reply. 'And I am convinced that you have many natural talents which will be revealed when you know us better.'

Ned's jaw dropped and Hugh choked on a morsel of fish. Mistress Rhodes reached for her wine cup and directed a slow smile full into the Captain's face.

'You are so understanding that I feel I know you already. And it is true that I am held to be skilled in certain matters.'

Justin smiled back at her. 'I don't doubt it.'

'And what are your skills?' asked Will, gently breaking the thread.

The glowing, auburn head was tilted slightly, exposing the rounded column of a creamy throat. 'The arts of healing, sir. I am experienced in the use of herbs.'

Exchanging a swift glance with Hugh, Will said, 'Are you familiar with the new fever – the one people call the influenza?'

'I have seen it. You have a particular reason for asking?'

'Very much so,' replied Will, grimly. 'Since the siege was raised, it's gone through the ranks like an epidemic and three men have already died of it.'

She nodded. 'Have you others you consider at risk?'

'Several. So if there is anything you feel you can do, I shall be most grateful to you.'

Something stirred in the beautiful face and then was gone.

'I'll do my best. Fortunately, however lightly I travel, I never move without the most essential of my powders and cordials. I'd sooner leave my fripperies behind.' She shrugged, smiling. 'Indeed, I had to. One can carry so little on horseback.'

Later, when she had gone with Sir William to visit the influenza victims, Ned looked respectfully at Justin and said, 'I'm beginning to believe what I hear about you. You certainly favour the direct approach.'

'I wanted to find out something,' replied Justin, absently.

'I know what you wanted, you dog, and I've the distinct impression that you're likely to get it!' Ned paused and then, when no response was forthcoming, said, 'You're very quiet. Indulging in pleasant anticipation, no doubt?'

'Not particularly.' Justin gazed enigmatically at his hands. 'I was wondering if our sultry windfall really does know of miraculous herbal cures. And I was thinking that, if my instincts about her are correct, we are in for an interesting few weeks.'

Three days later, the snow came.

Justin went into the town amidst large, swirling flakes in order to line his empty pockets with the sale of a set of pearl buttons which were his only possession of any value. He indulged Mr Atkins, the goldsmith, with twenty minutes of cheerful barter and Mistress Barbara, the goldsmith's daughter, with the same amount of discreet flirtation, then he struck a satisfactory bargain and left. Half an hour later, he had taken his horse from the stables and was riding to Bodicote with specifications of certain equipment needed for the Castle repairs.

The snow began to settle. His mind occupied with the probable effects of prolonged bad weather on the west wall, Justin did not immediately notice the cloaked and hooded figure trudging along the road ahead of him and by the time he did, the sound of his hoofbeats had made it turn to look back so that he was able, without difficulty, to recognize the face within the hood.

'Good God, Mistress Radford! What the devil are you doing out here on a day like this?'

Abigail brushed a snowflake from her nose and some of the tautness drained from her face. 'I don't mind the snow.'

'That's hardly the point,' said Justin impatiently. His eyes narrowed a little. 'But you mind something, don't you? What is it? You're not absent without leave again?'

She shook her head and managed a nervous smile.

'No. I'm going to Barnes' forge to collect a new spindle for the winding-jack and take Mistress Barnes some samples of linen.'

'Oh.' He stared at her in mild exasperation. 'Then, since I'm going to the forge too, I suppose you'd better come with me.'

It was scarcely a gracious offer but it brought a flood of gratitude and relief into Abigail's face. 'Can I? Thank you!'

Captain Ambrose raised sardonic brows.

'This is obviously my lucky day,' he drawled. 'Come. Give me your hand.'

It was Abigail's turn to stare for, stupidly, it had not occurred to her that he meant her to actually ride with him. And that, suddenly, was not all. Even coatless and dishevelled, the Captain had been an object of awed fascination, but sitting easily on his horse, with a short cavalry cloak dropping gracefully from his shoulders and the long, walnut hair glistening with snow and damply curling, he was Bayard, Galahad and Roland all in one.

'Your hand,' he repeated imperatively. 'Mistress Radford, I wish, just once, that you could do something without dithering. My horse is taking cold. What's the matter? Don't you want to come?'

'Oh yes – I do. But —'

'Then hurry up! Before we're up to our necks in bloody snow.'

His tone was one that sixty motley horsemen knew and obeyed instantly. Abigail reacted even quicker. Her hand was received in a firm clasp and she was drawn effortlessly from the ground to arrive in terrifying proximity before him on the saddle. The horse moved forward.

'There. That wasn't too difficult, was it?'

'No,' she whispered. An arm lay casually around her waist and her left shoulder was pressed against his chest. It was shockingly improper and alarmingly confusing. She felt thoroughly abandoned. 'No.'

Unholy amusement bracketed Justin's mouth but he merely asked, 'How is Samuel? Still alive and well and quoting Free-born John, no doubt? "Alas, poor Parliament – how art thou betrayed!" and so on.'

It was a quotation from the latest illicit pamphlet which Samuel had been distributing secretly around Banbury. She tensed and said hastily, 'That may not have been Mr Lilburne's work. It had no name on it.'

'The lack of a name,' observed the Captain, 'does not necessarily make a thing anonymous. Even if its anti-Presbyterian and pro-Cromwell sentiments didn't shout Lilburne, its coherence certainly would.' He paused. 'If your brother is involved in that direction, he'd do well to take care. Lilburne's always been an embarrassment to the King and he's become one to a goodly proportion of the Parliament. The rest – Cromwell and the so-called Independents – will probably follow suit soon enough when they find that even they can't live up to such radical ideas. If the wolves gather, they'll take his acolytes as well.'

'Thank you,' said Abigail, hollowly, 'but Sam isn't – he wouldn't – I don't think he has —'

'No? Then I humbly beg his pardon,' mocked Justin, plainly disbelieving. 'But if he isn't busy with politics, why isn't he walking to Bodicote instead of you? Come to that, why walk at all? You must have a cart or something?'

'We have. But Sam needed it to make a delivery. Of cloth,' she added guiltily. 'Jonas is busy in the shop with it being nearly Christmas. Mother is baking and Rachel is – is – isn't very well at present.'

Justin had no difficulty in interpreting this and a sudden laugh shook him. 'Well, well. But you can always hope it doesn't take after its parents.'

For a moment, Abigail was startled into silence. Then, with unconscious wistfulness, she said, 'Don't you think Rachel is pretty?'

'Oh yes. But so are icicles, frosted trees and marble statues.' He glanced at her averted face. 'Cheer up. Hasn't Jonas told you that beauty is only skin deep?'

'No. He says it's a snare of the devil. It leads to wickedness and vanity.'

Justin grinned. 'Dear God, Rachel must find him a charming lover. Or perhaps she was always sour?'

Abigail had never heard anyone speak like this before but, amidst her natural embarrassment, she discovered a dreadful impulse to giggle. She fought it because both it and the Captain's style of conversation ran counter to everything she had been taught.

The gates of the forge loomed out of the snow, bringing back all her former fears plus one new one.

'Please stop and let me down.'

He reined in with an impatient sigh. 'Don't tell me. Jonas

must not know. No doubt he'd sooner see you dead of an ague than sullied by my touch.'

'Yes.' Abigail slid breathlessly to the ground and looked anxiously up at him. 'You will follow me in, won't you?'

'I will if you make it possible. One can only follow from behind.'

The caustic note had returned to his voice. Abigail gathered her cloak in unsteady fingers and went. The yard was empty but the sound of hammering came from the forge and she trod reluctantly towards it. Inside, the boy, Endurance, worked the bellows while his father's massive arm rose and fell with rhythmic precision. Then the smith looked up and, straightening, laid down the hammer and advanced on her, rubbing his palms on the stained, leather apron.

'I've come for the spindle,' said Abigail, baldly. 'Is it ready?'

'Aye, Mistress. It's ready.' His hands continued to move and the pale, lifeless eyes fastened hypnotically on hers. 'Endurance will fetch it for you.'

The boy left the bellows and vanished like a wraith through a door at the back. The smith circumnavigated till he stood between Abigail and the yard.

'We haven't seen you in a fair while, Mistress.'

'No.' She resisted the temptation to retreat and fumbled in the pocket of her cloak. 'Here are the samples your mother asked for. I'm sorry I can't stay while she chooses but it's snowing and I'm sure she will understand.'

He ignored the proffered package and moved slowly closer. 'Now why are you always in such a hurry? It's not very kind, is it?'

Abandoning her attempt at bravery, she backed away from him. 'I'm sorry. Endurance is a long time. Perhaps you should —'.

'You're a shy little thing, aren't you? Modest, too. But I like that. A girl should be modest and humble. I don't know if you're humble enough, Mistress,' he sorrowed. 'Still, I reckon you could be taught.'

She stared at him, understanding nothing save that the expression in his strange, immobile face was somehow

111

unclean. She was at the wall and shelves bit into her back. He took another step and leaned his great hands against the wood on either side of her shoulders. The odour of stale sweat arose and engulfed her.

'Smith!' A diamond-hard voice cut through the air and brought Barnes wheeling to face its owner. Holding his horse with one hand, Justin rested the other negligently against the doorpost. 'Are you open for business? Because, if so, I suggest that you reserve your dalliance for another time and a more receptive lady.'

'God-cursed Malignant!' rumbled the smith. 'Mind your own business.'

'And you mind your tongue!' snapped Justin. His hand dropped from the door-jamb and both voice and posture suddenly acquired eight generations of seigneurial ice. 'Finish your transaction with this lady and be quick about it. I've no wish to spend half the day in this draughty pigsty.'

The pale blue eyes came abruptly to life and the spatulate hands tightened convulsively. Silence, unpleasant, raw and suffocating, stretched between the two men.

'Your spindle, Mistress Abigail.'

The half-whispered words exploded like a faulty petard as Endurance arose from the gloom at the girl's side. She gasped.

'What? Oh yes. Thank you.' Taking the metal rod, she pressed the package of samples on the boy in its place. 'Give that to your grandmother. And here's the money for the spindle.' Then she was off across the floor. 'Thank you, Mr Barnes. Good day.' And, without even glancing at the Captain, she fled.

She was half a mile down the road when he overtook her and stopped, holding down his hand in silent invitation. She took it without thinking and let him pull her up. She was still shaking.

He said, 'It's all right. Calm down. I gather what I saw was fairly typical?'

She nodded. 'Only today I thought he was going to – to touch me.'

Justin did not doubt it. 'Have you told anyone? Jonas?'

112

'No.' She shivered. 'I couldn't.'

'Then you'd better tell Samuel. No, don't argue. Just do it and make sure he understands. If it helps, tell him I've a feeling that our friend Mr Barnes is a little unbalanced.'

Abigail turned sharply to stare at him. 'What do you mean?'

'Exactly what I say. Now forget it and tell me how you will spend Christmas.'

She continued to gaze searchingly into his face. Snowflakes clung to the tiny curls escaping from her hood and melted against the pale skin of her cheek. Captain Ambrose smiled ruefully.

'Don't do that. It's temptation and opportunity all in one; and this is my day for playing Galahad.'

His meaning escaped her but the last word recalled other thoughts and she turned quickly away, flushing a little.

'Christmas? We go to church.'

'And that's all? No music or festivities of any kind? No gifts?' She shook her head and Justin said curiously, 'Don't you find that rather sad? The traditional pleasures were harmless enough.'

She tilted her head. 'I don't know. I've never experienced them. Our tradition here is to treat it as any ordinary day. I know that, elsewhere, this has only happened since the war began but most of Banbury has been of the Puritan persuasion since long before I was born.'

'Cakes, ale and zeal? I see. Well, that explains Jonas. The original Banbury Puritan. Do you have a cat or does he make do with you and Samuel?' he teased caustically. And then, seeing her blank look,

> *To Banbury came I, oh profane one*
> *And there I saw a Puritan one*
> *A-hanging of his cat on Monday*
> *For killing of a mouse on Sunday.*

'A gross exaggeration, no doubt?'

Abigail thought about it. And then, with confiding candour, she said, 'No. Only a small one. Jonas has very strict notions. I'm a disappointment to him. I was to father as well.'

Something flared in the grey eyes and he said harshly, 'His loss and not yours, I'm sure. But perhaps you are mistaken. Your name, if I remember correctly, means "Father rejoiced".'

This had the astonishing effect of startling Abigail into laughter. The dark eyes sparkled and a dimple quivered into being beside her mouth.

'Does it?' she said, on a delicious gurgle of amusement. 'Oh dear, someone should have told him!'

Chapter Ten

Christmas, the third since the war had begun, came decorously to the town and with the inevitable roistering to the Castle. And when it was past and the cold days of December flowed inexorably into the even colder ones of January, Charles Walrond quelled every vestige of good cheer by returning from Oxford in possession of the majority that Sir William had requested for Hugh Vaughan. Worse still, he brought news that, a mere month after being honoured with a well-earned knighthood, Lieutenant-Colonel Sir Anthony Greene had succumbed to the new fever and been buried on Christmas Eve.

Submerged in gloom and divided by internal bickering, the garrison embarked on a round of ruthless tax-collecting in which the village of Kilsby was dissuaded from a refusal to pay by the taking of hostages, and then robbed of sixty horses by way of a lesson. Justin, meanwhile, watched sardonically as the self-styled Walrondians flaunted their yellow ribbons and brawled with the red-tagged Comptonians and wondered if such lessons, like charity, should not begin at home.

Visitors came and went bringing news and gossip. Prince Rupert had made an unsuccessful attempt to retake Abingdon in which Sir Henry Gage had been mortally wounded, with the result that Colonel Will Legge was now Governor of Oxford in his place. At Westminster, Lieutenant-General Cromwell's digust with the dilatory Earl of Manchester had led him to propose an ordinance forbidding any member of either House to hold military office. Supported by the Independents and opposed by the Presbyterians, this measure would deprive the army, not just of Essex and Manchester, but also of Cromwell himself. But in practice, said the cynics, it was easier for Cromwell to resign from the Commons than the Earls from the Lords. Meanwhile, the peace negotiations in Oxford had ended in stalemate and the

Royalist cause in the North was weak unto death. Even Montrose and his Irish had vanished into the fastness of a Scottish winter.

Amidst the general air of discontent, Captain Ambrose found it increasingly difficult to maintain a sense of proportion and purpose. Christmas had seen him in a mood of withdrawn sobriety and, for all her charming ploys, Mistress Anne Rhodes found herself held politely at arm's length. In the third week of January, her luck changed.

The day began like any other with the usual round of routine tasks. Then letters bearing the Royal seal arrived from Oxford and a troop of horse paused for refreshment on its way south from Newark.

The letters concerned promotions and were not unexpected for Anthony Greene's death had left a considerable gap in the Castle command. The manner in which this was filled was no surprise either but it was not until he heard his suspicions confirmed that Justin realized he had been indulging in subconscious optimism. Sir William, as was only right, became a Lieutenant-Colonel and Walrond's vacant Captaincy went to Ned Frost but no new field-ranks were created. Even though Justin was well aware that Hugh had a better right to disappointment than he had himself, resentment still cut him like a knife and brought back all his old bitterness against George Digby, that golden, lisping favourite who would be Earl of Bristol one day and thus did not need to carve himself a career.

Because Ned and Hugh were his friends, Justin hid his frustration beneath a mask of urbanity. But even the very moderate degree of conviviality in the common-room grated his nerves and, for the first time in five years, he took refuge in the wine bottle.

The Newark men were still there. Aloof and deliberately forbidding, Justin sat in a corner while the evening became one of full-blown surmise and tedious Nottinghamshire anecdote.

'They say old Templeton is dying,' a chubby-faced officer remarked. 'Be worth a bit to the King if he does.'

'Oh?' said Captain Vaughan, politely. 'How is that?'

116

'Well, he's too old to fight so he's been digging deep in the coffers and sending money and that'll stop if Bernard French inherits.'

Hugh stifled a yawn. 'Bernard French?'

'Templeton's stepson. There's a pair of 'em and each as weasely as the other. Sail-trimmers, both. If you ask me, it's a pity the old man threw his own son out. Boy was a ne'er-do-well, of course, but that was years ago and they kept the scandal pretty much in the family.' A grin creased the soft face. 'And if the fellow's alive and still a rakehell, so much the better. No chance then of him turning out to be a cursed Roundhead.'

The talk encompassed half a dozen equally scintillating topics before the visitors finally took their leave and, by then, Justin was on his third bottle. Ned examined him warily and, perceiving a strange look in the too-steady gaze, said, 'Are you all right?'

'Perfectly. And soon I shall be even better,' replied Justin, rising and reaching for a fresh bottle. 'I'm merely rediscovering forgotten delights. Fear not, I'll continue my carouse in genteel solitude. Goodnight, beloved.'

His progress upstairs was slow but unfaltering and he eventually arrived, without mishap, at the door to his room.

'Wake up, Rex my boy,' he said opening the door. 'Your master is home, marginally drunk and in need of uncritical—'

He stopped abruptly for the dog was not there. Instead, seated calmly on the rug amidst glowing, tawny skirts, was Mistress Rhodes.

'Well, well. If it isn't the sympathetic widow,' drawled Justin.

The slate-blue eyes conducted an enigmatic appraisal.

'Yes. And finally, tonight, you need me. Don't you?'

'Do I?' He smiled oddly. 'Who am I to contradict you? And if you were sure enough of it to come, why ask me?'

'Perhaps because I wish you to acknowledge it.'

There was a pause and then he laughed and kicked the door shut with his foot. 'There, then. Satisfied?'

'No.' A tiny smile touched her mouth. 'But I can wait. Are

you going to offer me some wine?'

Justin looked at the bottle in his hand as if he could not remember how it had got there. 'If you wish.' He crossed to the washstand, picked up a cup and filled it. 'Tell me, was there really a husband?'

Her smile grew as she took the cup. 'I said so and who are you to contradict me?' He bowed ironically. 'Don't you think I am a lady?'

He looked at her. The magnolia skin was warmed by the light of the fire, the chestnut curls glowed and the tawny gown was designed to make every opulent curve an enticement. A remembered and very different picture invaded his mind, that of a soberly-dressed child with apprehensive dark eyes and a spaniel in her arms. The contrast was stark enough to be comical but he did not laugh. Instead, he looked at the woman on the rug and said, 'I know what you are.'

Her eyes narrowed. 'You think so?'

'Oh yes.' He dropped on one knee beside her, the blurred gaze focusing slowly on her face. 'You came here for one reason only and we both know what it was.'

'You're very sure of yourself.'

'It's finding sirens nestling on my hearthrug that does it. It's always happening.' He raised a hand and lightly traced the line of her jaw. 'They are not all, of course, as decorative as you. It's a pity I dislike being pursued, isn't it?'

She caught his hand in both of hers and a faint flush stained her cheeks. 'Dislike it? Look at me! You should be flattered.'

'Why? The shell is lovely, but what is inside it?'

Speechless for once, she loosed him and made to rise. His fingers trapped her shoulders, imprisoning her.

'No, no,' he soothed, his eyes steel-bright. 'Don't be hasty. You came to lick my wounds, remember? To commiserate with me on my misfortunes, the worst of which you know nothing about, of course. But that doesn't matter. Nothing matters.'

She said, 'You're drunk.'

'Drunk, yes,' he agreed cheerfully, 'but not incapable, sweetheart. Far from it.' With benign but discourteous briskness, he slid the gown from her shoulders, leaving her half-naked in his arms, and then began to pull the pins from her hair.

For the first time a flicker of doubt showed in her eyes. 'You are hurting me. There is no need.'

'Oh but there is, my angel, there is.' He filled his hands with the brilliant, auburn hair and drew her to him, still coldly smiling. 'Why pretend? You have a jaded palate and I am less of a gentleman than you thought. So cheer up. All is not lost, for I promise that you shall not be disappointed.' His teeth gleamed savagely white. 'After all, my greedy huntress, I too have a reputation to consider.'

Ten days later, riding westwards through the darkness at the head of his troop of horse, Justin drew a long breath and silently thanked God for a little action away from the stifling effects of Banbury.

'Heartfelt,' commented Will Compton, grinning. 'It must be tiring to be so sought after.'

Garrison life was not fashioned for the keeping of secrets. Everyone knew that Anne Rhodes had spent a night in Captain Ambrose's room. More intriguing still, everyone also knew that, after seeking unsuccessfully to repeat the experience, her attitude had undergone a sudden transformation.

Justin smiled grimly. 'It is. And next time I'm seen to be moving past the first bottle, I hope someone will knock me over the head for my own good.'

Will looked faintly startled but before he could reply, his elder brother Charles rode up from the ranks and said quietly, 'We're nearing Epwell. Best go on with caution. Don't want to stir up any fuss.'

'No, General,' mocked Will. 'What's the matter, Charlie? Do you think I don't know this road?'

'Fool,' replied Sir Charles, good-humouredly. 'I was thinking of billets.'

'Weren't we all?' sighed his brother. 'Especially the no doubt cosy ones occupied this night by James and Spencer while you and I are out in the cold trying to regain the family roof-tree. Ah well, it's all in a night's work, as they say and mother will be pleased. I take it you want to go in from the north-west over old Thompson's five-acre field?'

'Yes. And quietly.'

Compton Wynyates, childhood home of Will and principal seat of his brother James, Earl of Northampton, had been in Parliamentarian hands for several months. Tonight, Wednesday January 29th, Will and Charles hoped to repossess it. Because many of the three hundred horse and foot they brought with them were of Lord Northampton's own regiment, the entire expedition had the flavour of an antique family feud. Feeling rather like a Capulet bearing down on the house of Montague, Justin discovered the first impulse to laugh inside a month and began to recover his spirits.

They arrived at their goal around two in the morning and, not unnaturally, surprise did the first part of their work for them. With text-book precision, they overpowered the guards and possessed themselves first of the barbican and then of the stable-block from which they prudently removed some seventy horses. By then the Roundhead garrison was not merely awake but managing to conduct a remarkably orderly defence and any chance of an easy victory had flown.

Left with fifty troopers to hold the stables while the rest of the force moved on to the house, Justin took every measure available to him. He posted marksmen at all the windows, both upstairs and down. He sealed all the entrances with bar and bolt. He set men heaping all the bales of fodder well away from the doors. It was not his fault that there was just too much of it or that the main attack failed as quickly as it did or even that the stable-block was composed almost wholly of wood.

The first fire-arrows came almost immediately, aimed cunningly at the roof, and then the night was alive with swift, flaming arcs of light that bit into doors and tore expertly through windows.

'Stamp out what you can,' shouted Justin. 'For the rest, dip your cloaks in the water-butts and use them.'

It was useless and he knew it. The floor was strewn with

dried rushes and there were bales of straw everywhere, piled high against the walls. Enough winter feed for an entire cavalry regiment or to turn the place into a pyre that would not be quenched by even twenty times the water they had.

The rushes caught first and then a tight stack of bales in the gallery. Justin took the stairs three at a time, clutching his dripping cloak, and brought it swirling down in a vain attempt to smother the blaze before it took hold. Below him, tongues of flame licked slyly up one of the main timber supports. He roared an order and saw men leap to obey it while others rushed to help him with the straw.

Coughing, Justin tried to assess their situation. Flickering red and already out of control, the fires began to spread and merge while, outside, the enemy had closed in around them. He had lost nine men at the windows and three more were suffering from burns. There were two exits on the ground floor and one via an outside stair from the gallery, useless because of its narrowness and lack of cover. The thought took his eyes upwards in time to see five men rushing towards the upper door.

'No! You fools, stop!'

Too late. The door was flung back and a draught of air fanned the flames at the end of the gallery into a shimmering, orange sheet which enveloped the man nearest to it. He screamed and hurled himself back, hair and clothes alight, to plummet down over the rail while, above, the five fled on to the outer stair. Over the crackling of the fire came confused shouting and cries of 'Quarter!' There was the rattle of musket-fire and the fifth man reappeared in the doorway to collapse in grotesque surprise, blood pumping from his open mouth.

'Shut that door and get down here, all of you,' yelled Justin. 'Drench yourselves – hair, clothes, everything – and then listen.'

Choking, they did as he asked. And when they were with him, he said briefly, 'You saw what just happened. They're not going to let us surrender and if we stay here, we fry. So I suggest we go out and make a fight of it.'

Tom Mayhew said, 'They're all round, sir. At least a

hundred of them. We haven't a chance.'

Justin smiled. 'I didn't say we had. Once we open the door, it will be every man for himself but I'd like ten of you to stay with me and give covering fire. We may not get out but we can take a few of those bastards with us. Well?'

There was no question of refusal. Even when a dozen men were cut down in the first rush, the rest battled on with reckless daring. Several were taken, most died where they fell and three managed to melt into the shadows. Those left inside could no longer see to load their pistols. Smoke seared their lungs and eyes and, around them, the building was a tumbling mass of flame raining fragments of burning debris. Then the gallery collapsed.

'Other door,' gasped Justin. 'Out.'

Like the others, he was on his hands and knees, scarcely able to breathe or see. His palms were raw from beating out the flames that attacked his hair and clothing. There were only five of them now. Three crawled, as he had said, to the other door. The fourth collapsed, retching and Justin, who had not intended to leave, found himself forced into further, excruciating effort.

His chest screamed and the flesh of his hands sealed itself to Tom Mayhew's charred and smouldering coat as he began dragging him, inch by terrible inch, across the floor. A sequence of movements brought unimaginable torment, which was chased by an eruption of brilliant, molten heat. Then there was blessed darkness and peace.

Far, far away, beyond the reaches of mind and will, were voices that ebbed and flowed and mingled. The light was closer, only just behind his closed lids, but he did not want that any more than he wanted understanding of what the voices said. The light meant pain and understanding, recollection of something that would tear him apart if he let it in.

'Justin! Wake up. Come on, now. You can hear me. Try to wake up, Justin.'

'Oh no,' he thought firmly. 'No. That would be stupid.'

He drew breath, exerting every ounce of strength to turn

his head away. Then there was wave upon wave of tearing pain and a harsh, repetitive sound that frightened him. Something cool touched his lips and his mouth was filled with pungent sweetness. He swallowed, choking; and the darkness came again.

The next time he woke, the voice had changed to that of a woman. He heard it, dimly, through distorting mists that fooled him for a time into thinking he did not know it. Then the unremitting stream of lightly stinging derision parted the veils and sent time spinning to the place where memory and reality became one.

Suddenly, the dark was no longer safe. Contemptuous faces and accusing questions dragged him to the precipice of his father's disbelief where, last time, he had not been allowed to speak his defence. The hurt welled up and up until, finally unable to bear it, he exorcized it with his voice.

He talked, word by word, hour by hour and day by day for quite a long time. Then, as his body began to heal, he came slowly back from the demon-infested darkness and into the waking nightmare of pain and reality. Finally, he opened reluctant eyes on the blurred face of Mistress Rhodes and managed, on the third attempt, to say, 'How long?'

She smiled with hard brilliance.

'Eight days, my hero. You have been helpless for eight days.'

He closed his eyes again, frowning, and tried to force his mind clear of shadows. When he opened them again, Will Compton was beside him.

'Thank God you're better,' he said. 'We almost thought we'd lost you. Anne has nursed you single-handedly. She wouldn't even let me in, in case I disturbed you.'

Justin met the eyes of his tormentor with sardonic understanding. 'Thank you.'

She smiled again. 'It's been my pleasure, I assure you.'

'Quite.' Justin looked back at Will. 'How did I get out? I don't remember.'

'You were damned lucky. Two minutes earlier and you'd have walked into a troop of Roundhead musketeers. As it was, they must have thought there was no one left alive

123

because they moved off to recover their horses. Charles slipped back with half a dozen troopers just in time to see you dragging Tom clear – and then the lintel came down on you both.' Will paused, grinning ruefully. 'Well – mostly on you, actually. Tom is feeling pretty fit and panting to come and take your hand in gratitude. I've told him he'll have to wait a while for that.'

Justin raised his arms cautiously and surveyed his throbbing, white-wrapped hands. 'So I see.' He lowered them again and became aware, for the first time, of the tight strapping around his chest. 'And my ribs?'

'Just cracked, we think. You'll be fit again in no time.'

A bleakly ironic smile touched Justin's mouth.

'I can't wait. How . . . how many men did I lose?'

Will frowned. 'Now, Justin, that isn't —'

'How many?'

There was a pause. 'Forty-one. But we don't yet know how many of those were taken prisoner.'

A tremor passed over the still, haggard face and there was the sound of a harsh, tearing breath, suddenly checked. Swallowing, Justin said carefully, 'I think I would like to rest. Do you mind?'

'Of course not.' Will rose hesitantly. 'Try to sleep.'

'Yes. I will. And so must Mistress Rhodes. I'm quite safe to be left, you know.'

'Oh no,' said Anne, sweetly, her eyes watching avidly for the first fissure. 'I wouldn't dream of leaving you now.'

'Dear Christ!' White-lipped and shaking, Justin stared furiously at the Governor. 'Get her out of here, will you? Just get her out!'

Courtesy fled before compassion and, taking her arm, Will marched Anne smartly out of the room. The door snapped shut behind them, severing the last thread of Justin's self-control. Because of forty-one lives tragically lost and one uselessly preserved, he turned his face hard into the pillow and wept.

Chapter Eleven

'Abigail, you have far too much polish on that cloth. It is wasteful and will clog the carving of the furniture. I believe I have mentioned it before.'

'Yes, Rachel.' Submissively, Abigail scraped most of the substance back into the pot. 'I'm sorry.'

'And the next time you clean the silver, do try not to leave fingerprints all over it,' continued Rachel, irritated both by the enforced indolence of advanced pregnancy and the perpetual ache in her back. 'Have you spoken to Betty about the meat?'

'No, dear. I did that,' said Alice patiently. 'You must stop fretting, Rachel, it's very bad for you. Why don't you read to us from the news-sheet? There must be something about the new peace talks at Uxbridge and Jonas said there is a piece about the garrison here.'

Allowing herself to be diverted, Rachel picked up *Mercurius Britannicus* and coolly read out the appropriate passages, ending with that referring to Banbury.

'*Oh it is a cursed den or else it had been yielded up last summer. When all their gunpowder is gone they are able to maintain it on bare oaths and curses against an army of Saints at any time.*'

Laying the sheet down again, she said, acidly, 'Well, it is undoubtedly true but hardly constructive. Are we never to be rid of them?'

'Eventually. If these plans for a new army materialize,' said Jonas soothingly from the doorway. 'Abigail, go and help that frivolous Atkins child to choose her lace. I take it that Samuel is still in the stock-room?'

'Yes,' said Abigail, exchanging an anxious glance with her mother. 'Shall I call him?'

'No. I have to go up anyway.' He eyed her with dawning irritation. 'Well? What are you waiting for? I thought I told you to go into the shop.'

Pink-cheeked from the cold and with her golden hair framed by a sapphire hood, Bab Atkins looked even prettier than usual.

'At last!' she said, as Abigail appeared. 'I thought you were never coming. Have you heard the news? Isn't it awful?'

'What news?, asked Abigail, her mind on Samuel's habit of secret reading. 'I thought you wanted some lace.'

'That was just an excuse,' came the impatient reply. 'I had to talk to someone and I thought you might understand because I know you've met him. Besides, I could hardly speak of him to father or Aunt Jane, now could I?'

'I don't know. Who are we talking about?'

'Why, Captain Ambrose, of course! Do you mean you really haven't heard? They say he was quite dreadfully burned a week or so ago at Compton Wynyates and is lucky just to be alive. I'm so upset I could cry. The most attractive man I've ever met, even if he is a Cavalier, and this has to happen!'

Strange sensations were taking place inside Abigail's stomach and she forgot about Samuel. 'Who told you this?'

'Joseph Parsons. He's got some of Charles Compton's troop billeted in his house and he heard them talking. They said that Justin – Captain Ambrose – lost over forty men. Not that I care about them, but it does make you wonder why he didn't simply surrender.' Bab paused, looking curiously at the other girl. 'Are you all right? You've gone terribly white.'

'I'm fine,' lied Abigail. Raised, angry voices drifted in from the house, piercing her cocoon of worry. 'Shall I show you some lace?'

'Lace? Oh no. I'm not in the mood,' shrugged Bab, faintly disappointed in her audience. Her blue eyes raked the shelves. 'Where's that bolt of cherry taffeta? Never say you've sold it! I've been longing for a length of that ever since I first saw it.'

So, as it happened, had Abigail but she would have surrendered every yard of it to be rid of Mistress Bab. A door slammed and she could hear Jonas shouting. She said quickly, 'It's upstairs. No one will buy such a colour, you know that.'

'Well, save it for me,' laughed Bab, whirling to the door. 'I'd marry the Wizard Prince himself if he brought me a pink silk gown!'

For a long time after Bab had gone, Abigail remained very still and faced the fact that she could not go running down to the Castle while Jonas and Sam were in full spate. Indeed, she told herself logically, there was no reason to go at all. Cold and sick she turned towards the contumely in the parlour.

'How long?' Jonas was demanding balefully. 'How long has this sly disobedience been going on? Is this what you do every time my back is turned, waste your time reading the kind of books that you know are expressly forbidden in this house?'

'Since those you approve of reach a mammoth count of two – yes,' retorted Samuel, bitterly. He faced Jonas across the table where Abigail's polish now reposed amidst a litter of books and pamphlets. 'But the work gets done. And even if it didn't, you have absolutely no right to search my room as if I were some dishonest apprentice with my hand in your cash box.'

'You insolent young fool! For as long as you sit at my board and sleep under my roof, I have every right, including that of guarding your moral and spiritual welfare.'

'If that means keeping me as ignorant as you are yourself, I deny it you! And I'll continue reading anything I can get my hands on.'

'Not if I know it!' stormed Jonas, snatching up a book and then throwing it down as if its touch defiled him. 'Poetry! Vile immorality fit only for burning. And this – *Essays in Philosophy*. Dangerous ideas for idle minds. Is this what you call knowledge – a lot of heathen rubbish? As for this,' he pounced on Godwin's *The Man in the Moon*, 'it's an offence against the Creation and an abomination in the eyes of the Lord!'

'Don't be ridiculous!' snapped Samuel, white-faced and furious. 'It's a work of fiction, that's all. And as for the rest, the vile and immoral poetry happens to be Shakespeare and *the Essays* are by Thomas Hobbes. It's neither God's fault nor mine that your brain doesn't function beyond the confines of your sales ledgers and your self-appointed pulpit.'

'Blasphemy!' choked Jonas, alarmingly red.

'No. Honesty.'

'Sam!' moaned Alice. 'Please stop it.'

He swung round to fix her with a glittering stare.

'Why? It's time these things were said. I'm tired of having to do my reading in secret and I'm tired of seeing you being alternately bullied or ignored in your own home.' His eyes flashed to Rachel. 'And I'm especially tired of hearing you address my sister as if she were a servant.'

Before Rachel could open her mouth to answer this unexpected attack, Jonas said swiftly, 'Your sister is as undutiful as you are yourself.' Catching sight of Abigail in the doorway, he stretched out an arm and pulled her forward. 'Tell me, have you been filling your head with this ungodly drivel as well?'

'No she hasn't, so you can stop mauling her and confine your attention to me!' It was a lie but Samuel cared nothing for that. 'You can't stop me reading, you know.'

'Can I not?' Jonas released his sister and gestured to the books. 'We'll see about that. Abigail, take these works of the devil into the yard and burn them.'

There was a sudden, appalled silence.

'You wouldn't dare,' breathed Samuel. 'Most of them are borrowed and you know it.'

Jonas smiled coldly. 'That is your problem. Abigail, do as I bid you.'

She stared at him, rigid with fright. 'No.'

'No?' He was thunderstruck. 'What do you mean, no?'

'Careful!' taunted Samuel. 'You'll have a seizure if you don't watch out. And where would poor Rachel be then?'

'Oh!' gasped Rachel. Her eyes were bright and she had forgotten her backache. 'You wicked boy! How dare you joke about such things?'

'Take a look at your husband and you'll know.'

'This is unendurable!' Wrath and indignation kindled Jonas like a brand. 'I can scarcely believe that such dire intransigence is actually festering beneath my roof. You are as filled with deceit and sinful pride as if Satan's mark were printed clear on your brow, and you are so wilfully obtuse that you cannot even see the damnation that lies ahead. But I see it and I will not be disobeyed by either of you.' He wheeled on Abigail and his voice shook with temper. 'The next time you defy me, I shall take a stick to your back. Now pick up those accursed books and destroy them. As for you,' he turned back to Samuel, 'while they burn, you will go down on your knees and pray for humility and proper repentance!'

'I'm damned if I will!' With sudden savagery, Samuel swept polish and pamphlets to the floor as he gathered the books into his arms. 'You pray. I'm going out.'

'Sam?' hissed Abigail, tapping gently on his door. 'Let me in.'

The house was in darkness and, for the first time since morning, peaceful. Jonas had continued to rage in Samuel's absence and renewed the attack immediately he reappeared. Of the disputed books there had been no trace and, after uttering a selection of sarcastic retorts, Samuel had retired to his bedchamber and locked himself in.

'Sam, please!'

The bolt was withdrawn and the door opened to admit her.

'I'm sorry,' he said, closing it behind her. 'You've had a rotten day, haven't you?'

She nodded and, curling up on the foot of his bed, pulled her robe over her bare feet. 'He was livid when you missed prayers.'

'Naturally,' replied Samuel derisively. 'He's pathetic. He belongs in a Royalist cartoon – the perfect example of a joyless, canting, self-opinionated bigot. He even talks to God as if they were on an equal footing!'

'Sam, forget Jonas for a moment, will you?' Abigail toyed restlessly with the ends of her long, curling hair. 'I have to get into the Castle tomorrow to see Captain Ambrose and I'd like you to go with me.'

He stared at her. 'What on earth for?'

She explained and, at the end, said, 'I know he's a Royalist but he's been good to us. And I have to know how badly he's hurt.'

'Yes. Yes, I see that,' said Samuel, thoughtfully. 'I'll take you, of course, in the afternoon when Jonas is busy and Rachel rests on her bed. But you mustn't . . . you mustn't let yourself become, well, fond of him, Abby. Even if he were not what he is, it would still be impossible. You do see that, don't you?'

'Well, of course,' she agreed blankly. 'But there's no reason why I can't try to repay a kindness, is there?'

Samuel's reaction was duplicated on the following morning when, having no notion what comforts might be useful to a man suffering from burns, Abigail poured out the whole story to her mother. Alice listened to an impassioned recital of Captain Ambrose's favours and then said gently, 'You know that I should forbid you to go?'

'Yes.' Abigail met her mother's troubled gaze squarely. 'But I hope you won't for I should be sorry to have to disobey you.'

'I see.' Alice paused. 'I think you'd better tell me about him, Abby. Do you like him?'

'I don't know. He's sarcastic and short-tempered and he swears rather a lot. He says things he shouldn't and laughs when you least expect it, but he's unmistakably a gentleman, in the same way that Colonel Fiennes is. And he's kind; someone to trust. Does that sound stupid?'

'Not stupid,' replied Alice slowly. 'A little dangerous, perhaps.'

'But Jonas need not know anything about it,' urged Abigail, misunderstanding. And then, taking Alice's hand, 'Mother, help me.'

Alice looked back into pleading dark eyes and sighed. 'Very well. We'd best make up a basket.'

By the time Ned Frost met the two younger Radfords crossing the outer ward under escort, he was sufficiently concerned by Justin's unnatural lassitude to be glad of any possibility, however remote, of rousing him from it. Consequently, he greeted them warmly, dismissed their attendant guard and took them inside, talking all the time.

'It's good of you to come. I'm sure he'll appreciate it. They'll have told you he's awake again? Physically, he's not in bad shape. It could have been a lot worse. Just a couple of cracked ribs and those shocking burns on his hands, but all that will mend in time. What's worrying me is that he doesn't seem to care about anything any more. It's not like him.' He paused at the top of the stairs. 'Here we are. Will you excuse me while I make sure he's not asleep or anything?'

Alone on the landing with his sister, Samuel said, 'Shall I come in with you or would you rather go in alone?'

'I don't know. I haven't the faintest idea of what to say to him. He's going to think I'm mad. But you don't —' She broke off as the door opened and then stared speechlessly at the lovely red-haired woman who preceded Ned Frost through it.

'Well, well,' said Anne, looking first at Abigail and then at Samuel. 'What a surprise. And do you both wish to visit Justin?'

Samuel glanced fleetingly at Abigail and then said decisively, 'No. Just my sister.'

'I see,' came the amused reply. Anne directed an appraising gaze at Samuel and then bestowed a dazzling smile on him. 'Then perhaps you'll join me in a walk on the ramparts while she does so? I need some fresh air and you can tell me all about the town.'

Ned stared at her. 'But —'

She laughed at him. 'And why not? He'll be perfectly safe with me and I'm sure you are busy. And you, my dear,' she said carelessly to Abigail, 'may go in. He's wide awake and quite decent. I shall get my cloak. Come, Mr Radford.'

Dazed and thoroughly unnerved, Abigail pushed open the door and went in, desperately clutching her basket.

He was in bed, propped up by several pillows and, although he might have been decent by some people's standards, he was not so by hers for his torso was bare except for the bandaging around his ribs. She flushed and said stupidly, 'Who is that lady?'

'My nurse,' said Justin, indifferently. 'Didn't Ned introduce you?'

'No.' She shut the door and advanced on him a little way. His hands were bandaged too and lay with helpless stillness at his sides. 'How are you?'

'Alive.'

She looked into eyes empty of expression and shivered.

'Aren't you glad?'

'Ecstatic.'

Shock evaporated her embarrassment and she crossed to the bed. 'I brought a few things for you. Nothing much, just some calves-foot jelly and a pie of my mother's and – and —' She stopped abruptly and put the basket ungently on the floor. 'Please don't look like that!'

'Like what?'

'As if . . . you wished you were dead.' Her eyes widened in horror. 'You don't, do you?'

He shrugged and, wincing slightly, said, 'Why shouldn't I?'

She did not reply and something in her gaze finally succeeded in piercing his detachment. He gave her a smile which did not reach his eyes and continued lightly, 'And then again, why should I? Don't get carried away, my child. I'm well enough. Unlike you, since you seem to spend your life in imminent danger of incurring the wrath of Jonas.'

'He won't know. And Sam is with me, at least, he's with your nurse at the moment.' She paused, watching him frown. 'What is it? Is something wrong?'

'Where are they?'

'On the ramparts, I think.'

'Well, that should be safe enough. She can hardly seduce him and I see no reason why she should push him off.'

'What?' gasped Abigail.

'Nothing.' He leaned back, looking at her from beneath half-closed lids. 'Merely my rather warped sense of humour. What did you say you had in that basket?'

'Calves-foot jelly, a mutton pie, a bottle of cherry cordial

132

and something of mother's for your hands,' she recited, still staring. 'Why should she do either?'

He sighed, closing his eyes. 'God! Will I never learn? All right. She won't do the second till she's been balked in her attempts at the first. Satisfied?'

'No. I don't understand. Who is she?'

'Her name is Anne Rhodes and she is what Jonas would call a harlot,' he snapped, a sharp furrow beginning to crease his brow. 'And don't tell me you don't understand that.'

'Oh. No.' She eyed him uncertainly. 'How do you know?'

'How do you think?'

'Oh,' said Abigail again, wishing she had not asked. His eyes remained closed, allowing her time to notice the carved pallor of his face, the scattering of burn marks and the places where the long, walnut hair had been badly singed. The line between his brows deepened and something tightened in her throat. She asked diffidently, 'Do your ribs hurt?'

'Not unless I laugh. And I expect you've noticed that I'm showing commendable restraint in that department.'

'Oh stop it!' Suddenly, she was unable to bear it. 'Since you can't possibly care what I think, there's no need to put on a performance.'

The grey eyes opened slowly. They were hazy with pain but remotely smiling. 'And what do you think, Abigail Radford?'

'I think,' she began impulsively, then, changing her mind, 'I think I'd like to look at your hands. May I?'

He gave a brief, humourless laugh. 'Help yourself. I can't stop you. And you're quite right, of course. They hurt like hell.'

'I believe you,' she said grimly, her head bent over her work. 'These bandages are far too tight.' Then, when the last, reeking pads fell away, she froze, a tiny sound rising unbidden in her throat. 'What has that — that woman being doing?'

'Punishing me, I suspect.' Justin examined the cream-clogged mess of his torn and blistered palm with absent interest. 'Doesn't look very hopeful, does it?'

Swallowing her rage and sickness, Abigail stood up and

jerked the strings of her cloak undone. 'I want two bowls of clean water, one warm and one cold. Where will I get them?'

'Downstairs,' he said laconically. 'But I wouldn't bother, if I were you. I really don't need a good Samaritan.'

Abigail threw her cuffs on top of her cloak, rolled up her sleeves and faced him purposefully. 'You need something. But nobody asked you, did they?' And she stalked from the room.

A little later, she returned followed by Ned carrying the water.

'Well, well, it's a procession of gentle naiads,' observed Justin lightly. 'But I'd rather have brandy, you know.'

Abigail ignored him. 'Thank you, Lieutenant. Put them by the bed, please.'

Justin tutted. 'Don't insult him, dear heart. He's a Captain now.'

'Shut up,' said Ned. He looked at Abigail. 'Is there anything else that I can do?'

'Not in here. But you might make sure that Mistress Rhodes is kept away from Captain Ambrose's hands in future.'

'Shame on you, Abby,' reproved Justin. 'What a thing to say! And it's too late anyway. Much too late.'

'That's enough!' snapped Ned. 'Look, Mistress Abigail, are you sure you don't want me to stay?'

She shook her head. 'No. The cleverness is all for your benefit. But thank you, anyway.'

'My pleasure,' he said and left.

Having washed her hands, Abigail advanced on the bed and sat down without looking at its occupant. Then, dipping a pad in the warm water, she began the ugly business of cleaning Mistress Rhodes' sticky ointment from the lacerated flesh.

It took a long time to do both hands and, fully occupied with controlling his breathing, Justin made no more attempts at flippant conversation. But the silence was raw, destructive and so, to spare them both, Abigail filled it with a mechanical account of the previous day's cataclysm. Only when it was over did she permit herself to lift her gaze to his

134

face. It was entirely without colour and lines of strain were etched about his tightly-compressed mouth, but his eyes, though frowning, were open.

He said, 'Well done. What happens now?'

'Rest for a moment,' said Abigail, as white as he and shaking with the effort required to continue hurting him. 'I'm sorry.'

'Don't be.' He looked at her with mild curiosity. 'Why did you come? Out of gratitude?'

'I don't know. Partly. Bab said you nearly died.' And then, because something inside her shied away from the other things Bab had said, she picked up the bowl of cold water and held it steady on his knees. 'I want you to put your hands in this and keep them there.'

The instant of immersion stopped his breath. Then he said raggedly, 'Talk, Sheherazade.'

So she talked, this time about Samuel's involvement with John Lilburne and his secret pamphlet-spreading. 'So you were right, you see. But luckily there were none left for Jonas to find. There, you can take them out now.'

He did so, saying in a threadlike voice, 'You shouldn't have told me all that.'

She set the bowl aside and began, very gently, to dry his hands. 'I know. But you'd already guessed, hadn't you? And it was the best I could think of at short notice.' She paused and sought a new diversion. 'Where is your dog today?'

'Out. He doesn't like redheads!'

Silence fell as she dusted his palms with her mother's elder and burdock powder and began to rebind them loosely. Then, quite without warning, the floodgates opened and Justin began to talk so rapidly that the words tumbled over each other in their haste to get out.

'I lost forty-one men. Can you understand that? I'd been sunk in self-pity for failing to get a promotion and then I went out and allowed my troop to be decimated. And, as if that were not enough to bear, I had Tom Mayhew in here this morning, drowning me in thanks for saving his life when the real truth is that it was the other way about. All I wanted was to incinerate my failures without any further effort and then

Tom collapsed and I couldn't. God watched forty-one men die and then wrought a miracle for me. Don't you find it ironic?'

He stopped as suddenly as he had begun, spots of colour burning in his cheeks. Then, shutting his eyes, said desperately, 'Oh hell, I'm sorry. I don't know what made me . . . it was inexcusable, all of it. I'm so sorry. I think you should go.'

'Tell me how you could have saved them.' Abigail's face was wet and her arms ached to offer the simplest of comforts. 'Name one thing you should have done and didn't.' He was silent and she said, 'You see? You did what you could and it wasn't enough. But you can't blame yourself for that. No one is infallible.'

'You don't understand,' he began wearily, opening his eyes on her. And then, on an indrawn breath, 'My mistake. You do understand. Don't cry. It's a waste.'

'I know. It doesn't work with you. You told me.'

His mouth twisted. 'I didn't mean that.'

'No. I know you didn't.' She rose and began tidying away the things she had used. 'Will you eat some calves-foot jelly?'

'If you wish.' He lifted his freshly-bound hands. 'And if you're not tired of playing mother.'

She thought as she fed him, spoon by spoon, how humiliating he must find this utter dependence. Then, as he sipped the cherry cordial, she found herself wishing that she could stay.

'Thank you.' Justin leaned back and smiled at her with apparent cheerfulness. 'And thank you for sending Ned away. It would have served me right if you hadn't but I'm glad you did. I'm afraid the "performance" might have become rather shoddy.'

She let down her sleeves and replaced her cuffs.

'Why do you do it?'

'To keep a balance. And because I find that the only thing that matters to me just now is to spare my friends the kind of maudlin diatribe I inflicted on you just now. It's not a pretty sight, is it? No, don't answer that. I've suffered enough for one day. And the stupid part is that I actually feel better for it.'

'Do you?' Her fingers stilled on the strings of her cloak and she searched his face. 'Truly?'

'Truly,' repeated Justin gravely. 'And, since I can think of nothing else that will please you, you may tell Samuel that such books as I own are at his disposal.'

Abigail flushed with pleasure. 'That is kind!'

'On the contrary. It's the least I can do . . . for a friend.' He smiled at her, the swift, leaping smile that Abigail thought she had forgotten and that made him look so different. 'Or am I taking a lot for granted?'

She shook her head, suddenly shy again.

'No. Or no more than I did when I came.'

In the end, it took more than Abigail Radford to bring Justin to himself again but it was thanks to her that his hands, at least, began to mend.

The final spur came on the twenty-third, exactly twenty-four hours after the Uxbridge peace negotiations ended in failure and thus nullified their attendant armistice. Paying a fleeting visit to his brother, *en route* for Newark, the Earl of Northampton was joined, later in the evening, by another regiment. Its commander was a dark, young giant in a scarlet cloak who took the stairs three at a time and entered Captain Ambrose's room like a cyclone.

'My God,' said Justin, struggling to rise. 'Sir!'

'Quite,' said Rupert of the Rhine, pushing him unceremoniously back on to the bed. 'And now perhaps you'll tell me what it was you did to Digby that made him send you here and why the devil you didn't apply to me to get you removed. After that, you can explain why you're lying here like a consumptive milkmaid when you should be up and about.' He sat down on the stool and grinned sardonically. 'Go on. I'm listening.'

Chapter Twelve

Samuel accompanied Abigail from the Castle in a mood of unusual abstraction that she, equally busy with her own thoughts, took two days to notice. When she did notice it, the natural and regrettable conclusion that it was due to red hair and voluptuous white shoulders was not hard to draw. Discreet enquiries produced evasion and more obvious questions, a snub. Finally, Abigail was driven into saying flatly, 'Captain Ambrose says she's a harlot.'

Samuel's eyes remained perfectly impassive.

'Does he? Well, well. Anything else?'

She stared at him. 'Isn't that enough?'

There was a pause. And then, 'No. I imagine it's purely coincidental. But who am I to educate him?'

He would say no more. Nor did he give any sign that he was facing the difficult choice between performing a small service for the Parliament and repaying, by inaction, the kindnesses of an enemy. Mistress Rhodes' slim, white packet lay like a stone in his pocket and he wished that he could bring himself to solve his dilemma by opening it. But he could not and, in the end, forced himself to make a blind decision. Based on the premise that the contents of the letter could not possibly cause Justin Ambrose any personal hurt, Samuel did as he had been asked and despatched it, unread, to the garrison at Newport Pagnell and the hands of Parliamentary Scoutmaster, Sir Samuel Luke.

As February drew towards its close and a renewed outbreak of influenza gripped the town, the news from outside showed the scales of war to be still in the balance. The Parliament's Scottish allies suffered another ignominious defeat when the Marquis of Montrose crushed the pride and Covenanting might of the Clan Campbell at Inverlochy. But the Parliamentarian forces of Shropshire scored a major success by depriving Price Rupert of his Welsh recruiting base at Shrewsbury. The Royalists managed to take Weymouth, but they lacked the men to hold it and were soon driven out again.

Meanwhile, having wrangled throughout January, the Parliament continued its bickering through February. Though the Independent faction's bid to rid itself of Essex and Manchester continued to hang fire in the House of Lords, another ordinance for military reorganization had not only been passed but was well on its way to fruition. Designed to do away with the frustrating parochialism of local committees and bodies of men who regularly refused to fight outside their own counties, it laid the foundations for a single, professional force under direct Parliamentary control. The post of Commander-in-Chief went to Sir Tom Fairfax.

Officers were selected, regiments re-formed, and uniforms designed. Because the like of it had never been seen before, it was christened the New Model Army.

At the sign of the Ragged Staff, the Radford family continued to devote itself to its own individual concerns. Samuel received and began to circulate a new batch of pamphlets decrying the Upper House's inability to sacrifice two of its number to the common good; Jonas tormented the days with sermons while he worried about Rachel's approaching confinement; and Abigail was suddenly catapulted into a brief but particularly terrifying nightmare.

It was the first day of March and they had just finished dinner. Rachel had already retired and Abigail rose, as usual, to clear the table only to be waved back into her seat by Jonas who said coldly, 'Sit down. I have something to say which concerns you.'

She glanced from her mother's surprised face to Samuel's wary one and then looked nervously back at Jonas while she waited for him to continue.

He said, 'This morning I received what I can only describe as a most unexpected request. Have you any notion, Abigail, of any gentleman who might be disposed to ask for you as his wife?'

'Me?' stammered Abigail, incredulously. 'No.'

'I am glad to hear it.' He paused, portentously. 'You may

139

consider yourself both fortunate and honoured. Although he may not have quite the standing I would have liked, Thankful Barnes is an industrious man and one of God's elect.'

There was a sudden, appalled silence. Abigail felt the room begin to spin around her and she clutched at the table-edge.

'Who?' she asked faintly. 'Did you say Th-Thankful Barnes?'

'I did,' came the repressive reply. 'And while I am pleased to find you so obviously unaware of his intentions, I consider your tone unnecessarily dramatic.'

The colour drained from Abigail's face, leaving it almost transparent and her eyes filled with stark horror.

'I can't,' she said. 'I can't marry that man. P-please, Jonas, I'm afraid of him.'

'Utter folly! You talk like a child.'

Samuel said, 'No, she doesn't. The fellow's not right in the head.'

'I beg your pardon?' snapped Jonas. 'I realize, of course, that you will go to any lengths to help Abigail defy me but slander is surely going a little far?'

'It isn't slander,' replied Samuel, devoutly hoping that it wasn't. 'Thankful Barnes may be one of God's elect but he leers at Abby in the best Cavalier tradition. Last time she went up to the forge, he'd have laid hands on her if another customer hadn't turned up in time to stop him.'

'And how was it that *you* didn't stop him? I presume that, since you know so much, you must have been there?' asked Jonas sarcastically.

'Abby told me,' admitted Samuel shortly. 'Since then, I've collected the vegetables myself and it doesn't need a genius to see that Barnes doesn't care for the substitution.'

'And does that make him insane?'

'I didn't say insane, I said not right in the head,' responded Samuel, rising impatiently from his seat. Then, falling back on Captain Ambrose's words, 'A little unbalanced, if you prefer it. And I'm convinced that he is. Half the town could tell you how he treated his first wife.'

'If a man is unfortunate enough to marry a girl with

frivolous tendencies, it is his duty to teach her to forget them,' announced Jonas. 'Thankful Barnes did no more than that. And he will undoubtedly have it to do again if he takes Abigail to wife.'

'No!' Abigail came unsteadily to her feet. She had never felt so ill. 'I can't, I can't! He makes me feel unclean.'

'Then that is a fault in you,' said Jonas distastefully. 'But you have nothing to say in the matter and I shall give Mr Barnes my answer when I have had time to consider.'

Alice directed a warning glance at Samuel and then spoke for the first time. 'That is just as well, for there are many things to consider, such as whether, with Rachel and the new baby to think of, we can afford to let Abby go just now.'

It was a shrewd move and Jonas paused before saying thoughtfully, 'She need not, of course, be married at once. But you are right to mention it.' And then, rising, 'You may clear the table, Abigail. We will speak of this again in due course.'

Her body ached and nausea was tearing at her throat.

'Jonas – no! You don't understand. I won't do it, I can't! Not him, anyone but him. I – please say you will refuse him?'

The humourless, intolerant face darkened with anger.

'I will do as I see fit. And it is not for you to say what you will or will not do. Now control yourself and stop disturbing the house with your hysterical behaviour. I am going up to see my wife.'

There was a moment's deathly hush after he had gone and Abigail looked beseechingly at Samuel and her mother.

'What can I do?' she whispered. 'I can't live with that man. I'd rather be dead.'

'Abby!' said Alice, compassionate but shocked.

Samuel shook his head at her and limped round the table to put his arms round his sister. 'Don't, my dear. It will be all right, I promise. Mother knows how to handle Jonas and I can be remarkably lazy when I try, so that you will become indispensable. And if you can only convince Rachel that you can't wait to get away, she'll keep you out of spite. All you have to do is be quiet and patient. Is that so hard?'

'Yes,' said Abigail, against his shoulder. 'It is. I understand

Captain Ambrose now. I didn't know one could feel like this.'

Jonas kept her waiting three days before announcing his decision and, in that time, Abigail began to look like a wraith, worn away by a nervous inability to eat or sleep. Samuel and Alice watched with anxiety while using every deterrent except that of open confrontation. Finally, Jonas was moved to open his mind to them all.

He said merely, 'I have refused Thankful Barnes' offer for your hand, Abigail. I hope you do not give me cause to regret it.'

'I'll try not to, Jonas. Thank you,' replied Abigail, with difficulty. And crumpled quietly on to the carpet.

With characteristic efficiency, Rachel produced Jonas' son on Wednesday March 5th at the respectable hour of four in the afternoon. He was a sound little fellow, fair like his mother but equipped (as Samuel pointed out) with lungs that promised something of his father. Jonas, after kneeling with his family to give thanks for Rachel's safe delivery and the gift of a healthy boy, was sufficiently uplifted to open a bottle of his mother's cherry cordial and announce that the child was to be named Hallelujah.

Samuel stared at him in awed disbelief. 'You don't mean it.'

'Why not?' Jonas lost a little of his benevolence. 'I consider it most appropriate. It is a Godly name and less common than many others.'

'To which,' said Samuel later to Abigail, 'only an idiot would attempt a reply.'

'It could be worse,' offered Abigail. 'Sarah Fuller has called her youngest Sorry-for-Sin. Is that this week's news-sheet you have there?'

'Yes.' He continued to read, his face becoming unusually grim. Then he looked up and slowly passed the sheet to her. 'I think you'd better read this.'

Abigail scanned the paragraph he pointed to and then her eyes widened and she sat down to read it properly.

The Monster Captain of Banbury: A Revelation
Beware, O Banbury! *Protect your goods, guard your womenfolk and sleep not soundly in your beds for Apollyon is in your midst. A man of Blood and Curses, whose very breath pollutes the air; the devil's Henchman – incestuous, vile and base. Recently nurtured in robbery and unnatural practices by the Arch-Fiend Rupert, the Monster Captain began his vicious career in boyhood with lies, spiteful slanders and the theft of a jewel from his own Father. But of his greatest Crime, who shall dare speak? Who, in England, can believe that there exists a creature base enough to foully Ravish his own, innocent young Sister? And yet it is most shamefully so. Steeped in evil, Satan's son is at large in poor Banbury; and his name is Captain Justin Ambrose. Mark it well!*

Abigail's fingers tightened convulsively on the paper and she stared defiantly at her brother. 'There's not a word of truth in it. You know that, don't you?'

Samuel shrugged uneasily. 'A gross exaggeration is probably nearer the mark. These attacks have to have some basis—'

'Not this one!' Abigail's hands grew clammy and she discovered that anger could make you feel physically sick. 'It's a tissue of lies from end to end and no one who knows him could possibly believe it for even an instant.'

'Meaning that you don't?'

'Of course not. Never in this world! Do you?'

Samuel hesitated. And then, 'No. I can't honestly say I do. But it appears I'd be foolish to admit it if I did.'

'And exactly what does that mean?'

'It means I'd prefer you to be less emotional over the whole thing,' he replied bluntly. 'Try remembering who you are for once. He's nothing to you, Abby, and he never will be.'

Her throat closed painfully and she swallowed.

'I know. You don't need to tell me. It isn't what you think. I hate the injustice of it, that's all, and you agree, don't you?'

'Oh, yes,' said Samuel drily. 'I agree all right. But you and

143

I are mere drops in the ocean and I don't somehow see us turning the tide. Do you?'

Captain Ambrose did not see the Parliament's news-sheet until late that evening. Able now, with the aid of padding and gauntlets, to handle his horse, he had been given reluctant permission to accompany Sir Charles Compton's troop on a tax-collecting mission in Warwickshire and had thus gone on his first outing since the catastrophic raid on Compton Wynyates.

It had been a long and full day for, learning of a rebel convoy *en route* from Gloucester to Warwick, Charles had gaily turned aside to intercept it. The men, he said, were tired of digging trenches, building bulwarks and making gunpowder and they deserved a little fun. They had it. After a circuitous ride, the convoy was eventually discovered five miles east of Tewkesbury. Incapable yet of holding a sword, Justin watched enviously as his fellows swooped down on the enemy and routed them in one swift, fierce engagement. Then the Cavaliers rode joyfully back to Banbury with seventy-two sacks of broadcloth worth twenty shillings the yard, a quantity of money and silver plate and seventy prisoners complete with horses.

Justin returned white with exhaustion and badly chafed hands but in a mood of near-contentment. Then Hugh Vaughan gave him *Mercurius Britannicus* to read.

'I know your views on this kind of thing but, well, you're bound to see it sometime. Everyone else has.'

Justin read it slowly and then read it again, the sense of it reaching him by degrees, like bubbles bursting on the surface of a pond. Then the room darkened around him as sharp flashes of pain gathered themselves into monumental pressure behind his eyes. He said oddly, 'Why me? In God's name, why me?'

Hugh gestured uncomfortably. 'Why anyone? It's just indiscriminate claptrap, unpleasant, I know, but not worth worrying about.' He stopped as the door opened to admit Captain Frost.

Blessedly impervious to atmosphere, Ned grinned cheerfully at Justin and said, 'You've seen it, then? Beats me how they dream the stuff up – or who they think is going to believe it. Still . . . you have risen tenfold in estimation here. Our lads think you're a second Rupert. Which reminds me, he's supposed to be coming from Stratford tomorrow to spend the night, so you'll be able to nurture your vices together.' He paused, looking enquiringly from Justin to Hugh. 'What's the matter? Have I said something I shouldn't?'

'When,' asked Hugh acidly, 'do you ever do anything else? How would you like it if stuff like that was written about you and your Lucy read it?'

'Oh. Yes. I see.' Ned coloured faintly and said, 'But look, Justin, you don't think anyone believes this, do you?'

The blades in Justin's head were escalating to a peak of grinding agony. He said carefully, 'I'm sorry. I'm afraid I must trouble you to help me upstairs. I have a . . . a slight headache.'

The grey eyes were narrowed and opaque and the skin was stretched tight over his bones.

Hugh said, 'I'm not surprised. You shouldn't have gone out today. Give me a hand, Ned – and for Christ's sake keep your mouth shut!'

Justin was violently sick before they got him to bed and by then he could see almost nothing, but he managed one final piece of irony. 'It's a pity they can't see their monster now, isn't it? Another illusion down the drain.'

Outside on the landing, Ned looked gloomily at Hugh and said, 'I'm a fool, aren't I?'

'You're a fool,' agreed Hugh kindly. 'But you can't help it. Come on, I need a drink.'

Ned detained him with a hand on his sleeve. 'Is he taking that stuff seriously or is he just overtired?'

'Both, I imagine.' Hugh paused thoughtfully. 'But it might be as well if the men were discouraged from congratulating him on his notoriety. I saw his face when he read those accusations and, though he was shocked, there was something missing.'

'What?' asked Ned blankly.

The Welshman met his eyes squarely. 'Surprise. I'd have expected him to show some surprise. But he didn't.'

Having slept relatively little, Abigail rose very early on the following morning and sat at her bedroom window while dawn became day. The view was not inspiring. The cobbled depths of Frog Lane, the irregular carved gables on the opposite side of Shop Row and the broken remains of the Bread Cross at the near end of Butcher's Shambles. There was nothing she had not seen a thousand times before or wished to look at now. Sighing impatiently, she started to dress.

Fifteen minutes later, she drifted by Betty with an absent smile and out of the house into the street. The air was fresh and lightly misted with rain but it was not cold. She drew a long breath, pulled her hood over her neatly-braided hair and set off eastwards along Sheepmarket. Few people were about as yet and, of those who were, most were stall-holders preparing for Thursday's weekly market. Abigail passed them without a glance and continued along Bridge Street to the river. The town gallows, grim but mercifully unoccupied, stood to her right and, as always, her steps quickened until it was behind her. And then she was on the bridge, with the Cherwell flowing placidly beneath her feet.

Resting her hands on the ancient stone parapet, she gazed across Goose Leys to the Castle, dour, silent and forbidding in the early morning light. The new bulwarks lay stark against the original building and gave the place an unfamiliar appearance, for where the curtain wall had once run back at a polygonal angle, it now stood four-square with the moat. But to Abigail, the Castle was only the shell which housed the kernel and her thoughts lay, as they had all night, with the man who lived at the top of the south-west tower.

A gentle plop brought her eyes down to the drifting spread of ripples on the water. Just as the surface stilled, another stone arched downwards to repeat the process. Abigail leaned over the parapet and found herself looking on a familiar, walnut head. Shock pushed her upright again and then, sparing a moment to relocate her breath, she trod carefully down the sloping path to the river bank.

He was leaning against one of the crumbling archways and he was dressed, not in the usual buff leather, but in severely-cut claret broadcloth. His face was turned towards the opposite bank and everything about him looked damp, as if he had been there for some time. Then he heard her and looked sharply round so that she saw, for one throat-constricting second, the unguarded expression that previously only the river had been witness to. It vanished immediately. The grey eyes became shuttered and his mouth, hard and unyielding as he said coldly, 'Go away. There's only an hour before breakfast and I haven't raped anyone yet today so you're in acute danger. Haven't you read the paper?'

'Yes. I'm sorry.'

'For what? Unwittingly repairing my hands so they can commit further atrocities? Or missing your chance to benefit humanity by slipping a little something into the cherry cordial? If only you'd known!'

'I meant that I was sorry such lies were written about you,' replied Abigail steadily.

'Lies?' He uncoiled from the bridge and advanced on her with brilliant eyes. 'Abby, Abby, you aren't saying you believe me a poor, maligned victim of circumstance, are you? Whatever will you think of next? No wonder Jonas is disappointed in you.'

She stared at him helplessly and then said, 'I don't blame you for being bitter, but —'

His hands shot out, gripping her arms and, even through the thickness of her cloak, he made sure that it hurt.

'You are deluding yourself. Shall I prove it to you?'

There was a pause. And then, 'I'm not sure what you mean. But I do know you've no intention of hurting me.'

He looked down into dark eyes that, though troubled, held no fear and his hands fell slowly away from her. Then, in a very different tone, he said, 'There are days when even the best of us are inclined to be too clever for our own good and this is one of them. Go home, Abby. I'm not fit company for anyone and, if you are seen with me, my

147

unfortunate reputation will be enhanced at the cost of yours. Do you understand me?'

'Yes.'

'Then why don't you go?' She said nothing and he gave a sudden, humourless laugh. 'Of course, how stupid of me! You're waiting for a confession, aren't you? It's written all over your face.'

Flushing, Abigail tilted her head sharply and felt her hood slide off. She ignored it and said, 'I just thought it might help you to talk. I've already made it plain that I don't think you have anything to confess.'

'And I've already made it plain that the most helpful thing you can do is to leave me alone,' he snapped. 'Or, if you're really desperate to brighten my day, go and stew a few toadstools for Jonas' breakfast.'

She recognized his desire to be deliberately difficult but the manner of it was outside her experience and she cast around desperately to find the key. Then, thinking she had it, she said deviously, 'Jonas is a father. The baby was born yesterday and it's a boy. They're going to call him Hallelujah.'

'Really?' Justin folded sardonic arms. 'By all means, let's make polite conversation. Hasn't the weather been mild recently? It's quite like spring. And what a pretty spot this is! Do you come here often?'

His irony went on and on and, unable to either leave him or bear with him, Abigail wilted beneath it. Finally, in exactly the same abrasively courteous tone, he said, 'And what have you done with your cap?'

'What?' she said blankly.

'Your cap, that lamentably unflattering piece of white starch you usually wear on your head. Not that its absence isn't a distinct improvement. If you stopped torturing your hair into a severity that nature plainly never intended, the transformation would probably be complete. What, nothing to say? Aren't you even going to ask how my hands are?'

'Of course,' said Abigail weakly. 'Are they still painful?'

'Only when I grasp young ladies brutally by the arm. Here, see for yourself. Still decidedly tender but definitely on the

148

end, thanks to you.' He held out his badly flawed palms
or her inspection and added abruptly, 'I don't have a blood
ster, only one by my stepmother's first marriage. And I've
ever laid a finger on her.'

Abigail's eyes flew to his face and her breath leaked slowly
way. She wondered whether this appalling habit he had of
arowing things at her when she least expected them was a
alculated one. His eyes met hers and she knew that it was.

'Why do you do that?' she asked irritably. 'You are as nasty
s you can possibly be —'

'Don't depend on that.'

'— and then you tell me —'

'— something I'd every intention of continuing to keep to
nyself,' he cut in, drily. 'Quite.'

'So why did you tell me?'

He shrugged and said flippantly, 'You obviously have
omething of the confessional about you. Or perhaps it's a
natter of simple vanity. I'll cheerfully admit to being
profligate – so far as my frequently non-existent pay allows –
put I draw the line at being called a rapist. It's a slur on my
capabilities, damn it.' He gave her a jewel-bright smile. 'And
hat is quite definitely all for today. Are you going or must I?
've really no wish to have your name added to my list of
aypothetical victims.'

'I'm going.' She replaced her hood and eyed him
anxiously. If their conversation had left her feeling drained,
he looked positively ill. 'Are you on duty today?'

'No. My time is my own. And when I have had enough of
solitude – if, that is, I ever get any – I shall probably get
drunk.' Temper flared again and he said, 'Now, for Christ's
sake, leave me alone. For reasons you may possibly appreciate, I'm finding it hard, today, to forgive you for being sister
to the kind of foul-minded hypocrite who put me in the
public pillory. Or, to put it bluntly, all Puritans are
beginning to look the same to me.'

It was probably the most hurtful thing he could have said
and he recognized it with distant regret, but it was too late.
Abigail had already gone.

The knowledge that he had wounded her for no good

reason did nothing to improve his temper. It was even faintly alarming because he knew it to be a direct result of an uncharacteristic tendency to talk too much. The whole thing reeked of self-indulgence and indiscipline and it worried him.

He spent the afternoon in the oak-panelled splendour of the Globe Room at the Reindeer Inn in Parson's Lane. Added to the original building only eight years ago, it was a pleasant, airy room with an elaborately-carved fireplace and a honeycomb plaster ceiling but, as far as Justin was concerned, it might as well have been a coal cellar. He sat moodily in a corner of the large, mullioned window and found a sardonic enjoyment in the wary glances accorded him by the other customers.

He did not, however, get drunk and this was fortunate because, at just five past o'clock, the door was flung wide to admit the King's nephew.

Silence engulfed the room.

Briskly oblivious, Rupert strode across to push Justin unceremoniously back into his seat with a curt, 'Are you sober? Because, if not, I've at least a dozen more urgent matters to waste my time on.'

Justin's mouth curled faintly.

'Yes, sir. Damnably sober. I can't afford to be anything else.'

With a derisive grunt, the Prince threw himself inelegantly into the opposite corner and waved the pot-boy aside. 'Then it's not a completely ill wind that keeps our pay in arrears. And at least you have boots! Two of my fellows were actually sharing a pair at one point. And despite all the plundering I'm credited I never seem to have more than a couple of pounds to my name. The whole army is living off the country and discipline is going to the dogs, especially in the West.' He brooded on this thought and then looked back at Justin. 'They told you I was coming, I suppose?'

'Yes. In order that we might "nurture our vices together" was, I think, the exact expression.' Justin paused and then made a briefly contemptuous gesture. 'They think so, at any rate. Or is it just that they've finally recognized you?'

'Who cares?' Rupert's indifferent gaze skimmed the room

150

and set at least four stalwarts edging nervously towards the door while the remainder exchanged meaningful glances. 'If I took to the bottle every time filth was thrown at me, I'd never be less than half cut.'

'No, sir. Point taken.'

'I hope so.' The dark eyes examined him shrewdly. 'Do you want me to take you out of here?'

The blood rose under Justin's skin and he said flatly, 'I'd be no use to you. I can't hold a sword yet, or even stay in the saddle for more than a few hours. And I know the pace you set.'

'Needs must,' shrugged Rupert. 'But if and when the Parliament fields this new army of theirs, I'll need all my best captains so you'd best get yourself fit.' He stopped and then said, 'You never used to drink. I suppose it is this damned propaganda?'

'Amongst other things.'

'Hm.' The Prince yawned hugely. 'Well, look on the bright side. At least no one's accused you of eating children.'

'No.' Justin stared into his ale-cup. 'What will you do now that Shrewsbury has fallen?'

'Use Ludlow.' Rupert scowled. He had depended on his brother Maurice to hold Shrewsbury and its loss was still a sore point. He said tersely, 'I've some news for you. Your father died at the end of last month.'

A muscle moved in Justin's jaw. Then his eyes hardened and he said, 'I see. Thank you for telling me.'

'Well, no one else is in a position to, are they?' observed the Prince with caustic logic. 'What will you do?'

A strange smile crossed the chiselled features.

'The same as I've done these last ten years, Your Highness. Absolutely nothing. I won't even get drunk.'

Chapter Thirteen

As cold, blustery March gave way to uncertain April, Just
gradually regained both his physical fitness and his sense
proportion and Abigail marked the passing of her nineteent
birthday. They did not meet.

Inside the Castle, the programme of digging and rebuild
ing continued with new vigour and Sir William Compto
strove to reach agreement with Sir Samuel Luke on a
exchange of prisoners. Outside it, the 'Self-Denying Ord
inance' finally emerged triumphant from the House
Lords, forcing all members of Parliament to surrender the
military commands within the month. The disenchante
Earls of Essex and Manchester pre-empted the order b
resigning twenty-four hours before it was passed; Lieuter
ant-General Oliver Cromwell continued quietly in activ
service out of London.

While Sir Tom Fairfax led the raw divisions of the Nev
Model Army into the field for the first time, the Royalis
forces grew unruly with conflict and Rupert's tempe
worsened every day. He quarrelled with subordinate com
manders over supplies, announced his complete pessimisn
about the cause in the West and then failed, in the face o
Lord Digby's mischievous optimism, to convince the Kin
to save what he could by making peace while he yet retaine
some bargaining power. Charles listened courteously an
then, refusing to be dismayed by his gloomy nephew, lef
Oxford on May 7th for Stow-on-the-Wold and the cam
paigning season. Travelling discreetly in the baggage-train o
his army went the bright-eyed daughter of a peer of the realm
and one of the Queen's ladies, Captain Ned Frost's enterpris
ing Lucy.

Samuel Radford, meanwhile, received an unexpected an
flattering invitation to join Free-born John in London
Lilburne, it appeared, had chosen to resign from the army

sooner than violate his beliefs by swearing the compulsory oath to the Solemn League and Covenant. By the end of April he had the civilian freedom to pursue his goals of political reform and he wanted all his promising young adherents with him.

Samuel, though he desired nothing better than to go, had declined and, though she knew nothing of it, Abigail was the main cause. On the day after their nephew had been born, Samuel had found her sobbing her heart out over something she refused to explain and since then he had not known what to make of her. Paler than ever, she devoted herself solely to household matters and, when he tried to interest her in the books he had borrowed from Captain Ambrose, she had walked away without a word.

Samuel felt a little guilty about the books for the pretext of borrowing and returning formed a convenient means by which he had been able to receive three more packets from Mistress Rhodes. All had gone to Sir Samuel Luke and contained, so he was told, bread-and-butter information about the state of the Castle's defences and the number of Royalist troops in and around the town. Samuel continued to feel a sense of unease which deepened when he was privileged, one day, to catch the fair Anne in the very act of spying.

He was not alone. For obvious reasons, he was never left alone in the Castle and, since Justin was out, his escort on this occasion was Tom Mayhew. Together they climbed the stairs to Captain Ambrose's door and Tom opened it and there, *in flagrante delicto*, was Mistress Rhodes up to her exquisite elbows in the Captain's carved chest.

Staring blankly at her, Ensign Mayhew lost what little poise he possessed. 'My God! What the hell are you doing?'

She raised delicate brows, completely at her ease.

'Do you think that Captain Ambrose would consider that to be any business of yours?'

Flushing, he hesitated. He knew of Justin's brief affair with the lady but he was also aware, as no one else seemed to be, of the mutual current of dislike which ran, crackling, between the two of them. He said, 'If you are here at his invitation, no. Are you?'

'How gauche you are,' she smiled, drifting unconcernedly towards them. 'Why don't you ask him? A snub would do you so much good. And, in the meantime, you may stand aside.' The slate-blue eyes moved past him to rest, with significance, on Samuel. 'Mr Radford.'

'Mistress Rhodes.' His face empty of expression, Samuel bowed and held the door open for her. Then, when she had gone, he closed it and said, 'Will he snub you, do you think?'

Tom shrugged. 'Probably. But since she suggested asking him, there's no point in bothering.'

Samuel stared moodily at the floor and then assuaged the nasty taste in his mouth by saying abruptly, 'You don't think she might have been counting on that?'

'A bluff?' Tom considered it and then said reluctantly, 'No. No one is that cool when they've been caught red-handed. She didn't bat an eyelid, did she?'

'No,' agreed Samuel drily. 'She didn't.'

'Still, I think I might just keep an eye on her. Justin's a good fellow and I owe him something. Not that it's easy to see what she might have been doing.'

'No.' Samuel's eyes grew thoughtful. 'No. It isn't, is it?'

He said no more and, selecting a book at random, left. Despite the look she had given him, he took care to avoid Mistress Rhodes and was half-way home before he realized that he had come away with Cruso's *Military Instruction for the Cavalry*.

On the day that the King left Oxford with his army, Abigail saw Captain Ambrose for the first time in two months. Because fate was being typically perverse, he happened to have Bab Atkins folded close in his arms.

It was late afternoon and they were standing in deep shadow under the timber-pillared overhang of the Town Hall. A tiny sound attracted Abigail's attention and then it was held frozen while, over Bab's golden head, she found herself looking into a pair of quizzical grey eyes.

With unhurried calm, Justin released Bab and smiled.

'Why, Mistress Radford.'

'Abby?' Bab turned swiftly, rosy-cheeked with defiance.

154

'You – you won't tell, will you?'

Abigail drew a long, unsteady breath. 'No.'

'Of course she won't,' soothed Justin. His voice held a hint of laughter. 'Go home, Bab. And don't worry.'

She looked at him, opened her mouth to argue and then thought better of it. 'All right. But promise you'll come tomorrow.'

'Impossible.'

'The next day, then?'

He sighed. 'Don't be importunate. I'll come when I can.' Then, looking past her to Abigail, 'Mistress Radford? I've something to say to you if you'll —'

'No!' said Abigail violently. 'No. I don't want to hear.' Recovering the use of her feet, she walked swiftly away from them.

She was almost home when he caught up with her and pulled her purposefully into an inconspicuous corner at the top of Frog Lane, saying, 'Listen! I only want to apologize.'

'For what?'

'For the way I spoke to you the last time we met. It was rude and unfair and I didn't mean it.'

Something burned in Abigail's chest and she said stonily, 'No. Obviously not.'

'And what is that supposed to mean?' His eyes narrowed and his fingers tightened on her shoulders. 'You're not referring to that little episode with Bab, are you? Good God! Don't you know the girl's an inveterate flirt?'

'I don't care what she is or you either!' retorted Abigail, cold, sick and miserable. 'Let me go. This is pointless.'

'I am trying,' said Justin patiently, 'to say I'm sorry. What's the matter with you? I thought we were supposed to be friends?'

'Oh, we are. But only when it suits you, only when it's convenient and you're in the right mood.'

Abruptly, Justin released her.

'And the same, it seems, is true of you,' he returned coolly. 'Very well. Go home and stew in your own bad temper if that's what you want. I'm sorry I troubled you. I didn't know you were so shrewish.'

'I'm not shrewish at all!' she snapped, horribly aware that, for the first time in her life, she sounded it. Hot tears stung her eyes and she added, 'It's just – it's just that you would never have said it to Bab, would you?'

'Said what, for heaven's sake?'

'That she was like Jonas and the people who write *Mercurius Britannicus*.'

There was a long, enigmatic silence. Then Justin said, 'No. I wouldn't. But then, I don't say anything to Bab except the sort of superficial nonsense which is all she either expects or understands. I indulge her, that's all.'

'Oh,' said Abigail, weakly. 'I see.'

'No, you don't. How can you when I don't myself?' He paused, listening to the church clock chiming the hour and then a swift smile transformed his face and he said, 'I'm late. You might at least make it worthwhile by saying I'm forgiven.'

The stone in her chest melted into unimagined sweetness. 'You're forgiven,' she said simply. 'Of course you are.'

Captain Ambrose's arrival back at the Castle coincided with that of a small party of horse from Oxford. In the midst of them, like a wren among hawks, was a brown-haired girl in a threadbare and decidedly dirty cloak who was allowing her horse to fidget whilst she inspected the courtyard.

'Captain Ambrose! It is Captain Ambrose, isn't it?'

Justin looked up into a pair of bright, blue eyes and acknowledged his identity with a slight bow.

'I thought so.' She beamed at him. 'Ned described you very accurately. I'm Lucy Gilbert.'

Not unnaturally, it was the last thing he expected to hear and, tearing his fascinated gaze away from her, Justin looked enquiringly at the well-dressed young officer on her right. The fellow eyed him with cheerful understanding and said, 'She is, you know. That cloak hides a multitude of sins.'

Lucy chuckled. 'I borrowed it from Firework Lil. It's my disguise. I came with the baggage-train.'

'Amidst the other baggages,' remarked her escort. And then, to Justin, 'I'm Frank Gilbert, her cousin, and I

156

apologize for everything about her. I'm especially sorry for landing Ned with the responsibility of getting her back to Oxford, but —'

'I'm not going back to Oxford,' said Lucy, with calm finality. 'I'm tired of being treated like a child.'

'Then you shouldn't behave like one,' said Justin mildly. 'Tell me, does Ned expect you?'

She tilted a mutinous chin. 'No. But he'll be glad I came.'

'I doubt it. Take a look at your audience, Mistress Gilbert. In ten minutes from now, there won't be a man in the garrison who doesn't know why you came or how.'

Lucy cast a dubious glance at the groups of interested, grinning faces and then turned, with dignity, back to Justin.

'Perhaps, but it isn't for you to criticize my conduct. Please help me down.'

Reluctant amusement bracketing his mouth, he did as she asked. Then, before he could speak, she gave a startled squeak and was running like a hare across the courtyard.

'Ned! Ned! Oh, Ned!'

Captain Frost froze in his tracks.

'Lucy?' he said incredulously. And then she was in his arms, laughing and crying at once. 'Lucy, you madcap! What – how on earth did you get here?'

Justin drew Frank Gilbert with him in Lucy's wake.

'Ned, for heaven's sake, take her inside.'

'What?' Ned glanced vaguely about him and then came quickly to his senses. 'Oh God! What do they think we are, travelling mummers?'

The officers' common-room was mercifully deserted and, having taken the time to kiss his betrothed, Ned greeted her cousin with an accusing, 'How did she get here? You never let her bully you into bringing her?'

'Don't be an idiot. The first I knew of it was when we got to Chipping Norton and by then there was no alternative but to bring her with me here. I've letters for Sir William and I could scarcely leave her, could I?'

'Chipping Norton?' echoed Ned, blankly.

Frank nodded. 'Yes. She got that far in the tail of the army.'

157

'She what?' Captain Frost wheeled furiously on Lucy. 'Of all the mad, stupid pranks – careering across the country with the biggest collection of doxies in the kingdom! You must be out of your mind!'

'They were very kind,' she offered, suddenly subdued. 'And I had to do something. No one would bring me and I never see you these days and I thought that, if I came, we could be married.'

'Well, we can't. Where does your mother think you are?'

'With you. I left a note. I told her I couldn't bear it any more and – and —' She stopped and the blue eyes filled with tears. 'Oh Ned, say you're pleased to see me?'

'I've a whole lot to say to you,' he replied grimly, 'but that's no part of it. Come on. We'll continue this in private.' And, taking her hand, he hauled her from the room.

'Whew!' grinned Frank Gilbert. 'He ought to marry her. He really should. It would be the making of her, not to mention doing the rest of us a favour.' He met Justin's enquiring look and added simply, 'Ned's the only one who can manage her and always was, even when we were children. But she'd make a first-rate garrison wife for all that. Got the right spirit.'

'She certainly has a good deal of nerve,' commented Justin, as he handed him a tankard of ale. 'You say you have letters for Will. Anything we poor back-up boys might find exciting?'

It was a natural question. Everyone was aware that messengers always knew the contents of their despatches.

Frank drained his tankard and said laconically, 'Perhaps. His Majesty wants reinforcements; as many as can be spared. Do you fancy taking a bite out of the rebels' new army?'

There was a pause. Then, 'Yes,' said Justin. 'I'll try anything once.'

With Sir Tom Fairfax and the New Model Army marching into the West to relieve Taunton, there was no urgency attached to the matter of sending troops to the King. Consequently, it took nearly a week to select and equip the men and make all the necessary arrangements that would leave the garrison functioning as normal. At the end of that time, Lucy was still clinging tenaciously to her right to remain in Banbury.

'I won't go,' she told Ned, stubbornly. 'And if you send me back by force, I'll run away again. And again and again if I have to.'

'Stay then,' replied Ned, at last. 'But I won't be here.'

'Not?' she stared at him blankly. 'Why?'

'Because Justin and I are taking fifty men to His Majesty and there's no saying when we'll be back. So you might as well go home, hadn't you?'

'No!' Lucy stamped her foot and tears began to slide, unheeded, down her face. 'Why won't you understand? I'm not a fragile little flower to be cosseted and I'm not so stupid that I'd ever wish to interfere with your duty. But we've spent three years snatching an hour together once or twice a month if we're lucky – and enough is enough! I know you can't always be in one place but, in future, I intend to remain in the place you come back to and, at the moment, it's here.' She paused and added tautly, 'There's only one thing you can say that will change my mind and that's to tell me that you've changed yours. Have you, Ned? Do you want to be free of me?'

He looked back at her steadily, his face rather pale.

'No. And since you know it perfectly well, I don't see why you're asking.'

'So that you may ask yourself,' came the direct reply. 'I think it's time you did.'

It was a little later that day when Ned looked helplessly at Justin and said, 'What can I do? We're off in the morning.'

'Ask Trooper Swan's widow to look after her and go,' said Justin placidly. 'She'll come to no harm here. And when you come back, we can celebrate our first garrison wedding.'

Ned stared. 'You think I should marry her? Now?'

'Well, of course,' sighed Justin. 'You'd be a fool not to.'

Entering in time to hear this, Hugh Vaughan said grimly, 'And you can't send her home now, anyway. Word's just come in that Fairfax has halted his advance into the West and turned back. He's marching on Oxford.'

159

Justin was laying out his gear in readiness for the morrow when Samuel arrived, escorted by Tom Mayhew and clutching Cruso's cavalry manual. Justin eyed the book satirically, waved Tom away and said, 'Is Lilburne planning a counter-coup or are you merely broadening your horizons?'

'Neither,' replied Samuel, tersely. He glanced at the clutter in the room. 'Are you going somewhere?'

'Yes,' came the equally unexpansive reply. 'Did you read it?'

'Some.'

'And?'

The dark eyes flicked wide open. 'If you must know, I found it tediously unimaginative. No expertise, just plain common-sense.'

'Quite,' said Justin cheerfully. 'But don't despise it on that account. Common-sense has its uses, you know. And everything can't be written with steaming emotionalism.' Lifting one brow, he added, 'Why do I detect an air of hostility?'

'Because you're about to deliver another "Beware of John Lilburne" lecture and I've heard enough.' It was a continuous sore point between them; surprisingly, the only one. 'Abby should never have told you.'

'I didn't need telling. And if the string-and-clapper arrangement that serves Jonas as a mind was capable of logic, he wouldn't need telling either.'

'Is that a threat?'

'No, you young fool, it's a warning. And I'll give you another. Lilburne's eyes are fixed on Utopia and he delights in solitary opposition, a born martyr, if you like.' Justin paused, folding his arms. 'Face nasty reality, Sam. The man whose ideas are wonderful but so far in advance of their time that they can't be implemented is an embarrassment. The man who adds to that a persuasive tongue and his own brand of integrity is a threat. Whatever the government is after the war, it won't be able to leave Lilburne loose. It will have too many other problems.'

Samuel yawned, deliberately provoking. 'Have you finished?'

There was a long, chilly silence. Then Justin said gently, 'You will take that tone with me once too often and I shall forget myself.'

'You mean,' snapped Sam, 'that you'll forget I'm a cripple?'

The grey eyes grew unexpectedly harsh but Justin curbed his tongue and said merely, 'If I had meant that, you may believe that I would have said it. I think you had better go.'

'With pleasure.' Samuel laid the book on the bed and limped to the door. Then, turning back, he said, 'You might try remembering that you are not my keeper.'

Justin smiled slowly. 'No. If I were, you would have a more realistic attitude to life. And better manners.'

Silently seething, Samuel descended the stairs with more haste than sense and collided violently with a brown-haired girl in blue. Lucy gasped, clutched at him and regained her balance grasping a button from his coat. Then, when Samuel embarked on his apologies, she pressed the button into his hand and said breathlessly, 'It's all right. I was running too. Have you been with Captain Ambrose? Is he in his room?'

'Yes,' said Samuel, withdrawing from her a little.

'Good!' She smiled radiantly. 'I wondered, at first, why Ned likes him so much. Isn't that silly?'

'Not particularly,' began Samuel sourly. 'He —'

'But now, of course, I know,' she continued. Gathering up her skirts, she flew upstairs, calling a vague 'Goodbye' as she went.

Samuel blinked and then looked down to find Mistress Rhodes watching him.

'I see you've met our little bride-to-be,' she said lightly. 'How fortunate. I might have missed you again.'

'Yes.' He went slowly down to meet her. 'What is it this time?'

'The same.' She produced the usual sealed packet from the folds of her gown. 'They are sending men to Charles Stuart. Sir Samuel will wish to know.'

'And that's all?'

'Of course.'

Samuel took the packet with reluctance. 'Why were you

searching Justin Ambrose's room?'

'Curiosity,' she shrugged. 'You must have seen the piece in *Mercurius Britannicus*. Wouldn't you like to know more?'

'No.' The obvious question hovered on his lips but, because he could not quite bring himself to ask it, he changed it to another. 'That girl . . . is she betrothed to him?'

'To whom? Justin?' The slate-blue eyes filled with sudden, malicious amusement. 'Don't be naive. He'd as soon marry me.'

'I see.' Coldly. 'Is he your lover?'

This time she laughed, openly mocking.

'No, my gallant conspirator, he is not my lover. We hate each other. Didn't you know?'

Something curdled in Samuel's stomach and, making a curt excuse, he left her. He did not know that the half-closed door he passed at the foot of the stairs belonged to Tom Mayhew nor, though it was perfectly audible, did he hear it click shut. He was too intent on getting home.

The family ritual of evening prayers was half over before Samuel realized that he had given Abigail his coat for mending without first emptying his pockets. All thoughts of devotions fled and he knelt impatiently through Jonas' sermon, inwardly deploring his own carelessness. Then, when it came to an end and he attempted to follow Abigail upstairs, Jonas called him back to discuss a trivial error in the order book.

By the time he finally entered his sister's room, a single glance was sufficient to inform him that he was too late. The thick, shining fall of her unbound hair pushed back over one shoulder, Abigail sat on the bed with his coat bunched in her lap. Before her, lying starkly white against the blue coverlet, was Mistress Rhodes' flamboyantly inscribed packet.

He closed the door behind him and said, casually, 'Ah, there it is. I was wondering where I'd left it.'

'You left it in your pocket,' said his sister flatly. 'It fell out. I take it you didn't want me to see it?'

'Why shouldn't you? It's only a letter.'

'To Sir Samuel Luke?'

Her tone startled him. 'Yes. What's wrong with that?'

'Everything.' She pushed his coat aside and stood up. 'Sir Samuel collects intelligence and, since this isn't your writing, I suppose you've been given it to pass on to the carrier because the person who wrote it can't do so themselves. Well?'

He shrugged. 'Yes.'

'And you were at the Castle this afternoon, which only leaves one interpretation, doesn't it? That someone in the garrison is spying for the Parliament and has involved you as go-between. And if that is so, I can only think of one likely candidate, that red-haired harlot!'

Samuel stared at her coldly.

'I see,' he said, 'that you've got it all worked out.'

'Yes. That's what I do. I wash and dust and sew and, in between, I wonder what madness my brother will indulge in next. This isn't the first letter, is it?'

'No. But you're being too dramatic. Anyone would think I was running some kind of risk.'

'And aren't you? What if you're caught – or if she is? Will Compton could have you hanged – or do you expect Justin Ambrose to save you?'

'That's enough, Abby.' He said it quietly.

'No, it isn't, not nearly enough.' Her eyes were bright with fright and anger. 'He's lent you his books and said nothing of your dealings with Lilburne and you've used him. Worse still, you may even have had a hand in the cruel rubbish that was in the paper. Or has that possibility not occurred to you?'

He flushed, uncomfortably. 'Yes. But it's highly unlikely. And, anyway, I doubt he let that stuff bother him. He probably laughed.'

There was a brief silence. Then Abigail said oddly, 'What a stupidly insensitive thing to say. You sound like Jonas.'

'And you sound like a budding Royalist!' retorted Samuel. 'Or are you just dazzled by one of them?'

'No more than you are by Anne Rhodes, I hope,' she replied, flushing a little. And then, gesturing jerkily to the letter, 'Are you going to send that?'

'I don't know. Probably. But, to spare your conscience, I'll promise to accept no more. Will that do?'

Abigail nodded, weak with relief. 'Yes. I don't think I could face Captain Ambrose if —'

'You won't have to face him,' said Samuel curtly. 'He's off to join the King in the morning.'

'Is he?' She stared at him, wide-eyed and very still. 'For good?'

'How should I know?' It had been a bad day and Samuel did not feel inclined to be helpful. 'Ask the harlot. I'm only the errand-boy.'

The days of May drifted slowly by bringing fragments of news and rumour. The King was at Droitwich, Market Drayton, Stone, Tutbury. He was marching north to join the miraculously successful Montrose; he was marching south to save Oxford from the besieging might of the New Model Army. Banbury held its breath in anticipation of another Edgehill. And then came word that a third course had been adopted; that, on May 30th, Prince Rupert had stormed and taken Leicester.

Encouraged by this development and with high hopes of being a June bride, Lucy went shopping. 'For goodness only knows when my things can be sent up from Oxford and I can't and won't be married in either of the two rags I brought with me,' she told Jenny Swan, firmly. 'Take me to a mercer The best one.'

Capable Jenny had taken Mistress Lucy's measure inside five minutes and so she made no attempts at dissuasion. But because she took her duties seriously, she refused to stir without a male escort, which was how Tom Mayhew happened to go with them.

At the sign of the Ragged Staff, Jonas was busy elsewhere and Rachel, with her baby to care for, no longer demeaned herself by working in the shop. This was fortunate because, after one look at Samuel, Lucy said brightly, 'But I know you! And I thought you belonged to the garrison.'

Withdrawing his gaze from Tom Mayhew's still face, Samuel said calmly, 'Do I look like a Cavalier?'

The blue eyes appraised his dark coat and in-between

length hair. 'Well, no. But you don't look like a Puritan either. Are you one?'

He grinned. 'Of a sort. What are you?'

'She's a lady!' snapped Mistress Swan. 'And we'll have less of your sauce, young man!'

'Oh Jenny!' Lucy laughed and then, smiling at Samuel, said, 'My name is Lucy Gilbert. I'm betrothed to Captain Edward Frost and I want material for my wedding dress.'

Samuel bowed politely, one eye on Mistress Swan. 'I'm Samuel Radford and this is my sister, Abby. She is better suited than I to show you what we have.'

Lucy turned blithely to Abigail.

'I'd like silk but I'm not sure I can afford it just now. And I don't know what colour it should be.'

'Blue,' said Abigail, simply. 'And I think we have just the thing. Are you to be married soon?'

'I hope so. It depends when Ned gets back. Oh!', Lucy stared admiringly at the length of cornflower watered-taffeta that Abigail produced for her inspection. 'That's beautiful! How clever of you. Jenny, what do you think?'

'Very nice,' agreed Mistress Swan briskly. 'But I don't know who you'll get to make it up, Miss Lucy. I wouldn't dare cut it and that's a fact!'

'Yes. It would be awful if it were spoiled,' sighed Lucy. And then, brightening, 'Abby, I may call you Abby, may I not? Do you know of anyone who might sew it for me?'

Abigail hesitated and said diffidently, 'Well, I could do it myself, if you wish. I'm not a professional seamstress but I occasionally make for Mistress Cope of Hanwell and the Dryden ladies at Canon's Ashby.'

'But that's splendid!' cried Lucy. 'Will you measure me now?'

Mesmerized by the tidal wave, Abigail nodded. 'If you will step upstairs to my bedchamber?'

'Thank you. Tom, you don't mind waiting?'

Ensign Mayhew opened his mouth for the first time. 'Not in the least, but not all day. I'm on duty at noon.'

When the ladies had gone into the house, Samuel fixed Tom with a level stare and said, 'Well? What is it you want to say?'

'How do you know I want to say anything?'

'Because you've got disapproval written all over you. Why?'

'Guess,' snapped Tom. And then, heatedly, 'I'm disappointed in you. I thought that, of all Puritans, you were honest.'

'Ah.' Samuel drew a long breath. 'And I'm not?'

'You know you're not, damn it? You're in league with that bitch of a redhead and you're carrying reports from her to Sam Luke.'

'Can you prove it?'

'Not yet but I shall. As for you, if it wasn't for the fact that you half warned me about her, I'd have already had you taken on suspicion.'

'I see.' Samuel paused and then said distantly, 'If I told you I've severed my connections with the lady, would you believe me?'

'I don't know,' said Tom warily. 'Why should you?'

'Because I suspect her of waging a personal war on Justin Ambrose. And, although he and I are at odds on almost every issue, I wouldn't use her methods on my worst enemy.'

Tom examined him thoughtfully. 'Did you send that letter?'

'Not yet. But I'd need a very convincing reason indeed before handing it over to you,' returned Sam bluntly. 'We're at war. Remember?'

'Yes. My loyalties are perfectly clear. What sort of reason?'

'Proof that she's doing what I think she's doing. Find that and I'll give you proof that she's also a spy.'

'On condition, I suppose, that I preserve you incognito?'

'No,' said Samuel coldly. 'On condition that you don't expect any other help from me. Because you certainly won't get it.'

Jonas was not pleased to learn that his sister was making a wedding dress for Ned Frost's bride. In fact, it was not until Samuel had the wit to point out that the expensive blue taffeta might otherwise have remained profitlessly on the shelf like its despised red counterpart, that he was brought to give ungracious permission for the work to proceed.

While Abigail worked lovingly on the gown and dreamed of fashioning a similar one for herself in cherry, Sir Tom Fairfax lifted the siege of Oxford and led the New Model Army to Stony Stratford. The Royalist army, meanwhile, threw Lucy into a frenzy of excitement by arriving at Daventry and, by June 9th, it was closer still. There were detachments at Brackley and the King came in person to Banbury with a large party of horse. He did not, however, bring Captain Frost with him and Lucy made her curtsy, bristling with disappointment. Jonas Radford shut the shop for the day, forbade his family to step outside and entertained them with a dissertation on the fall of Lucifer in which the fallen angel became inextricably muddled with Charles the King.

The second week of June dragged by bringing no sign of the expected confrontation and on the tenth, Oliver Cromwell transcended his own Self-Denying Ordinance by being appointed Lieutenant-General of the Tenth Horse. Two days later the New Model was reported to be just south of Northampton while, five miles away at Fawsley Park, the King enjoyed a day's hunting. Banbury waited beneath a lethargic hush.

It was late on the night of June 14th that the town was woken by pealing bells and galloping messengers shouting that the day had seen a great battle at the village of Naseby in which the King had been utterly defeated. On the following morning came details of the New Model's glorious slaughter of the fleeing Royalist army. A horrified pall of silence hung over the Castle and a current of Godly rejoicing shimmered through the town. Lucy Gilbert clung, white-faced with fear, to stout Jenny Swan; Jonas Radford celebrated with jubilant psalms and his mother's cherry cordial; and Abigail thought of Justin and was sick.

Samuel felt ill that day too but not because of Naseby. It appeared that, during the night, Tom Mayhew had been inexplicably seized with violent stomach cramps and vomiting. Before dawn, he was dead.

Chapter Fourteen

'He's back! Oh Abby, he's back!' Brown hair flying and cheeks pink with delight, Lucy erupted into the shop and came face to face with Jonas. 'I'm sorry. I expected to find Abigail.'

'Obviously.'

He was stiff with disapproval but Lucy failed to notice. She smiled on him and said, 'You must be Jonas. I'm so pleased to meet you. I'm Lucy Gilbert. Abby is making my wedding gown, you know.'

He inclined his head coldly and said nothing.

'I am betrothed to Captain Frost,' she added, 'but I don't think you know him, do you?'

Jonas unsealed his lips and managed an entire sentence.

'I am happy to say that my acquaintance with the ungodly oppressors of this town is mercifully small.'

Even Lucy could not mistake the contemptuous distaste with which this was uttered and her eyes widened dangerously.

'Well, no doubt the happiness is mutual.'

Unable to think of a suitable reply, Jonas subjected her to his most withering stare and then stalked furiously away in search of his sister.

When Abigail entered the shop some five minutes later, she was rather pale and her hands, if one looked at them, showed more than a trace of unsteadiness. Lucy saw neither but said impetuously, 'How disagreeable your brother is! I don't know how you put up with him.'

Abigail smiled faintly. 'I think you upset him a little.'

'Nonsense! He was in a foul mood before he ever set eyes on me. And, I must say, that if he's like that all the time —' She stopped, shrugging. 'This is silly. Naturally, you don't wish to discuss him with me and I have happier things to think of.'

Abigail's restless fingers were suddenly stilled. 'Oh?'

Lucy laughed. 'Yes. Ned's back. Isn't it wonderful?'

'Wonderful,' agreed Abigail, hollowly. 'And did Cap—?'

'He arrived late last night, and without a scratch, thank God. But they are all so tired, Abby. Dispirited, too, as if all the heart had gone out of them. It's awful. I've never seen Ned like this, but at least he's safe.'

'And Captain Ambrose?' asked Abigail at last. 'Is he safe too?'

Lucy stared at her. 'Justin? Do you know him?'

'Yes. Is he —?'

'My goodness! How did that happen? Your horrid brother must be grinding his teeth into dust.'

'Jonas doesn't know,' came the tense reply. 'Lucy, will you please stop chattering and tell me if Justin Ambrose is alive or not.'

The blue eyes grew positively round. 'Alive and well and limping about the Castle from a bullet in his thigh. You care, don't you?'

Her major fears relieved, Abigail said unevenly, 'Of course. He's been very kind to me and to Sam as well. We're friends.'

'Are you indeed?' Lucy grinned. 'You believe in living dangerously, don't you?'

'What? Oh, you mean Jonas?'

'No. I don't mean Jonas. Or are you going to tell me you haven't noticed how attractive Justin is?'

'Well, I —'

'Or that you don't know of his reputation with women?'

There was a sudden silence. Then, 'No,' said Abigail. 'I don't. But I can't see what that —'

'I know at least two girls in Oxford who are mad for him,' Lucy continued. 'But everyone says he's never in the least serious, so you'd better be careful what you're about.'

Much to her annoyance, Abigail felt herself flushing. 'Don't be silly. It's not like that at all. I don't care how many girls are in love with him. Why should I? He's a friend and I care for him in the same way I care for Sam.'

'Don't say it! I should never believe it, you know. The girl

169

who could regard a man like that as a brother hasn't been born yet. And, if you ask me —'

'I didn't,' snapped Abigail.

'— she never will be,' Lucy finished calmly. 'Don't be cross. I want you to come to my wedding. Will you?'

'I don't know,' began Abigail, startled but pleased. 'I'd like to come but it's a little difficult. Jonas —'

'Is no excuse,' said Lucy firmly. Then, cunningly, 'And you'd like to see Justin, wouldn't you?'

Abigail hesitated, acknowledging the truth but reluctant to confess it. As she finally made up her mind to speak, the shop door opened and the words froze on her lips.

Justin stood on the threshold, his shadowed gaze sweeping past Lucy to settle on Abigail. Then, taking care to favour his wounded leg as little as possible, he advanced on her saying lightly, 'There's no need to look so shocked. Contrary to whatever you've heard, I'm neither a ghost nor a cripple.'

'I never said you were,' objected Lucy.

No one paid her any heed. Abigail's eyes did not leave the Captain's face and she said, 'The battle, was it very bad?'

'Bad enough.' His expression was bleak as a December sky. 'Jonas must be jubilant. First Naseby, then the surrender of Leicester and now four thousand Royalist prisoners marched ceremoniously into London by his friend Colonel Fiennes.'

'Yes.' Abigail stared bitterly down at her hands. 'He's had a good week.'

'It doesn't show,' muttered Lucy, interestedly watching them.

Justin's face softened. 'I'm sorry. That was unfair of me. Stupid, too, since I've come to ask you a favour.' He waited until she looked up again and then said, 'My shirts are in ribbons and, while I can still afford the necessary cambric, I was hoping you might make me a couple of new ones.'

'Of course.' The mundane request produced a tingle of entirely irrational pleasure. 'I'll be happy to do it. I suppose you need one for the wedding?'

'Yes. I'm to be groomsman and Lucy won't like it if I appear half-naked.'

170

'I don't care what you wear so long as you come and the same applies to Abby and Sam,' said Lucy positively. 'Tell her she must come, Justin.'

His swift charming smile appeared and he said, 'No. I can't do that. But I can tell her that I would be pleased if she did.' Then, with weary irritation, 'Oh God!'

'You!' spat Jonas, emerging unexpectedly from the house.

'Quite,' drawled Justin. 'And every other bisyllabic expression of theatrical pointlessness.'

Ignoring him, Jonas turned on Abigail.

'How long has he been here?' He seized her arm. 'And why didn't you call me? Have you no sense, no shame? Consorting with —'

'Leave her alone, Jonas.' Justin was surprised at how angry he felt but he maintained his light, mocking tone. 'You should be glad to see me. Or don't you want the chance to gloat?'

'I do, but only at your hanging!' Jonas pushed his sister to the door. 'Get into the house. I'll have something to say to you later, turning my premises into a meeting house for every vile Malignant in the town.'

'Just a moment,' said Lucy clearly. 'I came for a fitting.'

'And I to escort her home afterwards,' lied Justin smoothly. 'So the sooner it is done, the sooner we can leave your hallowed premises.' He watched Jonas' hands clench and, reading his thought, said gently, 'I wouldn't if I were you. I can be quite rough, you know.'

Jonas drew a long, fulminating breath and then gestured wrathfully to the open door behind him. 'Abigail! Take this – this person upstairs and be quick about it. You have precisely ten minutes.'

When they had gone, he glanced sneeringly at the Captain and said, 'I see that you managed to preserve your skin at Naseby?'

Justin shrugged. 'At least I was there. It's more than can be said of you. But then, three yards of tongue is little use on a battlefield, is it?'

'How would you know? They say the King's officers are chosen for their running speed these days. The higher their rank, the faster they run. How fast are you, Captain?'

'Fast enough,' replied Justin, the grey eyes at variance with his laconic tone. 'And you?'

Jonas recognized the warning and shifted his ground. 'You realize that you've lost the war, of course? The only part of your cause that God has not yet blighted lies far away in Scotland, and it will take more than a renegade nobleman and his accursed Irish savages to save you now.' He produced a pamphlet from his pocket and threw it down on the polished board. 'Charles Stuart should have made peace before his attempts to bring in foreign troops were made public. There'll be no sympathy for him now.'

Justin stared at the paper, reading and re-reading its title. 'The King's Cabinet Opened' could mean only one thing: that His Majesty's private correspondence, lost during the nightmare flight from Naseby, had been made public property by the Parliament. He looked again at Jonas and said softly, 'Have you the remotest idea of the harm this could do?'

Jonas smiled coldly. 'If it harms the King, he has only himself to blame. The honest, righteous men of this kingdom have nothing to fear and much, thanks to our stout and Godly new army, to be grateful for.'

'Then may God take pity on us all,' said Justin grimly, 'for you and your kind will have none. You spoke just now of Irish savages. Shall I tell you how your wonderful new army conducted itself after Naseby? It maimed and slaughtered and pillaged its way in pursuit of us to within two miles of Leicester; it gathered a king's ransom in gold and jewels and left a trail of bloody carnage every step of the way. And these honest, trusty warriors of yours didn't restrict themselves to massacring His Majesty's infantry. They demonstrated their superior manhood by butchering women as well.' Pale and infinitely contemptuous, Justin folded his arms. 'Have you ever witnessed the wanton mutilation of women, Jonas? No? You should have been at Naseby. It was an education. Your God-fearing boys sliced off hands and feet and breasts; they left faces without noses, heads without ears and mouths without tongues. And they and you have called that the Lord's work.'

172

'Whores and Irish recusants,' rapped Jonas dismissively.

'They were neither, you ignorant bastard!' Cold, untrammelled temper flared in Justin's face. 'But even if they had been, does that excuse it?'

'There is no need to excuse it, least of all to a depraved, incestuous libertine such as you.'

'Isn't there?' An unpleasant smile bracketed the hard mouth. 'You seem to forget that we still hold Banbury.'

Jonas gave a short, grating laugh.

'If that is a threat, you are wasting your breath. Your time here is on the wane and you know it. There is nothing you can do to me or mine and I'd like to see you try.'

'Would you?' The smile deepened and Justin's voice grew silky smooth. 'Then I'll have to see what I can do, won't I?'

Abigail looked around at the select gathering of wedding guests in the Governor's quarters and wondered how to ask Samuel to take her home. Outside in the courtyard, where the men were roasting an ox or two and consuming gallons of free ale, the noise had reached its peak. It was becoming decidedly lively inside, too, now that the boards had been withdrawn from the wedding-feast – an array of dishes that had left Abigail faintly stunned and made her wonder how many of the pastries and creams owed their existence to Mistress Welchman at the cake shop. But though the food had gone, muscat and canary wines continued to flow freely and the talk, laughter and music was bidding fair to rival the revelry without.

Abigail sighed. It had been all right until they left the chapel. She had even enjoyed it. Captain Frost, so obviously in love; Lucy, radiantly happy and exquisite in the corn-flower gown; and the surprisingly simple ceremony that had united them with each other. But then it had not seemed to matter that her best pewter damask contrasted sadly with the bright silks around her, neither had there been any need to talk with people she did not know. Sam had been safe from the beautiful, sinister woman who now held him trapped in conversation on the far side of the room. And then Captain Ambrose had been constantly within sight to reassure her.

173

She wished he were still; she wished Jonas had not driven Rachel to see her parents at Adderbury; she wished Sam would escape from Mistress Rhodes; she wished she were at home.

'Hello. Why so pensive . . . not to mention solitary?'

She turned swiftly and her gloom fled. 'You know I'm hopeless with strangers.'

'No. I know you imagine that you are.' Justin regarded her thoughtfully. 'I'm sorry I had to abandon you but Tom Mayhew's father arrived to collect Tom's things and he wished to speak with me.'

She frowned in an effort of memory. 'Isn't he the young man who used to escort Lucy to the shop? The one you pulled out of the fire at Compton Wynyates?'

'He was. He's dead.'

She looked searchingly at him for a moment and then said simply, 'I'm sorry. I didn't know.'

'How should you and why be sorry? You didn't know him.' His tone was harsh and, regretting it, he said, 'Forgive me, that was uncalled for. It's simply that, if he had to die, then fire was the easier way to do it. He was unconscious then, not throwing up in hours of torment. One of life's little ironies, you might say.' He paused again. 'Or no. Perhaps you wouldn't. And perhaps I should hold my tongue before I distress you further. Come and renew your acquaintance with Captain Vaughan. He's Welsh, of course, but he can't help that.'

His reward was a tiny choke of amusement and, looking down at her, he said, 'That's better. You should do it more often. Where has Sam got to?'

'He's over there,' replied Abigail, guiltily aware that she had forgotten all about him. 'I think . . . he seems to be quarrelling with Mistress Rhodes.'

'Well, well . . . so he does. Now why, I wonder?'

She drew a fortifying breath and said desperately, 'Perhaps he's like your dog and doesn't care for redheads.'

Justin grinned. 'Then he's either very remarkable or he's had unsuspected opportunities.'

'Why do you say that?'

'Because my experience is substantially wider than Sam's and she is undoubtedly the most beautiful woman I've ever seen. That she is also vain, spiteful and promiscuous is something that I would expect Sam to be blissfully unaware of and, at his age, few of us look beneath the surface . . . unless we are given a reason.'

'Oh,' she said again. 'I told him you said she was a harlot. Perhaps that was it.'

'If it was,' he replied, suddenly laughing, 'then he's not just remarkable, he's unique. Come along, here's Hugh.'

The dark-haired Welshman greeted her with easy charm and then, turning to Justin said, 'Go away and attend to your duties as groomsman. Ned has been trying to catch your eye for the past ten minutes.'

Justin gazed at him understandingly.

'You just want a chance to flirt with Mistress Radford.'

'No tact,' sighed Hugh. 'Do go away, there's a good fellow.'

Abigail watched Justin bow and cast him a glance of agonized appeal. It fell on stony ground. He responded with a decidedly wicked grin and then left her.

Her misgivings, however, were quite unfounded. Captain Vaughan was pleasant, courteous and extremely easy to talk to. He succeeded in making her laugh three times and never once let her suspect how skilfully she was being drawn out. Then Mistress Rhodes walked up to them.

'Lucy tells me that it was you who made her gown, Mistress Radford. It's absolutely charming, I envy you your talent.'

Abigail looked into lazily smiling slate-blue eyes and felt oddly chilled. 'Thank you.'

'I am fascinated to know how you contrived all those tiny ruffles on the sleeves. And the bodice embroidery too —' She broke off, laughing up at Hugh. 'I'm afraid we are going to bore you, my dear.'

'Impossible!' he declared dramatically. 'But there are two stools just behind you, and perhaps a glass of wine might not be unwelcome?'

'Perfect.' Waving him gaily away, Anne took Abigail's

arm. 'Now do sit down with me and we can have a frivolously feminine chat . . . and you can tell me why it is that you don't leave your brother to know his own business best.'

Abigail sank on to the stool more quickly than she had intended. Then she glanced round to see if help was at hand and, finding that it wasn't, gritted her teeth and prepared to make the best of things. She said, 'If you see a child about to put its hand in the fire, do you leave it to learn by experience?'

The delicate brows rose. 'Why no. But Samuel isn't a child, is he? He's an intelligent young man whose small services put him in no danger whatsoever.'

'Then I expect you'll find him easily replaceable.'

'That is hardly the point. These matters have to be handled carefully – ah, thank you, Hugh!' Anne smiled brilliantly on Captain Vaughan and, placing the two glasses on a small table at her side, said, 'But you must go away. We haven't touched on the embroidery yet.'

Abigail looked wistfully at the Captain's retreating back. Sighing, she said, 'If Sam were determined to help you, I could not stop him.'

'But you have already done so, haven't you? He was willing enough before you found out what he was about. But if you won't repent what you have done, I hope you will at least give me your assurances that what you have learned has gone no further.'

'Well, of course it hasn't. I'm not a complete idiot!' Abigail was suddenly annoyed. 'Do you think I'd betray my own brother?'

'Gently, my dear. Naturally I don't think you would do so deliberately but, having seen Justin Ambrose taking an interest in you, I had to ask. Come, take a little wine and relax your prickles.' Anne turned unhurriedly to the table beside her and, in the same lightly amused tone said, 'I know, you see, how devastating Justin can be. And you have only to glance across the room to watch him bewitching poor Lucy, and she not wed an hour yet!'

Abigail's gaze moved involuntarily to where the Captain was laughing down at Lucy and then came back, bright with anger.

'What a malicious thing to say! Or is it that you're jealous?'

The lovely eyes narrowed a little and then Anne gave a long, rippling laugh. 'No, silly child. Are you?' There was an enigmatic pause and then, 'Oh come, take your wine. I apologize for everything and can see that I was utterly mistaken in you. Will that do?'

Faintly bewildered, Abigail nodded and accepted the glass. Then, frowning into it, she said slowly, 'Yes. But in return for my continued silence, I'd like your word that you'll leave Sam alone.'

'And if I don't give it, you'll tell?'

'If you don't, I may have to.'

'I see.' Anne was still smiling. 'Then of course I agree. Let us seal our bargain with a toast to your delightful brother. May he prosper as he deserves!'

Unnerved by the ease of her victory, Abigail took grateful refuge in her glass. And then, even more thankfully, she looked up to find Captain Ambrose stalking stiffly and unsmilingly towards her.

Anne rose gracefully in a rustle of tawny taffeta.

'Your little friend and I have been getting acquainted,' she announced smoothly. 'I have met her brother too and found him equally refreshing. One wonders which of them you like best.' And, with a sweetly disparaging smile, she drifted away.

Abigail investigated the set of Justin's mouth and said doubtfully, 'What did she mean by that?'

'Mischief, as usual. Forget about it. What did she say to you?'

'Oh, nothing much.' Abigail turned despairingly to her wine. 'She talked about Lucy's dress.'

As always, Justin read the expressive face without difficulty and knew that she was lying but for once, he misinterpreted her reasons. 'And regaled you with anecdotes of my habits in the bedchamber, if your expression is anything to go by,' he remarked sardonically. And then, as she choked over the last of her wine, 'But don't get excited. She knows as little of me as you do – she just has a better imagination.'

Confused, breathless and extremely flushed, Abigail surged to her feet. 'I think,' she said carefully, 'that I ought to go home.'

Justin took her arm and glanced across the room to where his fellow officers were cheerfully competing for the bride-favours that adorned Lucy's gown. It was the point in the celebrations where bawdiness usually set in. Smiling a little, he said, 'I think so too. But I want to talk to you first, so let's get out of here for a few minutes.'

'Where are we going?' she asked, startled. 'I can't – what will people think?'

He turned a reflective grey stare on her. 'Does it matter? Jonas isn't here to see and no one is going to tell him.'

'Yes. But I —'

'You're dithering again.' He swept her effortlessly along with him. 'You'll have to stop it, you know. I can't tolerate indecision.'

'I wasn't being indecisive. I was trying to say no.'

'Then you were making a very poor job of it.'

They emerged suddenly into the bright heat of the ramparts. Blinking, Abigail allowed herself to be drawn to the wall and then stood rapt in silent appreciation, gazing out across the town.

Justin leaned lazily against the warm stone and contemplated her profile, his conscience pricking him a little. She was so very young and vulnerable. It really wasn't fair to use her as a means of damaging Jonas' domestic despotism along with some of his immense self-conceit. On the other hand, it would do Abby no harm to learn a little defiance, or even a lot of it, and he would naturally take good care not to hurt her. He would merely nurture a few weeds in the orderly garden of her brother's Puritanical hypocrisy, and Abby, he told himself firmly, would be all the better for it.

He said, 'Does Jonas go often to Adderbury?'

She nodded. 'When the weather is good. He takes Rachel and Hallelujah every Tuesday afternoon.'

Momentarily diverted, he said, 'Who?'

She turned, the dark eyes faintly mischievous.

'The baby. They called him Hallelujah. I did tell you but

178

you weren't noticeably impressed at the time.'

'I probably didn't believe you. My God, what will they call the next one?'

'Hosanna.' The elusive dimple played about her mouth. 'But only if it's a girl.'

He laughed and then said negligently, 'So you're free of doom, gloom and criticism every Tuesday afternoon. What do you do?'

'Nothing much. Sew perhaps or read a little. It's my day for being lazy.'

'I see.' His expression grew strangely intent. 'Then, next week, will you come and be lazy with me?'

Totally unprepared for it, Abigail made a small choking sound. 'What did you say?'

'I asked you to commit the dire impropriety of meeting me in secret and by appointment next Tuesday. Will you?'

She stared at him, half outraged and half regretful.

'I can't. You know I can't. You're joking, aren't you?'

'No. Whatever gave you that idea?'

'Then you've gone mad. It's impossible.'

'Why? We've been associating with each other quite merrily for the last seven months.'

'Yes, but by accident!'

'Not always.' Justin folded his arms and smiled reminiscently. 'You've sat on my hearthrug and ministered to me in bed and —'

'That was different! It wasn't a deliberate flouting of convention just for pleasure. Even Sam would have a fit if he thought I were —'

'Indulging in a clandestine relationship? But you won't be. You'll simply be sharing an innocent hour with a friend. And if Sam is likely to make difficulties, then don't tell him.' He paused and raised one ironic brow. 'Alternatively, if you really don't want to come, all you have to do is say so.'

And Satan took him up into a high place . . . thought Abigail, racked by temptation.

Lucy was right. He was attractive and dangerous and he had the power to shatter her peace of mind. Rachel would undoubtedly have said 'Get thee behind me Satan,' and a respectable girl with any sense at all would have given the Captain a swift and unequivocal refusal. Abigail found herself incapable of either.

'Yes, it is a beautiful shirt, isn't it?' teased Justin. 'I thought you'd never notice.'

She raised her eyes to his face and said, 'But why? Why me?'

'You think I should ask Bab Atkins?'

'It would make more sense.'

'On the contrary. It would make no sense at all. I want a companion, not a china doll; a friend, not a tawdry flirtation. In short, I want an hour with the one person who will neither bore me, catechize me, nor expect a perpetual flow of charm. You.' He smiled down at her, watching the colour rise to her cheeks and then added, winsomely, 'Say you'll come. Please?'

The peculiar sweetness of his smile was Abigail's undoing. Her heart turned over and temptation triumphed. To herself, she said, 'Just this once . . . '

Aloud she said, 'I'll try.'

'Thank you,' said Justin simply. 'And don't worry about Jonas. He's not God.'

'I know.' Filled with sudden, inexplicable lightness of heart, she laughed back at him. 'I know. But who's going to tell him?'

Chapter Fifteen

'Where on earth did you get to?' asked Samuel as they walked home from the wedding. 'You were gone ages.' And then, looking curiously at her, 'What's the matter? Your eyes have gone awfully peculiar. What is it? Guilt?'

'No,' said Abigail hazily. 'I feel rather odd. As though everything inside me wants to stop working.' Her footsteps slowed and she put out a hand to steady herself against the wall. 'I'm so tired.'

She swayed and Samuel grabbed her about the waist.

'Well you can't go to sleep here. Come on, lean on me. We're nearly home now. It's the wine, I suppose. You shouldn't have touched it. You know you're not used to it. How much did you have?' And then, when she did not reply, 'Oh Lord! I just hope Jonas isn't back, that's all.'

His prayer was answered and, with their mother in the kitchen, it was a relatively simple matter to get Abigail upstairs unseen. Panting a little, Samuel heaved her carelessly on to the bed and grinned down at her. 'You're remarkably heavy for such a little thing. I never realized.'

Abigail lay like a stone. Her face was white, her eyes closed and her breathing oddly noisy. Anxiety dawned in her brother's face and, taking her hand, he began to slap it, saying, 'Oh come on, Abby! You can't possibly have had more than a couple of glasses so sit up and pull yourself together. You can't appear at dinner like this and, if you don't come down, Jonas will demand to know why. And I can hardly tell him you're drunk, can I? Abby!'

Her eyelids fluttered open to disclose hugely dilated pupils and a complete absence of expression. Struggling with the words, she said, 'I . . . I . . . only one glass.'

He stared at her, half exasperated and half alarmed. And then, making the only sensible decision, he limped quickly downstairs to find his mother.

The maid, Betty, was with her, so he said carefully, 'I think you ought to come and take a look at Abby.'

Alice put a pie sharply on the table. 'What's wrong with her?'

'I don't know.' And then, suddenly inspired, 'But she may be contagious so Jonas and Rachel ought to be warned to keep away from her.' He met his mother's gaze defiantly. 'Well, we don't want the baby to catch anything, do we?'

Alice dropped her apron on the settle. 'No. You heard that, Betty? If Mr Jonas returns while I'm upstairs, tell him on no account to come up.' She followed Samuel through to the hall and then said, 'Now what's all this about? Contagious, indeed!'

'Well I had to say something to keep Jonas out of it.' He ushered her up the stairs. 'How good are you at sobering people up?'

'What?' gasped Alice. 'Samuel are you being flippant?'

'I wish I were. We slipped out to the Castle this afternoon so that Abby could see her precious wedding dress in its hour of glory and —'

'You did what? Oh Sam!'

'Yes I know. But Abby wanted to go and I didn't think it would do any harm. It never occurred to me that she'd come back cupshot.' He opened the door of Abigail's bedchamber and stood back to let Alice pass. 'Look at her. If it weren't for Jonas, it would be funny!'

Alice sat on the bed. 'Abby? Come along, dear, wake up.' She slapped one pale cheek quite lightly and then, when there was no reaction, repeated the action a little harder. 'Abigail!'

'She said she only had one glass,' remarked Samuel judicially. 'But it doesn't look like it, does it?'

'Help me sit her up,' snapped Alice. 'I don't like the way she's breathing. Abby, wake up. Open your eyes!'

Slowly, very slowly, Abigail fought back the tides of unconsciousness. Her lashes were leaden weights which had to be forced apart and her body no longer belonged to her, but she obeyed the ungentle summons and looked out upon the blurred face of her mother.

'Oh God!' Alice's hands crept up to her mouth. 'No.'

'What's wrong?' asked Samuel. 'Mother – what is it?'

'Get her up. Get her up. Make her walk. Do anything you like so long as you keep her awake.'

'But why? It's only the wine, isn't it?'

Alice was half-way to the door but she swung round, her face ashen but fierce. 'No, it isn't just wine. It's belladonna. And if we don't bestir ourselves, she'll die.'

On the following morning, Captain Ambrose had barely returned from a dawn patrol when Samuel found him in the outer courtyard of the Castle.

'I've got to talk to you,' he said baldly. 'Where can we be sure of being private?'

Justin glanced searchingly at him and then nodded.

'In there.' He led the way across to the ruined mansion house. 'No one comes here any more. Now, what did you want to say?'

'It's got to be quick,' came Samuel, in the same flat tone. 'I'm needed at home. But I couldn't leave it any longer. Not now. Abby nearly died last night. Mother says she was given belladonna.'

'Christ,' breathed Justin. 'Poison?'

Samuel nodded wearily. 'Yes. We think, we hope she's out of danger now but she's still very ill.'

'If your mother is right, I'm not surprised,' came the grim reply. 'You kept Abby awake?'

'Yes. All night long. I dragged her round and round the room, slapping and shaking her. It was horrible. Mother made her drink egg white and then she changed it to salt water so that – so that . . .'

'So that Abby was sick. Yes.' The harsh face relaxed a little. 'Your mother is a wise woman.'

'I know. But I doubt any of us can stand another night like that and it was made all the worse by having to hide it from Jonas.' Samuel paused and drew a long breath. 'But I came to tell you something quite different.'

'Ah. Your theory, perhaps, on how Abby came to drink nightshade?'

'Yes.' Samuel set his jaw. 'It was Anne Rhodes. I know it just as surely as I know she murdered Tom Mayhew. And though I can't prove she actually did it, I can prove why she'd try.'

There was a long, stunned silence and then Justin said distantly, 'Go on. I'm listening.'

'She's a spy. She's employed by Sir Samuel Luke and she's been sending him monthly reports all the time she's been here. Tom found out and so did Abby.'

'And how,' asked the Captain, 'do you know all this?'

'Because I've been delivering her letters to the carrier.'

The grey eyes remained coldly enigmatic. 'I see. You are a busy child, aren't you?'

Samuel flushed. 'I know what you're thinking and —'

'I doubt it.'

'— and I don't blame you.'

'That is kind of you.'

'Will you listen?' snapped Samuel. 'I'm not going to waste time justifying myself to you. It's bad enough that I'm here at all. What I came to say is this: if you can make Anne Rhodes confess to murdering Tom and trying to kill Abby, I'll give you proof that she's a spy.'

'Proof? You mean you'll testify against her?'

'If it's necessary. But I can do better than that,' replied Samuel, rigid with strain. 'You see, I still have her last despatch.'

It was a long time before Justin spoke and when he did his words were unexpected. He said, 'You obviously care a great deal about Abby.'

'Yes. Can you do what I ask?'

'Oh yes.' Justin smiled, but not pleasantly. 'In fact, it will be my pleasure.'

Within minutes of Samuel's departure, Justin stood outside Mistress Rhodes' door. It was slightly ajar. He entered without knocking and then, closing it behind him, slid the bolt home.

Startled, Anne looked up from the array of powders and potions that littered her table and came hurriedly to her feet.

'How dare you walk in here like this? Get out!'

184

Justin folded his arms and leaned against the door, his gaze resting meditatively on the bottles and jars. Then he said gently, 'Which one of those contains the belladonna?'

She sensed dangerous temper beneath his apparent calm and asked warily, 'Why?'

'Why do you think? I was wondering who you'd use it on next.' He strolled across the room and began lightly touching the bottles. 'Is it this? Or this? Abby Radford is still alive, you know. You should have chosen something less easily identifiable. Ah no!' His hands shot out, imprisoning her arm. 'No, my dear. You're going nowhere yet. We're going to have a little chat, you and I.'

'Let me go!' She twisted in his hold and brought her free hand up to his face, the nails poised to rip and tear.

Justin felled it using the hard edge of his palm in a downward, chopping movement that drew a gasp of pain from her. Then, smiling, he forced her down on the stool. 'As I said, a little chat about Abby Radford and Tom Mayhew and Sir Samuel Luke. You see, sweetheart, I know it all, or nearly all, and you are going to tell me the rest.'

She moistened her lips, her mind busy with possible courses of action. Then, recognizing their futility, she said, 'I'll see you damned before I tell you anything. And you'll never prove it.'

'Oh but I will,' he assured her calmly. 'You really shouldn't have poisoned Abby. Her brother is a little annoyed with you, and he still has the last letter you trusted him with.'

The shock of it set the blood coursing to her head and for a moment she could not speak. Then, 'That bloody little daisy. I should have seen to him.'

'You should indeed. Why did you kill Tom Mayhew?'

She curbed her rage, aware of the perils of saying too much. 'I didn't kill him.'

'You did. But not, I think, with nightshade. What did you use?'

'Nothing. And that's all you'll get from me.'

'You think so?' His fingers strayed at random through the clutter of the table until they encountered the bone handle of a small knife. 'You are taking me for a gentleman again and it's a mistake, particularly now. For you will talk, you know, one way or another.' His hand closed on the knife and, turning a glacial smile on her, he added conversationally, 'I learned a lot at Naseby.'

The blue eyes narrowed. 'You bastard. You wouldn't dare.'

'No? You don't know me very well, do you? I don't hold women sacred. I have known others like you, you see. And I don't make empty threats or balk at soiling my hands when the devil drives. So you will do well to believe what I say for I'll use any means I have to, short of actually killing you. And that is for the law to do.'

She did not answer but, instead, made another sudden dive for the door. Justin seized a handful of her hair and hauled her screeching back to him.

'Don't try that again. I'll pull it out next time. Now. Sit down and begin at the beginning. I want to know exactly who you are and who sent you – everything.'

Mistress Rhodes spat hard and accurately into his face.

For one second, perhaps two, Justin continued to regard her out of chilly, purposeful eyes. Then, without warning, he brought the back of his hand percussively up across her cheek.

'And that,' he announced impersonally, as she collapsed against the table sobbing for breath, 'concludes the pleasantries for both sides. Act One, Scene Two, same question. I suggest you answer.'

He halted and then, when she merely uttered a brief insult in the lowest form of gutter vernacular, he pulled her to her feet and, in a single, lithe movement, twisted her right arm high against her spine and laid the knife flat along one flawless cheek.

'Stop!' she moaned, her head forced back against his shoulder. 'You're breaking my arm.'

'No. You'd be surprised how much more it can hurt before I do that. Now let's start with your name.'

'You know it. Anne Rhodes.'

His grip tightened just a little. 'Sure?'

'Yes – no. It's Hannah, Hannah Rhodes. Don't!'

'Then answer truthfully. How did you poison Tom?'

'I – I – water hemlock. Let me go! I'll tell you —'

'And Abby? Belladonna in her wine yesterday afternoon?'

'Yes. Please, I think I'm going to faint.'

'Don't do that. The knife might slip. Tell me about your dealings with Samuel Luke. How long have you been doing this? As long as that? Really! And what information have you been sending him? Try again. I don't believe you.' Without effort, the inexorable inquisition gathered speed. 'And Sam Radford – when did he first get involved? Not till February? Then how did you contrive to warn Compton Wynyates that we were coming? Don't lie, they were expecting us. How did you do it? One of our exchanged prisoners? What enterprise! I'm impressed. And now you can explain where you gathered the exquisitely garbled version of my past history that you supplied to *Mercurius Britannicus*.'

Sudden, breathless silence. Justin brought his grip to the brink of bone-splitting agony and watched, unmoved, as tears of pain and rage rolled down her face.

'Don't stop now. It's just getting interesting. You did send it, didn't you? Didn't you?'

'Yes – yes! And I'm glad. I only wish I'd done as Bernard said and—' She broke off, aghast, and felt the tremor of shock that ran through the still body behind her.

'Bernard?' repeated Justin in an odd voice. 'Bernard French? Is he in this too?'

Inexplicably, her conviction that he would not use the knife evaporated and she was suddenly very frightened indeed.

'Yes, it was all him. He wants you dead.'

'So he sent you. Go on. Why you?'

'He – we are betrothed. He works for Samuel Luke too and he said I could kill two birds with one stone. He said he'd thought you already dead till he heard John Fiennes mention your name and then he told me that getting rid of you would do everyone a favour, especially him and me.'

'I see.' The crisp voice grew even more remote. 'And did he explain why?'

'No. But as soon as I saw you, I guessed.'

'Guessed what?' And then, as she hesitated, 'My next move will shatter your arm. What did you guess?'

'That you're the missing heir, Bernard's stepbrother. And that, if you ever were plain Justin Ambrose, you're not any more. You're the eighth Baron Templeton of Trent.'

He released her so unexpectedly that she almost fell. Her arm and shoulder were a burning torment and the knife had scraped her cheek a little but the look on his face outweighed both. He said, 'Very good. But you are misinformed on one vital point. I was disinherited ten years ago.'

'I know that. But your father changed his mind. Why do you think Bernard needs you dead? He can't inherit while you live.'

There was a white shade about Justin's mouth. He laughed oddly and said, 'Well, well, so they lost after all.' Then, his gaze focusing again on Mistress Rhodes, 'And is that why you were so determined to find a way into my bed?'

'Why else? Did you flatter yourself that it was for your body? No. I thought —'

'You thought I might prove a better proposition than Bernard. Quite. But, having discovered your mistake, why didn't you kill me while you had the chance when I was ill?' He stopped and then said, 'Of course. You couldn't. It would have been too obvious.'

'Not if rhubarb had been in season. But it wasn't – and then you gave me a new interest. You began to talk.' She gave a brief, unmusical laugh. 'So *Mercurius Britannicus* got it all wrong, did they? Yet you gave it to me yourself under the influence of opium.'

Nothing in the pale, chiselled face showed how very close she was to death by strangulation. Yet the temptation swelled up and up in Justin's mind like a tidal wave, drowning every thought save one: that, if she lived to come to trial, his ten-year-old cloak of anonymity would be wrenched from him and he would be back in the destructive vortex of endless, prying speculation. Just two minutes, he told himself. And with Sam's evidence, who would know it for personal vengeance?

Sam's evidence . . .

The wave receded slightly, admitting logic. Sam had asked for proof that Anne – no, Hannah – was a murderess. What he had just heard might not in itself be enough. Only a written confession would be certain to satisfy Sam's complicated sense of honour so that he would give up the letter. The letter was too important to be thrown away as the price of his own peace of mind.

Writing materials lay amongst the deadly harvest of the table and he pushed them towards her, saying, 'Sit down. You are going to write your confession. Three lines should do it: you are in Parliamentary pay: you killed Tom Mayhew and you attempted to kill Abby Radford. Then sign it.'

She stared at him, her eyes filled with the ugliness of hate. 'I won't. Why should I?'

'To prevent my having the inestimable pleasure of spoiling your lovely, lying face,' returned Justin deliberately. He came closer, the knife gleaming cold in his fingers. 'Now write.'

Hannah Rhodes allowed her gaze to fall to the paper. A confession signed freely in the presence of witnesses would unquestionably be her death warrant but this, if she wrote it, could be revoked later on the plea of duress. There were always bargains to be struck – information for Will Compton, her body for any man who would help her escape. The future was full of chances; the present held nothing but certain disfigurement if she refused. Slowly, she picked up the pen.

Of the first night of her illness, Abigail remembered only the endless battle to stay awake and the ever-increasing pain of incessant nausea. By dawn, she had been too weak to stand and the nerves of her stomach were so raw that a mere scent was enough to set her retching. Finally, they had let her rest – half blind in the growing light but too physically broken to care.

It was two days before she could see properly, four before she could eat anything without being sick and six before she had the strength to leave her room. For all that time, Alice and Samuel kept Jonas at bay by maintaining the fiction of an infectious internal disorder. It was the only bright spot in Abigail's world.

By the time a full week had elapsed and Tuesday had come again, she felt that she had been to hell and back but she had not forgotten her afternoon appointment at Bridge Bar and, expressing the intention of resting quietly in her room, she slipped calmly out of the house to keep it. He would not be there of course – she realized that. Sam had told her all about his early morning visits to the Castle, the second of which had seen him finally hand over the letter to Captain Ambrose. But none of it, not even the fact that Mistress Rhodes had tried to kill her, seemed to matter very much to Abigail. The only thing that did matter was that if the Captain knew her to be ill, he would not come to meet her and that would be the last, dreary straw.

By the time the bridge was in sight she had other things to worry about; the question, for example, of whether she could get that far without making a fool of herself by collapsing in the street. In the dubious belief that concentration could avert this disaster, she began counting her steps. She was still counting them when she arrived at the place where Justin had tethered his horse.

He had been sitting with his back against a tree, wondering why he had been fool enough to come. And then she was before him and shock brought him sharply to his feet.

'Oh Christ,' he breathed, staring at her transparent, fine-drawn pallor and the still dilated dark eyes. Then, quietly, 'Abby? You ought to be in bed.'

'Two hundred and forty-seven,' said Abigail, frowning a little. 'Two hundred and – and —'

In three strides he was beside her, lifting her easily in his arms. Then, after glancing round with a sort of furious helplessness, he carried her deeper into the copse and laid her carefully on the grass.

'Captain Ambrose?' she asked uncertainly. 'Is it you?'

'Yes.' Anxiety made him abrupt.

She sighed. 'I didn't think you'd come.'

'Since you were stupid enough to do so, it's just as well that I did, isn't it?'

'Yes.' The blurred gaze focused slowly on his face. 'You sound angry. Are you?'

'Yes.' With myself for the insane piece of mischief that brought you here; with your family for letting you out; with a God who leaves defenceless things like you to fend for themselves. 'Yes. Very angry. But not with you. Come, sit up. You're still having trouble breathing, aren't you?'

'Sometimes.' She let him raise her up and found herself comfortably installed against his shoulder. 'I'm glad you came. Thank you.'

'Don't mention it.' His mouth twisted wryly. 'It seems we're forever fated to meet under cataclysmic circumstances, doesn't it? I wonder what it will be next?'

'Don't.' She shivered. 'Sam says he's given you the letter.'

'Yes. You should be proud of him. It wasn't an easy decision.'

'No. Poor Sam.' Her head drooped against his chest. 'If there is a trial, will he have to give evidence?'

'No. Don't worry. I laid the facts before the Governor and he's grateful enough to leave Sam out of it.' He fell silent, bitterly contemplating the other things he'd had to say to Will, things he had not spoken of in ten years, except once, in a very different hour of discovery, to Rupert.

Explanations and excuses had never come easily to him and he hated making them, but not nearly as much as he had hated having to ask Will's connivance in a furtive and apparently ludicrous attempt to restrict, as far as possible, the knowledge that Captain Ambrose and the eighth Lord Templeton were one and the same. Stirring restlessly, he gazed down at the top of Abigail's head. It could have been worse. Will had been surprised – as well he might be – but his innate good manners had prevented him enquiring too closely into the reasons for such secrecy. That had been just as well, reflected Justin, for there were days when he could not explain them to himself.

'I'm sorry,' murmured Abigail drowsily. 'I'm not being much of a companion, am I?'

'No. But the same could be said of me. And you shouldn't be here at all, by rights. I ought to take you home. What the devil were Sam and your mother about to let you out in this state?'

'They don't know. And I was quite well when I left.' She tilted her head to look at him. 'Let me stay a little longer. It's so pleasant here, and I feel much better now. Tell me about Mistress Rhodes.'

'There's nothing to tell. She's safely under lock and key, awaiting her trial with well-concealed impatience.'

'But how did you persuade her to write her confession?'

A faint, grim smile touched his mouth.

'It's better that you don't know. Let's just say that I was forced to be a little rough with her.'

Abigail's eyes widened. 'Oh.'

'Does that surprise you? It had to be done and she deserved nothing better.'

'I know. But it can't have been very pleasant.'

'I've done worse things,' he shrugged. And then, reading her face, 'I'm a professional soldier, Abby. When something requires to be done, I do it.'

'Always?'

'Yes. There's nothing romantic about war and no room for sentiment or an over-developed degree of fastidiousness, not if you want to stay alive.' Against all reason, he was irritated. 'Or did you think we were all epic heroes galloping off to immortal glory?'

Stung by his tone, Abigail sat up and turned away a little. 'Of course not. I hate the war and everything it stands for.'

'I wish I could say the same. Unfortunately, it's my living.'

'You mean you were a soldier before the war started?'

'Yes, and will continue to be when it's finished. There's always a war somewhere and the higher the rank I can achieve in this one, the higher the pay I can command for my services in the next. The Galahads of the army,' he added trenchantly, 'don't make very good officers. A leader who lets his emotions rule him has a nasty tendency of getting his men killed.' He stopped on a sudden indrawn breath and then added, sarcastically, 'Hoist with my own petard, as they say. Don't you want to point out that it serves me right?'

'No,' said Abigail, flatly. 'I want to go home.'

'To mother?'

'No, to Jonas. I know where I am with him.'

A long silence followed this observation. Finally Justin said, 'I'm sorry. Self-indulgent histrionics. I'd better take you home.'

'I don't need you to take me home. I can go myself.'

'Don't be a fool. You're as weak as a kitten and so bloody thin that a moderate wind would blow you away.' A tiny, strangled sound escaped her and he said, 'Oh God! You're not crying, are you?'

'No!' Abigail repudiated the suggestion with every sign of loathing and hunted frantically for her handkerchief.

'Liar.' Justin produced his own and tossed it into her lap. 'Here – use this.'

'Thank you.' She buried her face in the snowy folds as the involuntary sobs came harder and faster. 'I never cry! It's only – it's only —'

'Because you've been ill. Yes, I know.' His voice held amusement mingled with concern. 'Don't cry. Tell me I'm a thoughtless bastard, if you like, but don't cry. I'm not used to it. The ladies of my acquaintance are more inclined to throw things.'

'I don't blame them!' wept Abigail. 'And if you dare to laugh —'

'Shh. I'm not laughing.' Reaching out, he drew her firmly back into his arms. 'Now stop upsetting yourself and say you'll come again next week if I promise to be on my best behaviour.'

'I can't.' The sobs faded against his chest.

'Yes you can. Same time, same place?'

'No. It's all wrong and if someone sees us and tells Jonas—'

'Oh, Jonas.' Justin snapped dismissive fingers. 'I've quite lost my faith in him since Sam told me how frightened he is of infection. I thought he was the trust-in-the-Lord type.'

'He is.' Abigail lifted her face and a watery smile dawned. 'He is. But he likes to tie up his camel as well.'

Chapter Sixteen

While John Lilburne expertly aggravated the differences between the Presbyterian and Independent factions in Parliament, Lord Digby continued to enrage Prince Rupert by blaming him for the disaster of Naseby while simultaneously claiming it to be no great loss. Help, he said airily, would come from my Lord Ormonde in Ireland or my Lord Montrose in Scotland – or both; and Rupert, watching his uncle believing it because he wished to believe it, promptly lost his temper. There would be no troops from Ireland, he shouted. And as for Montrose – he hadn't enough men to hold the places he took in Scotland.

But Charles refused to be disheartened. His cause was just; the Parliament, itself divided, was again quarrelling with the Scots; and Montrose's star was still firmly in the ascendant. There was no reason for despair and Rupert's gloom was displeasing to him. Rupert, he therefore intimated gently, would do better to take his disturbing presence elsewhere.

Fuming, Rupert did so. While the King moved on to Raglan Castle to play bowls, he joined the Prince of Wales at Barnstaple and then, reluctantly leaving Somerset in the frequently cupshot hands of George Goring, took himself off to the vital task of holding Bristol. Within the week his trust was proved misplaced. Goring was defeated by the New Model at Langport and then abandoned Bridgwater to its fate so that it too fell. Rupert cursed him with versatile ferocity and then threw himself into preparations to strengthen Bristol – lifeline of the Royalist cause and their only gateway to the outside world.

News of Langport arrived in Banbury on the day appointed for the trial of Hannah Rhodes. Out of consideration for Justin, Will Compton had decided that the business should be dealt with quietly in his own quarters. Only those officers holding the rank of Captain or above were bidden

194

attend and the proceedings, though formal, were kept as brief as possible.

Mistress Rhodes, still beautiful despite her two-week incarceration, faced her accusers with defiant splendour. They had dissected the evidence against her with frightening efficiency and all her ploys had failed her. Will had refused to barter freedom for intelligence and her jailers, carefully chosen from amongst Tom Mayhew's friends, had declined even to speak to her outside the line of duty. All that remained was to publicly revoke her confession whilst casting doubt on Justin Ambrose's motives and methods and this she now fully intended to do.

Sir William, aware of her design, was ready and the moment she launched into her denunciation of Justin, he said, 'I am aware of these facts, Mistress, and do not find them related to the matter in hand. As for your confession, we are all agreed that it shows no sign of having been written under the violent circumstances you describe and are therefore satisfied that it is valid.'

'Valid? It's no more valid than if I'd been put on the rack! Less, in fact, because apart from my own, the only signature it bears is that of a man who doesn't exist. There is no Justin Ambrose, only Lord Templeton!'

A silence that was part baffled, part stunned greeted this triumphant declaration. To some, like Ned Frost, it meant nothing but in Hugh Vaughan and two or three others, it struck a chord of shocked fascination. Will Compton glanced enquiringly at Justin and waited, as they were all doing, for him to speak.

An oddly mocking smile touching the corners of his mouth, Justin rose and looked unhurriedly at the faces about him. Then, turning to Mistress Rhodes, he said clearly, 'You are mistaken. Justin Ambrose not only exists, but is standing before you.'

'It's a lie!' she shouted, her eyes brilliant.

'No. I was christened Justin Ambrose Templeton, Ambrose being my mother's maiden name. I shed my father's name ten years ago and have had neither need nor wish to resume it since. But if it will simplify matters, I am willing to add it to the document in question here and now before you all.'

'You bastard,' said Hannah. 'You bloody, stinking bastard!'

Ignoring her, Sir William directed a bright stare at his officers. 'Well, gentlemen? Are you satisfied with the signature as it stands or do you wish Captain Ambrose to add to it?'

There was another pause. Then Hugh Vaughan rose and said evenly, 'Unless anyone objects, I would suggest that we leave that decision up to you, sir. Speaking for myself, I am content to let the matter rest.'

There was a murmur of agreement and Will inclined his head courteously. 'So be it, then. The document shall stay as it is and I am sure Captain Ambrose will be as grateful for that as he will be of your future discretion.'

'God,' thought Hugh, startled. 'So we're not even to speak of it, are we? Well, well.'

'This is not a trial,' cried Hannah, contemptuously. 'It's a puppet-show with that perverted madman pulling the strings.'

'You are being tried in accordance with the rules of war,' said Will coldly. 'The matter of the confession is a trivial one for it tells us nothing we cannot substantiate from other sources, such as the nostrums in your bedchamber which included enough poison to wipe out the entire garrison and the letter in your own hand informing Sir Samuel Luke of our stores and defences. It is my duty to inform you that; having examined these things most carefully in your presence here today, I find the conclusions inescapable. But any of these gentlemen are entitled to disagree with me. If you have anything to say in extenuation or any new facts to lay before us, I can truthfully promise you a fair hearing. You may now speak your defence.'

Hannah spoke but very little of what she said was any form of defence. She railed against Will Compton, Samuel Radford and Abigail; she prophesied doom for the Royalist cause in general and dire reprisals on the Banbury garrison if they dared touch her and she spat every venomous curse she knew at Justin Ambrose.

Sir William sat patiently until her tirade exhausted itself and then, rising, he asked his officers if they wished time to discuss their verdict. One by one, they shook their heads.

'Very well. Then rise in turn and declare your findings so that the accused may hear.'

'Guilty!' said Major Walrond.

'Guilty!' echoed Hugh Vaughan.

'Guilty!' repeated five other voices, consecutively.

'Guilty!' said Justin, his expressionless gaze resting squarely on Hannah's face.

The room seemed suddenly hot and airless. With measured deliberation, Sir William said, 'Hannah Rhodes, you stand convicted of treacherous dealings with the enemy and the foul murder of one of His Majesty's loyal subjects – the penalty for both of which is death. I therefore sentence you to be hanged on the public gallows of this town and may God have mercy upon you.'

'No!' The lovely face was contorted with fear. 'No!'

Will faced his officers.

'Sentence to be carried out, six days from today, on Wednesday July 23rd at noon. Thank you, gentlemen. You may now return to your duties.'

Abigail sat on the grass and watched the shifting pattern of dappled sunlight move over Captain Ambrose's face. It was the Tuesday of their second meeting and she had discovered that being wicked did not feel nearly as dreadful as she had always supposed. Instead of feelings of anxiety and guilt, she was filled with a sensation of exquisite awareness and a golden, boundless content. She did not care that Justin did not speak. It did not even matter if he had fallen asleep for that only proved that he too was at peace. His hat and coat adorned a nearby bush, his sword lay on the ground beneath them and, relaxed and apparently oblivious, he himself lay full length on the turf with his hands clasped behind his head and his eyes closed.

'You're very quiet,' he said lazily. 'Nothing to say?'

She smiled. 'I thought you were asleep.'

'Not at all.' He opened one eye on her. 'I'm not so rude and

197

didn't I promise you my best behaviour.'

'Yes. You did. And I'm looking forward to seeing it.'

'Little cat.' The other eye opened and he grinned at her. 'I suppose that means you're waiting to be entertained. Find me something suitable and I'll juggle for you, if you like.'

Smiling sceptically, she opened the bag of apples at her side. 'Go on then.'

He sat up. 'Is that a challenge?'

'Yes,' said Abigail, shying the fruit at him.

He caught it deftly and then raised one considering brow. 'And what's the forfeit for failure?'

'Three answers to three questions,' she said promptly.

'And the prize for success?'

'That you take that horrendous thing off your head,' returned Justin, frowning severely at her cap. 'The very sight of it gives me the marthambles.'

'Done!' She laughed, still convinced that he was teasing. Anyone could catch but it took rather more skill to juggle.

Whatever it took, Captain Ambrose undoubtedly had it and his hands became a blur of activity as he sent the apples spinning high into the air. Then, without stopping or fumbling, he came to his feet and somehow whisked the despised white cap up to join the whirl of flying fruit before despatching everything, piece by piece, into her lap.

'Well?' he asked quizzically. 'Are you suitably impressed?'

'Yes.' The dark eyes regarded him with awed appreciation. 'What else can you do?'

'Oh, I've a whole collection of useless skills.' He dropped neatly back on to the grass. 'I can mix cosmetics, filch the odd fowl, pacify a magistrate, even, at need, deliver a baby. And before you ask – no, it was not mine. It just so happened that Nan Pollet went into labour during the first scene of *Antony and Cleopatra* and gave birth during the last while everyone else was still on stage.' The grey eyes were alight with amusement.

'One of my fondest memories is of Mistress Wilkins, in full Egyptian regalia and clutching her asp, hissing instructions to me from the wings. Not, of course, that it was very funny at the time. I remember being in a state of pure panic.'

Stunned into silence, Abigail's stare grew wider than ever. Finally, she said feebly, 'Do you mean you were an actor?'

'Not exactly.' He smiled suddenly. 'I spent nearly a year with a troupe of players in York but candour compels me to admit that I never rose above the role of second gravedigger. And my only really creditable performances, so Manager Wilkins continually told me, were those given as a corpse. I think they only kept me because my knowledge of swordplay was useful for the fight scenes.' He leaned back and propped himself on one elbow, looking at her. 'Are you shocked?'

'Yes. I thought . . . I've always imagined you in a big country house with a park, like Canon's Ashby or Broughton. You don't look like someone used to earning their living. You don't behave like one either.'

It was not the reply he had expected and he searched for signs of the unqualified horror all Puritans felt for the theatre. It was not there. She had not, he realized, even thought of that aspect of it. She was too busy equating the implications of his words with his person.

'Manager Wilkins must have taught me more than he thought, then, for I've supported myself since I was sixteen.'

His customary reserve coupled with something in his manner made Abigail pause but she could not resist saying cautiously, 'And before that?'

'Before that I was bred to be idle in the sort of surroundings you describe,' he replied, coolly careless. 'I left it behind me ten years ago and haven't been back since but I suppose it accounts for any residual aura of gentility.'

The warning was clearer this time so she said merely, 'I've never seen a play. Did you enjoy being an actor?'

He shrugged. 'In a sense, I suppose I did. The company was vulgar but lively and it was certainly an improvement on the months I'd spent previously.' The worst months of his life; often cold, frequently hungry and always alone. He passed over them and said, 'But it was in my mind to go abroad as a mercenary so I made my way to London and spent another year as a dock hand to earn both my passage and enough money to buy a decent sword – that one. It wasn't new even then but it's seen me through a few German campaigns and a battle or two here and I've grown quite attached to it.'

Silence fell for a moment and then she said, 'Is it true that you know Prince Rupert?'

'Yes. I came over with him and de Gomme and the others. I was part of his cavalry until – until circumstances conspired to send me here.' He smiled at her. 'You want to know what he's like.'

She nodded. 'Is he really as wicked as they say?'

'He's not wicked at all. He's just a very large young man with the energy of ten who happens to be extremely good at his job. He loathes drunkenness, despises inefficiency, hasn't an ounce of sophistication or tact and is ridiculously shy with women. You'd probably like him.'

'And that really would put me beyond the pale, wouldn't it?'

She clasped her arms about her knees and surveyed him keenly. 'Will you tell me about York and London and all the other places you've been to?'

'It's something of a tall order – but I suppose I could try. Why are you so interested?'

'Can't you guess?' She spoke with the first hint of personal bitterness he had ever known her show. 'I've never met anyone like you before and I probably never will again. You're my window on a world I'll never see and, more than that, you represent the half of England that isn't like Jonas. I thought that, if I listened to you, I might begin to understand why there is a war.'

'Hasn't Jonas educated you?' he asked, lightly probing.

'Oh yes. Ship money, the Scots war, the new Prayer Book, the dissolution of Parliament,' she recited. 'I know all about why Jonas is at war. What I don't know is why you are.'

'Do you care? It won't last much longer anyway. Naseby finished us and, sooner or later, the King is going to have to face it.'

Her eyes widened a little. 'That's what Jonas says.'

'Well, for once he's right. With no money, bits of our armies scattered uselessly all over the country and more of our strongholds surrendering every day, we haven't a chance

200

in hell of winning. All we can do is play for time by holding on to trump cards like Bristol until the King sues for terms. And let us hope,' he added grimly, 'that he does sue for terms. For if he chooses exile, the fanatics like Jonas will make England the sorriest country in Christendom.'

'And that is why you are fighting?'

'Yes. The only basic difference between myself and – John Fiennes, shall we say? – is that he is defending one set of liberties and I another. His, you have lived with all your life. Mine have the advantage of being more cheerful.'

She met his eyes and smiled ruefully. 'You mean that yours would allow me to let my hair curl and wear a cherry taffeta gown.'

'Yes. You could laugh and dance and give presents at Christmas. You could visit the play, pick flowers on the Sabbath and learn the art of flirtation without wondering if you are wanton.'

'Jonas says I am wanton,' replied Abigail thoughtlessly. And then flushed painfully as she realized what she had said.

A spark of pure temper smouldered in Justin's eyes.

'Jonas,' he said savagely, 'should have been drowned at birth. It would have spared him a world of sin and us a wealth of mindless, gutter-bred suspicion.' He drew a long breath and then, in a more moderate tone, added, 'Your brother, my dear, would find fault with the Archangel Gabriel, and if you continue to pay him the slightest heed, he'll make your life an utter misery.'

She sighed, her head bent over her hands.

'I know. But what can I do? He isn't easy to ignore.'

'Perhaps not. But you could at least start taking yourself at your own valuation instead of his. When all's said and done, the man's no more than a —'

'A puffed-up pig's bladder?'

'Quite. *What* did you say?'

The dimple quivered into being and the great dark eyes laughed up at his astonishment. 'A puffed-up pig's bladder. It's what Nancy Lucas called him.'

'Is it indeed?' Justin knew a devastating impulse to laugh. 'And what do you know of Nancy Lucas, pray?'

'Not much. I once sold her some cambric behind Jonas' back. I liked her.'

He stared at her for one last, priceless second and then gave way to boundless hilarity. Finally, still sobbing for breath, he said, 'Oh Abby! You don't need me. You'll never make a good Puritan if you live to be a thousand. You're like one of de la Roche's damned fireworks – perfectly safe until a spark gets in.'

'You make me sound dangerous,' she complained.

'I'm beginning to think you are. Will you come next week?'

A translucent glow lit her skin. 'Yes.'

'Good.' He rose and, reaching out a hand, pulled her to her feet. Then, growing suddenly serious, he said, 'I'd like you to promise to stay at home tomorrow and tell Sam to do the same. Will you?'

'If you wish. But why?'

'They're hanging Hannah Rhodes at noon,' he said bluntly. 'And I'd like to be sure that you won't be there to see it.'

Chapter Seventeen

The citizens of Banbury watched the hanging of Hannah Rhodes in sullen silence and the garrison, who had been prepared for trouble, cut the body down the same night and despatched it for hasty burial in an unmarked grave. Her belongings were cleared from the Castle and burnt and, before midnight, nothing was left of her existence except the damage she had wrought in the hearts of men and a single line, laboriously written in the parish register. *July 23rd Hannah Roads executed this day as a spy by the garrison.*

The beginning of August brought a heatwave and news that Scarborough, Pomfret and Carlisle had all surrendered to the Parliament, thus completing the isolation of Montrose. Faces in the garrison grew correspondingly grim but little was said and the work of tax-collecting and plundering convoys went on much as usual. Then Bath fell and Sherborne, and word came that the New Model was turning its feet towards Bristol.

'Will it fall, do you think?' asked Abigail of Justin.

'If Fairfax is left alone long enough to form a siege and maintain it, yes. Rupert's not a miracle worker and we took the place from Nat Fiennes with a lot less at our disposal than Fairfax has at his.'

'Won't the King send help?'

'I doubt it. He and his roving cavalry – the only army he has – are too busy pillaging Huntingdon. If that has any point to it other than as a rude gesture to Cromwell, I'd like to know what it is.' He paused, looking at her. 'I hear that Lilburne's in Newgate again for his attack on Speaker Lenthall.'

'Yes.' The expressive face clouded. 'And Sam is not only distributing tracts of it but also writing endless letters on Lilburne's behalf.'

'What sort of letters?' asked Justin sharply. 'Defence or agitation?'

'Both. He's in touch with someone called William Walwyn and he's frightening me to death.'

'Stupid young fool! I've more than half a mind to arrest him for his own protection. He'll be a damned sight safer with us than if the Presbyterians lay hands on him.'

'I know – but please don't. He'd never forgive me. It means a lot to him, you know.' In an attempt to change the subject, she pulled *Mercurius Britannicus* from her pocket. 'Have you seen this?'

Justin's eyes scanned the paragraph she pointed to. It was a simple advertisement asking for information about a wanted man named Charles. The man might be recognized, it said, by his slight stammer and an inability to speak the truth. Justin screwed it up in his fist and pitched it into the nearest bush, saying contemptuously, 'The Windmill Tavern strikes again.'

'What?'

'It's where the hottest sectaries hold their meetings. Men like Lilburne and Rainsborough, and Cromwell, if he were more open and less careful of appearances. There's a whole gaggle of them, mostly officers of the New Model and all Independent to the core. Their activities are giving the Presbyterians a headache and thereby doing the King a small favour.' He surveyed her with sardonic warning. 'It's where Sam will probably end up, one of these days.'

On the day Justin learned that Fairfax had opened his siege of Bristol, he met Bab Atkins for the first time in six weeks. His expression should have told her that it was a bad time for importunities but she was too pent up to notice it and plunged recklessly in with, 'You've been avoiding me. Why?'

'Avoiding you?' repeated Justin absently. 'No. I don't think so.'

'Yes, you have. It's been weeks!'

'Not as long as that, surely?'

'Longer!' His obvious indifference infuriated her and the blue eyes sparkled with determination. 'Why haven't I seen you?'

'I've been busy.'

'All the time?'

'Yes.' Faintly exasperated boredom began to creep into his face. 'I'm sorry if you've been disappointed, Bab, but I'm equally sure you haven't wanted for company. Half the young men in Banbury must be at your feet.'

She shrugged petulantly. 'Shopkeepers and country boobies? As if I cared for them! When can you meet me?'

'I can't.'

'But you must be off duty sometimes?' she protested, still unable to grasp the full extent of his coolness. 'Say when and I'll manage to give my aunt the slip somehow.'

His patience, always precarious, became stretched to the limit. 'You won't need to. We had a charming flirtation, my dear, but it's over. I've absolutely no intention of making an assignation with you.'

'What do you mean, it's over?' Her astonishment was so complete as to be comical. 'It can't be! You love me.'

'What on earth gave you that idea?'

'You did! You said I was the only ray of sunshine in this dismal town and far too pretty to waste on a clod-hopping tradesman.'

'Did I?' Justin grinned unrepentantly. 'But so are dozens of girls, you know. And I can't possibly fall in love with all of them. It isn't reasonable.'

'Oh!' Indignation flamed in her cheeks. 'But you were serious, I know you were! And I thought that, when the war is over, we'd be married.'

'You what?' The grin became a ripple of laughter. 'Then I fear you deluded yourself, sweetheart. I'm never serious and I've no intention of saddling myself with a wife, particularly one with your lively imagination.'

'You're hateful!' shouted Bab tearfully, heedless of who might be listening. Then, eyes narrowing in suspicion, 'Is there someone else?'

'In this benighted place? Don't be ridiculous.'

'Then why?'

His momentary amusement vanished and he regarded her with impersonal coldness. 'Because even if I wished for emotional entanglements – which I don't – I've the greatest dislike of being chased, catechized or smothered. And you, Mistress, do all three.'

At the exact moment when Royalist despondency was reaching its peak, came news that Montrose had done the impossible and won Scotland for the King. After a year which men were already calling the *Annus Mirabilis*, his little army had destroyed the Covenant forces at Kilsyth and taken Glasgow so that Scotland lay suddenly and unexpectedly at his mercy and, knowing it, the hitherto uncommitted or hostile lairds were flocking to present the Marquis with protestations of loyalty and support.

'It's the greatest achievement of the war, by God!' said Ned Frost jubilantly. 'If he marches south, it could change everything.'

'It could,' allowed Justin cautiously. 'But first let him hold what he has taken, and then we'll see.'

'Don't be such an old sour-guts. Just think what a general he must be to follow.'

'I am thinking of it,' came the quiet reply. 'And that's the only reason I'm not laughing my boots off at the idea that he might possibly save England.'

August gave way to September. Bristol remained under close and active siege, Montrose was rumoured already to have crossed the border and Captain Ambrose continued to encourage the seeds of insurrection in Jonas Radford's sister.

He told her about the cheerful bustle of London as it had been before the war, the crowded gaiety of Oxford since it had become the Royalist capital and discovered, without surprise, that she had never been further than Brackley. He told her about the King, whom he described as quiet, dignified and bewildered by this war but with a streak of obstinacy that would probably be his undoing; and the Queen, not pretty, her skin sallow and her teeth sticking out. He even spoke of Digby and the offence that had resulted in his transfer to Banbury.

'I merely said that I hoped his love-making showed a better

grasp of tactics than did his military advice, for the latter was unsubtle, ineffective and frequently catastrophic.'

Abigail stared. 'You're nothing if not direct, are you?'

'I only say what I think. And my sole regret is that, since I'm sure he'd have found an excuse for my removal anyway, I didn't say it to his face instead of letting that gossip Wilmot repeat it for me.' He cast an anxious glance at the sky. 'It is going to rain, you know.'

It was September 16th and all morning the air had been heavy and thundery. But when Jonas and Rachel departed as usual for Adderbury, Abigail had been too relieved to care what the weather would do. She said, 'It's all right. I'm perfectly well again now and I won't dissolve in a shower of rain.'

'Possibly not. But we've walked farther than usual and you haven't even brought a cloak.'

'Neither have you. It's too hot.' She searched her mind for a diversion and then found it. 'William Walwyn has got up a petition to free Lilburne. Did you know?'

'No.' The grey eyes surveyed her with amused understanding. 'But then I don't have access to privileged sources. Is Sam still —?'

His words were drowned by a deafening clap of thunder which reverberated through the sky directly over their heads.

'Hell!' He came swiftly to his feet as the first spots of rain pattered ponderously down. 'Come on, out of these bloody trees. We'll make straight for the Southam road. It's a longer way back and we'll probably be soaked but better that than be struck by lightning.'

'But your horse?' protested Abigail, already moving quickly at his side, her hand held firmly in his. 'Shouldn't we—'

'He'll bolt and make for his stable. Stop arguing and save your breath for running.'

By the time they reached the road, the thunder was an almost continuous roar and jagged flashes of lightning were tearing the sky. Then the heavens opened and the rain became a torrential downpour that drenched Abigail within minutes and turned the road into a sea of mud.

Pausing to let her get her breath, Justin said, 'Your mother is going to have a fit if you go home like this. You'd better come into the Castle till the rain stops.' His voice held an unexpected note of laughter. 'We can try drying you off a bit and it's nearer anyway.'

Abigail peered at him between descending snake-like coils of hair. 'I don't think I should.'

'Why not? You needn't worry about Jonas. He'll be lucky if he gets home at all today with the roads like this. Come on, before we start to sink in.'

The Castle precincts were almost deserted. Justin whisked Abigail upstairs virtually unnoticed and then, shutting his door behind them, said briskly, 'You'd better get rid of that wet gown and do something about drying your hair. Take a blanket to wrap round yourself and you can change in there.' He pointed to the inner door. 'It's full of all sorts of rubbish but I daresay you'll manage. I'll get a fire going.'

Shivering a little, she did as he suggested. The room was little more than a closet and contained, as well as the assorted debris he had mentioned, a narrow bed with its mattress folded double on the boards. Abigail removed her collar and cuffs and set about undoing the wet laces of her gown. When finally she emerged again, wrapped in her blanket and without either petticoats or shoes, Justin had not only lit a fire but was busy mulling wine.

'Come and sit on the rug,' he called, without turning round. 'I'll have this ready in a minute.'

Abigail hitched up the folds of her blanket and waddled towards him. Then he looked up, smiling, and she stopped, suddenly afflicted with paralysing shyness. He had discarded his coat and the long brown hair lay damply curling against the white shirt that was one of her own making. His skin was deeply tanned from the summer sun and the remarkable, light grey eyes were full of blithe unconscious charm. She found that it was strangely difficult to breathe.

'Madam?' He held out an imperious hand. 'Your robes, vastly elegant though they are, appear to be inconveniencing you somewhat. Pray allow me to assist.'

Her constraint ebbed and she gave him the tips of her

fingers, laughing a little at his foolery. Then she sat gracefully on the rug and spread the mantle of her hair around her to dry. Thick, curling and dark as night, it rippled over her shoulders and fell past her waist to the floor. It was beautiful hair and, unprepared for the sheer luxuriance of it, Justin allowed the wine to bubble and spit while he simply stared.

It looked, he thought, as if all the vitality of her growing had gone into it and, left loose, it changed her completely. Finally, he said lightly, 'My goodness! I had no idea that you were Godiva in brunette. It must take hours to dry.'

She smiled. 'Rachel says it's immodest. She's always telling me to cut it.'

'That would be a pity. There's nothing immodest about it and I imagine she's merely jealous.' He poured out the wine and handed her a cup. 'Be careful. It's hot.'

'Jealous?' echoed Abigail, startled. 'How could she possibly be jealous of me? She's a hundred times prettier than I am.'

'Is she?'

'You know she is, just as well as you know I'm perfectly plain.'

'I wish you wouldn't put words in my mouth,' complained Justin. 'Who told you that you were plain?'

Abigail regarded him patiently.

'No one told me. It's not the kind of thing people say to you. But the evidence is fairly conclusive. You, for example, had met me three times before you were able to recognize me.'

There was a moment's pause. Then he grinned and said, 'All right, you win. I'll allow that, under normal circumstances, you don't particularly catch the eye. But the man who could call you plain at this moment is either as cold-blooded as Jonas or uncommonly hard to please.'

The dark eyes looked back at him with childlike uncertainty. 'You're just being kind.'

Justin laughed. 'You ought to know me better than that. And I didn't say you were pretty, you're not. You'll never be pretty. But you could be beautiful. The only thing missing,' he finished calmly, 'is a smile.'

A tide of colour rose beneath her skin and it was a long time before she spoke. Finally, with her eyes downcast to avoid his gaze, she said, 'I'm sorry. I didn't mean you to . . . I didn't think you would say something like that. No one else ever has.'

'No. Well, I don't suppose anyone else has seen you wrapped in a blanket with your hair tumbling down your back,' he replied, amused. 'But if it will restore your equilibrium, I'm willing to add that I find your clothes appalling and can't understand a religious persuasion that hides and despises the things which God created to be beautiful.'

'Because beauty is a snare,' she explained, sadly. 'And it is. I shouldn't care how I look, and yet I've a positively wicked desire to see myself in cherry taffeta.'

Justin viewed her consideringly. Then, 'Apricot,' he announced simply, 'would be better.'

Lost for a reply, Abigail stared at him. And then a fist hammered on the outside of the door while an urgent voice called, 'Justin? Are you in there?'

Justin frowned but before he could speak, the door swung open to reveal Hugh Vaughan.

'Justin – oh!' The Welshman's gaze took in both Abigail's presence and her obvious state of undress. He stiffened and said coolly, 'I beg your pardon. I didn't mean to intrude.'

'Don't be a fool, Hugh.' Justin came easily to his feet. 'She got wet, that's all. What was it you wanted?'

'I just came to tell you that Bristol has fallen,' came the deliberately curt reply. 'I thought you'd like to know.'

Abigail watched Justin's face and waited for an expletive of some kind. Instead, he said expressionlessly, 'When?'

'Last Thursday. Fairfax made an assault and took the town. Rupert withdrew to the Castle and then surrendered – presumably to save his men. He got good terms and apparently got on remarkably well with Fairfax, with the result that people are saying there was collusion; that Rupert – being a mercenary and a foreign one at that – sold the place for a hefty fee.'

'Then damn them to perdition!' snapped Justin, white

with fury. 'Christ! Rupert's the only man in this entire bloody fiasco who's never even thought of lining his pockets.'

'Quite possibly,' agreed Hugh. 'But the King isn't behaving as if he believes that. He's revoked Rupert's commission.'

'He's done what? He's mad! Who the hell does he think can replace him? That toad Digby – whose hand, I am sure, is behind this damnable lie? The army would mutiny. And I,' he concluded harshly, 'would join it.'

'You're coming very close to talking treason,' said Hugh.

'Then let me come even closer.' Justin's chest was beating with anger. 'If, after all Rupert has done for him, this King allows George Digby to persuade him into abandoning the Prince without a hearing, he is not fit to spit on. And we have put this land through a blood-bath for nothing.'

Hugh's hand clenched on the door-latch.

'I think you would be advised to master your temper before you speak of this again,' he said frigidly. And with a slight bow to Abigail, he was gone.

For a long time Justin did not move. Then he turned slowly to look at Abigail out of strangely glittering eyes and said, 'I don't wish to seem rude, but I think it would be better if you left.'

'Of course.' She rose, confused and a little wistful. 'I – I'm sorry.'

'Why? You've done nothing.'

'I meant that I was sorry about Prince Rupert.' Without knowing why, she felt a desperate need to comfort him. 'But the King is his uncle, isn't he? So he's sure to at least let him explain.'

'You would think so. And yet . . . and yet I have known fathers who did less.'

Shocked, she took a step towards him, heedless this time of her blanket. 'Why do you see your father everywhere? He can't have hurt you that much.'

Justin gazed absently at one slender calf and the blue-veined delicacy of her bare foot. The primitive unreliability of temper which had prompted him to send her away now stirred again and channelled itself. His glance flicked back to her face and he said blandly, 'What an instructive day we're having. Shall we complete it?'

What have I said? thought Abigail. *This is how he was at the river.* She said, 'I only want to help.'

'Do you?' He closed the space between them to draw her smoothly and deliberately into his arms. 'Then you shall, sweetheart, you shall.'

His eyes were jewel bright and thoroughly alien. Abigail rammed her hands hard against his chest in a moment of sudden panic before his head blotted out the light and his mouth found hers. There was terror, delight and a solitary second of recognition in which these and every other feeling he had ever inspired in her became one and then the world dissolved into unimagined sweetness. His arms pressed her close against the length of his body while the fingers of one hand slid up the bare skin of her nape into her hair. His mouth solicited her response by invitation and by demand but with a tenderness that was purely instinctive. Abigail's hands crept involuntarily round his neck. It was her first kiss. She was lost.

Slowly, he released her mouth and raised his head to look at her. Then the world dropped back into place and, sick with shame, his hands fell away from her as if they were burning.

'Abby? I'm so sorry. I swear I never meant to – that I didn't bring you here for that.' And then, wearily, 'Oh hell! Why is it always you?'

She said nothing for she did not think she could trust her voice. Neither was she sure she knew what he was saying.

'My dear, I haven't frightened you, have I?'

Dumbly, she shook her head.

'Then why won't you speak to me?' He stood frowning helplessly but making no move to touch her. 'I give you my word that it will never happen again.'

Tears stung her eyes as, silently, she implored him not to say any more.

'Never again, I promise. It was just my accursed temper as usual.' He paused and then added, 'Don't look so tragic, Abby. It was only a kiss, after all.'

212

She swallowed and said huskily, 'Yes. I know.' *Only a kiss? Only? How can I have grown to love you so much without knowing?* 'It's all right. Don't worry. I understand.'

A faint smile bracketed his mouth.

'You're a terrible liar, my child, but I daresay you're right and it's best forgotten. That is what you want?'

'Yes.' She tried to pull herself together. 'I ought to get dressed. I shall be late.'

He glanced at the window. 'It's still raining.'

'It doesn't matter. And the thunder has stopped.'

Justin hesitated, baffled by her remoteness and half inclined to keep her with him until it faded. Then the decision was taken out of his hands as, for the second time, someone knocked energetically on the door.

'Hell and damnation!' He stormed across to it and jerked it open. 'Well?'

Ensign Harding quailed. 'You're wanted below, sir. There's reports of a rebel convoy near Chacombe.'

The grey eyes surveyed him unpleasantly for a moment and then Justin snapped, 'Very well. I'll be down in five minutes. Have my troop ready to go out.'

He was already closing the door when the ensign said nervously, 'Please, sir?'

Justin swung back to him. 'Damn it, what now?'

'It's Captain Tirwhitt, sir. He was to have gone with you only – only he isn't to be found.'

'Not again!' muttered Justin. Then, impatiently, 'Well use your brain, man. Get Captain Frost.' And, without waiting for a reply, he closed the door and turned back to Abigail. 'I'll have to go. Will you be all right?'

'Of course.' Her hand was on the latch of the inner door. 'I'll just dress and go home. Goodbye.' And she slipped swiftly into sanctuary.

Two minutes later she heard the outer door slam behind him, but still she sat on the bare boards of the bed and made no move to dress. What she felt for him was by no means new, she realized it now. But it would have been so much easier to have gone on in ignorance for the little time that was left. For the summer was over and in one week, or perhaps

213

two, the weather would make their Tuesdays impossible. Soon the war would end and he would leave Banbury behind him forever. It would have been easier not to know. Easier not to have to face the understandable but incredibly painful fact of his indifference or contemplate, uselessly, all the things that stood between them.

'It was never possible,' she told herself firmly. 'Even if I were beautiful, even if we were on the same side, no gentleman is going to fall in love with the sister of a shopkeeper. Be sensible. Use your brain. Go home and forget it ever happened. For it didn't, except in your mind.'

But it was too late and she knew that it was. Her world was inside out and she had no means of righting it. Wearily, she began to dress.

Chapter Eighteen

During the last week of September the Royalist cause dwindled closer and closer to a state of insanity. Devizes fell to Cromwell; Berkeley Castle surrendered to Fairfax and, when the King tried to relieve Chester, his northern cavalry were defeated at Rowton Heath. Worse still, the Parliament ordained a day of thanksgiving for a victory of which the King, as yet, knew nothing: the complete routing of the Marquis of Montrose at a place called Philiphaugh.

Aghast at the possibility of such a disaster, His Majesty turned to the ever-optimistic Digby and was not disappointed. Reassured, he allowed himself to be steered adroitly away from Worcester where Rupert's brother Maurice was Governor and headed instead for Newark, the place of safety which lay furthest from Oxford, Rupert and Rupert's angry grievances.

The last day of the month was one of light breezes and spasmodic sunshine. Abigail looked dismally through her window and wished for rain. It was Tuesday.

At a little after noon, Samuel went in search of her and eventually ran her to earth in the linen closet. He said, 'I've just seen Captain Ambrose.'

Her breath stopped. 'Oh?'

'And he sent you a message.'

'Did he?'

'He did. He said to tell you that he looked for the sweetbriar last week and couldn't find it but that he hopes to do better today.' He folded his arms and inspected her sardonically. 'What's going on between you two?'

'Nothing.' She busied herself again with the sheet she was mending. 'Nothing at all.'

Shrugging, he left her and she let the sheet fall back into her lap. The devil was at her elbow again, prompting her to set aside all her sterling resolutions and snatch one last, bitter-sweet hour with Justin while the chance was there. It had been hard enough to stay away last week but now she knew that he had been there and would be so again today, her good intentions crumbled into dust. She had thought she could be strong and cut him from her life only to find that all he need do was beckon. His friendship, because she knew he did not give it lightly, was too precious to be cast aside.

He was there before her, pacing restlessly to and fro across the grass. She watched him silently for a moment before saying lightly, 'Will you recognize the sweetbriar when you find it, Captain?' And then he swung round to face her and her bones melted.

He said abruptly, 'I've brought you here under false pretences. I can't stay. Christ knows why, but Lord Northampton had Will Tirwhitt discharged from duty this morning, and I'm needed. I'm sorry.'

Disappointment cut her like a knife but she tried not to show it. 'Another convoy?'

'No. An enemy patrol. They have a talent for appearing at inopportune moments.' He paused, smiling ruefully and then said, 'Why didn't you come last week? Was it because you were still angry with me or because you don't trust me any more?'

'Neither. It just seemed better not to come. I didn't mean to come today, either.'

'So why did you?' The grey eyes watched her intently.

'Because I couldn't just leave you here to wait.'

There was a space. Then, 'No. I suppose you couldn't. Anyone else, but not you.'

She tensed with sudden doubt but, before she could ask what he meant, he said, 'I have to go. Dare I ask you to come next week?'

The anxiety vanished from her face and her mouth widened into a smile of singular charm. 'You already have, haven't you? And, what's more, I've a distinct feeling that you'd be astounded if I said no.'

'In other words, you think me both egotistical and selfish.' He grinned, untethering his horse. 'And you're right, I admit it. Are you saying no?'

216

'Not this time,' she replied magnanimously. 'But only because I feel that you need an example of selflessness.'

On Saturday October 4th, the Castle's titular commander, Lord Northampton, arrived to hold a council of war and the garrison was swamped by a flood-tide of speculative excitement. It was well known that Sir William and his brother the Earl existed in a state of almost perpetual discord and the quarrel that followed the passing-over of Hugh Vaughan in favour of Charles Walrond had been vitriolic in the extreme. Now his Lordship had overruled Will again by dismissing Captain Tirwhitt, so it was small wonder that the officers gathered for the council in the expectation of seeing the fur fly.

For a while, it looked as if they were to be disappointed. The Earl was his usual calm, pedantic self and Will presented a façade of icy formality. The year's work since the great siege was reviewed in a series of detailed reports — monies raised by taxation, goods seized from passing rebel convoys, the present state of the Castle's defences and levels of powder and match in the arsenal. And then, when his Lordship had apportioned praise and criticism in equal measure, Lieutenant Blencoe was instructed to rise and receive his promotion.

It was when the new Captain had returned bashfully to his seat amidst the good-natured chaffing of his fellows that the Earl commanded instant attention by saying mildly, 'And now we come to the case of Captain Tirwhitt.'

Will Compton sat up a little straighter and Justin and Hugh exchanged glances.

'As I am sure you are all aware, Captain Tirwhitt was relieved of his duties last Tuesday on my orders and is now, as I understand it, no longer resident in the Castle.'

'No he isn't,' cut in Will, swiftly. 'He's in Oxford lodging an appeal against his dismissal, on my advice, I might add.'

Lord Northampton eyed his younger brother with chilly placidity.

'Then you might have spared yourself, and him, the trouble. My reasons for removing him from his post admit no possibility of redress.'

217

'And what exactly are your reasons?'

'Firstly, that the Captain has neglected his duty by frequent spells of absence and also allowed his company to fall under strength.'

Will's temper began to rise. He said, 'We all know that Tirwhitt is occasionally a touch unreliable but he's a good officer for all that. And if running a company of less than regulation numbers is a dismissible offence, you'd better sack every officer in the whole bloody army. So what else has he done?'

Angry colour touched his Lordship's cheeks but he kept his voice even.

'He has demeaned me both in word and deed and shown a constantly mutinous and seditious attitude.'

Will looked blank. 'How?'

'So plainly that I see no need to elaborate the point,' came the curt reply.

'Well, I do. He's under my command, after all.'

'No. He is under mine – as are you. And it is my decision that he be cashiered and his company immediately dispersed.'

'Damn it to hell!' Will rammed both hands against the table-edge and exploded to his feet. 'You can't! I won't permit it!'

There was an unpleasant little pause and then the Earl said blightingly, 'You forget yourself, sir. This is a council of war and if you cannot conduct yourself suitably, we will be better served by your absence.'

This time the silence was catastrophic. Walrond shifted slightly in his seat, Ned drew a long, soundless breath and Justin and Hugh stared fixedly at the bright Turkey rug which covered the table. The others remained in a state of glorious anticipation.

Finally, Will resumed his seat and, folding his arms, said sardonically, 'Very well, sir. By all means let us play this scene by the rules. I therefore suggest, with all due respect, of course, that the matter be postponed, for military regulations clearly state that no officer may be cashiered in his absence.'

'Checkmate!' thought Justin, looking up at last.

But Lord Northampton was not to be beaten. He said flatly, 'Normally, no. But the circumstances are unusual and I have no time to wait on Captain Tirwhitt's pleasure. It is, perhaps, a pity you sent him to Oxford. In any event, I intend to proceed today and will require all your signatures on the charge-sheet.'

'Well, you won't get mine!' snapped Will. 'It's iniquitous.'

'I see.' The Earl looked slowly around the table. 'Do we have any other objections, gentlemen, or may I count on your loyal support and recognition of duty?'

It was a subtle tug at the leash and every man there knew it. A ripple of acquiescence ran round the table as far as Hugh Vaughan; and after a moment's grim-faced hesitation, he complied with a brief nod and Ned Frost uneasily followed suit.

Justin removed his gaze from Will Compton's stormy face to the Earl's implacable one. Then, rising from his seat, he said clearly, 'I fear, my Lord, that you will have to excuse me. I can't subscribe to something that condemns a man unheard, and, if that constitutes disloyalty, I can only say that I find it regrettable.'

Lord Northampton considered him with growing distaste. 'Be very careful, Captain. If, as I suspect, that remark was intended as a criticism not only of me but also the King's dismissal of Prince Rupert, you may possibly find yourself treading the same path as Captain Tirwhitt.'

The grey eyes gleamed mockingly. 'For what, my Lord?'

The Earl discovered he had no answer and frowned.

'I think,' he said, frigidly, 'that you would be wise to remove yourself from this meeting.'

Justin saluted smartly.

'I think so too, my Lord.' And he went.

By the time the following Tuesday came round, Cromwell had taken Winchester and was marching on the Cavalier stronghold of Basing House with its large population of Royalist refugees.

'I wish to God,' said Justin grimly to Abigail, 'that some of the eternal optimism would give way to plain common-sense.

If Montrose still had an army, we'd have heard of it by now and no fortress in this land is impregnable. Yet everyone seems determined to believe that Montrose will sweep south in a blaze of glory and that Basing House is no more than a means of wasting Cromwell's time. It's crazy. We've achieved nothing all year so what hope do we have now His Majesty has embittered half the army with his treatment of Rupert?'

'Have you heard from the Prince?' asked Abigail, snatching at the flying edge of her cloak. It was a chilly day of grey, windy skies and, since it was too cold to sit down anywhere, Justin had taken her up before him on his horse and was cantering up Cherwell Edge.

'No. As far as I know he's still kicking his heels in Oxford.' He bent a satirical brow on her. 'And how is that other popular hero, Lilburne? I heard he's been let out again.'

'He has and he's already written a new pamphlet. It's to be called *England's Birthright.*'

'And you've already seen a copy.' It was not a question.

'Yes. It says the Merchant Adventurers are a vile, illegal monopoly and an offence against the free-born subject. I don't think Jonas is going to be impressed. He used to deal with them quite a lot before the war because they control the buying, selling and exporting of cloth in London.' She smiled wryly. 'His connection with them used to be his second greatest source of pride.'

Justin laughed. 'And what's the first?'

'His respectability. If something damaged that, I don't think he could be trusted to stay sane.'

They breasted the rise overlooking the small stone and thatch village of Chacombe and Justin reined in, suggesting that they walk a little. Abigail nodded and let him help her down, relief warring with regret at being released at last from the terrifying delight of his nearness.

For a while they walked on in silence and then, attempting to escape her thoughts, Abigail asked about Captain Tirwhitt.

Justin's face hardened. 'He went to Oxford to appeal and was cashiered in his absence. Will Compton's foaming at the mouth over it.'

220

'Oh.' Silence fell again until, finally, she said abruptly, 'When the war is over – what will you do?'

'Go abroad – to France or Germany, perhaps. Wherever the best prospects appear to be.'

The dark eyes grew bleak. 'It must be a strange life.'

'Strange?' He considered it. 'I suppose you would think so. It's certainly no life for the man who is fond of his hearthstone. But if you've a reasonable amount of ambition and no desire for the ties of permanent relationships, it's probably as good a life as any. At any rate, it suits me.' He grinned suddenly. 'But then, as you've observed for yourself, I'm selfish.'

She stopped and, turning away from him a little, gazed out over the scattering of cottages below her. 'You speak as if you never intend to marry.'

'I don't. Firstly because I regard marriage as a species of slow strangulation and secondly because mercenaries' wives inevitably fall into one of two categories; they weep and wail and cling or they seek consolation in some other fellow's bed, and I couldn't tolerate either.'

'I see.' There was a certain implied contradiction in his words but she did not trouble to point it out. 'You have a very low opinion of women, haven't you?'

'Of a good many of them, yes.' Irony deepened in his voice. 'I learned it early and it's saved me many a disappointment. You should understand that, at least, for your own expectations are pretty low, aren't they?'

Startled, she said, 'Yes. But that's different.'

'Is it?'

'You know it is. Girls have so few alternatives. My future will be decided by Jonas and it will either be that of a merchant's wife or a useful spinster aunt. Neither is a stunning prospect but I won't even be allowed to choose between them.'

The grey eyes rested on her with an air of mild discovery. 'And if you were free, what then?'

'I don't know.' She grimaced. 'The only thing I'm sure of is that I don't want to marry someone like Jonas.'

'Now there's an appalling thought,' commented Justin

flippantly. 'But you don't dislike the idea of marriage in itself?'

'No.' A hint of colour touched her cheeks. 'Not if it was with someone I loved and who loved me. But that's not very likely.'

Her wistful tone seared something inside him and he said bracingly, 'I don't see why not. You're young yet. You've plenty of time to meet the man you'll care for. As long as you don't choose a confirmed bachelor like myself, I imagine you'll make him a good wife.'

This was too close for comfort and she did not even attempt a reply. Instead, she said, 'I think we should go back. Jonas comes home earlier now the evenings are drawing in.'

He looked at her, watching the wind whip the tiny curls that edged her face. 'What have I said to send you into retreat? You surely don't think I was warning you off?'

'Warning me off what?' she asked blankly.

'Me,' came the laconic reply.

She drew a ragged breath. 'No. Were you?'

'Don't be silly.' He smiled with sudden, ridiculous charm. 'I think you're the only female I've ever met who had neither schemes nor artifice and who has never made demands of me. You've no idea how pleasant it is. Do you really want to go back?'

'Yes,' said Abigail, hollowly. And to herself, 'Preferably to a point before this conversation took place.'

The return ride was accomplished largely in silence and, seated once more in the circle of his arm, with her every nerve stretched and tingling, Abigail was glad of it. She had not known that physical attraction could be so strong and it alarmed her. Perhaps Jonas was right after all. Perhaps she was wanton.

Inconspicuous against the shadowed curve of the bridge, Bab Atkins watched their approach out of hard, blue eyes. He had lied to her then. He had told her there was no one else when all the time he had been seeing that plain, mealy-mouthed Abby Radford. It was the worst insult he could have offered. But she would teach him a lesson, him and that deceitful little cat he was hugging so close up there on his horse. Her fingers clenched tight on her cloak and, turning her back on the objects of her wrath, she walked swiftly away towards the town.

Justin, meanwhile, had reined in and lowered Abigail from the saddle. He looked down at her, moodily aware that the afternoon had signally failed to restore the natural balance between them as he had assumed it would. She was still faintly on edge and uncharacteristically remote and he had discovered that he could no longer see her as a child. For while he had successfully ignored the questing, sensitive mind, the compassionate warmth and the wise tolerance, he found that he could neither ignore nor quite forget her unchildlike response to his mouth. It was bloody annoying because there was absolutely no reason why, out of a thousand kisses, he should be inconvenienced by the memory of this one.

'What's wrong?' asked Abigail, puzzled by his expression. And then, when he did not answer, 'Captain Ambrose?'

'I thought,' he said irritably, 'that I'd asked you to call me Justin.'

'No.'

'No?' His brows soared. 'Why the devil not?'

'No, you haven't asked,' she explained placidly. 'And if you're going to speak to me in that tone of voice, I'm more likely to call you sir.'

His mouth relaxed. 'I beg your pardon. Please, dear Abby, will you do me the honour of using my given name?'

She grinned. 'I'll think about it. Is that all that was bothering you?'

'Not quite. I was wondering how old you are.'

'Twenty next April. Don't tell me, you thought I was a precocious thirteen.'

'Something like that,' he agreed absently. 'But don't let it trouble you. You'll be glad of it when you're thirty and still passing for twenty-one.'

'Will I?' she asked with sudden irony. 'What on earth for?'

She arrived home later than she had intended to find Jonas' cart already in the yard. She smoothed her hair as best she could, prayed that neither he nor Rachel was in the parlour and slipped quietly into the kitchen. Betty looked up from her cooking pots and surveyed her with round eyes but did not speak. Abigail crossed to the parlour door, listened for a moment and, hearing nothing, opened it and passed through. Then she came to an abrupt halt.

They were all there, waiting in utter silence. Alice sat in her usual corner, her eyes strained and anxious and her hands twisting nervously in her lap while Rachel faced her with an expression of smug anticipation from the other side of the hearth. Flushed with anger, his mouth set in a mulish line, Samuel leaned against the carved dresser. Jonas stood motionless before the mantelpiece dominating the room, his hands clasped behind him and his face white with suppressed fury. Abigail looked round at them all and felt her stomach cleave to her ribs.

'Where have you been?'

It was Jonas who spoke and his voice crackled in the charged atmosphere of the room. Abigail felt the chill of animal danger and began to shake.

'I went for a walk.'

'Where?'

'The other s-side of Bridge Bar.'

'And were you alone?'

'Yes. Of course.'

Slowly, Jonas crossed to stand in front of her.

'So you went for a walk alone. That's all?'

'Yes, Jonas.'

For a moment he continued to stare at her out of oddly gleaming eyes. Then he lifted his arm and struck her savagely across her mouth. 'You lying, brazen slut!' Alice and Samuel cried out in protest but he did not even glance at them. 'Do you think I don't know that you've spent the afternoon in the arms of your paramour?'

Abigail's head was ringing and the imprint of his hand lay stark against the pallor of her skin. She said shakily, 'I have no paramour.'

'Spare us your lies,' said Rachel acidly. 'It's too late for them. You were seen.'

'Seen?' whispered Abigail, warily.

'Yes, seen!' Jonas wrenched her cloak from her and dragged her into the centre of the room. Fragments of leaf clung to the hem of her gown and her hair was escaping from her cap. 'Seen by Barbara Atkins, riding shamelessly along the road in the embrace of your Cavalier lover. Are you going to deny it?'

She shivered and said the only thing that was not a lie.

'He is not my lover.'

Alice made a small, stifled sound and said, 'It's true then, that you've been meeting Captain Ambrose?'

Abigail's mind was still paralysed with shock. She swallowed and said painfully, 'Yes. It's true. I'm sorry.'

'You will be.' Jonas' fingers bit into her arm. 'You will be. How long has this lascivious relationship been going on?'

'It isn't lascivious. It's —'

'How long?' He shook her until her teeth rattled.

'Since July,' she gasped. 'But —'

'Four months?' he shouted, incredulously. 'You have been creeping off to lie with that God-cursed Malignant for four months?'

'No! It's true that I have been meeting him, but there has never been anything wrong between us.'

'Do you seriously expect us to believe that?' demanded Rachel.

'Let her speak,' snapped Samuel. 'Apart from the fact that Abby is not a liar, I shouldn't think the Captain would be stupid enough to seduce her.'

'What do you know of it?' sneered Jonas. 'He would do it out of malice. Not, I imagine, that it was made very difficult for him. It seems that our sister is a born harlot.'

'I'm not.' Abigail was shaking from head to foot. 'I know it was improper of me to meet him but it isn't as you think. I haven't – he has never —'

'Be silent! You soil this house with your presence and our ears with your lies. Were it not that your disgrace would fall upon the entire family, I would gladly see you whipped through the streets at the cart's tail. But, as it is, my duty is clearly to save our name and deal with you myself.'

'Jonas, please!' begged Alice. 'If she says she is untouched, may we not believe her?'

'Are you mad? She would say anything. And what other reason can you suggest to explain why a notorious libertine should waste his time on her? For the pleasure of her conversation? Or because she is a promiscuous little whore who was willing to give him anything he cared to take?' His voice trembled with rage. 'Look at her. She comes to us fresh from the arms of her lover, a man from whom decent people shrink, and she is not even repentant. She has shamed us all before God, and, for all we know, she may already be carrying that incestuous devil's bastard.'

There was a sudden, appalled silence. Then, with dragging reluctance, Alice said, 'Abby, you have to tell us. Is what Jonas says possible?'

Abigail's eyes widened with hurt. Then the numbness left her brain and her nerves were suddenly steady. She said, 'No. Justin Ambrose is a gentleman and my friend. I don't believe he has ever once thought of making love to me and the only sin I am guilty of is meeting him in secret.' She lifted her head with a hint of new, inflexible pride. 'But I had no choice in that, did I? And I don't regret it. He is a good man and I'm not ashamed of liking him.'

'You hear her?' choked Jonas. 'He is a foul-mouthed, lecherous drunkard, an enemy and a thief, but none of that matters to her. He has sullied her honour and —'

'He has not!' Abigail tore herself free and faced him, flushed with temper. 'He has done no more than talk to me, sometimes with laughter, sometimes in anger but never of love. In short, he's done something that you will never understand, Jonas. He has given me kindness and companionship, and he is a better man than you, for all your pious talk!'

A vein throbbed in Jonas' temple and he drew back his arm to hit her again but before he could do so, Samuel was beside him, grasping his wrist.

'That's enough, Jonas! Control yourself!'

It was the last straw. With a violent jerk of his elbow, Jonas sent Samuel crashing back into the dresser amidst a shower of falling pewter and horrified cries from Rachel and Alice.

'Stay out of this,' he warned, 'or it will be the worse for you. I'll have no wanton wickedness in this house and, since all else appears to have failed, I intend to beat it out of her.'

'Jonas, no!' It was Alice who spoke, her face haggard with misery. 'If you won't believe Abby, why not get old Mother Caudle to examine her?'

He stared lividly at her. 'And have the whole town know?'

'And end by being proved wrong?' added Abigail drily. 'Of course he won't call on Mother Caudle. He wants to believe me sinful, so he will. In some peculiar way of his own, he's enjoying this.'

This time the silence hovered on the brink of cataclysm. From his place by the dresser, Samuel looked across at his sister and recognized that, for the first time, she needed neither his defence nor his encouragement. She had grown up and she had strength of her own. He felt strangely sad and proud.

Finally, Jonas moved, his hand going out to close like a trap around Abigail's wrist. The force of his wrath impeded his breathing. He said, 'If you think to provoke me into disowning you so that you may cast yourself upon your vile, sottish lover, you are wasting your time. You are a base abomination in the eyes of the Lord but I shall not evade my duty in the battle to save your soul. One thing I can promise you: you will never see your dissolute Captain again. As soon as I am assured that you are not with child by him, I shall get you out of this house and into marriage with the first God-fearing man I can persuade to take you.' His grip altered and he pulled her to the door. 'Now come with me and learn repentance.'

Though what followed was both brutal and humiliating, Abigail endured it all in stubborn, hard-held silence. Even when she was left alone in her room, bruised, aching and sick, she did not cry. Her physical pain was nothing compared to the black demon of fear that was growing in her mind; fear of the one thing that she knew – and that Jonas knew – she could not bear.

'Please God,' she whispered desperately into her pillow. 'Please don't let him think of it, don't let him remember. For if he does, he will not hesitate and I would rather be in hell.'

227

Chapter Nineteen

Unaware of Abigail's troubles, Justin set out early on Wednesday for a tax-collecting mission in Northamptonshire, and when he returned at past nine in the evening, he found the Castle stables bursting with strange horses.

'Visitors?' he asked resignedly of Sergeant Cole.

'The Princes, Sir. Prince Maurice arrived this afternoon with twenty or so from Worcester and Prince Rupert's just come in from Oxford with another eighty.'

Justin's gaze quickened. 'Coincidence, Archie, or a rendezvous?'

'A rondyvoo, sir. They're dining in Sir William's quarters and Prince Rupert said you'd to go on up and join 'em as soon as you arrived.' The sergeant hesitated and then said, 'The men say they've volunteered to ride with His Highness to the King at Newark, sir.'

'Through eighty miles of enemy country? Bloody hell!'

'Yes, sir. So I was wondering if Sir William might be agreeable to some of us riding along with 'em, if he was to be asked, sir.'

'You did, did you?' Justin turned to move away and then, looking back, added, 'It's suicide, of course, you realize that?'

Sergeant Cole exhibited a gap-toothed grin. 'Yes, sir. Do you?'

For a man whose Royal guests had arrived without warning, Sir William had done remarkably well. The long table was spread with crisp white linen, meat steamed appetizingly on silver platters and canary wine glowed red through sparkling glass. Justin bowed to the Princes and, with a murmured word of apology, slid into the vacant seat beside Hugh Vaughan. The atmosphere was formal, even a little strained; and if the ride to Newark was fact and not fantasy, it was plain that everyone was taking a good deal of

228

care to avoid discussing it. As if reading his mind, Prince Maurice, a fairer, more stolid version of his brother, whose shy manner was often considered merely sullen, caught Justin's eye and winked.

But tongues became gradually loosened as the meal progressed and the evening began to show faint signs of conviviality until, that was, Major Walrond foolishly introduced George Goring's name into the conversation.

'The last I heard, he was raising fresh levies in the West,' he remarked. 'Has anything been heard of them?'

'No, and never will be!' snorted Maurice. 'The fellow's no more than a talking sponge.'

'Shut up,' growled Rupert, softly.

Maurice was hurt.

'Well, it's no more than you've said yourself,' he argued. 'You said he's forgotten all about the war and only sobers up long enough to pursue his feud with Richard Grenville. Yes, and you said that if steps weren't taken to protect the Prince of Wales, either Goring or Grenville was quite like to s—'

'Maurice, shut up!' snapped Rupert again, this time with force. He had learned, even if his brother had not, that this type of damning honesty did more harm than good; and Goring, incomprehensibly to Rupert, who had neither the time nor the inclination to look for good points beneath the unreliable exterior, was surprisingly popular.

Belatedly aware of his blunder, the Major attempted to repair matters. 'Perhaps Your Highness would favour us with your opinion of Lieutenant-General Cromwell? I believe you met him at Bristol, whereas we have had no opportunity to . . .'

Groaning inwardly as the inane words flowed inexorably on, Justin folded his arms and slumped in his chair. Then, chin on chest, he looked up the table at Will Compton and raised one satiric brow.

Rupert's mouth had set like a trap and he stared down his high-bridged nose at Charles Walrond for a long moment before saying icily, 'Cromwell is a good soldier of no particular genius but with an immense capacity for organization. By the time he's done, England will have a fine army, but woe betide any that get in his way for he'll not stomach them. And the fine army will be in the hands of a sanctimonious fanatic who's afraid to give credit to his enemies. I trust that answers your question?'

'Oh yes, sir, indeed!' enthused the Major. 'But what I was wondering was how he set about the . . . er . . . '

'Christ!' muttered Hugh. 'He's going to ask him how he lost Bristol.'

'How he set about the . . . '

'Charles.' Sir William spoke quietly. 'I'd be obliged if you'd make a check on the gate sentries. They've become a little slack lately.'

'Of course.' The Major was bewildered. 'Now?'

'If you please.' The dark eyes swept round the table. 'And I'm sure the rest of you all have matters requiring your attention, as do Their Highnesses and myself.' His officers rose amidst a scraping of chairs and Will smiled faintly. 'I bid you goodnight, gentlemen.'

It was a full hour before Rupert walked unannounced into Justin's quarters and said baldly, 'What a lousy bloody evening. I suppose you've heard?'

'That Your Highness is going to Newark? Yes.'

'That My Highness is going to Newark against the King's express orders,' corrected Rupert sardonically. 'I've promised myself I'll put a bullet through Digby. Want to come?'

'Please.' And then, wryly, 'I suppose it had to be Newark?'

'Since we no longer hold Carlisle, yes.' Rupert stood at the window, one long-fingered hand lying clenched hard against the stone. 'I had to give up Bristol, you know. There wasn't any choice. It was undermanned and you can't hold a town when the town's against you. But I'm a foreigner, and no matter what I do, I'll never be anything else, so I'm accused of treachery and taking bribes. Eighty thousand yellow boys, it's a joke! I haven't fifty pounds in the world.' He paused, broodingly.

'I'm disgraced, finished. It's ironic, isn't it? The only ones not busy spitting on my honour now are the bloody Roundheads!'

'That's not true, sir,' said Justin quietly. 'You've more friends than you realize.'

Rupert gave a short, mirthless laugh.

'They'd best beware then. Look at Will Legge, removed from his post as Governor and placed under arrest in case he throws in his lot with me and sells Oxford. It's a dangerous pastime these days being a friend of mine. For example, this little jaunt to Newark could be called mutiny. Any man with ambition and a mind to his career would do well to stay out of it.'

'Yes. I can see that.' Justin smothered a yawn. 'What time do we leave?'

'First light.' Some of the strained harshness evaporated. 'And I've Will Compton's leave to take any twenty that volunteer.'

Justin nodded. 'I'll see to it. And if we get there, what then?'

'I'll make the King give me a court-martial,' replied Rupert with grim simplicity. And then, differently, 'What do you mean – if? With Maurice, you, myself and a hundred and twenty volunteers, who's to stop us?'

'Fairfax – Cromwell – the New Model Army?'

'Bogeymen!' grinned the Prince, snapping dismissive fingers. 'Which reminds me, it's time you went home and faced up to yours, isn't it?'

'Perhaps.' Justin gazed absently into the fire. 'But sufficient unto the day is the evil thereof . . . so let's just say I'm going along for the ride.'

They set off into the grey October dawn expecting to meet with adventure and they were not disappointed. The first trouble came at Burghley where a pistol, aimed at point-blank range into Rupert's face, reinforced all the myths by refusing to go off. Rupert smiled grimly at its renegade owner and shot him dead.

By dint of night marches and his usual frenetic pace, Rupert kept his little force clear of serious resistance until they reached Belvoir Bridge. There, only twelve miles south of Newark, they ran into three hundred Roundhead cavalry, but they gave a good account of themselves and might even have emerged victorious had not reinforcements come up and made Rupert take evasive action. Sending the bulk of his troop along the main road to Belvoir Castle, he turned to Justin and said, 'There's a cross-country route, isn't there? I went that way shooting rabbits as a boy, but it's ten years ago and you'll know it better than me, since this is your country.'

There was a pause and then Justin said drily, 'It's ten years for me as well, sir, and more. But I'll do my best.'

The memories of childhood are strong and a mere decade is nothing to land which changes little in a century. So Justin led them faultlessly along narrow, winding lanes flanked by tangled thickets of hawthorn and let his mind follow other paths entirely.

They were no more than four miles as the crow flew from Trent House but he did not think of it as home. It had never been that since the day his gentle mother had eloped with the estate manager sooner than spend an unsuccessful lifetime attempting to match the inflexible perfection of her handsome lord. Justin had been seven then and had not understood. But the next five years of trying to please his superb, forbidding father had done much to teach him. Nothing, he discovered, was ever quite good enough; not his academic studies, not his horsemanship, nor even his table manners. Gradually had come the knowledge that, beneath the river of icy reserve, lay a rock of actual dislike that was rooted in the fact that beautiful, unworthy Catherine looked out of his own light grey eyes.

He had been almost thirteen when hope had finally been extinguished by the news that she was dead. Within three months, purgatory had become hell when his father brought Cordelia French home as his bride, Cordelia and the three children of her first marriage: sixteen-year-old Bernard, strong and a born bully; fourteen-year-old John with his clever, lacerating tongue; and twelve-year-old Jenny, dainty, golden and rotten as a poisoned peach.

Justin's fingers tightened involuntarily on his bridle. He still carried the scars of some of Bernard's pleasant little pastimes and John's derisive speculations on his paternity were enshrined in his mind like flies in amber. *You're nothing but a bastard, are you? And with your mother's fondness for bailiffs and grooms and the like – who's to know who begot you?* But it was Jenny – sweet-faced, smiling Jenny who had triumphed in the end and sent him into bitter exile.

'They're after us again,' said Rupert, breaking sharply into the unpleasant pattern of Justin's thoughts. 'Keep close formation, gentlemen, and be ready to turn when I do.'

Tired, dirty but safe, they arrived at Belvoir Castle in time for a belated dinner and were told that the King, still with no word from Montrose, had set off northwards to join him. Digby, of course, had gone too. A contemptuous smile lit Rupert's eyes. 'Heard I was coming and bolted, did he? Well it won't do him any good. I'd follow him to hell, let alone Scotland.'

The following morning, surprisingly, brought a letter from the King which Rupert crumpled carelessly in his hand while he asked after Digby.

'He's taking the northern horse into Scotland, Your Highness,' replied the messenger nervously. 'His Majesty has sent him to help my Lord Montrose, who, it now seems, is in full retreat and not marching south as we thought. The King himself is returning to Newark and Lord Digby is now Lieutenant-General of all the forces north of the Trent.'

The blaze of fury in the dark eyes prompted Justin to remove the King's envoy from earshot. Then he said quietly, 'You'd best read the letter, sir.'

Rupert told him, in the vernacular, what he could do with it.

'Quite. But that won't get you your court-martial, will it?'

'Neither will this,' growled the Prince, throwing the letter down on a table and striding off to the window. 'It will be an order to stay away. My uncle has a nice touch with a pen. You should have seen what he wrote to me immediately after Bristol, when he told me to "seek my subsistence somewhere beyond the seas" and sent me a pass signed by Digby. I still don't know why I bothered to read it. I swore, after the one he sent me before Marston Moor, that I'd never mind his letters again. But we won't talk of that. I fought and lost and nothing has gone right since.' He turned his head and fixed a sombre gaze on Justin. 'Do you remember the last time we entered Newark together back in '43?'

Justin nodded. The town had been closely beleaguered and Rupert had effected a brilliant relief. Then a chance meeting had revealed his own dark secret and the Prince had held it in trust for him ever since. 'Yes. I remember.'

There was a silence and then Rupert said abruptly, 'I told you to go home then and you didn't do it. This time you will. Ten years is too long to be hag-ridden. Once this court-martial is over – if, that is, I get it   you'll go back if I have to drag you there at pistol-point.'

After an unpleasant interlude in which he forced his way into the King's presence only to be totally ignored, Rupert was finally granted a court-martial to enquire into his surrender of Bristol. While it progressed through its two sittings, Justin lodged with the Princes in the house of Newark's Governor, Sir Richard Willys, and found that time hung heavily on his hands. He could quite easily have ridden out to Trent but he did not go. He was afraid, he suddenly realized, of how he might conduct himself.

The court found Rupert 'Not guilty of the least want of courage or fidelity' but did nothing to reconcile him to an uncle who could forgive neither his disobedience nor his rudeness. Vindicated, therefore, but not reinstated, Rupert relapsed into a bitter depression. Through the wet October evenings, his friends gathered before Richard Willys' roaring fire and began cautiously to examine the possibility of making Rupert their King.

Into this charged and potentially explosive atmosphere came two pieces of news. Basing House had fallen at last to the pillaging lust of Cromwell's soldiers and Digby had found a dramatic way to escape from Prince Rupert's bullets. He had lost the northern cavalry near Dumfries and fled to the Isle of Man.

Gripped by a sudden, inexplicable restlessness, Justin took his horse from the stables and rode out of town. He paid little heed to the direction he was taking and it was not until he halted for a mug of ale at a dingy wayside tavern that he realized that another mile would bring him into the village of Hawksworth and four would see him at the gates of his old home.

Something inside him shivered at the uncanny chance that had brought him this far and on this day. October 24th. His twenty-seventh birthday. Shrugging it aside, he rode resolutely on. There was nothing to fear, nothing to avoid and nothing to force him anywhere he chose not to go. He was master of his destiny and the notion that his journey today was pre-ordained was sheer nonsense.

It was mid-afternoon and fog was beginning to thicken the air. Tall, ornate and heavily wrought, the gates of Trent House loomed up with an unexpectedness that trapped the breath in his throat. He stretched out tentative fingers to touch the coat-of-arms embossed on the great lock and watched the gate swing back in silent invitation. Then, because there no longer seemed anything else to do, he nudged his horse forward and entered.

The drive was less neat than he remembered and the house – an ancient, moated manor – wore an air of faint dilapidation. Justin sat for a long time before he dismounted, then he tethered his horse, crossed the bridge over the murky water and passed under the gate-arch to the door. His hesitation was gone now and, without troubling to knock or ring, he lifted the latch and walked inside.

The vaulted hall smelled noticeably of fish and there was dust on the long, oak table: small things, but ones which spoke loudly of his father's passing. Justin curved his hand absently around a tarnished silver candlestick and heard a familiar, high-pitched voice say sharply, 'If you are a thief, sir, you have come to the wrong house. There is little enough here worth taking.'

He turned slowly and stared at her without speaking. The golden hair was untidy, the porcelain skin had grown florid and the daintiness had vanished beneath a good deal of extra flesh. She looked ten years older than she was and as vulgar as a pothouse bawd. Scowling at him over her shoulder was a youthful replica of everything she had once been.

His cold grey gaze remaining fixed on the child, Justin spoke at last. 'Well, well, Jenny, and is that the little bastard you tried to foist on me? Or have you several?'

Her eyes widened warily. 'Who are you?'

'Don't you know?' He smiled and walked deliberately into the light of a window. 'I'm surprised at you. A girl ought to remember the men she's ruined, if only in the spirit of self-preservation.'

The high colour fled, leaving her ghastly white.

'You!' she whispered, one hand creeping to her throat. And then, to the child, 'Find your uncle, Meg, quickly!'

Meg's scowl became more pronounced. 'Why? Who's that man?'

'Never you mind!' Jenny rounded on her. 'Just do as I say, and hurry up about it!'

Wisely, Meg turned and fled.

A malicious smile curled Justin's mouth.

'Frightened, Jenny? Now why, I wonder?'

She swallowed. 'Why have you come?'

'For revenge? To pass a dull Friday? To reacquaint myself with my birthright?' he offered lightly. 'It must have been a shock when father reinstated me.'

The gentian gaze flickered. 'You know, then?'

'Yes. I know. A little gull told me. And since I don't somehow see his late, unlamented lordship falling prey to sentimental melancholy, I can only assume that one or all of you must have been careless enough to offend him. Unless,' he added with deceptive negligence, 'he discovered the error of his ways?'

'I don't know why he did it,' came the pettish reply. 'He changed his will five years ago but the first any of us knew of it was about six months before he died when he had a terrible quarrel with Bernard over the money.'

'Oh? What about the money?'

'The fact that there wasn't any. The cunning old devil was busy making sure that the King got the lot.'

236

An arrested gleam lit Justin's eyes but when he spoke his voice was like the flick of a lash. 'I see. Well, no doubt he preferred pouring it down the drain to dropping it into the midden.'

Jenny gasped. Then she said, abruptly, 'You've changed.'

'So have you.'

He surveyed her mockingly. And then, just for an instant, the years rolled back and she was again the girl she had been in that fateful summer of 1635. He saw her with tears sparkling on her lashes and the golden hair falling in disarray over the torn bodice of her gown as, with halting, heart-rending innocence, she poured her tale of rape into his father's cold, receptive ear. He saw her leaning against the gate on the following day, laughing at him and sending him on his travels with the useless truth ringing through his head. 'I'm pregnant, you stupid creature, and I could hardly say I'd been lying with the gamekeeper, could I? Now, when they find out, they'll assume it's yours and no one will blame me because I was forced. Don't you think that's clever?'

He drew a long breath and said again, 'So have you. And if degeneration runs in the family, I can't wait to see the others. Where are they?'

Her colour came flooding back but she was still wary enough of him to mind what she said. 'Mother's in London with John. He's a secretary to the Committee of Both Kingdoms.'

'Is he? Well that should suit him to perfection,' replied Justin derisively. 'And Bernard, Sam Luke's master-spy?'

'How do you—' She stopped short, biting her tongue.

'How do I know?' Justin laughed harshly. 'My little gull was most informative. Her name was Hannah and Bernard sent her to kill me. Didn't you know?'

'Oh God,' breathed Jenny. 'No. He didn't tell me that. Was? She's dead?'

'And buried. Something else Bernard forgot to mention.'

'Perhaps he doesn't know.'

'Very unlikely. But if not, then I shall have the pleasure of enlightening him.' He paused, smiling coldly. 'He is here, isn't he? You told the gamekeeper's brat to fetch her uncle, and John, you say, is in London.'

'Yes, damn you, he's here. And he'll make minced meat out of you.'

Justin raised one ironic brow. 'He's welcome to try.'

'You're sure of yourself, aren't you?' She eyed him bitterly. 'Are you married?'

'No. Are you?' She did not reply and he said sweetly, 'What, all that passionate beauty gone to waste and no name for the little bastard? What a shame.'

'Damn you!' said Jenny again, her voice rising to an eldritch screech. 'What do you want?'

'A little entertainment. Can you blame me? And this is my house, sweetheart, or had you forgotten?'

She gave a hysterical laugh.

'That's what you think, my clever lordling!'

'What do you mean?' asked Justin quietly.

'You'll find out. Bernard will – oh, thank God!' She turned sharply away to the sound of approaching footsteps. 'And about time! I thought you were never coming. Look who's here! It's —'

'The bastard,' said Bernard French flatly. He paused in the doorway, massive and blond as a Viking, his gaze fixed unwinkingly on Justin. 'The Monster Captain of Banbury. Did you enjoy that, brother?'

'Not nearly as much as seeing your whore hang,' came the bland reply. 'Tell me, did she learn her technique in your bed or in someone else's? I've often wondered.'

The heavy, expressionless face darkened and Bernard advanced into the room. 'Why? Were you a disappointment to her?'

'Since I still live, I leave you to draw your own conclusions,' shrugged Justin. 'You will have guessed that she broke the glad tidings of my father's change of heart. I am here to find out what prompted it.'

There was a pause. 'I should have known,' said Bernard. 'I should have known that curiosity would bring you. Nothing we ever did hurt as much as the speed with which the old man believed ill of you, did it? And now you want to know if he died knowing you innocent or if he restored your inheritance merely because you'd become the lesser of two evils.'

'Exactly,' agreed Justin, coolly. 'And you know, don't you?'

'Yes, I know.' Bernard smiled. 'I'm reminded of the day that goldsmith fellow walked in with your mother's picture and told the baron that you'd sold it to him. Do you remember it, a pretty little thing set in gold and emeralds?'

'Yes,' said Justin quietly, seeing again the expensively-framed miniature that had been painted of his mother the year before her marriage. 'I remember it.'

'I thought you would. But what I remember is the look in your father's eye. For years he'd wanted a reason for disliking you, and suddenly there it was, being laid in his hand like a present. And he was so bloody glad he didn't ask a single question or allow you a word in your own defence.'

'And you found his attitude a godsend,' finished Justin. 'I know. Did you steal the painting or was it John?'

'John took it. I just bribed the tradesman. Didn't you find our choice ironic? Even if you hadn't been too damned honest for your own good, you'd never have sold that picture. It meant too much to you.'

'I find most things ironic,' replied Justin, folding his arms. 'Are you determined to reminisce at random, or can we come to the point?'

'The point, my cockerel, is this. I'm the only one who can tell you whether or not your father discovered the truth, and I don't intend to do it. You can go to your grave wondering.'

Nothing changed in the shuttered face but Justin's eyes were like flint. He said gently, 'How predictable you are. But the estate is still mine, you know. How do you plan to keep it?'

'Very simply. You're an active Royalist, a delinquent, and I've made sure that the Parliament is aware of it.'

'Ah.' A muscle twitched in the hard jaw and then was still. 'Of course. Sequestration.'

'Bright, isn't he?' Bernard directed a mocking smile at his sister. Then, looking back at Justin, 'As you say – sequestration. Every acre is under seal to the Parliament and assigned, in the meantime, to me.'

'Until I compound. I can, you know.'

'Of course. You can swear your oath to the Solemn League and Covenant and pay your fine. But the fine's been fixed at one third of the estate's pre-war value,' announced Bernard with slow satisfaction. 'A third. Have you any idea of how much land you'd have to sell to raise that?'

There was a long, inimical silence.

'If it put you back in the gutter,' replied Justin deliberately, 'I'd sell the last square inch. And you know it perfectly well.'

'You see?' Breaking her long silence, Jenny turned fretfully on her brother. 'He's going to compound. I told you he would. He'd be mad not to. And what will become of us then?'

'Nothing,' said Bernard, smiling. 'Nothing at all. You're a fool, Jenny. You don't imagine I'm going to let him leave here, do you?'

Justin did not move but the grey eyes flamed with sudden savage brilliance, as though the words were what he had been waiting for. He said softly, 'Do you think you can stop me? I'm not a child any more. Or are you expecting help?'

'Help?' Bernard gave a bark of contemptuous laughter, and pulled out his sword. 'The little bastard's become a braggart! I took a crop to you on one occasion, as I recall? Have you forgotten it? Or that I could break you with my hands? And I can do it still. But this time, this last time, I'll let you strut in your own pride and show me what you've learned. And then, for Hannah and the land and my own satisfaction, I'm going to kill you.'

Very slowly, Justin unfolded his arms and moved away from the wall. His gaze remained locked with his stepbrother's and for an instant their mutual and implacable hatred rose like molten lava trapped in a conduit of ice. In one fluid movement, Justin drew his sword and discarded his baldric. With a smile like splinters of glass, he said, 'If you talk much more, I'll die of pure boredom.' And launched his attack.

Yelping, Jenny dived for cover behind an ancient box-chair and only just in time for, a second later, her brother's sword sliced the air where she had been as he whipped up his guard. Steel sparked on steel and Bernard felt the jarring impact of the blow shudder through his arm. Then Justin disengaged, feinted and lunged in bafflingly quick succession and Bernard gave ground before him, furiously aware that the laces on his sleeve had been cut clean through.

It was the first surprise of many for Justin's swordplay was a fast and disconcerting blend of Continental styles. Furthermore, he wasted no time testing his opponent's skill but pressed an immediate, ruthless assault loaded with a hundred small tricks designed to shatter the other man's confidence. He scratched buttons and slit cloth whilst driving Bernard into hard-pressed retreat around the great oak table.

Booted feet rang on the stone floor. The swift, irregular chime of the swords echoed through the vaulted hall. With sweat already beading his brow, Bernard recognized that he could not stand this pace for long.

He tried a vicious sweeping pass and then another. His blade met nothing but the opposition of Justin's. The grey eyes were alight with silent mockery and the point of Justin's sword came to rest lightly against his throat before withdrawing again. He retreated more swiftly, pulling down stools and torchères into his wake. Justin came nimbly over them, his sword unwavering in his hand. His heart began to pound unpleasantly in his ears and, with crisp clarity, Justin spoke.

'Why did my father change his mind?'

The sweat prickled cold on his skin. He did not reply. The darting point snicked along his forearm.

'Why?' repeated Justin. 'Did he learn the truth?'

His breath was beginning to come in uneven gasps. He sucked in air and let it wheeze noisily out. 'Yes.'

The blades slithered into a disengage. 'All of it?'

He attempted a time-thrust and watched it go awry as his sword-hilt slipped in the wetness of his hand. He swore.

'All of it?' If Justin was tired, it did not show. His movements retained their neat economy and his breathing, though fast, was well controlled. 'About the painting and about Jenny?'

'Yes.' His arm ached from wrist to shoulder.

The hard mouth curled in something not quite a smile. 'When?'

'Years – ago,' same the laboured reply. 'In '41.'

Justin pushed him back towards the stairs. 'Who told him?'

'Don't know.' His lungs were a hot, searing agony and his defence a leaden travesty. He parried too late and felt Justin's blade puncture the cloth above his heart before withdrawing again. He gasped. 'He wouldn't say and I'm glad. You bloody bastard!'

Justin's teeth gleamed. He said, 'For years I've carried your scars on my back and on my mind. Now it's your turn.' And, breaking effortlessly through Bernard's guard, his point flashed delicately on and up through the skin and flesh of his stepbrother's cheek.

Bernard's sword fell clattering across the stone and he dropped to his knees, sobbing for breath, his hands clamped over the bleeding ruin of his face. Justin looked down on him and slowly lowered his own blade to the floor. His breathing was light and fast and his hands not quite steady as he replaced the plain, leather baldric and sheathed his stained sword. Then, walking unhurriedly to the door, he said coldly, 'See to him, Jenny. I want him to remember me.' And, with that, he was gone.

Outside, the fog had lifted a little. He untethered his horse but, making no move to mount, stood with his fingers clenched in the coarse mane and his brow resting on the saddle, sick, tired, lacking in purpose. Then, lifting his head, he collected the reins in one hand and began to walk.

It was quiet and the trees dripped dampness upon him. Every stone and path was achingly familiar, every blade of grass, every root. He had not known how much he loved the place or that the desire to hold it could burn through his bones like fire. For the first time in many years he experienced a sensation of intense loneliness, and it was then that he wanted Abby.

Abby. Her face rose up before him out of the mist, grave, trusting, gentle. If she were here, would she understand what he had just done? Or would she turn away, disgusted less by

242

his action than by the violent hatred that had prompted it? But no. A faint smile touched his mouth. She would not turn away and, though she might not understand, she would wrap him in the balm of her constant, undemanding affection. And he would no longer have to bear the emptiness of isolation.

It was the last thought that jerked his mind back into full awareness and caused the breath to catch in his throat for it brought the astounding and unpalatable truth in its wake. He had not lured her to defy her brother solely out of a desire to make mischief but because he had come, without suspecting it, to depend on her. She gave him the kind of peace and warmth that he had not known in twenty years and had not thought he needed. But she had shown him the myth of that and it now seemed that, from what had begun as no more than respect and a strong urge to protect, had grown a kind of caring that he could not understand.

He had never been in love and what he felt now was far from being any species of grand passion. There was no overwhelming desire to discover the sweetness of her body and make it his; no tormented longing to know that his hunger was hers also. But what did undeniably exist was a deep, subtle binding and the inexplicable conviction that saying goodbye to her was going to cost him some small but fundamental part of himself.

He rode back to Newark through the swiftly deepening dusk and arrived to find Rupert alone by the blazing fire.

'I threw 'em out,' the Prince volunteered simply, in response to Justin's enquiring glance. 'I got sick of hearing them babble about the amount of support I'd have if I chose to act the traitor so I told them to leave.'

'Even Prince Maurice?' asked Justin, aware of the strong bond between the brothers.

'Especially Maurice. He ought to know better, instead of which he's the worst of the lot.' Rupert grinned suddenly. 'But you can stay if you like and if you promise not to plague me with talk about crowns and thrones. Where have you been?'

'To Trent.'

'Ah.' The heavy lids were suddenly raised. 'Sit down and tell me about it.'

Justin sat and, in his habitually economic fashion, related the story of his day.

Then, when he had finished, the Prince said laconically, 'So. And will you compound?'

A satirical gleam lit the grey eyes. 'Will you let them try to make you King of England?'

Rupert groaned. 'No. But it's hardly the same thing, is it? Trent is yours and you have a perfect right to take it.'

'I know. And I want to take it,' admitted Justin wryly. 'But I don't think I can stomach their damned oath, not even tongue in cheek. I'm surprised at myself. I didn't think I was capable of falling victim to a principle. Do you think I'm going to end up a follower of Free-born John?'

'Christ knows where you'll end up,' replied Rupert, yawning hugely. 'Do you intend going back to Banbury?'

'Eventually, yes. Oddly enough, I've become quite fond of the place.'

Rupert rose and eyed him sardonically from a great height.

'I should have guessed. Is she pretty?'

'Not in the least,' retorted Justin, without thinking. 'She's beautiful.'

It was three days later that, through the open doorway of a mercer's shop, his eye was caught by the rich brilliance of apricot silk and, following a ridiculous impulse that he did not even try to deny, he walked in and bought it.

Chapter Twenty

Abigail leaned her brow against the small, leaded panes of her bedroom window and wondered how much more she could bear. It had been almost a month now, four weeks of imprisonment broken only by church on Sunday for appearance sake; twenty-nine days of being watched, harangued and prayed over; and a century of loneliness and stupid despair since Samuel had managed to tell her of Justin Ambrose's departure for Newark.

It was the fifth day of November and the street outside was remarkably busy but she looked down on it without curiosity. Animation was suspended in foreboding about the future, her future, which Jonas was busy arranging but of which he had so far said nothing.

The door opened and Samuel said softly, 'Abby? Are you all right?'

She turned and regarded him indifferently. 'Yes.'

'Then why don't you come down? It does no good to sit brooding on your own, you know.'

'No. But I prefer it.' She turned back to the window. 'You'd better go down or Jonas will think you're in league with me.'

He stared helplessly at her averted cheek. Then he said, 'I can't help this time, can I?'

'No.'

'And you blame me for it.'

'No.'

'Then why won't you talk to me?'

'Because there's no point. We both know I can't escape.'

'I didn't mean that. Tell me what it is you're so afraid of.'

Her hands clenched in her lap. 'Marriage.'

'In general?' He frowned. 'But that's silly. You always knew Jonas would arrange a match for you sometime and you never minded before, except when it was Thankful Barnes, of course. And that was different.' He paused and then said slowly, 'Is that it? You think Jonas may —'

'Don't!' She rose, wheeling swiftly to face him. 'Don't say it!'

He drew a long breath.

'All right. But you're worrying about nothing. After being turned down last March, I shouldn't think he'd have you.'

'On the contrary. He's the one man who would.' The dark eyes were haunted. 'Think about it.'

The noise from the street suddenly changed to an ominous rumble of voices, overlaid by the clattering of horses' hooves. Samuel dived to the window and opened it, admitting a blast of icy air. 'Come and look.' He pulled Abigail down beside him on the window seat. 'It's the King.'

'What?' She stiffened and leaned perilously out to see. 'But he was at Newark.'

'I know. That's what I came up to tell you. He and his party rode into the Castle a couple of hours ago. He must be going back to Oxford. Look!' He pointed. 'That must be him . . . the one in grey.'

Abigail's eyes swept over the cavalcade of elegantly accoutred gentlemen, searching in vain for one dear face before coming to rest on the neat, miniature person of Charles Stuart. And then disappointment faded into something sharp and unexpected as she watched him ride through the hostile, muttering crowd. He sat very straight in the saddle, looking neither to the right nor left, his face seemingly expressionless. Yet the remoteness of his dignity was somehow so piercingly forlorn that it produced the second most shattering impulse of Abigail's life.

'God protect Your Majesty!' she called, with sweet, disastrous clarity.

Samuel jumped, choked and hauled her inside – but not before she had glimpsed the startled warmth of the swiftly upraised face.

'You're mad!' hissed Samuel, shutting the window. 'Absolutely mad!'

'Perhaps.' She eyed him with a sort of confused defiance.

'But he looked so sad that I just wanted him to know that everyone doesn't hate him.'

'Is that all?' He ran distracted hands through his hair. 'Well, either the anniversary of Guy Fawkes has gone to your head or Justin Ambrose has a lot to answer for.'

Her head drooped defeatedly. 'He wasn't there.'

'Of course not. If he's back at all, he'll be in the Castle.' He paused grimly. 'I do hope he's back. I've a number of things I'll enjoy saying to him.'

'No!' Abigail's voice was sharp edged. 'I don't want him told, Sam. It isn't his fault —'

'No? Whose, then?'

'Mine.' She looked down at her hands. 'He can't help any more than you can, and I won't have him blamed and made to feel responsible. He's quite likely to lose his temper and do something stupid.'

'Oh fine! By all means let's preserve his peace of mind and save him from himself. It doesn't matter who else suffers the consequences of his selfishness, does it?'

'No. It doesn't.'

The firm simplicity of her reply stunned Samuel into silence and for a long time he stared at her as if he had never seen her before. Finally, he said slowly, 'You love him.'

'Yes.' Her gaze was level. 'But it changes nothing.'

'That rather depends, doesn't it?'

'On what?'

'On whether he loves you.'

'He doesn't. But he – I think he's fond of me – in a quite different way. And if he knew about all this, he'd worry.'

'Good.'

'It isn't good!' Suddenly she was angry. 'I met him because I wanted to, because it gave me pleasure. And, since I don't regret it, why should I be made to? As for the way I feel about him, that's my business. Not yours, not even his. All I will say is that you can't possibly disapprove of it more than Justin would if he were told and that, if for no other reason, is why you will leave him out of it.'

Five days later, the long fuse of uncertainty finally exploded into realization of all her worst fears when Jonas coldly announced that she was to be married on the second Sunday of December.

Abigail faced him, as she had done through all her weary waiting, with an air of ironic detachment.

'And who,' she asked, 'is the fortunate groom?'

'Hold your tongue!' he snapped. 'It's Thankful Barnes, and I want no hysteria about it this time.'

'You'll get none.' Her skin had lost every vestige of colour. 'I wouldn't give you the satisfaction.'

'And what possible satisfaction do you think I found in having to explain that you've been giving yourself to an accursed Malignant?'

'Since you had no need to say any such thing – a good deal, I imagine. I only hope he had the wit to strike a hard bargain. Did he?'

His face darkened with anger. 'That is not your affair.'

'No?' She smiled sardonically. 'Well, whatever you're paying, I'm sure it's worth it. Just think, if it weren't for Mr Barnes, you'd have had to hunt around for a beggar or a simpleton or a hunchback. And that could have taken months.'

There was a long silence. Then, in a voice that shook, he said flatly, 'The only man low enough to deserve you is the one who has soiled you in body and mind – and him you will never have. Thankful Barnes is too good for you and, when he comes here tomorrow, try remembering how few men would knowingly take a whore to wife.'

Fear plucked at Abigail's spine. 'He's coming here?'

'Yes. For some mystifying reason, he wishes to talk to you. So keep a dutiful tongue in your head and be grateful.'

Thankful Barnes towered over Alice, smiling blandly and twisting his hat in his hands. 'I've already spoken to Mr Jonas, ma'am. And he says I can have a few minutes alone with Mistress Abigail.'

Alice glanced dubiously at Abby, pale and silent in her corner, and then looked back at the smith. She did not particularly like the man but neither did she understand her daughter's aversion. He seemed harmless enough.

'Under the circumstances,' he added, with gentle significance.

Alice flushed and struggled in a morass of half sentences.

'It's all right, mother,' said Abigail colourlessly. 'If Jonas has given his sanction, you'd better go.'

After a little hesitation, Alice went out leaving the door slightly ajar behind her. The smith walked over and shut it with a little snap. Then he turned back to Abigail without any trace of the blandness that had deceived Alice and said, 'Your brother says you've disgraced yourself with one of them drunken lechers from the Castle.'

'Yes,' replied Abigail, employing her only small hope. 'Does your mother know?'

He ignored the question and said sorrowfully, 'You didn't ought to have done that, Abigail. That was wicked. You ought to have wed me when I asked you. Now you've spoiled everything.'

'Then perhaps you should think again and withdraw your offer.' She recognized the look in those pale eyes now. She had seen the cat look that way when it cornered a mouse. 'I'm sure your mother would prefer it.'

'And you're spoiled too,' he continued, just as if she had not spoken. 'You're not so timid any more, are you? Almost brazen, you are. Too much to say for yourself and nowhere near as humble as you should be. I don't even think you're grateful.'

'I'm not. You must know I'm being forced to marry you. I wouldn't do it from choice.'

The strange gaze altered and drifted unhurriedly over her body. Then he said, 'I'm being kind, Abigail. I'm saving you from the shame of your sin. You'll have to learn to be grateful for that, you really will. Mother doesn't like it, of course. But she'll come round. And between us we'll save you from damnation and teach you your duty.'

The crawling fear that she had been fighting to deny since he had first arrived blazed into new life and she rose from her stool saying quickly, 'Why are you doing this? Why me?'

'You're afraid of me.'

For a moment she thought it a mere statement of fact. Then, sickeningly, she realized that it was an answer. 'And that pleases you?'

He smiled obliquely. 'I like small, helpless things. You are afraid, aren't you? You're trying to hide it from me but you mustn't do that. I don't like it.'

Abigail shivered. 'You're insane.'

He was beside her in two strides, his eyes suddenly opaque and one hand grasping hers so that her thumb was twisted painfully across her palm. 'Don't say that. Don't ever say that.'

The pressure of his grip was still increasing and she gasped. 'No. I'm sorry. Please! You're hurting me.'

He looked down at her hand and then slowly released it.

'You've so much to learn,' he said fretfully. 'And there's so much harm to be undone. But it will all come right once I get you away to Bodicote and if your lover comes sniffing round you there, I'll break his neck.'

'He won't come,' she said unevenly. 'That's all over now.'

'And you've forgotten him?' One great hand came to rest against her neck. 'I hope you've forgotten him, Abigail. It wouldn't please me if I thought you hadn't. And it's better if you try to please me, much, much better. You are going to try, aren't you?'

His other hand was searching out the curves of her waist. Abigail felt the stirrings of nausea and tried to free herself.

'I don't know what you mean.'

'Don't you?' His fingers stretched, then clamped themselves about her neck and the pale gaze grew strangely mesmeric. He whispered, 'Shall I tell you?'

Frozen in the black, swirling waters of her fear and revulsion, Abigail was beyond speech or movement or even constructive thought. She could only hear the coarse, ugly whisperings of things that she scarcely understood but recognized, dimly, as unnatural; she saw the heavy, glistening face that had begun to waver oddly before her eyes and she felt the hard, intrusive hand that pinched and squeezed and groped its way about her body until she could stand it no longer and began to retch.

A tremor passed through Barnes' muscular frame and his fingers closed convulsively on her thigh. Then, with slow reluctance, he released her and Abigail, her hands pressed over her mouth, fled unsteadily into the kitchen.

She was still there, heaving helplessly over the sink, when Samuel came in. For a moment he stopped short, staring then he crossed the floor to take her shoulders in a firm grasp.

'Abby? What is it? You look terrible.'

She drew a long, shuddering breath. 'Has he gone?'

'Barnes? Yes.' He stiffened. 'Why? What did he do to you?'

'Nothing. I can't talk about it.'

'Don't be stupid. If he's responsible for this, you've got to.'

'I can't!' She broke away from him to sit huddled in a corner of the settle. Her face was ashen and the dark eyes were full of lingering horror. 'And if I did, you wouldn't believe me.'

'We'll see about that.' He sat purposefully at her side. 'Did he touch you?'

'Yes.' She laced her fingers tightly together. 'But that wasn't as bad as – as the things he said.'

'What things?' And then, when she did not answer, 'Accusations? Threats? Look, if you don't want to repeat what he said, at least give me some idea of what it was about.'

'Lessons,' said Abigail, tonelessly. 'Lessons I must learn in order to please him. He likes fear and humility, you see, and he has his own ways of getting them. He explained them to me.'

Comprehension dawned slowly and brought disgust in its wake. 'He's mad, of course?'

'Quite mad. And dangerous because he half suspects it.'

'Then you can't possibly marry him. Jonas will have to . . . or no. That's pointless. He'd never believe that the man could be a lunatic, let alone a mass of perversions. It'll have to be Justin Ambrose.'

His sister's head jerked up. 'No. I won't have it.'

'You haven't any choice. He's the only one in a position to do anything.'

'I don't care.' Her mouth quivered. 'Barnes threatened to break his neck.'

'So?' Samuel lifted one irritable brow. 'The Captain's not exactly frail, is he? I think you can trust him to take care of himself. He's had plenty of practice, after all.'

There was silence and then Abigail finally put into words the only real difference that had ever divided them. 'You don't like him.'

Samuel sighed. 'Actually, I do. But I'll never agree with him politically and, more importantly, I disapprove very strongly of the changes he's brought about in you. You're neither fish nor fowl any more and he's to blame for it.' He came to his feet and looked sombrely down at her. 'But that's beside the point now. If he can help, I'll be grateful. I only hope he's back and not still careering about the country with the Wizard Prince.'

On the following day, Samuel paid what was to be the first of many visits to the Castle and came back depressed. No, said Ned Frost, Justin was not back; no, he had not been in touch; and no, they hadn't the faintest idea of his present whereabouts.

'He may still be with the Prince,' came the unhelpful conclusion, 'or he may have stayed on in Newark.'

Samuel frowned. 'Why would he do that?'

'Oh, personal matters,' said Ned, airily evasive. 'You know.'

Samuel did not know. Nor did he know quite what he was going to do about Abby if the Captain did not reappear in time.

As November slid by bringing the first flurries of snow and no sign of the errant Cavalier, while Abby grew thinner with every passing day, the weight of his anxiety began pressing down on him like a medieval torture.

December arrived and Captain Ambrose did not. The wintry sky was heavy with the threat of impassable roads. For the first time, Samuel began to understand the meaning of panic. Then, on the fourth day of the month, just as the snow started to fall in earnest, he met his quarry face to face in Parson's Lane.

It was so completely unexpected that the shock of it stopped his breath. Then he said furiously, 'And where the hell have you been till now?'

'Woodstock.' One dark brow rose in amused surprise. 'I got back last night and Ned said that you wanted to see me. But I must confess that I hadn't expected it to be urgent enough to make you swear.'

'Don't be flippant!' snapped Samuel. 'It's urgent enough to make me do more than swear. Where can we talk?'

Justin grinned mischievously and gestured to the Reindeer tavern. 'In there?' And was amazed when Samuel merely nodded and limped ahead of him through the gates.

It was market day and too early for custom. The elegant Globe Room where Justin had met Rupert the previous spring was deserted and, stalking into it without a glance for its splendour, Samuel declined Justin's offer of refreshment and came immediately to the point. 'Jonas knows about you and Abby. And naturally he's convinced that you're lovers.'

'Naturally?'

'Well, of course. With your reputation and his little mind, what else would you expect? He regards Abby as a whore and a blot on his respectability. And if that comes as a surprise to you, I can only assume it's because you've been too busy to consider the matter.'

'Don't mince words, Sam.' Eyes and voice were totally enigmatic. 'Say what you mean.'

'All right, I will. You're selfish and arrogant and uncaring. And you've probably never once stopped to wonder what Abby would go through if Jonas found out about your little meetings!'

'And what, precisely, is she going through?'

'Torment. She's not been out of the house for eight weeks except to go to church. Rachel makes clever little remarks and watches her like a hawk. Jonas prays over her with a look in his eye that suggests he'd prefer to do as he did the first day and resort to violence.'

For a moment there was silence. Then, his face suddenly not expressionless at all, Justin said softly, 'Are you saying

253

that he had the temerity to touch her?'

'Touch her?' Samuel laughed harshly. 'He took his belt to her. And where does temerity enter into it? He has an absolute right to do as he likes with her and he's using it. She's contracted to marry Thankful Barnes in ten days' time.'

A knife twisted in Justin's stomach and he turned abruptly away to the ornately carved fireplace. Beside him stood the great globe which gave the room its name. He spun it, watching the world whizzing past beneath his fingers and was distantly surprised at how sick and angry he felt.

'Did you hear what I said?' demanded Samuel.

'Yes. I heard.'

'But you're not terribly interested. I see.' Samuel stared explosively at the broad, buff-covered shoulders. 'The man is a lunatic and perverted and you couldn't care less.'

One badly scarred palm came down hard and flat on the smooth surface of the globe. 'What did you say?'

'Why? It doesn't concern you, does it?'

Justin swept round, white with anger.

'Stop trying to be clever. How the devil can you know about Barnes' personal habits?'

'I don't but Abby does. He apparently described them to her in glorious detail. I don't know exactly what he said. I do know it made her physically sick.' Samuel paused and then added bitterly, 'That was a month ago. Since then she's hardly slept or eaten and I'm at my wits' end. You, of course, weren't here.'

'All right.' Justin drew a long, painful breath. 'Let's take the arraignment as read, shall we? You think it's all my fault and I agree with you. Now what do you want me to do?'

'Help her. How is up to you. Just do something to prevent this farce of a marriage. You owe her that much at least.'

The grey eyes kindled dangerously.

'What kind of bastard do you take me for, damn it? This isn't a question of trade and, if you think I need to be bludgeoned into getting Abby out of this mess, you must be as blind as your bloody brother! Of course I'll help. And I give you my word that she'll never marry Barnes. Satisfied?'

'Yes.' Samuel coloured a little. 'I'm sorry. What will you do?'

'I haven't the remotest idea – yet. When did you say the wedding is fixed for?'

'Sunday the fourteenth.'

Justin nodded coolly. 'Very well. I'll deal with it. All you need do is stop her worrying and get her to eat properly.'

Feeling as though an immense burden had been lifted from his shoulders, Samuel nodded. 'I'll try. And – thank you.'

'Don't mention it. Just one more thing. I assume that someone told Jonas about Abby's friendship with me. Do you know who it was?'

'Yes. It was Barbara Atkins though I can't for the life of me see why she'd be so spiteful.'

A slow, disquieting smile touched the hard mouth.

'I can,' said Justin gently. 'And I'll remember it.'

Chapter Twenty-One

In the long hours of a sleepless night, Justin examined the problem of Abigail's future from every conceivable angle and discovered how restricted were his options. Any sort of appeal to Jonas was plainly useless, even supposing he could control his own temper long enough to make it, and would probably only succeed in making the situation worse. Barnes was an easier target. It should, for example, prove a relatively simple matter to have him arrested on some pretext or other, but the man could not be locked up indefinitely without good cause and a temporary solution was no solution at all.

Coolly, he reviewed the various ways in which Barnes might be persuaded to change his mind and then rejected them. With a sane man certain subterfuges might be made to work but with Barnes nothing could be relied on. In any case, such ploys were tortuous and time consuming. The only permanent answer would be to contrive the fellow's death and even that was not foolproof since Jonas Radford was quite capable of choosing an equally unsuitable substitute.

Justin walked to the window and gazed, without appreciation, at the gleaming, magical whiteness outside. It was still snowing steadily. Even if he had money or knew of some trustworthy household in Oxford to which he could send her, it was already too late. By tomorrow the roads would be impassable and it might not thaw for weeks.

'Damn it to hell!' thought Justin, prowling restlessly back to his stool by the fire. 'There has to be a way. I won't leave her to be broken on the wheel of Jonas' fanaticism.'

There was, he realized, more than a measure of guilt in his feelings but that worried him less than the other forces that were driving him: a compulsion to protect, which, though by no means new, was suddenly intensified; an illogically crude desire to beat Jonas into pulp; and the discovery that the mere thought of Abby being frightened or hurt was unbearable to him. None of it accorded with what he had thought of as his mild, undemanding affection for her and the knowledge was profoundly disturbing. Strong emotions had no place in his life. He could not afford them, neither did he want them. Yet here he was, utterly committed to God knew what folly for the sake of a girl he had not even bedded.

'I ought to be put away,' he sighed, running light, rhythmic fingers over one of Rex's long ears. 'And if I end up having to put a bullet through Thankful Barnes, I probably will be.'

It snowed almost continuously for two days and then it froze. By the following Wednesday, inactivity was beginning to make the men fractious and so Justin duly organized snow-shifting details to clear the Market Place whilst simultaneously working off some of his own frustrations. Then Hugh Vaughan bore him off to the Reindeer for a noonday quart of spiced ale and he was granted a far more satisfying means of appeasing his temper.

From the window of the cake shop, Bab Atkins watched them enter the tavern and made a quick, bold decision. She was wearing her velvet cloak with the fur-trimmed hood over a new sapphire-coloured gown and she knew she was looking her best. So she smiled brightly at her friend Mary and, over-riding the girl's horrified protests, swept her across the road and into the forbidden precincts of the inn.

Justin watched her trip blithely into the room and was filled with pleasant anticipation.

'Oh!' Bab gave a start of well-feigned surprise. 'I hadn't expected to see you here, Captain Ambrose. We thought this room was empty, didn't we, Mary?'

Mary turned scarlet and muttered something indistinguishable.

Justin strolled towards them, smiling blandly.

'Then this must be my lucky day,' he drawled, 'because you are the very girl I most wished to see.'

She eyed him speculatively from beneath her lashes. 'You do surprise me.'

'I'm sure I do,' he agreed cordially. 'You look extremely

charming today. A new gown, surely?'

'Yes. Do you like it?'

'It's perfect.' The grey eyes gleamed with sudden, icy contempt and, raising his arm, Justin emptied the contents of his ale cup liberally over her head.

Bab choked, Mary screamed and Hugh Vaughan shot towards them with an astounded, 'Bloody hell!'

'Keep out of it, Hugh,' warned Justin coldly. And then, to Bab who was spitting with rage amidst dripping hair and stickily stained velvet, 'That was for telling nasty tales to Jonas Radford. You should have taken your spite out on me instead.'

'I hope Thankful Barnes kills her!' howled Bab. 'Look at my fur, you've ruined it!'

'Be grateful for small mercies,' he replied. And walked out of the room and away into the snow.

He had nearly reached Cornhill when Captain Vaughan caught up with him and said, 'What the devil was all that about?'

'Don't ask. It's a long story.'

Hugh surveyed him thoughtfully, a gleam of humour appearing in his face. 'What an eventful life you lead. I sometimes wonder if I'm not missing something.'

Justin grinned wryly. 'Take my word that you're not. And I can assure you that I don't collect complications from choice.'

'In that case Nemesis must have a grudge against you.'

The grin became a laugh.

'Naturally. She's a woman, isn't she?'

They returned to the Market Place where Justin's sergeant was busy organizing a change of shifts. Then, just as Hugh was suggesting that he take over the task of supervision, Justin looked up to see a broad, familiar figure approaching them.

'Well, well,' he murmured softly. 'You chose the right day, Hugh. I think we're in for another dramatic interlude.'

'With that blacksmith fellow? I must say, you've some very peculiar friends. Not that he looks very friendly, does he?'

'No,' came the suspiciously mellow reply. 'He doesn't.'

Thankful Barnes circumnavigated the piles of banked-up snow and planted himself firmly in front of Justin. He said, 'I've come to give you warning. Stay away from Bodicote.'

Justin folded his arms and smiled provocatively.

'Now why should I do that? The district is just beginning to appeal to me.'

'Thou shalt not covet!' declaimed the smith, fiercely.

'Covet what? Thy neighbour's wife? But you are not my neighbour, Mr Barnes, nor do you have a wife. Yet.' The smile grew. 'And who knows what tomorrow may bring? Life, you must know, is full of uncertainties.'

'Not mine. On Sunday I wed A—'

'Pray lower your voice, Mr Barnes, and try to remember that a gentleman doesn't bandy a lady's name in public. As you see, we have an audience.'

They had indeed for Barnes' threatening stance and rumbling tones had caught the interest of the newly-dismissed working-party and they stood around in expectant groups, waiting.

'So,' mused Justin smoothly. 'You are to be married on Sunday. I congratulate you. Your bride is entirely charming, a pearl beyond price. What is it the Scriptures say? Ah yes, "Who can find a virtuous woman? For her price is far above . . ."' he ducked as the smith's fist drove at his jaw, '". . . rubies." What is it, Mr Barnes? Have I said something to upset you?

'You flaunting demon!' roared Barnes, storming into the attack. 'I'll make minced meat of you!'

The Captain sidestepped, flinging his hat and cloak at Hugh Vaughan. 'What kind of Godly sentiment is that?' he taunted, and, sending his sword spinning into a heap of snow, closed in.

Thankful Barnes was a big man and his trade was one which built strength and muscle. A blow like the recoil of a cannon took Justin in the stomach and sent him staggering back, gasping. Then he recovered and, as the smith surged forwards, he twisted neatly to avoid the outstretched hands and brought his own interlocked fingers smashing upwards under the heavy jaw. A murmur of approval rippled through the unashamedly partisan members of the garrison.

But Barnes had no intention of making this a fist-fight. Neither as quick nor as well trained as his opponent, his aim was to use his advantage of weight and size in a wrestling bout and presently, turning an initially imperfect grip into an arm-lock, he achieved it. Rumbling with satisfaction, he braced himself to complete the move that would dislocate Justin's arm.

He never made it. With two vicious, backward jabs of heel and elbow, Justin gained the second of relaxation which was all he needed to twist free. Then, grasping Barnes' coat with both hands, he took a single, cross step and brought him crashing to the ground over his hip. Someone cheered their encouragement but Justin, already on one knee and desperately searching for one particular hold, was too busy to notice. He rocked the smith back against his body, hooked his right arm about the thick neck and, locking his hand into the crook of his other elbow, jammed the back of his left wrist down behind Barnes' nape. Barnes heaved forward and brought up his hands to wrench free. Justin countered with a scissor-like jerk that placed sudden, sharp pressure on the windpipe. Barnes gasped and froze into wise immobility.

The men burst into expressions of noisy appreciation and nearer at hand, Hugh Vaughan said lightly, 'That's a nice move. I must remember it.'

Bound up in his own thoughts, Justin scarcely heard him. He had Barnes entirely at his mercy. All he had to do in order to snap the fellow's neck was to swivel his left wrist and push but he could not quite bring himself to do it and, fortunately, there was an alternative. An alternative that he did not want and one which he had deliberately avoided facing but an alternative for all that. The only one. He loosed his grip and came abruptly to his feet, leaving the smith breathing heavily on the snowy ground. Then he turned on his heel and strode wordlessly through the ranks of grinning troopers to the Castle.

Samuel had heard — as, indeed, had the whole town — of

Captain Ambrose's fight with Thankful Barnes and could see no point to it. His anxiety mounted with every passing day and, when Saturday arrived and still the Captain had done nothing, he made a last-ditch attempt of his own to convert Jonas. As he expected, it failed and he went upstairs to Abby in a mood of steaming resentment that admitted only one, negative ray of satisfaction. He had not told her that Justin had vowed her release, only that he had promised to try.

She sat in apparent contemplation of the dark blue wedding dress that she had never even touched, a faint frown creasing her brow. Ever mindful of appearances, Jonas had insisted on a new gown and provided the material. Because Abigail would neither cut nor sew it Alice had eventually done it for her. Now it was finished and it lay in symbolic ugliness across the foot of her bed. Abigail looked at it with no more expression than if it had been a dirty dish-cloth.

'He won't budge,' said Samuel flatly. And then, giving way to his feelings, 'I wish to God I knew what Justin is up to! Surely he's had time to do something by now?'

'Such as what?' Abigail turned a remote gaze on him. 'What can he do? Kill Thankful Barnes? Carry me off over his saddle-bow? Turn Jonas into a humanist?'

'Nothing so extravagant.'

'What, then?'

He shrugged irritably. 'I don't know.'

'No. Yet you expect so much.'

'One of us has to,' he snapped. 'You seem to have given up.'

A quiver passed over the pale, still face and then she bent her head over her hands. 'Yes. Can't you see that I no longer have a choice? If I go on hoping, if I continue thinking of Justin, I only make it worse.'

'Can it be made worse?'

'Oh, yes.' She looked up out of eyes that were no longer empty. 'Yes. You have no idea. Try to understand, Sam. I have to find a way of enduring it.'

His mouth tightened. 'And this is it? Indifference and withdrawal?'

'Yes.' Her voice was firm now and clear. 'As long as I have

control over myself, I am free. Thankful Barnes may have a right to – to my body, but he can't hurt *me* unless I let him.'

There was a long silence. Then Samuel said, 'If you really believe that, you are stronger than I thought.'

She smiled faintly. 'Perhaps. At any rate, we shall know, shan't we, tomorrow?'

The evening meal was a strained occasion that would have passed in complete silence but for Jonas. And by the time the board was cleared, even he appeared to have run out of conversation and retired moodily into his bills and ledgers. Samuel disappeared into the shop; Alice and Rachel took up their sewing; and Abigail vanished, as usual, into the fastness of her chamber.

Samuel sat staring into his candle, wondering if Justin Ambrose really had failed them and, if so, why. He had seemed so positive that even now, with time fast running out, it was hard to accept that he would do nothing. And yet, as Abby had said, what could he do, for dramatic, eleventh-hour rescues were surely not his style?

He was drawn from his meditations by a light rapping on the door and, surprised that anyone should call so late, moved round the trestle to open it a crack.

'Good evening,' said Justin, his voice disembodied in the darkness. 'The *deus ex machina* has arrived. Are you going to let me in?'

Samuel jerked the door wide. 'And about time too! What's the plan?'

'The simplest one possible.' Justin flicked his cloak back over one shoulder. 'Where's Jonas?'

'In the parlour with mother and Rachel.'

'And Abby?'

'Upstairs.'

'Fetch her, will you? And point out the parlour door as you go.'

Samuel stared. 'Jonas will have an apoplexy.'

'That,' came the cool reply, 'would simplify matters no end. Come on, and don't let Abby waste time asking questions.'

'Much good it would do if she did,' grumbled Samuel,

leading the way into the house. 'Can't I come in with you? I'd love to see Jonas' face.'

'I daresay but this is no time for frivolity. Go on!'

It was Alice who looked up first to stare blankly at the tall, elegant stranger who had invaded her parlour. Then Jonas erupted violently to his feet with a strangled cry of horror and most of her questions were answered. She said, 'Captain Ambrose?'

He swept off his hat and bowed.

'Who else?' choked Jonas. 'How did you get in here?'

The ghost of a smile lit the grey eyes and they continued to rest almost companionably on Alice. Then, without haste, they turned to encompass Jonas and Justin said, 'I knocked and the door was opened to me. Try and stay calm, Jonas. I know that we each hold the other in total aversion but we ought to be able to manage five minutes of reasonable conversation.'

'About what? The shameless effrontery of this intrusion?'

'No,' replied Justin patiently. 'I am sorry for that. But I came because I understand you to be labouring under a misapprehension about the nature of my conduct towards your sister.'

'Misapprehension?' snapped Jonas. 'When a girl spends four months creeping slyly from her home to meet a notorious libertine such as yourself, the conclusions are painfully obvious!'

'Not when the girl is Abby.' The crisp voice became unmistakably severe and his gaze took in Alice and Rachel. 'She is a hopeless liar and transparently innocent. Her family of all people should know it best.'

Alice's heart sank beneath a wave of shame and fear. Shame for the single instant of doubt which had prompted an unforgivable question and fear of what depth of feeling Abby might cherish for this austerely attractive young man.

Rachel said acidly, 'You will be telling us next that you are innocent too.'

'No. What you think of me is unimportant except, perhaps, in one small detail. I don't seduce virgins.' He broke off as the door opened and then froze, looking at Abigail.

263

Her thinness and the carved pallor of her face hurt him and the lost expression in her shadowed eyes stopped the breath in his throat. Everything was suddenly changed and, jettisoning all the sensible, persuasive phrases that had been designed as much for his own protection as for hers, he cast into the void the only thing he valued and said, 'Get your cloak, Abby. I'm taking you out of here.'

The shock of it wrenched a tiny sob from her and she would have gone to him had not Jonas prevented it by seizing her arm.

'You are going nowhere except back to your room!' he roared. 'Rachel, take her upstairs and stay with her.'

'Take your hands off her.'

Justin spoke very quietly but something in his face made Rachel sink automatically back into her chair and brought a strange chill to the air. Samuel glanced anxiously at his mother and discovered that she was watching the Captain with thoughtful and astounding composure.

A muscle moved in Justin's jaw.

'I won't tell you again, Jonas. Let her go.'

Slowly and with the utmost reluctance, Jonas relaxed and withdrew his hold. Justin held out a hand and, like one in a dream, Abigail crossed to his side. She leaned against him, turning her face into his shoulder and his arm closed tightly around her. Over her head, his steely gaze remained fixed on Jonas and he said clearly, 'I'd hoped, for all our sakes, to avoid this. I came here prepared to allow you to insult me in whatever way you chose if, in the end, I could convince you of all the things you seem incapable of recognizing for yourself. But none of it matters now. I wouldn't leave her here if you went down on your knees and kissed her feet and if you try to stop her going with me, I shall be delighted to use violence.'

An angry tide of colour rose under Jonas' skin but, even as he opened his mouth to frame a furious retort, his mother said, 'One moment, Jonas. Captain, where do you intend to take her?'

'The only place open to me, Madam. The Castle.'

'I see.' Alice surveyed him coolly. 'You realize that, if you

264

do this, she will be utterly cut off from her family? My son will never permit her to return here.'

'Nor would I allow her to do so,' he replied curtly. 'I've no wish to offend you, Madam, but the plain truth is that you can't protect her whereas I both can and will.'

'Are you planning to marry her?' It was Samuel who spoke. 'I think we have a right to ask.'

'You do and I'm not. There is no need for it and, once the roads are open again, I'll arrange matters more suitably.' He paused, looking at Alice. 'Will you accept my word that I'll take good care of her? For I will, you know.'

It was a moment before she replied but, finally, she said on a slight sigh, 'Yes. I believe you will.'

'Are you bewitched?' shouted Jonas, unable to remain silent any longer. 'He has debauched her person and her loyalties and you are content for her to compound her sins in his bed?'

'Be quiet.'

He choked. 'I beg your pardon?'

'I said be quiet.' Alice rose purposefully to her feet. 'I think it's time you exercised a little of the respect that is due to me as your mother. I have borne a great deal from you, Jonas, but now you have gone your length. You've become a sanctimonious and uncharitable bigot with a mean mind and no warmth whatever. You have turned this house into a prison and the simplicity of our religion into a penance. You have made Abigail's life a misery and driven Sam into the dangerous intrigues of John Lilburne.' She glanced fleetingly at her younger son's stunned face. 'No doubt you thought me as unobservant as Jonas.'

'No.' A faint smile touched Samuel's mouth. 'I merely thought myself adept at concealment. It was foolish of me.'

'What is all this?' demanded Jonas, recovering. 'You scarcely know John Lilburne!'

'Wrong,' said Samuel. 'I've been working with him for over a year. And once I know Abby is safe from you and that lunatic Barnes, I intend to join him in London, as he's asked me to do.'

Abigail stirred at last from the shelter of Justin's arms. She said, 'You stayed for me? Why did you never tell me?'

'It wasn't the time.' He held her gaze with his own. 'Will you go with Captain Ambrose?'

'I don't know.' She turned uncertainly to Justin. 'Why are you doing this? You can't want to be burdened with me.'

He smiled at her. 'Don't worry about that. It's more important that you realize exactly what your position will be if you come. I have Will Compton's permission for you to take up residence in the Castle but not, in view of past events, for Samuel or your mother to visit you there.'

'What past events?' Jonas rose like a hound to the scent. 'Is my entire family enmeshed in this web of deceit and corruption?'

'It would appear so,' responded Rachel tartly. 'And, for the sake of our child, I think it's time you rooted it out. There is no question of allowing Abigail to bring disgrace on us all. She must stay and be married as planned. As for Samuel, it seems he has a good deal of explaining to do.'

'But not to you, Rachel,' observed Alice. Then, turning to her daughter, 'Abby, listen to me. If you stay here and Jonas is set on your marriage, I can do nothing to stop it.'

'I know.' Abigail moved slowly towards her. 'But how can I go? If Sam leaves, you will be alone.'

'I shall have my grandchildren,' came the firm reply, 'and they will have me. I want to be sure that Hallelujah, and any others that follow him, grow into more satisfactory human beings than their father. And what good will it do me if you go to Bodicote as a second Mary Barnes?' She took Abigail's hands. 'I want something better for you than that. But all that really counts is whether or not you want to go with the Captain.'

'I do.' The dark eyes were candid with longing. 'Very much.'

Alice swallowed. 'Then go, my dear.'

'Yes, go!' Jonas pulled Abigail round to face him. 'The house will be well rid of you. But, before you decide, understand this: you will never enter this house again while I live and you will take nothing but what you stand up in – no, not even a cloak! Let your lover clothe you; let him feed and

266

shelter you; let him demand the kind of payment that it seems you are only too eager to give!'

'Excuse me,' said Justin pleasantly to Alice and moved in to pole-axe Justin with one thoroughly satisfying blow to the jaw. Then, gently massaging his knuckles amidst the utter silence of shock, he said, 'My apologies, ladies. But I've wanted to do that for a very long time, and I did warn him not to maul Abby in that vulgar fashion.'

'You've killed him!' cried Rachel, kneeling beside the sprawling body. 'Murderer!'

'Don't be a bigger fool than you can help,' said Samuel. 'He's knocked out, that's all. And it serves him right. I wish I'd done it.' He grinned at Justin. 'Correction, I wish I could do it!'

'If you join the Windmill Tavern set, you'll learn fast enough.' Justin paused, holding out his hand. 'Go carefully, won't you? I'd hate to think that all my strictures were wasted.'

'Nothing is ever wasted.' Samuel gripped the proffered hand. And then, looking across to where Abby was clinging wordlessly to Alice, 'You ought to go.'

'Yes, I know.'

Justin turned away to draw Abigail gently from her mother. Then, taking off his cloak, he wrapped it closely about her and said, 'It's cold outside and I'm afraid we have to walk. Now, say your goodbyes.'

She stared at him with dry-eyed misery. 'I can't.'

'Yes, you can. It's not forever.' Samuel gave her a swift hug and kissed her cheek before moving to put a comforting arm around Alice. 'Take her away, Justin. This is awful.'

'No!' Abigail struggled against the arm that was drawing her to the door. 'Not yet, please!'

'This minute or I leave you here,' said Justin deliberately. 'Well? Which is it to be?'

She gasped and tears welled up into her eyes. Justin shook her. 'Are you coming?'

'Yes.' Sobs crowded her throat and she glanced pleadingly back at Samuel and her mother. 'Yes.'

'Very well.' He bowed briefly to Alice and put on his hat.

'Goodbye, Madam, and don't fret. I'll see she's well looked after.' Then, over his shoulder as he swept Abigail with him through the door, 'Good luck, Sam. Write to us from London.'

Chapter Twenty-Two

It was more than cold; it was bitter and the tears froze on Abigail's cheeks as Justin took her through the dark, icy streets to the Castle. He did not speak and she could not but he held her close within the circle of his arm and she was dimly grateful for that. Then they were being challenged by the sentries and finally they were alone in the warmth of his room.

She stood like a stone, letting him take the cloak from her and draw her to the fire. The brown and white spaniel nuzzled her hand and she knelt beside him, numb and frost-bitten as the night outside. Then, quite slowly, she became aware that Justin was breaking the silence and she lifted her head vaguely.

'I'm sorry. I didn't hear what you said.'

'It wasn't important.' His tone was placid but his eyes frowned a little. 'Your room is on the floor below if you think you could sleep. Would you like me to take you down now?'

'No.' She drew an unsteady breath. 'Please, I don't want to be alone just yet.'

'Very well.' He sat on the edge of the bed, watching her. 'Do you want to talk?'

'I don't know what to say.' She bent her head over the dog, shivering a little. 'It's all a bit of a shock. But I didn't mean you to be involved in it. It wasn't your fault.'

'That's a matter of opinion.' He rose again and came to pull her to her feet. 'You're cold. You ought to be in bed.'

'I'm all right. It's just nerves. Don't send me away.'

He looked into the wide, confused eyes and sighed. 'Then come here and be wrapped up. It's not very proper but I suppose there's no actual harm in it.' He tucked her up, fully dressed, under the quilt on his bed and then sat down beside her. 'Perhaps this is as good a time as any to make one thing crystal clear. Despite what Jonas said to the contrary, I

269

haven't brought you here to seduce, ravish or otherwise molest you and neither do I expect any demonstrations of sacrificial gratitude.'

'Of course not.' The numbness was beginning to melt into pain. 'So why did you do it?'

'Because I couldn't leave you where you were. But cheer up. It's only temporary. When you're feeling better, we'll make some plans. It may even be possible to send you to London with Sam.'

A tear splashed on to her hand and she hid it in a fold of the quilt, hoping he hadn't noticed. She said hastily, 'I saw the King last month. Did he forgive Prince Rupert?'

'Eventually. That's why I was so long away. I was at Woodstock for weeks, helping persuade Rupert to apologize for forgetting his party manners before the court-martial.'

'And did he?' Another tear followed the first one.

'Yes, but not to His Majesty's satisfaction,' replied Justin caustically. 'His answer was a lesson in the correct way to express penitence, so he sent back a sheet of paper, blank but for his name, and said his uncle could fill in the rest. It was a gesture of pure sarcasm which the King mistook for humility. They say it brought tears to his eyes.' He stretched out a hand to touch her wet cheeks. 'There is no shame in it, you see.'

'I know.' She swallowed a sob. 'But it annoys you.'

Something tightened in Justin's chest. He said ambiguously, 'No one's perfect. And I'm willing to put up with it just this once, on one condition.'

'What?' asked Abigail, her throat raw and aching with the effort of suppression.

Smiling crookedly, he gestured to her head. 'That you give me the pleasure of ceremoniously burning that bloody cap, at midnight, under the next full moon.' And gathering her into his arms, he bound her in wordless, passive warmth while the storm inside her finally broke, shattering her into a thousand pieces.

She woke to the gleam of wintry daylight and found herself thoroughly dishevelled and alone amidst the rumpled, twisted quilt. For a moment she lay very still, remembering what today should have been; and then, turning her head, she saw the note on the pillow beside her.

'Duty calls. Sorry. Make yourself at home. J.'

Abigail sat up, disentangled herself from the quilt and went to the mirror. Her hair was a mass of tangles, her collar was dirty and her gown looked like a duster. She groaned, wondering how she was going to make herself presentable. Then the door opened.

'At last!' said Lucy. 'I've been up twice already and thought you were never going to wake. My goodness . . . you look awful.'

Abigail eyed her gloomily. 'Thank you. I had noticed.'

'Well, don't be depressed. Help has arrived. I've been in and out of your room all morning like a bird with twigs in its beak, so come downstairs and let's get started.'

'On what? And I can't go anywhere like this.'

'No one will see you.' Lucy seized her hand. 'Hurry up! We're going to have fun.'

The room on the floor below was much like the one Justin inhabited but Abigail saw nothing but the widespread evidence of Lucy's activity. She stared around her and said, 'What's all this?'

'Gowns, petticoats, shifts, night-rails. See for yourself. Justin says you haven't brought anything with you, and, if you don't mind my saying so, I think you were wise.'

'But I can't take your things!'

'Why on earth not? My mother sent every ribbon I own up from Oxford as soon as the siege was lifted and heaven knows I've more than enough! Besides, I'm glad you've come. I was beginning to miss having a friend to gossip with. And I'm going to enjoy transforming you.'

A slow smile lit Abigail's eyes. 'You think it can be done?'

'Of course.' Lucy spun her round and began briskly unlacing her gown. 'Now stop asking silly questions and let's get to work. Everything will have to be taken in and shortened but you can deal with the tricky stuff while I do the hems and, if we work hard, we ought to have you ready in time for dinner. What do you think?'

'I think,' replied Abigail, stepping out of her gown and turning to face the other girl, 'that I don't deserve such generosity.'

Lucy pulled a face. 'What nonsense! Try the violet taffeta first. I've never worn it because it makes me look liverish but it ought to suit you perfectly.'

Abigail stared at the gown Lucy was holding out to her. 'I can't wear that!'

'Why not? What's wrong with it?'

'Nothing. It's beautiful. But —'

'But nothing,' said Lucy, casting it over her head and settling it on her shoulders. 'Ah – yes. It's going to be superb. *En avant, mon capitaine.* We've got a busy day ahead of us.'

But no matter how busy her hands were, nothing could stop Lucy's tongue and she drifted blithely from the latest fashion in trimmings to daily life in the Castle and finally into news of the war.

'You heard about Basing House, of course? I hope that man Cromwell is thoroughly ashamed of himself for letting his men run amok in that disgraceful way. But I don't suppose he is and Justin says our men are just as unruly now Prince Rupert's no longer in command.' She paused, frowning over her sewing. 'I wish it were all over. Ned says we've only got Cornwall, a bit of Wales and a handful of other garrisons like this one and more towns are falling every day so I can't understand why someone doesn't make peace. Goodness knows, the King is always negotiating with someone or other so he might as well talk to the Parliament and have done with it. I know it's horrible for him but one has to be practical about these things. And I really would prefer Ned's son and heir to be born respectably at home.'

Abigail let the violet gown slide unchecked to the floor. 'You're pregnant?'

'Yes.' A brilliant smile curved Lucy's mouth. 'Isn't it wonderful?'

'Wonderful,' agreed Abigail, laughing a little. 'You like surprises, don't you? When is it due?'

'Not till June. So there's ages yet for Ned to come out of the army and learn to be a gentleman again.'

By the time the gown and its petticoats were ready, Justin had been turned from the door three times and there was less than an hour before the evening meal. But Lucy refused to be hurried.

'No one is seeing you until I'm satisfied that you look absolutely perfect,' she said firmly. 'And if we're late, they'll just have to wait for us. Now stop fidgeting while I finish your hair.'

'I'm going to be sick,' announced Abigail. 'I can't go down.'

'Rubbish! You'll go if I have to drag you.'

'Be reasonable, Lucy. It's a lovely dress, but what chance has it got? Justin is going to laugh himself silly.'

Lucy grinned. 'He'd better not. Now, keep still!'

It was Lucy who entered the officers' room first to a good-humoured chorus of complaint which she silenced with a wave of her hand. Then, drawing Abigail forward, she said lightly, 'Best behaviour, gentlemen, or Abby and I will dine upstairs.'

There was a moment of utter astonishment as six pairs of male eyes encompassed Abigail and then Hugh Vaughan said, 'Don't do that. Not after all the trouble we've been to.'

'What trouble?' scoffed Lucy.

'This.' Hugh drew them in to look at the table. 'Holly, Will's candlesticks and one of Lord Saye's best damask cloths. You're not the only one who's been busy.' He turned, smiling, and kissed Abigail's hand. 'A small token of welcome.'

She flushed. 'Thank you. It – you are all so kind.'

'Not at all. Now, I don't think you've met Major Walrond or Lieutenant Poulteney?' He gave her time to smile shyly at each in turn and then said, 'But you know Ned, of course, and here is Justin.'

Abigail raised a reluctant, anxious gaze and was relieved to find that the Captain showed no sign of wanting to laugh. Instead, the light grey eyes were wide with something she did not recognize but which disrupted her breathing. She said, 'I don't feel decent.'

He smiled. 'It's an illusion.'

'It's not. Or if it is, the whole room is sharing it with me,' she retorted distractedly. 'I wish I'd never let Lucy bully me into this. I wish I had a shawl. Look how much of me is showing!'

'I am looking,' came the frank reply. 'It's difficult not to.'

Behind the lightly drawling words, he was in limbo. It was stupid to be so shaken, even more stupid to be lost for the simplest expression to tell her how she looked. Such a thing had never happened to him before and there was no adequate reason for it now. The incredible mass of night-dark hair, now cunningly coiled and twined with silver ribbon, was no surprise. He had known how it could gleam blue in the candlelight and frame the pointed face with tiny curls. And if he had been fooled by ill-fitting clothes into mistaking the delicate perfection of her body for thinness . . . well, there was nothing in that to account for the loss of his poise. Nothing at all, until one added exquisitely fine-boned shoulders, translucent creamy-white skin and the temptingly shadowed hollows at the base of a slender throat; and then, he reflected wryly, it was enough to explain palsy, apoplexy and paralysis of the lungs.

The meal was accompanied by a good deal of talk and laughter, both of which were as foreign to Abigail as was her appearance. But she gradually relaxed enough to respond to Hugh Vaughan's easy conversation and managed to eat a little of what was put in front of her. She might even have contrived to come to terms with the alarmingly decolleté gown had it not been for Justin watching her almost continuously whilst saying virtually nothing. He had, she decided, a capacity for stillness and silence that could either be companionable or downright unnerving; and tonight was a prime example of the latter. The others, fortunately, were more forthcoming and their gossip was peppered with largely unfamiliar names.

'They say Goring's gone off to France,' remarked Ned with faint disapproval. 'I know his career hasn't been brilliant lately but I never took him for a rat.'

'Probably drunk the West dry and moved on to fresh supplies,' grinned Hugh. 'And did you hear about his father?

He asked the King to give him the governorship of Pendennis Castle and said he'd prepared himself for the responsibility by reading a good many romances!'

There was a general burst of laughter into which Charles Walrond announced that he did not find idiocy amusing.

'You don't find anything amusing,' muttered Ned into his wine-cup and then grunted as Lucy kicked him.

It was left to Lieutenant Poulteney to fill the awkward pause by saying quietly, 'I wonder how they're faring in Chester? It must be hell to have a whole town starve while you try to defend it.'

'Are they besieged?' asked Abigail.

Hugh nodded. 'Byron, the Governor, is desperate. He even sent his new bride down to Oxford to plead for help, but it's useless, of course. Even if the King had men to send, who could get that far north in this weather?'

Silence fell as everyone stared guiltily at the well-stocked table. Then Lucy said brightly, 'Come, this won't do! Isn't anyone going to remark on how ravishing Abby looks?'

Abigail started and cast a wary downward glance at her décolletage.

'Well, naturally,' replied Ned. 'We'd all noticed but words failed us.'

'That'll be the day!' scoffed Lucy, pushing aside her plate to lean both elbows on the board. 'In my experience, you all have far too much to say for yourselves and it's usually rude.'

'If you please, ma'am, we're only nasty common soldiers,' pleaded Hugh, meekly. And then, raising his cup to Abigail, 'But we find Mistress Abby charming and drink to her new life amongst us – may it be a happy one.'

Flushing, Abigail studiously avoided Captain Ambrose's gaze and managed a shy smile as the toast was drunk.

'Thank you. I'm sure it will be.'

'And on that felicitous note,' drawled Justin, rising abruptly from his seat, 'you may say goodnight. You look worn to the bone.'

Abigail looked back at him, nettled. 'Is that why you were staring at me? I was beginning to think I'd a smut on my nose.'

There was a ripple of amusement.

'Not at all. Just shadows under your eyes. Come on, everyone will excuse you.'

She went, in the end, because she did not know how to frame a dignified refusal. But once outside the room, she turned on him and said crossly, 'Do I look like a child?'

He lifted a burning torch from a wall sconce and held it up while he considered her. 'No.'

'Then I wish you wouldn't treat me like one.'

He grinned suddenly. 'You must forgive me. It's confusing to find my tear-stained waif transformed into an elegant shrew.'

Effectively silenced, Abigail stalked ahead of him up the stairs in hot-cheeked affront. Then they arrived at the door of her room and her heart sank as she followed him through it and watched as he placed the torch in an empty bracket. She did not, she realized, want to sleep here and she did not want him to go, leaving her alone, but she had made it quite impossible to say so. She swallowed and said challengingly, 'You haven't said whether or not you like the way I look?'

He turned to her, his face in shadow. 'Haven't I?'

'No. And Lucy will ask because I said you'd laugh.'

'You wronged me then. I never felt less like laughing.' He paused and the air grew strangely still. 'So you want a compliment that you can deliver to Lucy.'

'I – no. Not exactly,' she floundered, feeling extremely gauche. 'I – I just wanted to know what you were thinking all through dinner.'

'The same thing I'm thinking of now,' he replied broodingly. 'This.' And, drawing her lightly towards him, he dropped a brief kiss on her parted lips.

Sparks fled tingling through Abigail's veins and she drew a ragged breath. The grey eyes widened a little and then Justin stepped back saying pleasantly, 'There. Quite reprehensible, of course, but an undeniably economic alternative to the usual hackneyed compliments. Goodnight.' And he was gone, shutting the door behind him with a gentle click.

Abigail sank weakly on to a stool and began pulling pins and ribbons from her hair with shaking fingers. It did not mean anything; it was just a rather extraordinary way of saying something very simple, and all of a piece with sitting down to dinner half-naked amongst people who gave no sign of remembering that she was the ruined sister of a Puritan shopkeeper. She would never, she decided edgily, get used to it.

Upstairs, Justin prowled moodily about his room. Where, he asked himself irritably, was the gentle binding he had contemplated under the trees at Trent? It was so far away now that he doubted it had ever existed at all except in his imagination. He was enmeshed in a caring that was anything but mild and tonight, after all his noble posturing, he had been brought face to face with the ultimate irony of physical desire. Abby was no longer his safe harbour. She was his need, his torment, his delight. She had laid waste every rigid tenet until all he was left with was the will to hide from her what he could no longer hide from himself, and the hope that, in time, it would merge into the other distant impossibilities of his life.

He took care, in the next few days, to meet her only in the company of others but by the time Saturday came again and she had been in the Castle for a week with the flat marks of exhaustion still in her face, he began to fear for her health. She ate like a bird. She did not look as if she slept – and he did not know why, since in every other way she appeared to have made a remarkable adjustment.

He was passing her room in the early hours of the morning after completing a spell of duty when he heard the muffled sounds that gave him his first clue. And, almost glad of the excuse, he opened her door without a second thought.

Illuminated only by the dying glow of the fire, she was sitting bolt upright in bed, gasping for breath. He said softly, 'Abby? I'm sorry. Did I startle you?'

'No. It wasn't you,' she said unevenly. 'I had a dream.'

'And not a very pleasant one, I take it?'

'No.' She shivered. 'Can you stay a minute?'

'Of course.' He shut the door and came to sit beside her on the edge of the bed. Her skin was damp with sweat. 'This isn't the first time, is it?'

She shook her head, miserably. 'It . . . I feel so silly.'

'You were silly not to tell me,' he agreed. 'Does it happen every night? Is this why you can't sleep?'

'Yes. I dream about Thankful Barnes and mother and Sam. It's all very mixed up.' She bent her head over nervous fingers. 'I'm sorry. After all you've done, it seems so ungrateful.'

'No. It's perfectly natural. Give yourself time, Abby.' He paused and then said wryly, 'I haven't been much help, have I?'

She looked up at him. 'You've been busy.'

'That's no excuse.' His mouth twisted at the thought that it was also untrue. 'Tell me what will help you and I'll do my best to arrange it.'

She grew very still and a slow flush stained her cheeks. 'I can't. It's too great an imposition and you won't like it.'

'Let me be the judge of that. What is it?'

She hesitated for a moment and then said, 'I know it's unreasonable – childish, if you like – but I don't like being alone here. I thought it would pass but it hasn't or not yet, anyway. And I'd prefer, if it were possible, to have the little room that adjoins yours.'

He stared at her in enigmatic silence for a long time. Finally, he said, 'Wouldn't having Jenny Swan or one of the other women sleep here with you do just as well?'

The forlorn head dropped again. 'Yes. Yes, of course.'

'Which means it won't,' said Justin drily. He hesitated and then added carefully, 'It would be a mistake, you know, to become too dependent on me. As soon as the snow melts —'

'I know,' she said quickly. 'It's temporary. I do understand that.'

'And do you also understand that if you move upstairs with me the entire garrison will assume that I'm your lover?'

'Oh.' She drew a long breath. 'But would you mind? They probably think it anyway and thinking doesn't make it true.'

An odd expression flickered in the grey eyes and Justin said, 'You take a lot for granted, don't you? But never mind. Are you sure this is what you want?'

She nodded. 'Oh yes. But wouldn't you find it very tiresome?'

'Probably.' He stood up, a faintly satirical smile bracketing his mouth. 'But not as tiresome as worrying about you. And we all have to make the occasional sacrifice, don't we?'

By the following night the tiny room was ready and Abigail retired into it with a grateful determination to make him forget she was even there. She had, of course, no way of knowing that her mere presence on the other side of the door was a constant thorn of temptation or that it grew daily more difficult for him to maintain his usual manner. She only knew that there was a security in his closeness that let her sleep again. She began repaying her debt by secretly repairing his shirts.

On Christmas Eve the men went out into the countryside and came back laden with greenery to decorate the great hall. The whole Castle was suddenly alive with cheerful bustle, snatches of seasonal song and the odour of roasting meats. Abigail found herself caught up in a whirl of bewildering preparations for her first traditional festival.

She woke early on the following morning and lay for a while, letting her thoughts stray wistfully to her mother and brother and listening to the familiar chimes of St Mary's. Then, for the very first time, the door opened and Justin looked in on her.

'Hello,' he said, smiling in a way that made her heart turn over. 'This is no time to lie about brooding, we've a lot to do.'

She sat up. 'Have we?'

'Certainly. There's divine service in the chapel in an hour and you'll hardly want to attend in your night-rail, will you? But first you've to stay where you are and close your eyes.'

'Why?'

'Do it and you'll find out.'

Laughing a little, she did as he asked and heard him cross the floor to her side. Then something settled weightily across her knees and he said, 'You can look now.'

She opened her eyes on the living brilliance of apricot silk and blinked, forgetting to breathe.

'Merry Christmas,' said Justin, gently.

Slowly, very slowly, she touched the gleaming material

with awed fingers. Then she said dazedly, 'It's for me?'

'Yes.' His throat tightened but he went on lightly, 'I know you have a yearning for cherry but I hope you'll like this just as well.'

'It's beautiful,' she whispered huskily. And then, raising her eyes, 'You make me ashamed. I have nothing to give you.'

All Justin's stern resolutions crumbled and he sat down, taking her hands in his. 'No? Do you think I haven't noticed the wizardry you've been working amongst my shirts or that I always come in to a good fire these days?'

She sniffed. 'But that's nothing. I enjoy doing those things.'

'And I shall enjoy seeing you robed in a silk gown of your own creating. But if you're set on giving me something now, a smile wouldn't go amiss, even a small one. God knows, I didn't cherish this stuff all the way from Newark just to —' He stopped, his gaze locked with hers. 'Ah. That was foolish of me. Now you're going to ask why I bought something that, at the time, I couldn't possibly have given you.'

'And why did you?'

Shrugging, he released her hands. 'I haven't the faintest idea.'

There was a long silence and then Abigail snarled every nerve and fibre of his body by putting her hands about his neck and laying her cheek against his own. She said, 'I can't smile yet. Do you mind?'

'No.' Involuntarily, his arms closed about her. 'No. You do know, don't you, that I bought it for you?'

She made a tiny sound that might have been laughter.

'Yes. Unless, of course, you tell all the girls they'd look better in apricot.'

It was a magical day and music rippled through it like water. They sang in the chapel and then again, differently, in the hall. From amongst the men appeared a motley collection of instruments: flageolets, drums, guitars. And when the boards were cleared and voices had grown hoarse on wassail songs, the tunes became insistent rhythmic dances that made it a crime to be still.

280

Perched like a familiar spirit on the arm of her husband's chair, Lucy watched Justin guide Abigail expertly through the wild intricacies of the couranto and said, 'Have you noticed how she looks at him when she thinks he's not looking at her?'

'I might have,' grinned Ned, 'if I knew who you were talking about.'

'Don't be difficult.' She turned a defensive gaze on him. 'She's not his mistress, you know. He treats her like a brother would. I've watched him. It's sickening.'

'Sickening,' he agreed. And then, flatly, 'No.'

'No what?'

'No, I won't talk to him about it. Isn't that what you were about to ask me?'

'Well, yes.' She tucked her hand into his. 'Why won't you?'

'Because it wouldn't do any good and would probably earn me a black eye,' he told her firmly. 'There are things you don't know and Justin don't take kindly to interference. Shall we dance?'

It was while Abigail was moving through a gigue with Charles Walrond that Justin looked smilingly away from her to find Hugh Vaughan at his side. He said, 'Remarkable, isn't it? Like watching the birth of a butterfly?'

'Yes.' The dark gaze rested thoughtfully on the graceful, violet-clad figure. 'Do you still intend to send her to London with her brother?'

'If I can. Why?'

'I thought you might have changed your mind. It's not easy to see why else you should have moved her into your own quarters.'

The smile vanished.

'Into my quarters, Hugh, not into my bed. And my reasons are not your concern.'

'No. But she's a nice child and I wouldn't like to see her hurt. I wondered if you might be planning to marry her.'

Justin gave a brief, derisive laugh. 'Hardly. You know my views on matrimony.'

'I see.' The Welshman surveyed him coolly. 'Then it's not

281

very fair of you to encourage her to grow fond of you, is it?'

'I'm not.' A tinge of colour stained Justin's cheekbones and he turned to move away. 'This is a ridiculous conversation.'

'Is it?' Hugh detained him with a hand on his arm. 'Think about it. Just tell me one thing – does she know who you are?'

'Unless some well-meaning friend has chosen to enlighten her, no.' The grey eyes were like ice. 'Are you going to remove your hand or do I take it with me?'

Although he tried to ignore them, Hugh's strictures lingered like a chill on Justin's mind; and when, long after midnight, he was alone with Abigail and about to bid her goodnight, he heard himself say abruptly, 'Are you happy?'

She smiled. 'Yes. Don't I look it?'

He searched the beautiful, dark eyes and drew a slightly unsteady breath. 'You look as though someone has given you the moon.'

The smile became a gurgle of laughter.

'Not the moon. Just a length of apricot silk.'

For a long time after she had gone to bed, he sat watching the fire burn lower and lower while the truth eddied and flowed through the channels of his mind. Useless to continue forbidding the words when the reality was so evident. He loved her and wanted her and needed her, and if the land could be locked in perpetual winter, he would be glad. But it couldn't, any more than he could ask her to share the rigours and uncertainties of his life abroad. Unless he violated his conscience and claimed Trent, he had no other home to offer her.

He stared down at the tightly-latticed cage of his fingers. There was no simple, perfect answer; no dragon to slay except that of his own terrible temptation to discover exactly how close she was to loving him in return. Only the emptiness of denial and the Dead Sea fruit of his own, once-prized freedom.

Chapter Twenty-Three

Twelfth Night came and went bringing no sign of a thaw and Abigail worked lovingly on the apricot silk whilst rejoicing in the frozen wastes outside. News no longer travelled along the empty roads and a strange tranquillity settled over town and Castle as people stayed huddled around their hearths. The war had begun to seem like a distant memory, buried deep beneath the snow and it was the first time of peace that Abigail could remember in almost four years.

Thanks to hours of patient, chilly lurking on Justin's part, she managed to exchange letters with Samuel and so discovered that all was well at home and that he too was waiting on the weather. More importantly, he also wrote that he could scarcely have her with him in London until such time as he had secured employment and found a home for them both. Justin received this news with a frowning nod and the grudging admission that it was logical. Abigail smiled secretly over her flying needle and celebrated with snatches of quiet song.

She finished the apricot gown late one afternoon in the middle of the month and, sighing, held it up for Lucy's inspection. 'There. What do you think?'

'I think you've sewn your heart into it,' came the perceptive reply. 'Put it on. I can't wait to see how it looks.'

'Neither can I,' said Abigail slowly. 'But I'm half afraid to. Isn't that ridiculous?'

'Utterly!' Lucy grinned wickedly. 'Especially as it isn't my verdict you care about.'

The gown fitted like a dream and its clever simplicity was startling for, wisely relying on the richness of the silk to be its own ornament, Abigail had used neither slashing, panning nor pleating. Soft, full sleeves fell from the edge of her shoulders to end in falls of creamy lace at the elbow; a feathering of delicate embroidery traced the wide, curving

283

décolletage and was echoed on the neat tassets at her waist; the glowing folds of the skirt flowed gracefully into a demi-train of molten gold.

Lucy drew a breath of pure appreciation.

'It's perfect. The gown, the colour, everything. And if Justin Ambrose can look at you without melting, then he isn't the man I take him for and doesn't deserve you. No, don't say anything! Just arrange your hair and wait for him. I'm going.'

By the time Justin came in Abigail had twisted her hair into a mass of tumbling curls and her nerves into pulp. As soon as she heard his step outside the door, she fled back into the sanctuary of her own room in a fit of inexplicable shyness.

'Abby?' Justin crossed towards the bed, pulling off his sash as he went. 'Are you there?'

She moved slowly to stand watching him from the doorway.

'Yes. Did you want something?'

'Not unless you'd care to give me a hand with this.' His head was bent over the task of unlacing his buff-coat. 'I've spent the last hour on the ramparts and my fingers are frozen to the bone. Oh hell!'

A slow, sweet smile invested Abigail's mouth and she advanced on him with restored confidence. 'I'll help if you promise not to swear at me. Has someone upset you?'

'Not especially. And since you must, by now, be perfectly well-acquainted with the unreliable nature of my temper,' began Justin, glancing irritably up at her. And then stopped, blindly staring.

With leisured calm, she unfastened his coat and stepped back, head tilted in courteous enquiry.

'There, it's done. Now, what were you saying?'

'Nothing. I don't know.' He paused, suddenly helpless. 'I'm a fool. Why didn't you tell me?'

'That you are a fool? I wouldn't dare. As for this,' she smoothed the silk with tender fingers and pivoted gracefully, 'I was waiting for you to notice. Do you like it?'

It was a long time before he replied. And then, in a voice she scarcely recognized, he said, 'How could I not? You are so beautiful. You always were even in Jonas' sackcloth. But I'm glad I chose apricot.'

Her breath caught and, for an instant, she seemed to be drowning in his eyes. Unconsciously, she took a step towards him and would have taken another if, with an effort that could be felt, Justin had not shattered the spell by wheeling abruptly away from her, saying, 'Don't, Abby! God knows I'm already having enough trouble remembering —'

He stopped and she prompted gently, 'Remembering what?'

'Nothing.' He turned back, smiling with forced cheerfulness. 'I'd better change, hadn't I? Not that I have any hope of matching your elegance but I think the occasion warrants something better than second-hand buff leather.'

She eyed him wistfully, aware that he was retreating from her but unsure of how to prevent it. Finally she said gravely, 'I'll leave you, then. You'll find your sashes in the chest. I pressed them this morning.'

'Thank you.' He hesitated, oddly discomposed. 'Have I said something to upset you?'

'No. It's what you haven't said that bothers me.' And with an uncharacteristically brittle smile, she was gone.

Justin heard the door close behind her and then walked aimlessly to the washstand. With beautiful detachment, he considered how close he had come to self-betrayal. Looking down at his hands, he found that they were shaking.

Three days later it began, almost imperceptibly, to thaw. Two days after that Nancy Lucas brought herself, her girls and her baggage unannounced to the Castle and demanded to see Captain Ambrose.

'Well, Nan?' Justin leaned against the guard-room door and regarded her with quizzical tolerance. 'What brings you here? Not, of course, that it isn't always a pleasure to see you and especially after so long.'

'And whose fault is that? You know where to find me if you've the mind to.' She examined him critically, noting the tiny lines of strain around his eyes. 'You look done to a cow's thumb. Been having a busy time, have you?'

He shrugged. 'No more so than usual. And things have been quiet enough this last few weeks.'

'Well, they're moving again now if what I hear is right,' she replied grimly. 'That's why I've come. I want to bring the girls back here for a bit if it's all right with you. It could be no more than a buzzard's bogey but I don't want to take no chances. And all my trade's in here, anyway. So —'

'Hold on, Nan,' cut in Justin crisply. 'Are you telling me you've reason to expect enemy action in this area?'

'Closer than that. I've been told, never mind by who, that they're coming to have another go at this place.'

He stared at her. 'But the roads won't be fit for artillery for weeks. How sure are you?'

'Sure enough to pack and come here. Look, is it going to be all right for us to stay?'

'What? I expect so,' said Justin absently. 'I'll have to ask the Governor but I can't see him casting you out, though God knows what he's going to make of this talk of an attack. No commander in his senses would embark on a siege in weather like this unless —' He stopped.

'Unless what?' asked Nancy.

'Unless he had reason to hope for a quick surrender. Damn it to hell! I wish we knew what's been happening outside this thrice-blasted town. It's high time we sent out some scouts. If you wait here, I'll go and see Will. I suppose your old quarters will suit?'

'Well enough,' she grinned. And then, as he turned to go, 'By the way, what's all this about you and the little Radford girl?'

He looked back at her, his eyes glinting with irony.

'You tell me. You're the one who knows everything. What am I popularly credited with?'

'Seduction, rape, kidnapping and marriage, depending on who you listen to.'

'I see.' A cold smile curled his mouth. 'Then let's hope the rest of your information is equally inaccurate.'

'She's not here, then?'

'Oh yes. But unwed, unconstrained and relatively unsullied.'

'And what's that supposed to mean?' snorted Nancy. 'It's like saying a girl's "relatively pregnant".'

Justin was not noticeably amused.

'It means,' he said blandly, 'that, though she is living in my quarters and generally held to be my mistress, she is nonetheless pure, untouched and blissfully virginal. And now, if you've no objection, I'll see what can be done about accommodating you.'

He gained Sir William's permission without difficulty and also found him surprisingly unsceptical of Nancy's story.

'It would make sense, wouldn't it? "Oxford cannot fall while Banbury flourishes" and all that. And the Committee of Both Kingdoms must be panting to finish the war this summer. Thank God we're well provisioned this time.'

'Can I send some of my fellows out?' asked Justin. 'They can at least report on the state of the roads and they might bring back something, even if it's only a broadsheet.'

'By all means,' nodded Will. Then, grinning, 'I wonder if Saye and Sele is in on this? There's a rumour in the town that he's asked Parliament to compensate him for his losses and I'm sure they'd far rather return his Castle.'

After he had despatched the reconnaissance party, Justin went in search of Abigail and eventually found her brushing the tangles from Rex's long fur. He said, 'If he lets you comb his ears, you'll have worked a miracle.'

'I know and he won't.' She smiled invitingly up at him. Unless you'd like to hold him for me?'

'If I must.' He sighed with mock reluctance and dropped on one knee beside her to take the dog's head in his hands. Nancy Lucas has just arrived to take up residence.'

'Nancy?' She was surprised. 'Why?'

'That's what I wanted to talk to you about.' He kept his eyes strictly on Rex. 'She's been warned that the Parliament mean to make another attempt on the Castle and it's only fair to say that she has a knack for good intelligence.'

'I see.' Abigail's face grew pensive. 'Another siege?'

'Perhaps.'

'Soon?'

'I don't know. Not before the Oxford road clears, I hope.'

He frowned a little. 'Do you understand why I'm telling you?'

'Yes. Thank you.'

Her tone was so serene that he glanced sharply at her and said, 'You're sure?'

'Yes. You're saying that, if there's a siege before you can find a home for me elsewhere, I'll be here for the duration,' she replied calmly.

Reluctant amusement lit the grey eyes.

'I can see,' he remarked, 'that you're overcome with alarm at the prospect.'

'Oh no.' She favoured him with a kindly apologetic smile. 'But I expect I would be if it weren't that you seem worried enough for both of us.'

The reconnaissance party brought back nothing but the news that a small amount of traffic was now abroad on the road. Two days later on January 21st, the first Parliamentary detachments of horse and foot arrived in the town. There were about a thousand of them – not enough to completely blockade the Castle – and they brought scarcely any ordnance. But their commander, Colonel Edward Whalley, had begun the war as a cornet in John Fiennes' troop and was therefore familiar with the Castle's defences. Furthermore, he scored an immediate victory over a troop of Lord Northampton's flying cavalry and took sixty of them prisoner.

Abigail looked interestedly down on the spreading pattern of tents and trenches and tried hard not to bless the Committee of Both Kingdoms for granting her a reprieve. She had wanted so badly to stay and now, with Colonel Whalley busily making it possible, her only sorrow was that Justin seemed more elusive than ever. He was also extremely busy, though she was not at all sure why for so far neither side had opened more than a sporadic burst of musket-fire. Indeed, the Parliamentarian army seemed largely content to shout up depressing fragments of news: the fall of Hereford and Dartmouth and Chester and the King's latest diplomatic failures. Yet Justin spent less and less time in his room, often coming and going while she slept. By the end of the first week in February, she came at last to the painful and bewildering conclusion that he was deliberately avoiding her.

He was. It was all he was left with. Because he had to pass his off-duty hours somewhere, he took to spending them in the north turret with Nancy Lucas.

On the night that the taunting voices outside announced that Fairfax had taken Torrington, he lounged in a chair before Nancy's fire with an untasted cup of wine in his hand and silently contemplated his crossed ankles. Nancy endured it as long as she could and was finally driven to say, 'You're not enjoying it any more, are you?'

'No.' He stirred a little but did not look up. 'I shall be glad to go.'

She grimaced. 'It's the Radford child, isn't it?'

This time the grey eyes rose to encompass her, wary and very bright. 'I beg your pardon?'

'Why? Are you deaf?' She came to her feet and faced him, arms akimbo. 'You come here to hide, don't you? And when a man can't trust himself near a girl, there's only one reason that I know of. Well?'

His fingers tightened on the cup. 'Leave it, Nan.'

'I'm damned if I will! I'm tired of sitting watching you eat yourself up from inside without a word to say why.'

'Very well.' He uncoiled from the chair and was at the door in two strides. 'Then I'll go.'

'Fine,' snapped Nancy. 'And I'll tell Abigail exactly what her precious virtue is doing to you.'

Justin froze on the threshold. Then, using both hands and the full force of his body to send the door crashing shut, he turned back, white-faced with temper and said unevenly, 'All right. But has it occurred to you, has it ever occurred to you that if all I wanted was a body I would have solicited yours?'

An odd smile flickered across the comely face. 'Don't be a fool, Justin. Why else d'you think I'm meddling?'

'For fun? It can't be because you believe this is helpful.'

'It might be if you'd let it. How long can you go on like this?'

His anger drained suddenly away, leaving him tired and

empty. He said, 'I don't know. It's all such a bloody mess. I can't go near her for fear that one day I'll discover that she feels as I do.'

'If you think that,' said Nancy slowly, 'I don't understand what's to stop you marrying her.'

'Poverty,' he replied flatly. 'That and the fact that you can't ask a girl who hates war to live from one foreign battlefield to the next. And then, of course, there is the problematical question of my . . . or no. I'm talking too much. Goodnight, Nan.'

'Wait!' She drew a steadying breath and smiled at him. 'You know, don't you, that I've always had a fancy for you? So don't go. Stay here and share my bed for friendship's sake.'

Justin's face softened and he said, 'My dear, I really wish that I could. But I thank you with all my heart for the thought.'

There was silence. Then Nancy said quietly, 'You must love her very much.'

'I do.' A terrible, relentless longing filled his eyes. 'That's why I can't discuss it. I'm sorry. Goodnight.'

He entered his room with caution and, finding it empty, silently discarded his clothes and got into bed. It was a little after midnight and he felt extraordinarily wakeful but sleep was both a military requirement and a discipline long since perfected so he finally achieved a fitful and uneasy doze which ended abruptly in a roar of orchestrated cannon-fire.

He catapulted instinctively out of bed and over to the window to look out, aware from the grey light in the room that it was already dawn. Then the inner door was jerked open and Abigail shot through it in her night-robe.

'Justin? What's happening? It sounded like —' And there she stopped, frozen into wordless immobility by the mind-cracking discovery that he was naked.

A single glance into her face told Justin that she was too shocked even to think of looking away and somewhere, unrecognized at the back of his mind, was amusement. But his first conscious reaction was a slight, ridiculous flush and his second, to reach for a blanket with a studied lack of haste.

Then, with the thing wrapped toga-like about him, he said carelessly, 'It's all right. At a guess, I'd say Colonel Whalley is merely announcing the completion of his lines. But there's nothing to worry about. He hasn't enough ordnance to demolish a hencoop.'

Deceived by his nonchalance, burning with embarrassment and totally incapable of speech, Abigail took the line of least resistance. She fled.

For a moment, Justin stared blankly after her. And then, without warning, he dissolved into helpless, crippling laughter.

'Abby?' he called, unsteadily. 'Come back here this minute!'

Silence.

'Abby!' Still sobbing for breath, he opened the door and looked in on her. 'Don't be an idiot. Something of the kind was bound to happen sooner or later and it's my fault for sleeping in the buff. Come on, smile. I'm not laughing at you.'

She peered gloomily at him through the veil of her hair.

'What then? What else is there? I'm so ashamed!'

'Why, for God's sake?'

'Because I – I just stared!'

'So?' He grinned. 'I'm flattered.'

'Oh!' Indignation swept her to her feet. 'You're too brazen to care!'

'I'm not. I blushed.'

'Rubbish!'

'I did!' His eyes were bright and strangely carefree. 'You obviously weren't looking or not in the right place.'

Response tugged at Abigail's mouth but, before she could speak, the air exploded again in the roar of cannon.

'I'd better go,' said Justin, sighing. 'It sounds as if it could be a busy day. You, of course, can go back to bed. You may not sleep with this row going on, but at least you'll be warm.'

He went and Abigail sat gazing into space, harvesting her thoughts. The noise disturbed her not at all; and if she was cold, she did not know it.

Chapter Twenty-Four

Two days later, Justin led a sortie on the enemy works and returned, charged with euphoric good cheer, at four in the morning to find Abigail sitting fully dressed by the fire. Her eyes were stark with fright but she said merely, 'Are you all right?'

'Never better. You haven't been sitting here worrying?'

Her brows rose irritably.

'Well, of course I have. What do you expect? There's bread and cold meat if you want it. I'll go to bed now. Goodnight.' And she was gone, leaving him in a state of astonished approval at her lack of fuss.

For some illogical reason things were easier between them now and he no longer felt impelled to avoid her. Laughter, it seemed, was remarkably good for one's sense of proportion and the daily routine of defence, combined with the occasional excitement of a sally, gave him little time to brood.

But the siege, when compared to John Fiennes' investment of 1644, was a tame affair. February became March and, although he now had some three thousand men, Colonel Whalley still lacked the artillery necessary to pose a serious threat and was therefore pursuing his attempts to demoralize the garrison with carefully selected bits of news. In a sense this worked for with no other source of information, it was hard for the garrison to know truth from fiction. But while the general trend continued to be one of determined optimism, Justin found no difficulty at all in believing that the King was making simultaneously naive overtures to both Presbyterian and Independent leaders in the frail hope of having one offer to support him against the other. It was, Justin decided, depressingly typical that, having stumbled into the war almost by accident, Charles should retreat from it in the same untidy manner. But there was no point in repining. The day of reckoning was not – could not be – far off and, in the meantime, they had a castle to keep.

On March 9th Abigail stood on the ramparts and watched reinforcements file into the camp below. Then, turning, she saw Justin bearing down on her and instinct warned that she was about to be ordered inside.

'We've got a new Colonel,' she said cheerfully, accustomed now to the way her stomach lurched at his approach. 'Do we know him?'

'We do. His name's Rainsborough and he's one of Sam's fire-eating Independents. What are you doing up here?'

'Extending my education.' She paused. 'I wonder if Sam has gone yet.'

'Probably. If he had any sense he'd have gone as soon as the roads cleared. That was the plan, wasn't it?'

She nodded, her gaze travelling absently across the town. 'It's just strange not knowing. We were always so close.'

'I know.' He watched her thoughtfully for a moment and then, gesturing to the Parliamentarian camp, said, 'Is all this hard for you? Do you mind being on the wrong side of the walls?'

She turned, smiling a little.

'Am I on the wrong side? I hardly know any more. My loyalties are not – have never been – political and I've never found anything in either cause to justify this war. I thought you knew that.'

'I do. But getting unexpectedly caught up in the crossfire might reasonably alter your ideas.'

'You think I should regret it?'

'Don't you?'

'No.' Her smile became infinitely sweet. 'And I wish that you didn't either. I'm not anxious to leave, Justin. I never was.'

It took him by surprise and he replied without thinking, 'Then you should be. Or do you imagine that I'm a born monk?'

Just for an instant, his meaning eluded her. Then her breath leaked slowly away and she stared at him in fascinated astonishment.

'No. I know you're not. You spend too much time in the north turret for that.'

There was a catastrophic silence while Justin, already cursing himself, tried to put a curb on his tongue and failed.

'I do not sleep with Nancy Lucas.'

'Oh.' Abigail looked down at her hands. 'Who then?'

'No one, and I'm trying rather hard to keep it that way!' he replied with an air of mild desperation. Then, half laughing, 'This is the devil of a conversation.'

'I know. Perhaps we shouldn't be having it here.'

'On the contrary – this is the only place to have it.'

Considering and faintly wistful, the dark eyes rose to meet his and she said unevenly, 'Are you saying that you want to make love to me?'

'The thought has occasionally crossed my mind,' he admitted lightly. 'It would be a miracle if it didn't. But I think what I'm trying to say is that you're too trusting and, though I didn't bring you from one impossible situation to put you in another, it would be nice if I sometimes had a little help.'

'I see,' said Abigail vaguely, her mind hopelessly adrift. 'Would it be an impossible situation?'

The shock that rippled through him had nothing to do with the sudden crackle of musket-fire but the latter gave him the excuse to say satirically, 'I think you'd better go inside before misfortune overtakes you.'

'Speak for yourself,' said Abigail shortly and went.

The subject was not renewed and for two weeks she brooded over it like a sparrow with a cuckoo's egg. She had known for a long time that, if he ever showed the slightest inclination to take her, she would not resist. Her virtue was an empty thing if she could not give it to him and the only time that counted was now, while he was still with her. It did not matter that his desire for her was not as hers for him, that it was transient and probably impersonal. It only mattered that he felt it at all. If she had possessed the remotest idea of how to lure him into forgetting his scruples, she would have done it without a qualm but she had no such knowledge and the days sped by bringing Colonel Whalley's summons to surrender and with it – unbelievably – a note from Samuel announcing his departure.

'How?' asked Abigail. 'How did he do it?'

Justin shrugged. 'You know Sam, he has a talent for nefarious dealings. Whalley's ensign brought it in, unsealed, as you see. I'd have brought it up before, only we've been rather busy.'

She folded Samuel's letter in her lap and looked across at Justin. 'What happened?'

'The same as always. Whalley told us we haven't a hope of holding out or getting relief and asked to be given the Castle before he occasions "the effusion of Christian blood". And Will wrote back that he'd no intention of delivering up his trust to rebels and desired the Colonel to "forbear any further, frivolous summons".' He smiled cheerfully. 'The honours are even. We'll get no help but unless they get some decent ordnance, we won't need it.'

'So what do we do?'

'Carry on as usual till His Majesty decides to whom he's going to surrender.'

Abigail thought of the small, sad-faced King. 'Surrender? Is that what it's come to?'

'Yes.' Justin gazed down at his clasped hands. 'Belvoir has fallen and Corfe and Lichfield, and his friends are melting away to compound for their estates. He has nothing left to fight with and nothing to offer in the market place. It's over. All he can do now is choose the time and place to say so.'

Four days later Colonel Whalley sent in word that Lord Astley's newly-recruited army of Welsh infantry had been routed at Stow-on-the-Wold on its way to Oxford and the King. It was, Abigail realized, looking at the curiously resigned faces about her, the last straw, the end of the King's forlorn hope of staving off surrender until help came from France or from Ireland or until Montrose conquered Scotland again.

'Balderdash!' said Justin irritably. 'We might as well wait for the Roundheads to turn Royalist. And two thousand untrained boys against the New Model, what chance could they have?'

As little as I do, thought Abigail later as she paced restlessly round the confines of the inner ward. *This can't go on. I've got to do something but first I need help. And I know where I can get it, too.*

Nancy admitted her hospitably enough but with blunt surprise and, waving her to a chair, said, 'Well, well, what's brought you up all them stairs?'

Abigail clasped her hands tightly in her lap. 'I've come to ask the favour you once promised me.'

'Have you indeed? And what is it?'

Abigail drew a long, steadying breath and met the brown eyes squarely. 'I want you to teach me how to seduce Justin.'

There was silence while Nancy gaped and collapsed absently on to a stool. Then she began to laugh. 'If I knew how to do that, my duck, I'd have done it for myself long since!'

It was Abigail's turn to stare but, becoming suddenly brisk, Nancy gave her no chance to speak.

'Tell me why.'

'I love him.'

'My God!' The bold gaze widened. 'Have you told him?'

'No. There's no point and he seems to have enough burdens already. If he felt less responsible for me it would be easier but, as it is, he's too hedged about by his own stupid promises to lay a hand on me. And so I need help.'

Nancy examined the expressive face with apparent calm while thoughts jostled with each other in her mind. Then, finally deciding that loyalty to Justin made it impossible to repeat his confidences but did not preclude her giving Abigail a little advice, she said, 'All right. I'll offer a few suggestions if that's what you want but I reckon the best thing you can do is tell him how you feel. He's going to guess it anyway.'

'Oh.' Abigail swallowed. 'I hadn't thought of that.'

'No. Well, you ain't exactly experienced, are you?' sighed Nancy. 'Oh Lord! This is going to be like teaching the King to black his own boots. Are you really set on it?'

'Yes. It's all I have.'

'All right. Then listen.'

So Abigail listened and, by the end of the second sentence,

her cheeks were burning with embarrassment for, though prosaic in the extreme, Nancy was nothing if not explicit. Finally she rose abruptly and said, 'Stop it! I can't do any of that!'

'That's what I thought,' agreed Nancy patiently. 'The only thing you might possibly cope with is to plant yourself in his bed one night and hope he's too pleased to ask questions, but I wouldn't care to depend on it. Not with Justin.'

Reluctant amusement touched Abigail's mouth. 'Nor would I. So what's left?'

'Court ladies' tricks. You put on a pretty gown, flutter your eyelashes, droop over his arm and turn your smile into a discreet invitation. It might work. No?'

'No,' replied Abigail regretfully. 'I've tried it, more or less, and I don't think he noticed.'

Nancy dropped her face into her hands and laughed. 'You've been brought up all wrong, love.'

'I know. And so, unfortunately, does Justin. I think that's why he's intent on preserving my chastity as if it were a national treasure.'

Nancy rose slowly. 'Then you'd better tell him it isn't, hadn't you? Or shall I do it for you?'

'No!' The dark eyes reflected utter horror. 'You mustn't say a word of this to him!'

'But —'

'No, Nancy. Promise me!'

Nancy groaned. 'Oh all right, all right! But if mistaking my door for the confessional is going to become a bloody habit, I might as well get myself a nun's veil and have done with it!'

A few nights later there was another sortie and Abigail sat taut as a bowstring, waiting for Justin to return from it. There had not, thankfully, been many such expeditions for Will Compton was keeping his men close until they could wreak the greatest havoc but Abigail lived in secret dread of them and invariably passed them in a state of nastily imaginative fear.

He came in wet from the rain. The long hair curled

damply on his shoulders and his buff leather was dark with moisture. He looked tired and she rose quickly, saying, 'If you take off your coat, I'll put it to dry.'

'There's no need. I can do it.' His voice was edged with impatience and he stayed by the door, one-handedly discarding his baldric. 'It's long past your bedtime, isn't it?'

'Yours too, by the look of you,' she retorted, turning to get a towel from the washstand to hide the acuteness of her relief. 'But you'd better dry your hair a bit first and —'

'For Christ's sake stop fussing!' snapped Justin. 'I've managed for years without a nursemaid and I'm damned if I need one now. Just go away and leave me in peace.'

She stared at him, at first hurt and then increasingly suspicious. Stepping towards him, she saw what his behaviour and the shadows had previously hidden from her. The towel fell unheeded to the floor and she said shakily, 'Why do you have to be a hero? Let me see it.'

'It's nothing. I can deal with it myself.'

'With only one hand? You won't even get your coat off.' She closed the space between them and set to work unopposed. 'What was it, a sword?'

'No. A musket-ball.' He winced a little as she drew his coat from him. 'I think you'll find it's gone straight through. I'm sorry I shouted at you.'

She smiled wryly at him. 'That's all right. I'm used to it. Now come into the light and sit down so I can see.'

Gingerly, she peeled back the torn, blood-soaked edges of his shirt sleeve to examine the unpleasant gash in his forearm, then, crossing swiftly to her own room, she returned with a pair of scissors and proceeded to cut the cambric from wrist to elbow.

Justin sighed. 'Another shirt down the drain. I knew it.'

'Be grateful it's only a shirt.' She rose again and set about assembling water and strips of linen for binding. 'How was the raid?'

'Wet,' he replied, watching her move lightly about the room. 'And informative. They've constructed a defensive line right round the outskirts of their camp.'

'Oh?' Abigail sat down beside him on the bed and began

298

cleaning the wound. 'Is that unusual?'

'Only when, as now, there's no possibility of being attacked from the outside.' He caught his breath and then released it. 'Their engineer must have got bored. Abby, that hurts.'

'Keep still then.' Her tone accorded ill with the greenish pallor of her face. 'I do this for fun, you know.'

'Yes? Perhaps I ought to come back in holes more often then.'

Abigail cast him a glance of cryptic reproof before setting the bowl of water on the floor and restoring her attention to the task of bandaging. Silence fell. Justin found himself dwelling on the silky sweep of her lashes and the line of concentration between her brows. Then she looked up at him and the world melted.

He watched her eyes change and her breathing shorten as the thread between them tightened and then, with dreamlike slowness, he used his sound arm to gather her to him so that he could find the sweetness of her mouth.

Her hands rose to touch his face, his hair and her body blended into his with a lithe willingness that demolished whatever remnants of logic he had left. His kiss grew more demanding and, unmindful now of his bandaged arm, he drew her down with him into the softness of the feather quilt, holding her closer and closer against him until it was impossible to tell her heartbeat from his own.

His fingers were at the laces of her gown when his foot inadvertently kicked over the bowl of water and brought him to his senses. His eyes flicked open and he lay absolutely still for a moment then, releasing her with an abruptness that made her gasp, he was up and away across the room.

He heard her sit up. Then she said huskily, 'Justin? What's wrong?'

'Everything.' He remained with his back to her, staring into the fire. 'Go to bed, Abby.'

There was a long silence. Then, 'I thought,' she said, softly, 'that we were doing just that.'

Something inside him gave a dizzying lurch and he turned slowly to face her. The half-awakened dark eyes looked back at him with candid longing and he said harshly, 'Don't be such a child. You'll regret this tomorrow.'

Her gaze did not waver. She said, 'I won't. I love you.'

This time the floor seemed to shift beneath him but he kept his head. 'Of course you do but as a friend.'

'If you can believe that after what just happened —'

'Forget that.'

'Why?' She came sharply to her feet. 'I'm not entirely naive, Justin. I know it's different for you but I'm not asking for words and promises. I'm only asking you to let us share something that you want as much as I do. Or are you,' she finished bitterly, 'going to deny that as well?'

The knife twisted and he gave her a crooked smile.

'No. How can I? But it isn't that simple.' He drew a long breath. 'Sit down, Abby. I think it's time we faced the wolf so that we can fight it together.'

She walked uncertainly towards him and sank gracefully on the rug at his feet. 'I don't understand.'

'No.' He hooked the stool forward and sat facing her. 'I'd hoped to avoid this but I didn't bargain for tonight. And we've gone too far for me to leave you thinking that I don't care for you or that it was easy to walk away just now.'

She drew up her knees and clasped her arms tight about them. She was shaking. 'Go on.'

He said simply, 'You are – you have become – the other half of me and if I could marry you, I would. But I have no future in England and no home to offer you and, because of that, I don't have the right to touch you. In any way.'

She stared up at him, almost afraid to breathe.

'Can't we take things one at a time?' she asked unevenly. 'You're going too fast for me.'

'Deliberately,' came the austere reply. 'The facts are inextricably linked and the sooner you accept that, the easier it will be for both of us. I love you but I can't marry you and I won't take you on any other terms – and that is final.'

Despite the disturbance in her chest and the agony in her throat, Abigail said calmly, 'Not quite. I think I have some rights too . . . and perhaps you should know that I'd live in a hole in the ground if it was the only way to be with you.'

A sudden flame flickered in his eyes and then died. 'No.'

'Why not? What would I be giving up?'

'That isn't the point.'

'Then what is?' He did not answer and presently she said, 'Very well. If you won't allow us a future, let's see what can be done with the present.'

'No,' he said again. 'No, Abby. There are . . . things you don't know. Try to understand.'

'I do. You want me to make it easy for you – but I can't.' Her voice shook a little. 'You expect too much.'

'I'm sorry.' He was white with strain. 'Perhaps I shouldn't have told you. But it's done now and if we apply a little common-sense, the situation shouldn't become intolerable.'

'It already is!' retorted Abigail, her vision suddenly blurred. 'And I don't want to be sensible. I want to seduce you if it takes all Nancy's suggestions to do it.'

'What?' asked Justin quietly. 'You've been to Nancy?'

'Yes.' She came awkwardly to her feet. 'She was very helpful.'

'I'm sure.' He also rose and stood looming over her. 'But if you try any whore's tricks on me, I should warn you that the effect may not be quite what you had in mind.'

His anger confused her but only for a moment.

'Then I'll be myself and perhaps that will be enough.' She smiled up at him through her tears. 'I love you. What will you do when you find me in your bed or when I come close to you or touch you?'

He remained perfectly still, letting her lay her hands flat against his chest. Then he said stonily, 'I shall leave you. If you persist, if you continue trying to force me in this way, I shall move downstairs and lock my door against you. Is that what you want?'

Her bones grew icy cold. 'You don't mean it.'

'I do.' He stepped back from her, choosing his words with care. 'We can have total separation or we can go on as we did before without ever referring to this again. I would prefer the latter but the choice must be yours.'

She had begun to shiver. 'Please, I can't bear it. Not now.'

'You can.' Pressure was building up behind his eyes and he

301

frowned at her, trying to concentrate. 'If you won't decide, I'll go.'

'No!' She caught his hand and then, looking despairingly into his face, released it. 'All right. I'll try.'

'Not good enough,' he replied with difficulty. 'Promise me. No tricks, yours or Nancy's.'

Anguish tore her in two. She promised.

Chapter Twenty-Five

April arrived and the days became weeks without bringing any material change to the general situation. The Parliament quarrelled again with its Scots allies and Exeter, bulwark of the Royalist cause in the West, fell to Fairfax but still the King made no public move towards surrender. By the middle of the month Lucy was becoming gloomily resigned to the prospect of giving birth in the Castle. Tiring of unconfirmed Roundhead tales, Will Compton sought Colonel Whalley's permission to write to the King. He did not get it and was sufficiently aggravated by the refusal to order a sortie – which, though it did the enemy very little harm, made the garrison feel a good deal better.

Still lacking even one mortar, Colonel Whalley let his engineer take over and the nature of the siege changed as sapping and mining became the order of the day. His men dug irregular, twisting trenches aimed obliquely at the walls only to have the garrison shower them with stones and grenadoes. They constructed tunnels designed to hold explosive devices and had one such turned against them when the garrison counter-mined. But they could not, they found, get inside and they no longer expected to.

In the midst of it all, Justin and Abigail trod a cautious path through the briars of their personal life. It was not easy for the balance was at best precarious. There were days when they forgot everything except the simple joy of being together; days when they talked and laughed and recaptured for a while the old carefree pleasures of their earliest meetings. And then a careless word or unwary glance would shatter the peace and bring awareness flooding back to leave them stranded in an airless void until one of them left the room.

It was on the last day of the month that Colonel Whalley sent in the most startling piece of news that anyone had heard since the dismissal of Rupert. It seemed, incredibly, that the King had vanished. Slipping quietly out of Oxford on the 27th with only a handful of attendants he had left Rupert to hold Oxford against the might of Fairfax's approaching forces and, for all that had been seen of him since, might have disappeared in a puff of smoke.

Alone in the garrison, Justin seemed unmoved by the mystery and while others speculated, he remained silent. And when the talk became loaded with individual plans for a future which did not include the war, he still said nothing until his friends conspired to force his hand.

They were gathered around the dinner table when matters finally came to a head and the candlelight flickered fitfully over the planes and angles of Justin's face while Ned, Lucy and Abigail listened to Hugh Vaughan bombarding him with a series of flagrantly inquisitive broadsides.

'Come on, Justin, you must have some theory to offer. Where do you think the King has gone?'

Justin shrugged irritably. 'How the devil should I know? The West, perhaps, or possibly to France.'

'God, I hope not!' groaned Ned. 'If he's left the country, we'll be left with nothing but unconditional surrender.'

'Quite,' said Hugh. Then, again to Justin, 'I suppose you agree that a general surrender in the next few weeks is inevitable?'

'Obviously.'

'Ah.' Hugh saw his chance and took it. 'So what will you do?'

'What do you think?' snapped Justin. 'That I'm likely to embark on a one-man crusade?'

'Don't be obtuse. I meant where will you go?'

There was a long silence while Justin stared mutinously down at his half-empty plate. Finally he swept it to one side and said coldly, 'I'll go abroad. What else?'

'And Abby?' asked Lucy, sharply. 'What about her?'

He looked bleakly into his love's dark eyes. 'When it is possible, she will join her brother in London.'

'And in the meantime?' It was Ned this time.

'In the meantime you can mind your own bloody business!'

304

Justin rose angrily. 'What is all this, the Inquisition?'

'No,' said Ned curtly. He lifted one brow at his wife and then said, 'It's an offer. Lucy and I would like Abby to come home with us and if you can control your blasted temper, there's nothing to stop you coming too.'

The shock of it stopped Abigail's breath and she stared pleadingly at Justin, willing him to smile, to agree. But his face grew, if anything, more impervious and, in a tone completely devoid of expression, he said, 'Thank you. You are very generous, and if you will care for Abby I shall be more than grateful.'

'And you?, asked Abigail, rising abruptly. 'Will you come too?'

'No.' He kept his eyes on Ned. 'I can't. But I thank you for suggesting it. And now I'm afraid I have to check the guards.'

It was late when he came in but Abigail broke all the rules by waiting up for him. She said flatly, 'I didn't know Ned was going to say that. Do you believe me?'

'Of course.'

'Then why won't you accept his invitation to you? Why?'

He looked unutterably tired but he said patiently, 'Because neither of us can take much more of this. And it would solve nothing.'

'There's nothing to solve. You are suffocating us both with your own pride.'

The grey eyes reflected bitter hurt.

'I'm sorry you think that. But perhaps it will make it easier for you.'

She froze and then, choking a little, said, 'I didn't mean it. How can you think that I . . . Justin, I love you so much.'

'I know.' His mouth curled in something that was not quite a smile. 'I know. Forgive me, Abby, but I'm going to sleep downstairs.' And he was gone before she could stop him.

On the morning of May 6th Abigail awoke slowly to the realization of two strange facts; the sound of gunfire had been replaced by the distant rendering of a triumphant psalm and Justin stood in the doorway of her room. It was the first time he had been near her in five days. She sat up.

'Something's happened?'

'Yes.' His face was like granite. 'We're surrendering.'

It was, stupidly, the last thing she had expected to hear and her stomach heaved. 'When?'

'Today.'

That was all. No explanations, no attempt to soften it, just a bisyllabic death knell. 'Just like that? Why?'

'Because the only point in not doing so has been removed,' replied Justin remotely. 'Yesterday the King made a gift of his person to the Scots Covenanters at Southwell and today, at his order, the Newark garrison is demonstrating his good faith by opening its gates to the enemy. The war is over and we are surrendering.'

'But it's so sudden,' said Abigail weakly.

'Yes. It is, isn't it? But wise, no doubt.' His voice was faintly bitter. 'I have to go. Whalley's commissioners will be arriving soon and I'm supposed to receive them.'

'Wait!' She rose abruptly. 'Will you promise me something?'

'If I can.'

She stood very still, the long hair tumbling over the straight fall of her night-robe. 'Promise me that, when the time comes, you won't go without saying goodbye.'

He looked at her with renewed longing and recognized that he had lost his will for restraint, that he was bound only by his word. The seconds ticked by in silence and finally he said, huskily, 'I promise. Of course I do.'

It was a long, strained day which the Castle spent wrapped in an unnatural hush. Abigail walked aimlessly on the ramparts for a time and then, deliberately avoiding Lucy, went back to sit alone in Justin's empty room. Even the spaniel, she noticed dismally, appeared to have decamped.

Dusk came and then dark. The evening grew chilly and she lit a fire for its cheer and warmth only to find herself incapable of absorbing either. And then the door opened and Justin came in.

He was carrying a tray loaded with food, wine and two glasses and, kicking the door shut with his foot, he came across to place it before her on the hearth. His expression was profoundly irritable.

'What the devil are you playing at, missing your dinner to sit here in the dark? Do you think I haven't enough to do without following you about to make sure you eat?'

She shrugged and turned her face away towards the fire. 'I'm not hungry.'

'Nevertheless, having carried this lot up here, I intend to watch you eat it.' He unsealed the bottle and poured her a glass of wine. 'Drink that.'

'No.' His abrasive tone added resentment to her misery. She watched him reach down a torch from the wall and said, 'Don't. I like the dark.'

'Possibly. But I don't recall having asked you.' He lit the torch from the fire and returned it to its sconce. 'It's only fair to point out that I too have had a hellish day. Now will you drink your wine or do I have to pour it down your throat?'

She did not need to look at him to know that, although he was fully capable of it, he would not do it but her head jerked round and she said breathlessly, 'Go on, then. You might as well add physical assault to everything else.' And only then did she see the aching anxiety that overlaid his irritation. She pressed the heels of her hands hard over her eyes and said, 'I'm sorry, I'm sorry. That was unfair.'

'Not particularly.' Justin stared down at her, his soul awash with seething rebellion. His hands clenched at his sides and he said carefully, 'Please drink your wine. For me.'

Slowly, she lifted her head and even managed a smile as she picked up the glass. 'For you I'd drink hemlock.' And then, before he could reply, 'Tell me about your day. Have they settled the terms?'

'Yes.' He sat down beside her on the brightly-coloured rug and pushed a plate of bread and cheese towards her. 'They have.'

Abigail broke off a token piece of cheese. 'And?'

'And Colonel Whalley has shown his gratitude by being inexpensively generous,' he replied, with irony. 'We are required to swear no oaths and are offered passes to any place of our choice with the exception, I'm afraid, of London. The sick and wounded will be cared for here until they can travel and all officers are graciously permitted to retain their swords, one horse and half their money.' He smiled sardonically. 'They are not, I rejoice to say, going to make much out of me. For the rest, we are bound to hand over the Castle as it stands and leave behind all muskets, pistols, cannon, powder, shot and colours. Oh yes, and they want hostages against our good behaviour.'

'Not you?' asked Abigail sharply.

'No, not me.' He paused and then said simply, 'We're to leave on Friday morning.'

Her hand shook and she put the glass clumsily down on the hearthstone. 'The day after tomorrow?'

'Yes. You'll have to start packing.'

Her eyes were wide and dark. She said, 'What about Lucy? The baby is only a few weeks away.'

'They haven't far to go. And Ned has been promised a carriage.' As if from a long way off, he heard himself add, 'You'll travel in style.'

She flinched. 'And – and you?'

'I've applied for an overseas pass from any port.'

'So it's goodbye, then. Forever?'

The question brought him up short.

'I – yes. I imagine so,' he said unevenly. And then stopped as the mind-cracking truth pushed him, without warning, to the edge of the precipice.

He could not go on with it. However honourable, sensible or right, he could not bring himself to part with her. There was no good reason for it, no logic, only a knowledge deep inside himself that he was not, and probably never had been, capable of giving her up. And though he could not take her abroad, there had always been a place where he could take her at the price of one, very small sacrifice.

He looked at her out of eyes that were suddenly brilliant and wondered how best to explain. And then he realized that he did not have to explain, that the words could come later. For now, all he need do was stretch out his hand.

He did so, gently pushing aside the midnight hair to lift her chin. She looked up at him, surprised and a little wary; and then, before she could speak, he drew her slowly into his arms. Her breath caught on a tiny gasp and he felt the echo of it ripple through her body in the second before her piercingly sweet response parted her mouth beneath his and turned her to liquid fire in his embrace.

Without either haste or hesitation, his fingers sought and freed the laces of her gown to slide it from her shoulders so that his mouth could follow his hands in a burning trail across her skin. He explored the tender hollows at the base of her throat, the delicate line of her clavicle, the curve of her breast and, when she clung to him, sobbing his name, he said huskily, 'I love you . . . I love you. Heart of my heart . . . say that you love me too.'

'I love you.'

'Forever? No matter what you might learn of me?'

'Yes, yes.'

He rose, taking her with him to gather the fragrant softness of her closer and closer against him while his mouth brushed hers with tantalizing lightness. 'And you'll marry me?'

'Yes.'

'Say it, promise me.'

'I'll marry you.' She twined her fingers in the thickness of his hair, lost and drowning in a tide of sensation. 'I promise.'

Her gown slithered to the floor, followed by the ruffled petticoats. Then the light, disrobing hands were suddenly stilled and, holding her cradled against his shoulder, he said raggedly, 'I want you so much. But if you wish to wait —'

'No.' She smiled, drawing his head down to hers. 'No. I've waited too long already.'

His breath caught and his hands were unsteady against her skin. For a single, encapsulated second, he searched her face with hungry, grey eyes. Then thought vanished with the space between them as he lifted her high against his heart and carried her to his bed.

His care for her was infinite and the joy he taught her was returned to him a hundredfold. Together they shared the tingling explosion of delight that came with the first, unimpeded meeting of their bodies and, when his hands dissolved her bones beneath an intricate pattern of pleasure, he too was left scorched by the fires he had created. Only then, with the time for continence long past, did he guide her delicately over the final threshold where the song of their loving grew effortlessly into the music of the spheres.

Abigail awoke to dancing sunlight and a feeling of delicious lassitude that deepened with returning memory. As once before, she was alone, but this time there was no note on the pillow beside her, only the imprint of Justin's head and a couple of long, walnut hairs that she twisted foolishly about her fingers. She stretched a little, discovering the flagrant disorder of the bed and an unfamiliar stiffness in her muscles that made her search for some sense of shame at the long hours of sweetness that had caused them. But there was none and the only thought that brought a flush to her cheeks was the hope that tonight would be no different.

An hour or so later she walked slowly into the frenetic activity of the outer ward to find Justin briskly supervising the collection of firearms. His hands were full of papers and the ground around him was an arsenal of pistols, muskets and powder-flasks. He looked across at her and all his crisp efficiency vanished with his smile. He thrust his lists into the hands of the nearest man and moved swiftly to pull her into the dark privacy of a doorway so that he could take her in his arms.

He kissed her mouth, her eyelids, her hair and finally, sighing, he said, 'I'm sorry I had to leave you to wake alone. But there is so much to be done before tomorrow.'

'I know. It doesn't matter.' She melted against him and felt his hold on her tighten. 'I'm so happy.'

'And I,' he whispered, kissing her again. Then, 'There is so much to say, but not now. I have to go. Will you . . . may I come tonight?'

The diffidence in his voice made her ache. She said, 'Of course. If I see about some food, do you think we might avoid dinner? I don't know what to say to Lucy.'

'I'll take care of that.' Laughter stirred in his eyes. 'Though if she sees you, I imagine you won't need to say anything.'

The truth of this remark was proved when, on her way back inside, Abigail encountered Nancy Lucas and found herself subjected to a shrewd brown stare.

'Well,' said Nancy, at last. 'And about time too.'

Abigail gave a tiny laugh. 'It's as obvious as that?'

'Yes. You look like a first-day bride. And how does Justin look?'

'Busy,' retorted Abigail, cheerfully. And then, becoming suddenly grave, 'What will you do, Nancy? Jonas and his friends will close the town to you. Where will you go?'

'Into keeping,' came the prompt reply. 'I've had an offer – and a good one, at that – so you don't need to worry about me. I'm going up in the world. You just look after the Captain. He's a good man and you're lucky.'

'I know,' said Abigail simply. 'And I'll do my best.'

After several hours spent packing up her new wealth of belongings and tidying both rooms, Abigail visited the kitchens, changed into the apricot gown and left her hair optimistically loose. Then, in the same mood of sweet expectancy that had possessed her all day, she sat down to wait.

He came sooner than she had dared hope, entering the room quietly to gaze at her with faintly smiling reticence. He said, 'You are so beautiful, and I am very dirty. Will you excuse me for a moment?'

She rose and came to stand before him.

'No. Your work is done. Let me do mine.' And, lifting her hands, began to unbuckle his baldric.

A pulse quivered in Justin's throat and the grey eyes dilated a little as she laid his sword carefully on the carved chest and returned to unwind the silk sash from about his waist. He watched her fold it with an air of grave wifeliness and then stood very still while she unlaced the grease-smeared buff-coat. Finally, she looked up at him and said, 'There is wine, if you want it.'

'I want only you,' he replied simply. And then, still making no move to touch her, 'But perhaps the wine is a good idea. This time we have to talk.'

311

'Do we?' She sensed but could not understand his anxiety. 'Why?'

'Because I have to explain to you about last night.'

Smiling, she shook her head.

'You don't. I understand that you changed your mind – and I'm glad. You don't have to provide me with reasons.'

It was a long time before he spoke. Then he said slowly, 'I think, in all my life, you are the only person who has ever held me in perfect trust and I could worship you for that alone. I only wish I were more deserving.' His mouth twisted wryly. 'Pour the wine, Abby. We're going to need it.'

Apprehension clawed at her spine but she did as he asked and then sat patiently on the stool while he washed his hands. Then he came to sit at her feet on the hearth, frowning a little and still silent until, looking up, he said abruptly, 'Last night you promised to marry me. Before you do, I think you should know that my full name is Justin Ambrose Templeton and that my father was Lord Templeton of Trent.'

Silence stretched out on an invisible thread. Finally, Abigail said weakly, 'Was Lord Templeton . . . ?'

'Yes. He died just over a year ago.'

'I see. So that makes you —'

'The eighth baron,' supplied Justin, with irony. And then, differently, 'It's a long and complicated story, and the details, if you want them, can come later. For now all you need to know is that my mother ran off with the bailiff when I was seven and that my father later married a widow with three children – Bernard, John and Jenny. They were grasping and devious, and still are. Because my father disliked me, it was easy for them to discredit me in his eyes. I was sixteen when the inevitable finally happened and I was disinherited. I won't bore you with the reasons, but —'

'Jenny,' said Abigail flatly. 'Jenny was one of them. Wasn't she?'

'Yes.' He looked at her, pale and intent. 'I wasn't sure if you'd remember. But I swear to you that I didn't —'

'Stop it!' Sliding swiftly from the stool, she dropped to her knees beside him. 'Even if you hadn't already told me that you never touched her, do you think I could ever believe that of you? Or don't you trust me at all?'

'Oh God!' He pulled her against him, burying his face in her hair. 'I'm sorry. But all this must come as a shock and you have every right to feel deceived and betrayed. My only defence is that, after eleven years, secrecy becomes a habit.'

Abigail put her arms around him and held him close.

'Finish the story.'

'Like this?'

'Yes.'

'Very well.' He drew a long breath and felt the tension seep from his body. 'When I left Trent, I shed my father's name and went off to earn my own living, you know how. Then fate organized a chain of events which resulted in Bernard becoming aware of my presence here in Banbury. And because, by that time, my father had changed his mind and reinstated me as his heir, Bernard sent Hannah Rhodes to kill me.'

Abigail flinched and her hands tightened about him.

'I thought she was a spy.'

'She was. And so, as it happens, is Bernard.' He paused and then said, 'I paid him a visit when I was in Newark – one which he's unlikely to forget. He informed me that Trent is under a sequestration order and, at the time, I decided against compounding. Now, however, I've changed my mind.'

'Because of me?'

'Because I can't give you up,' he corrected gently. 'I thought I could but I can't. So I'll take their damned oath and sell as much land as I have to in order to pay the fine – I should perhaps have mentioned that there's no money. The King had that. So I'll have to learn to be a farmer and we won't be much better off than we are now. Will you mind?'

'Yes.' Abigail drew away to fix him with a troubled gaze. 'I'll mind very much if you're doing this just for me. If it were all as simple as you make it sound, you'd have told me about it two months ago instead of – of —'

'Of putting us both through hell? I know. I've been a fool.'

'No. But you must take me for one. It's the oath, isn't it?' she said broodingly. 'You don't want to take the oath because you know you won't mean a word of it. And that's why you decided to let the estate go.'

'Yes. But that was before I had a reason for claiming it.' He held her gaze with his own. 'I can't take you abroad, Abby. Apart from the fact that it's no life for someone like you, the chances of you ending up a young widow or encumbered with a crippled husband, are fairly high. No one's luck lasts forever, even mine. And it's not a risk I'm willing to take.' He smiled at her and took her hands in his. 'Few things come absolutely free, you know. And since I love you too much to lose you, I'll put my tongue in my cheek and swear the oath. It's no sacrifice, believe me. And even if it were, I'd still do it because I can't bear to be alone again. Not now.'

It was the simple truth, prosaically stated and it brought Abigail back against his shoulder. 'There is no question of that. You know I will go anywhere.'

'Good. Then you'll come with me to Trent.' He fell silent for a moment, savouring her closeness. Then, with a hint of laughter, he said, 'Do you realize I've been worried sick about having to tell you who I am?'

'That was silly of you.' She coiled a strand of walnut hair about her fingers. 'But perhaps you should consider a little. About marrying me, I mean.'

Justin was suddenly still. 'Why?'

'Because Lady Templeton shouldn't be a shopkeeper's sister.'

There was a long pause. Then he tipped her head back with an ungentle hand and said flatly, 'If you ever say such a thing to me again, I swear to God I'll beat you.'

Presently and with difficulty, Abigail said, 'Are you sure? Are you sure about going to Trent?'

'Yes.' He kissed the hollow beneath her left ear. 'Yes and it's all arranged. Why must you go on about it?'

'To make you think what you are doing.'

'I have thought. I'm tired of thinking. And what's more, I'm tired of having you think.'

'I'm sorry.' Breathless under the delicious assault of his hands, she managed one final flicker of provocative mischief. 'What's all arranged?'

'Passes . . . Ned and Lucy . . . everything. Are you going to talk all night?'

'No.' Her mouth quivered against his throat. 'No. I hope not.'

For Abigail, the day of the evacuation began at a little after dawn when she woke to the honeyed promise of lazily drifting hands. She stirred, her fingers stretching responsively against the warmth of his chest and said sleepily, 'Is it time to get up?'

'No.' Justin turned to her, smiling. 'Not just yet. I'm sorry. I didn't mean to wake you.'

'Didn't you?' The dark eyes opened, wide with love for him and her arms slid up around his neck. 'Why not?'

Something changed in his face and he said quickly, 'I want you to know that . . . that it's never been like this before. And that, despite my variable past, there will be no others.'

'I know. Haven't I told you that I love you?'

'Yes.' He drew her hard against him. 'But not today.'

After joy came the practical realities of the day, the first of which was Justin's duty to see the Castle firearms safely delivered into the Parliamentary camp by nine of the clock. He dressed hurriedly whilst issuing Abigail with instructions.

'Pack only the essentials, we can't take much on horseback, and put everything else in the chest. I'll try and arrange for the carrier to collect it. I'll shave later, so leave my razors out and I'll be sending someone up to polish my boots. I'll wear the claret coat and you can throw the other away. I won't be needing it again.' He headed for the door, coatless and faintly dishevelled. 'Ah yes, and if you can find any old bits of soft cloth, I'd like to clean my sword.'

'Yes, sir!' Abigail was still sitting up in bed with her hair tumbling wildly about her shoulders. 'Are we out to make an impression?'

'Yes.' He smiled suddenly. 'Something like that.'

Despite what he had said, she folded his buff-coat neatly away in the chest in obedience to an illogical inner prompting of her own. Then she brushed the claret coat, laid out his grey silk sash and set out to work on her own appearance.

He returned at a little before ten and proceeded to ready himself with startling rapidity while Abigail wandered about the room, aimlessly touching things. Finally twitching the folds of his sash into place, he reached for his cavalry cloak and said, 'What is it, Abby? Regrets?'

'No.' She smiled at him. 'I believe I was storing up memories but it's done now. Is it time to go?'

'Yes.' He crossed to her side and put his arm about her. 'It's time. In fact, we're probably a little late.'

'For what?'

'You'll see.' And, whistling for Rex to follow them, he swept her from the room.

They emerged from the shade of the Castle into the brightness of the north ward and for a moment Abigail was dazzled by brilliant sunshine and a vivid blue sky. Then the air drained slowly from her lungs as, for the first and last time, she saw the entire garrison arrayed with formal splendour in the fortress that it had held so long and so stubbornly. Pikes, helmets and breast-plates glittered amidst an ordered forest of green and buff. Silk sashes gleamed, colours fluttered gently in the breeze, horses shuffled in a jingle of harness. Every still face and upright figure bore a stamp of pride that brought a lump to Abigail's throat.

'Come,' said Justin softly. 'They're waiting for us.'

She accompanied him without question until she saw the Castle chaplain and the Governor waiting beside Ned and Lucy and Hugh. Shock brought her to an abrupt halt. 'Justin?'

He smiled down at her. 'I thought . . . I thought that now seemed as good a time as any. And can you honestly think of anywhere better than here, with our friends all around us?'

And, of course, she couldn't.

It was Lucy who took her cloak and handed her a tiny posy of silk flowers and Hugh Vaughan who placed her fingers on his sleeve as he prepared to take the part of her kinsman. Then she was standing beside Justin before the upturned drum.

The ceremony was brief – no more than a simple

exchanging of vows – and there was no music. But all around was the familiar creak of leather and muffled chink of armour and somewhere a bird was singing. A clump of broom glowed gold against the worn grey stone of the Castle and, far above it, the lions and lilies of England floated serenely in an azure sky as Justin took Abigail for his wife.

He kissed her amidst a surge of cheers, whistles and laughter and then, over the noise, said, 'I wish I could tell you that it will be easy when we get to Trent but I can't. It may be months before we even have the place to ourselves. Perhaps . . . perhaps I should send you with Lucy after all, just until I can get rid of Bernard.'

'No.' Abigail smiled up at him. '"Entreat me not to leave thee . . . for whither thou goest, I will go." Always. As long as you love me.'

'Always, then,' replied Justin simply. 'For I swear I'll love you till I die.'

After the good wishes and farewells came the final ritual of surrender. Bareheaded and grimly silent, the undefeated ranks of the Banbury garrison watched the massing of their colours and the lowering of the King's standard. Then hats and helmets were replaced while, for the first time in four months, the gates were opened wide, revealing the red-coated lines of the New Model Army. A crisp order tore the air, followed by the staccato tuck of drums. With cool, leisured dignity, Sir William Compton led his people out across the moat and into the wider world beyond.

Susannah Kells

The superb, dramatic chronicles of the Lazender dynasty, set against a brilliant picture of England through the centuries. Susannah Kells is a major new British talent, writing in the great storytelling tradition of Daphne du Maurier.

A Crowning Mercy   £1.95

Four intricately wrought seals – each owned by a stranger, each holding a secret within. These are Campion Slythe's key to the inheritance from her unknown father – her chance to escape from the worthy marriage which awaits her. But to claim her inheritance, and to find again the love she discovered on one golden summer afternoon, Campion must follow the course her father's legacy charts for her. And it is a road full of both peril and enchantment.

The Fallen Angels   £1.95

Secure beneath the prosperous English sun, the 'little kingdom' of Lazen is unaware it is a house under siege. From the heart of Revolutionary France, the Fallen Angels – the most dangerous men in Europe – spin their web of intrigue, seeking the fall and the fortune of the Lazender family. Only the beautiful Lady Campion Lazender can save the great estate. But one man stands between Campion and disaster – Gitan, the mysterious gypsy – a man who could as easily be her enemy as her lover . . .

'Excellently done . . . Susannah Kells is a natural story teller' *Catherine Gaskin*

FONTANA PAPERBACKS

Fontana's Sagas

Almost Paradise £2.95 Susan Isaacs

'*A joy to read and remember*' COSMOPOLITAN

Jane Cobleigh gave up her ambitions to nurture her husband's rise to stardom. His success brought them glamour and riches, but to her – loneliness, until she began her own career. But could any marriage stand the price of such success? A rich, moving story of love, joy and heartbreak set in New York, Hollywood and London in the glittering world of the film industry.

The Diamond Waterfall £2.95 Patricia Haines

'*In a class of her own*' TIMES

The Diamond Waterfall is a necklace, a magnificent object of wealth and beauty. But it is also to the three women who wear it a symbol of bondage and tragedy. This is a vivid and turbulent family saga that follows three generations of a Yorkshire family from glittering Edwardian England through to the drama of World War Two.

A Fragile Peace £2.50 Teresa Crane

'*A story of great skill and vitality – I really loved this book*' SARAH HARRISON

It was a lovely summer's day – perfect for a garden party. But when the Jordans' party was over their tranquil, traditional life would disappear too. It was 1936. Only young Allie thrived amid the turmoil. But one day she fell in love – with Buzz Webster, a lively, lovable RAF pilot. was 1941 . . .

FONTANA PAPERBACKS

Fontana Paperbacks: Fiction

Fontana is a leading paperback publisher of both non-fiction, popular and academic, and fiction. Below are some recent fiction titles.

- [ ] THE SERVANTS OF TWILIGHT Leigh Nichols £1.95
- [ ] A SEASON OF MISTS Sarah Woodhouse £1.95
- [ ] DOUBLE YOKE Buchi Emecheta £1.50
- [ ] IN HONOUR BOUND Gerald Seymour £1.95
- [ ] IN SAFE HANDS Jane Sandford £1.95
- [ ] SHARPE'S ENEMY Bernard Cornwell £1.95
- [ ] A WOMAN OF IRON Sheila Holland £1.75
- [ ] FAIR FRIDAY Peter Turnbull £1.50
- [ ] THREE WOMEN OF LIVERPOOL Helen Forrester £1.95
- [ ] FRIENDS OF THE OPPOSITE SEX Sara Davidson £1.95
- [ ] KNAVE OF HEARTS Philippa Carr £1.95
- [ ] THE SECOND SALADIN Stephen Hunter £1.95
- [ ] ECHOES OF WAR Joan Dial £1.95
- [ ] MAKING WAVES Liz Allen £1.95
- [ ] GLIDEN-FIRE Stephen Donaldson £1.25

You can buy Fontana paperbacks at your local bookshop or newsagent. Or you can order them from Fontana Paperbacks, Cash Sales Department, Box 29, Douglas, Isle of Man. Please send a cheque, postal or money order (not currency) worth the purchase price plus 15p per book for postage (maximum postage is £3.00 for orders within the UK).

NAME (Block letters) _____

ADDRESS _____

_____